Praise for the Diana Tregarde

"Mercedes Lackey's work is as sharp—and as scary—as the suddenly revealed fang of a vampire. She'll keep you up long past your bedtime."

—Stephen King

"Diana Tregarde is intelligent and resourceful—with a most charming and unusual associate."

—C. J. Cherryh on *Children of the Night*

"A very enjoyable thriller with a sense of humor."

—*Locus* on *Children of the Night*

"Diana has a wry, practical sense of humor. Anyone who likes their supernatural yarns laced with intelligence will find this novel more than satisfying."

—*Dragon* magazine on *Burning Water*

"I loved *Children of the Night*. It's a delight to know that a writer whose work I've loved all along has written something so fresh and original."

—Marion Zimmer Bradley

Mercedes Lackey

JINX HIGH

A Diana Tregarde Investigation

TOR®

A Tom Doherty Associates Book
New York

JINX HIGH: A DIANA TREGARDE INVESTIGATION

Copyright © 1991 by Mercedes Lackey

Jinx High was originally published in 1991, in mass market by Tor Books.

A Tor Book
Published by Tom Doherty Associates, LLC
175 Fifth Avenue
New York, NY 10010

www.tor.com

Tor® is a registered trademark of Tom Doherty Associates, LLC.

Library of Congress Cataloging-in-Publication Data

Lackey, Mercedes.
    Jinx High : a Diana Tregarde investigation / Mercedes Lackey.—1st trade pbk. ed.
        p. cm.
    "A Tom Doherty Associates book."
    ISBN-13: 978-0-765-31319-5 (pbk.)
    ISBN-10: 0-765-31319-7 (pbk.)
    1. Tregarde, Diana (Fictitious character)—Fiction.   2. Witches—Fiction.
3. High school students—Fiction.   4. Tulsa (Okla.)—Fiction.   I. Title.

PS3562.A246 J56 2006
813'.54—dc22

                                                                        2006044636

First Trade Paperback Edition: November 2006

Printed in the United States of America

0 9 8 7 6 5 4 3 2 1

Dedicated to
Melissa Ann Singer
for helping to bail!

JINX HIGH

ONE

uffie Gentry pounded the steering wheel of her brand-new Miata, and cursed—though what she really felt like doing was crying her eyes out like a little kid. It *couldn't* have stalled. Daddy had *just* picked it up today. There was nothing wrong with anything, it had a full tank of gas—

But it had died way out here on 101st, and now it wasn't responding at all.

And this was a spooky place to get stranded past midnight. You might as well be in West Texas instead of less than twenty miles from downtown Tulsa. There wasn't anything out here but cows and cicadas, mysterious shadows, and an awful lot of dark.

Visions of the Rainy-day Rapist and the Southside Strangler kept popping into her head, making her look over her shoulder as she tried to get the *damn* car started one more time.

No luck. And now the tears did come; she sobbed in what she told herself was frustration but felt more like fear. *God, this is like the classic slasher-movie setup, girl stuck out on a deserted road at three A.M.—next thing I'll see is a guy in a hockey mask—*

She shivered and told herself not to be stupid. There was a gas station not a half mile behind her—it was closed, but there *was* a phone there. She could call the auto club. That was why Daddy had a gold card with them.

Resolutely—though it took every bit of courage she had—she

left the protection of the car and started the long trudge back toward the Kerr/McGee station. But she kept seeing things out of the
corner of her eye, things that vanished when she looked straight at
them, and before long she wasn't walking, she was running.

She'd never been so grateful to see a gas station in her life.

She fumbled the last quarter out of her purse—this was one of
those phones where you couldn't use a charge card, and you had to
put a quarter into it even to call 911. She was just glad she hadn't
dumped all her change, back at the mall, when Fay Harper had
sneered at her for putting cash in the liver-transplant box. Fay had
made her so damn mad—just because she'd beaten the senior out
on the Teenage America finals, that was no reason for Fay to imply
she'd gotten that far by sleeping with one of the judges—

Well, neither of them made it to the regionals, so there.

Buffie just wished Fay hadn't said what she did, when Buffie had
retorted with the truth nobody ever said out loud.

*"You should know, Fay Harper. You get everything you want by
sleeping around and passing out nose candy."*

And Fay had said something horrible, whispered it in Buffie's
ear. So horrible Buffie couldn't remember exactly what it was—
just some kind of threat.

Or promise. Because it had ended with—*"And when you see
what's coming for you, remember I sent it."*

Buffie shoved her coin into the slot with hands that shook so
hard she could hardly dial the number, and prayed for a quick
answer.

"God damn it." Sharon LeeMar looked at the phone resentfully. It
would ring, now, when she'd just gotten a new coat of polish on her
nails. It was probably nothing; some drunk, like last night, wanting
the auto club to pull the car out of the ditch where *he'd* put it. Or
some stupid kid who'd missed her ride home from some rich-bitch
party, and wanted *them* to provide her with one.

Well, there was a way around that. It wasn't like she hadn't done it before. She hit the button with her elbow. "Big A Auto Club," she said. "Will you hold?"

And before the caller could say a word, she hit the hang-up button.

Buffie stared at the phone in gut-wrenching shock, unable to believe she was hearing a dial tone. "No—" she whispered, a panic that she knew was irrational starting to take over. "No, you can't—"

She scrabbled desperately in her purse, hoping for one more quarter. Nothing. With a sob, she upended the whole thing on the pavement, pawing through a tangled mess of makeup, jewelry, credit cards, and odd bits of paper, praying for a quarter, a dime, anything—

Then she heard the sound; a kind of growl. And looked up.

And the scream died in her throat before she could utter it.

"What?"

Derek Kestrel half closed his lids against the wind that was drying his eyes, and gathered breath for another bellow. "I *said*," Deke yelled, trying to make himself audible over the bellow of the TransAm's engine and the painfully howling guitars of Motley Crüe, "I can't *hear* you!"

Fay Harper shook her head, her blond shag whipping wildly about her cheekbones. Her hair looked like spun frost under the fluorescent streetlamps, her pale skin glowed in the moonlight, and her eyes were turned to crimson embers by the reflections from the panel lights. "I can't hear you!" she screamed back, turning the volume up another notch until the TransAm's floor panels shook from the bass.

Deke sighed and gave up, leaning back into the padded headrest of his seat. It was custom-leather upholstered, of course, in deep burgundy to match the rest of the car; Fay Harper was never seen in less than the very best. Nothing was going to compete with *those* speakers. Nothing natural, anyway. A B-52 at full throttle, maybe.

Hanging out with Fay was hazardous to the eardrums. He wished now he'd brought earplugs or something. First had been the concert, front-row seats, now it was Fay's ass-kicking stereo; he was going to be deaf before the night was over.

Then again, hanging out with Fay Harper was hazardous to a lot more than the eardrums.

The TransAm tore down Memorial, Fay daring anything to pull into her path. Deke squinted against the headlights of the oncoming cars, assessed his blood-alcohol level by how fuzzy they looked, and came up with an answer the Parental Unit wouldn't like. It was a good thing his dad couldn't see him now. Hell, it was a good thing his dad hadn't seen the concert! While Deke hadn't shared anything but the bottle Fay'd brought, grass had been the mildest of the recreational pharmaceuticals making the rounds tonight. Funny. Dad may have been a wild-eyed hippie back when he was Deke's age, but he didn't know the half of what went on these days. Deke said the word "concert," and he could almost see nostalgic visions of Woodstock drifting through his dad's mind in a sunshine-golden, artistically backlit haze. *The Summer of Love. Peace, pop. Like, it's a happening. Oh, wow.*

He laughed out loud, and Fay gave him a funny look, then cranked the stereo up the last notch. His whole body throbbed and vibrated with the song. He could feel the amplifier overheating—

Or maybe the heat he felt was the effect of her hand sliding up his leg.

There was a drunken howl from the back seat, and Sandy Foster, football bohunk extraordinaire, leaned forward and handed them both cold beers, after throwing his own empty through the open T-top.

"Kick ass, Fay!" he shouted, as Fay gave him a smile that dazzled in the hellfire glow from the instrument panel, and a long, wet kiss in exchange for the beer. She never once took her foot off the gas, but she never swerved, and she hadn't missed a light yet.

There was a flash of headlights in the left lane as a couple of hopped-up metal-heads in a chop-top Cougar pulled alongside.

The driver shouted something, lost in the howl of engines and the screech of feedback. Fay tossed back her head in laughter, rapped on the horn once, contemptuously. Then she gave them the finger, and blew the doors off their pitiful poser-custom.

Deke wondered if his spine was going to have a close encounter with the back seat. The speedometer was in three digits by the time his stomach caught up with the rest of him.

Sandy howled again, and another bottle hit the pavement behind them.

Deke looked back at the Cougar eating their dust. For a minute, the guy on the passenger's side looked a little like his buddy Alan.

He bit his lip, and wondered what Alan was doing tonight then looked at the bottle in his hand. His conscience awoke, and sanity reared its cold, ugly head.

What in the hell am I doing here? How did I ever get mixed up with Fay's crowd?

Sandy was screaming along with the Crüe; the simpleminded lyrics of any popular song were all he needed to cover *his* questions.

Yeah, but Sandy's got three answers to deal with everything he runs up against—drink it, screw it, or tackle it. Every Bud's for him.

Jillian McIver, Fay's best friend, was nuzzling Sandy's neck like a toothless vampire. *The rest of them pretty much match Sandy. Jill's got no life outside the mall. Fay's got anything she wants. I'm the oddball here. So what the hell do they want with me?*

He glanced over at Fay; she smiled and licked her lips, and her hand reached the Promised Land. Questions began to seem pretty immaterial. . . .

However, Fay's luck with the lights ran out at just that moment. She pulled her hand away as the light changed from yellow to red. She *might* have tried to run it—but there was a little something bearing down on the intersection.

Deke wasn't so gone that he couldn't see the semi—and his reactions weren't too blown to grab for the "aw-shit" bar on the door as Fay cursed, locked all four wheels, and put the TransAm into a sideways drift, stopping just short of the intersection.

And as the front swung around, the headlights glared right into the eyes of the metal-brains still trying to race them. They *didn't* see the semi, or the red light—and if their music was as loud as Fay's, they couldn't hear the air horn blasting at them, either. They headed straight into the free-fire zone.

The Cougar dragged against the side of the semi's cab in a slo-mo shower of glass and plastic, fiberglass pelting down like candy-apple-red hail—the impact inaudible over the hellish guitar.

Fay wasn't fazed in the least. She bared her teeth, mouthed something, and down-shifted; gunned the car, and fled the scene in a cloud of tire smoke.

Smiling.

Jill and Sandy were in a heap somewhere on the floorboard, mingling with what was left of the cold case Fay had brought to finish off the concert.

All that Deke could think of for the first, shell-shocked minutes, was—*Sandy's probably enjoying the hell out of himself.*

Deke pried his fingers off the bar, one at a time. Fay's hands were on the wheel and the shifter, giving him a moment of thought unclouded by raging hormones.

He looked back at the wreck, and in a break between songs yelled, "What about *them*? Aren't you gonna—"

"They weren't fast enough," Fay shouted back, interrupting him. "They got what they were asking for. They weren't good enough, and they weren't fast enough."

She gave him a long, sideways look, measuring him against some unknown standard. Her eyes narrowed, and she licked her lips, the barest hint of her tongue showing between them. "So how about it, Deke? Are *you* fast enough?"

Shit. He looked back at the wreck; Fay shoved the stick up into fifth and slid her hand over to his leg. Again.

Christ. She's crazy! I think that wreck made her horny! Or— hornier— Deke suppressed a wince.

"*Fay!*"

Jillian McIver had a voice like a ripsaw, but the harsh whine was music to Deke's ears about now. Fay pulled her hand away.

"What?" she snarled over her shoulder.

"What the *hell* were you doing?"

Jill's disheveled head rose over the seat back, her dark curls falling over one eye; her lower lip was swollen and cut a little, and she sucked at it petulantly. Deke watched as Sandy's hand came up and made a grab for her, and she elbowed him away. "I about broke my *neck*, Fay," she complained, raking her hair out of her eyes with talonlike fingernails. "An' I cut my *lip*. It's gonna be a mess for a *week*. What d'you think you're doing, anyway?"

My God. The guys in that Cougar could be dead, and all she's worried about is her lip!

"Livin' life in the fast lane, girl," Fay replied with poisonous sweetness. "'Smatter? Can't you take the pace?"

"But my *lip*—"

"Sandy'll kiss it, and make it all better," Fay cooed. "Won't you, honey?"

"You bet," Sandy said thickly, from somewhere below the level of the seat back, and Jill vanished in the direction of his voice with a muffled yelp.

Deke hunched his shoulders and tried to become part of the upholstery. *Yeah. Life in the fast lane. And me a Yugo. Neep, neep. Oh well; the wreck wasn't that bad. At least those guys walked away from it.*

Fay had just hit a bad stretch of road on the winding back way into Jenks, and she needed to keep one hand on the shifter, one on the wheel, and both eyes in front of her. Fay was a foot-to-the-wall driver, but she wasn't suicidal. Even this late at night, you never knew when some drunk cowboy was going to pull out in front of you from one of the kicker bars around here.

Trees and bushes blurred past, sparked with the occasional flickers of fire that were animal eyes staring, mesmerized by their speeding headlights. Deke blinked.

So Fay caused a bumper-bender. Big deal.

As he watched the shadows blur past, the memory slowly faded from his mind. All he was thinking about was the speed, the night, and Fay.

Seems like there was something I should remember. . . . Aw, hell. Forget it. It's a damn good thing I'm *not the one driving,* he thought muzzily. *This road's right out of* Grapes of Wrath. *God only knows why Fay's using it. Your county taxes at work. What was it Alan said? The difference between Chicago and Tulsa County is that Chicago politicians steal the money* after *the roadwork's paid for? Yeah. Then Dad laughed and said that was why we live in Jenks. Good ol' Jenks, Oklahoma. All the benefits of Tulsa, none of the drawbacks.*

Twenty years ago, Jenks had been Hicksville, and Tulsa wouldn't give the residents of Jenks the time of day—now it was the bedroom community that Tulsa would *love* to incorporate, and Jenks wasn't having any part of the idea.

Now Jenks was the haven for some of the area's wealthiest professionals—doctors, lawyers, top management—who didn't want to give up their well-maintained roads or their autonomously funded school district, thank you. Jenks money stayed in Jenks. Because of that money, the Jenks schools were as good as the private academies over in Tulsa, and a far cry from the Tulsa public school system. That was a big selling point; yuppie parents believed in expensive education. From computers in the classroom to Olympic pools, what Jenks High *didn't* have wasn't *worth* having.

And a mere fifteen minutes up the interstate from your job. Shit, I sound like a real-estate ad.

A yuppie paradise. Every acquisitive dream come true, and no slums to mar the landscaping; no low-income housing, no porno rows, no bag ladies, no "undesirables."

It harbored those who lived a sheltered, pampered life. The kids who went to Jenks were used to living their parents' fine lifestyle to the hilt, used to the goodies that came without asking.

Like Fay, Sandy, Jill. More money than they knew what to do with, and parents too busy clawing their way to the top to pay *too* much attention to what their kids did with that money. They'd had expert nannies as babies—the finest shrinks money could buy to get them through their early teens—and once they reached sixteen or seventeen, most Jenks parents figured their kids could take care of themselves. Sort of the ultimate latchkey children. So long as they didn't bring the law down on them, so long as they kept their grades up and *looked* like they were straight, everything was cool.

Parents seemed to rely a lot on appearances in Jenks.

In Fay's case, there were no parents at all. Daddy was long gone to wherever dead oilmen went; Mummy was sucking up tranks in the loony bin at Vinita. All Fay had was some guy in a bank making Mummy and Daddy's trust-fund dollars produce baby trust-fund dollars, and a "guardian" who spent all her time watching the soaps, making herself invisible whenever Fay wanted to party.

Deke felt more than a twinge of guilt about that. Dad knew Aunt Emily existed—and assumed she was keeping an eye on the proceedings every time Deke was over at Fay's. Tonight was no exception; he'd said something about it being nice that this aunt didn't mind hanging out with the kids.

When all the time Aunt Emily was not only letting them do damn near anything they pleased short of burning the place down, *she* was the one who'd bought the booze.

It's a good thing Mom's in Japan. She's got radar, I swear she does, she knows every damn time I get shit-faced. I bet she's the one that put Dad up to giving me that grass and making a video of me making an ass out of myself. He blushed, glad that it wouldn't be visible in the scarlet lighting from the dash. *I've never been so embarrassed in my life. God. I wanted to die.*

He couldn't even imagine Aunt Emily doing what Dad had done. *No way anybody's ever done that to Fay. No way anybody'd dare do that to her. She gets what she wants, and that's it. What the hell am I doing with her, anyway?*

Back to the same old question. It didn't make any sense. It hadn't made any sense when she asked him if he wanted to go with her. Fay Harper, head cheerleader, a senior, the prom queen, and the hottest roll in the sheets in Tulsa County—and *she* wanted *him*? Derek Kestrel, a junior, a guy who wasn't even on the basketball team for

Chrissake, a guy who didn't even have a *sports car*, just a Chevy Citation. It didn't make any sense at all. And that she'd stuck with him for two whole months was way outside probability.

He couldn't figure out what Fay wanted, what kind of prestige she was getting in going with him. It couldn't be his family—Dad was a pretty high-fee architect, but no Frank Lloyd Wright. Mom was as far up in the hierarchy as she was ever going to get—or wanted to get—with Telex. Fay had more money *now* than Mom and Dad put together, and when she hit eighteen—it was no contest.

And it wasn't like his parents gave him *any* extra on his leash, either. Fay didn't need him to do whatever she wanted; she just did it, and got away with it, just like tonight. The concert party had been her idea; the whole evening was *her* little treat. She'd wanted to raise some hell, and nothing was going to get in her way. She'd bought the tickets from a scalper, prices that had made Deke blanch; now she'd haul them all home with her, there'd be more booze, and she'd hinted she had some really hot videotapes.

All without a single word of opposition from anybody. Anytime Fay wanted anything, good old Aunt Emily okayed the credit card charges, bought the damn booze, and wouldn't poke her nose out of her room from the moment they all came in through the front door.

Aunt Emily doesn't give squat what Fay does. So long as she's got her soaps and Fay's trust fund keeps her life cushy, she's happy. She sends so many excuse notes to the principal's office you'd think Fay cranked 'em out on the Xerox. Shit, sometimes I think Fay only shows up at school 'cause cutting is more boring than going to class. Damn if I know how she stays head cheerleader. Or how she keeps from getting flunked out. Not that Aunt Emily would care.

God, how am I going to stay out of the doghouse? Derek suddenly realized that his dad would probably still be up when he came home—Mom and Dad were both night owls, given the chance—and he began trying very hard to think of a way to sneak in without Dad finding out he'd been putting a few down. It wasn't like Dad would *say* anything, or even *do* anything. He'd just give Deke that look—

The one that says, "I thought you had more brains than that." The one that says, "I still have that video, remember?" Christ. Good old straight edge Dad. You'd think he never got fucked-up in his life You'd think giving me that dope and letting me get shit-faced and making that tape was legal. So I put down a few, so what?

So I figure I'm making an ass out of myself, that's what. Worse; I'm being a shithead. We should have stopped at that wreck—Fay caused the wreck. I let her get away with running out. I was too blown—or too scared—to stop her. And Dad doesn't have to tell me what a chickenshit I am.

He sighed. He really didn't belong in Fay's crowd; *they* didn't care what their parents thought of them. He really kind of wanted his folks to—to respect him.

He just didn't fit in, no matter how hard he tried.

But Fay wanted him anyway.

I like the way the other kids look at me. Like I'm some kind of— of—superstar, to get Fay. I want to keep her—but what's the attraction? he asked himself, sneaking a look at the devastating blond out of the corner of his eye. *I don't think I'm that good in bed.*

She seemed to sense his eyes on her, and gave him a sideways glance of her own, a proprietary look that made him feel very uncomfortable, even though he grinned back at her.

One of those stoned cowboys pulled out right in front of them, and Fay cursed, pulled her attention away from Deke, and skidded around him. Warm, wet wind slapped Deke in the face as they rolled past the jacked-up pickup so fast it might just as well have been parked.

Deke slumped down in his seat, his hands clenched around the warming bottle of beer. For a moment, he'd been mesmerized by those eyes, but the minute she took her gaze off him, his mood sank again. *When she looks at me like that, I feel like a boy-toy, some kind of prize she can show off in front of everybody. Like a piece of meat. And I still don't understand why* me. *Why not Bob Williams? Shit, Mr. Touchdown, big-time quarterback, Senior All-Star. He's more like her speed. More than a match for her in the looks, too.*

Muscles all over, including between his ears, blond—shit, guy looks
like a recruiting poster for the Hitler Youth.

He turned away, brooding out the window at the shadows in the
fields and the vague hints of outbuildings going by. They were past
the Jenks "downtown" now, all two blocks of it, and everything but
the bars locked up tight; out in the country, heading for Fay's place.
Warp Factor Four, Mr. Sulu.

It ought to be Bob sitting here. No, that's backward—it'd be Bob
in the driver's seat, Fay over here; in his Porsche, not her TransAm.
Bob doesn't take the back seat for anyone.

Bob's old man was the basketball coach—one reason why Deke
had never even bothered to try out for the team. He got all the ex-
posure he wanted to the Williams family just avoiding Bobby-Boy
and his idea of what constituted a joke. Bob had a way of finding
exactly the most humiliating thing to say or do to you, and he liked
picking on what he called "brains." Deke had gotten dumped on a
couple of times by Bobby-Boy. He didn't need to put up with
Coach and the Gestapo Method of Basketball Training.

He runs that team like a concentration camp. Hell for the outcasts,
paradise for the Chosen. And a raise every year, even when the teach-
ers don't get one. Not that Coach Big Bob needs the job, or the money.
Mrs. Bob has enough loot for twelve. And Bobby-Boy spends it like it's
Argentinian pesos, throws it around, makes like hundred-dollar bills
were pocket change; just the kind of guy you'd think Fay would dig.

More than that, Bob's parental leash was as long as Deke's was
short. Big Bob let him get away with literally everything, with rule-
breaking that would get any other kid bounced from the team for
the rest of his school career. In fact, Bobby had gotten a girl from
Union pregnant last year—Big Bob got the pregnancy hushed up,
then got the family lawyer to scare the girl into an abortion.

Then had the balls to sit front-row center at the Mabee Chapel
over at ORU every Sunday, and campaign for Right-to-Life.

Deke had overheard his parents talking about the story one
night—Mom had been ready to fry nails, she was so hot. Seems
that Big Bob had been boasting about his boy's "prowess" over at

the club bar, and Mom had overheard. *And* given him a piece of her mind, right in front of his cronies in the bar.

Which makes for another good reason not to try out for the team. Thanks, Mom.

Deke rubbed his thumb along the wet side of the beer bottle. Bobby-Boy's mom would never have *dared* do anything like that. Deke kind of admired his mom's guts, but he wished she'd found some other way to take Big Bob down. One that wasn't so—public.

No, that would never have happened to Bobby-Boy. Not good old Bobby Williams, apple of his mother's eye, pride of his daddy's stable, master of all he surveyed.

Maybe that's why Fay didn't move in on him. She doesn't like to take second seat to anybody, any more than Bobby-Boy does.

Still . . . sometimes, it seemed like it would be nice to have a dad a little like Big Bob. Deke would lay odds that when Bobby-Boy came home shit-faced, not only would his dad hand him a beer, he'd want to know how many notches Bobby'd carved on his gearshift that night.

Fay was taking the long way home tonight. Deke stared up at the full moon pouring pale light down through the T-top, and wondered why she'd decided to tour the county. Not that it mattered. The end of tonight's ride was as predictable as the full moon. Fay's house, Fay's living room, Fay's movies; then Fay's bedroom, Fay's bed.

Life in the fast lane.

And somehow, some way, he was going to have to figure out how to cope with it all—Fay, money, lifestyle. Before he said or did something that would make it all fall apart and turn her against him. Because if she turned on him—he might as well try to talk his parents into getting a transfer for him, because life at Jenks would be unbearable. Fay would see to that.

You can't go back, isn't that what they say? I sure can't, not now. I'm doing stuff now I never even dreamed about.

Used to be, though, weekends would be over at one of the guys' houses, often as not. Either George Louvis's place, or Alan's. If

George's, they'd listen critically to the band; give George their two cents' worth. Sometimes he'd even take their advice, like when he got rid of the third Fender and picked up a Gibson. If Alan's, they'd do some computer stuff—Alan was too together to be a nerd, but he knew his micro like most guys knew their cars. Some of the games he'd come up with were pretty incredible.

Used to be, when he went out with a chick, the farthest he got was some really heavy petting.

Used to be, he knew who his friends were.

Now—well, since he'd taken up with Fay, George wouldn't even talk to him. George hated Fay, though he'd never say why, exactly. But he didn't let that show—he just avoided her like she was contagious. And since now Deke was constantly in her company, he avoided Deke, too. The only time Deke ever saw him anymore was at dances.

Alan was still his good buddy—except—

Except he figures Fay is Trouble. Keeps bugging me to drop her. Even when he doesn't say anything, it's like with Dad, like I can hear what he's thinking. That she's gonna get me in deep. And that when she does, she'll bail out on me, leaving me stuck up to my ass.

Deke grimaced. *Hell with it. They don't have a clue.* Because, God, it was worth it—Alan couldn't even guess. His life was so exciting. . . . Fay'd done things with him he hadn't even fantasized before he got involved with her. Some things he hadn't even known were anatomically possible! She was incredible, insatiable, a real sexual athlete—

Takes the gold in the water-bed races, not to mention the pole vault. . . .

In short, so far as Deke understood the meaning of the word, Fay was a genuine nympho.

There was only one problem. He was beginning to have trouble keeping up with her.

—as 'twere—

The real problem was, when he failed to come through with the goods, she really knew where to put the knife, and how to twist it to make it hurt the most. Her standards, and her expectations, were high. *All* the time. No coffee breaks, no vacations, no sick leave.

And when Fay didn't get what Fay wanted, there was hell to pay. *Oh hell. No pain, no gain. Right? Maybe more vitamins.*

Deke could see the lights of the cars on the interstate beading the horizon; that meant the turnoff to Fay's driveway wasn't too far away. He began to hope, desperately, that Fay *did* have some video-porn planned. Between the bottle that made the rounds at the concert and the beer he'd drunk in the car, there wasn't much rising tonight except hope.

I'm going to need all the help I can get, he thought unhappily.

A sudden lurch threw him against the door and broke into his preoccupied thoughts. Fay was weaving pretty badly, though she hadn't slacked up at all, speed-wise. Deke knew that the steering on her car was touchy, but this wasn't touchy steering, this was DWI. Her foot was *still* right down against the firewall, and she was taking up every inch of her lane, and then some.

Fay was pounding out the tempo on the steering wheel, just a hair off the beat, nodding her head in time to the music. She never did that except when she was well and truly polluted.

Deke closed his eyes and hoped that the driveway wasn't too far away.

"*Fay!*" Jill shrieked, five inches away from his ear, startling him so badly that he lost his grip on the beer and dropped it.

Oh, great, he thought, groping for it. *Terrific. In the morning, when she smells beer all over the car, she's going to have my ass for a rug.*

Fay just laughed at nothing, and took another swig from her brew.

"*Fay!*" Jill howled, her hair blowing into her wide, alarm-filled eyes as she leaned forward over the back of the seat.

"What?" Fay shrieked back, still laughing wildly.

Jill waited until the pause between songs. "I think you've had too much, Harper," she screamed, gesturing at the beer in Fay's hand. "You oughta let somebody else drive before we—"

Fay flung the empty out the top of the car, her face twisted with an anger Deke knew only too well.

Oh, shit. She's going to have a tantrum, right here and now, at warp speed.

She'd had a few of those tantrums at *him*, when he didn't bow to whatever whim of the hour she was embracing. They were not among his most cherished moments.

He usually wound up feeling like he'd been skinned and dipped in boiling lead. He'd *rather* have been skinned and dipped in boiling lead. It would have hurt less.

"It's *my* goddamn car," Fay screamed, twisting the wheel viciously as they rounded a curve, throwing both Jill and Deke against the right-hand side. "I'll drive it any way I fuckin' want!"

Jill clawed her way back up to her position between Deke and Fay. "Yeah," she wailed, "but we're gonna get stopped!"

Fay's teeth were bared in a snarl. "I never get stopped!" she countered.

"Yeah, but—"

"You callin' me a liar, McIver?" Her eyes glittered, hard and cold, and it seemed to Deke that not all the red in them was due to reflections from the dash lights.

"No, but—"

That was one "but" too many. Fay whipped around to face the girl, her expression a distorted mask.

"All right!" she screamed. *"You* drive!"

And suddenly—there was no one behind the steering wheel.

Derek couldn't move. He *tried*; tried to grab for the wheel, tried to vault the shift into the driver's seat. He *could not* move; something outside of him was holding him in place.

Jill screamed and bailed over the back of the seat, grabbing desperately for the wheel. The wheel wrenched to the left, just as she got her hands on it.

By itself.

It was enough to make his breath stop and the hair to rise on the back of his neck. Derek watched the wheel actually fighting her, like the car was steering itself.

The last obstacle on the way to Fay's place loomed up in front of them—an overpass with a little county road running underneath. The motor roared as the car impossibly accelerated.

Jill screamed, still clawing at the wheel.

The tires echoed her screams, in terrifying harmony.

Deke tried to break the paralysis holding his body as he realized they weren't going to make it past the overpass—

The left side of the car dropped sickeningly as the wheels left the road.

"*Fu*—" was the only sound from the rear seat, indicating that Sandy had at least noticed they were all about to die.

It was the phone call every parent is afraid he'll get anytime his kid goes out.

"Mr. Kestrel? This is Officer Ridell of the Tulsa County Police. There's been an accident—"

Larry Kestrel's hand spasmed on the handset; his heart stopped beating. He stared at a single pale-beige Art Deco rose on the kitchen wallpaper. And in his mind only one thought was clear. *Not Deke. Dear God, not Deke—*

"—your son's all right," the stranger's voice continued. "But you'd better come on down to Hillcrest and pick him up. He's cut up and bruised, and—real shook up. It was a pretty bad wreck, and one of the other kids was killed, one of the girls in the car."

His heart started again, leaping with relief and something shamefully like joy. His eyes blurred; his knees went to jelly. He wanted to laugh and cry at the same time. One of the other kids. *Not* Deke. Not *his* son.

He stammered something to the police officer on the other end of the line; it must have been all right, or else the cop was used to incoherent parents. Probably the latter. Whatever, the cop told him he'd get all the details when he got Deke from the emergency room, but no, the kids weren't in trouble and there weren't any charges being filed; it was just a hideous accident.

Somehow he got out to the car; he didn't notice that he was driving until he was already rolling past the Jenks downtown district. It was a damned good thing that the bars hadn't closed yet; if he'd had to play dodge-'em with a bunch of drunks, he'd have been wiped out before he got past Seventy-first Street. Shook up as he was, the drive to Hillcrest passed in a blur. He began to notice, but only after he'd passed them, that at least half the lights he hit were red. He slowed down a little, tried to relax by telling himself that the cop *had* to have been telling the truth—if Deke was at Hillcrest he couldn't be *too* badly hurt. He'd have to have been coherent enough to tell someone to take him there; otherwise he'd be someplace closer to Jenks rather than the hospital Larry had told him to ask for if he had a choice.

The parking lot was nearly empty, but lit up like a tennis court; Larry pulled the BMW across two spaces, flung the driver's door open, and raced for the emergency room without bothering to lock it—

He hadn't expected an automatic door; it had been years since he'd been to an emergency room. The double glass panels suddenly gaped wide for him, like the doors of the Starship Enterprise. He found himself in the anteroom, people turning to stare at him, most of them dressed in white, while he stood there blinking stupidly in the fluorescent lights.

Movement to his left; a dark tan-and-brown shape. He blinked again. A portly security guard approached him, a man obviously past retirement age, moving slowly, cautiously. Larry wondered what it was in his expression that made the man walk toward him so carefully, as if *he* was dangerous.

"I'm—" He coughed. His throat was too dry to talk easily. He swallowed, and tried again. "I'm Larry Kestrel. The county police called, an Officer Ridell. My son—"

The guard's anxious expression cleared. He nodded a balding, age-spotted head. "No problem, Mr. Kestrel," he said. "Your kid's okay; he's all patched up and ready to go home. We've got him over here." He gestured that Larry should follow him down the blindingly white corridor to his right, a corridor lined with closed and open doors. Larry glanced inside one of the open doors, looking for some sign of Deke. There were curtains on ceiling runners, some open, some making little partitions around waiting gurneys, some entirely closing off little alcoves. Examination areas?

Probably; from beyond one of those curtained-off alcoves he could hear voices, fragments of conversation. One, female, young but tired sounding: ". . . Christ, they oughta call it *Jinx* High, there's been so many accidents. That's the second one tonight, and three DOA. . . ."

Not my boy. Thank you, God. Not my boy.

There was a cop—a *real* cop, in a real Tulsa County uniform—waiting outside one of those closed doors.

"This's the boy's father," the paunchy old man said, and shoved him slightly in the cop's direction when he didn't move.

The cop took his elbow—this was a middle-aged man, maybe a little younger than Larry, but as lean as the rent-a-cop was paunchy. And he knew his business. Larry dazedly discovered himself being gently steered toward a bench and pushed down on it. The cop eased down next to Larry with a weary groan. Larry looked at him anxiously, and found himself staring right into a pair of tired, but friendly, brown eyes.

"Okay, here's the scoop," the cop said, the weariness that showed plainly in his eyes making his voice a little dull. "I'm the guy that called you; I'm the guy that got called to the scene. I'm the guy who's writing this up. I've stayed with these kids the whole time. First of all, your kid is fine. He had a scalp cut that took about three stitches, and he might be concussed. What he *is*, he's scared, he's shocky, and he's pretty well shook up. One of the two girls took a header through the windshield, practically in his lap, and—well, that's the one I told you about on the phone. The doctors are with her folks."

The man shrugged, but the look in his eyes told Larry everything he needed to know. It hadn't been pretty. And the girl's parents wouldn't want to see the father of one of the survivors.

"The other girl, the driver, she says the steering went out on her. Right now we don't see any reason to call her a liar. Things are a real mess under what's left of that sumbitch." He shook his head. "Things pretty well tally with what she told us. You can figure we ran blood and Breathalyzer tests on all of the kids, anyway. That's SOP for a case like this, that's part of why we couldn't call you right away. We were waiting for the results. All three kids came out straight. Nobody was doin' anything, no drugs, no booze. So, no charges. Not like the other one—two private-school kids out drag racing on Memorial, stoned to the gills. Glad the town boys got that one, I hear there wasn't much left."

Larry let out the breath he had been unconsciously holding in, and inhaled a lungful of harsh antiseptic. He hardly noticed as it burned his throat.

So Deke's not only okay, he wasn't fucked-up. "Then—what happened?"

The cop sighed, and rubbed his eyes with the back of his hand. "I don't know; the kids weren't real coherent. The other boy, Sandy, he can't remember anything after they left the concert—doc says it's traumatic amnesia, and he probably won't ever get that memory back. The other gal says her girlfriend was probably unbelted; she was leaning up between the front buckets to talk, anyway. You know kids—all over the damn car, yakking, and no way to convince 'em to stay belted. The other three were buckled up, but not the McIver kid. My guess is she was half over the front seat when the steering went out. Odds are they were probably speeding some, but since there's no skid marks, there's no way to tell for sure, and after this—hell, I may file a report, but *I'm* not gonna book 'em."

"But Deke's all right?" Larry wanted that reassurance again, though a part of him reflected on the irony of a former flower child begging for reassurance from The Man.

"As all right as he's going to be," the cop said, then hesitated. "Look, I'm no psychologist, and it's none of my business, but your kid just had a friend die, about as ugly a death as you can think of, and within inches of him. It was real messy. I don't think you want to know *how* messy. Go easy on him, okay? Give the kid some space."

"What I'm going to give him," Larry said slowly, "is the most convincing hug I've *ever* given him; I'm going to tell him I love him, and that I'm thanking God he's okay, and that anything else doesn't matter squat."

The cop grinned, his tired face wrinkling with smile lines for a moment, and he slapped Larry on the back lightly. "You're a good dad, Mr. Kestrel," he replied with sincerity. "You go in there and take your kid home."

They both rose and started for the examining room, the cop reaching the door a little ahead of him and opening it for him.

Larry stepped inside; Deke was sitting on the edge of a green plastic chair, slumped over. For the thousandth time since his son hit puberty, Larry was struck by the incredible likeness he and Deke shared. Same bone structure, same wavy hair—only the green eyes were Miri's. For Larry, looking at Deke was like looking into a time-reversing mirror. He wondered if Deke realized.

The boy looked up quickly at the sound of the door opening, his face white, his eyes like a pair of hollows in a snowbank. His clothing was torn, mud and blood splattered, and there were bruises on his forehead and neck. Under the harsh fluorescent light the kid looked like a corpse himself.

Then the blank, strained look Deke wore vanished as he realized who was there. "D-dad?" he faltered.

And threw himself into Larry's arms.

Legacy of the sixties; Larry and Miri Kestrel had taken no small amount of pride in the fact that they'd raised a boy who thought it no sin to show how he felt. Now Larry was deeply grateful they'd been able to do that. As the cop closed the door of the tiny cubicle to give them some privacy, the two of them shivered and cried together, and held each other tightly.

Deke couldn't speak at all for a long time, and Larry wasn't in much better shape. His throat was knotted with conflicting emotions, and he was trembling just as much as his son. Finally the tears seemed to ease something inside his boy, and the young body began to relax. "Dad—" Deke sobbed. "Dad, I'm sorry, I'm sorry—"

What it was he thought he had to be sorry for, Larry had no idea. At the moment it didn't matter. All that really mattered was that Deke was safe—

—*for the moment.*

The thought came out of nowhere, unbidden. As if it wasn't his.

A chill threaded Larry's spine at that alien, unguarded thought. A chill he hadn't felt for years.

Until now.

He held Deke a little tighter, and he stared over the boy's shoulder at the cold, blank, antiseptic wall. There was nothing there. Nothing that could be detected by the five senses.

But Larry Kestrel was not necessarily limited to five senses. He closed his eyes, and let his mind open, just a little.

Danger.

The feeling was unmistakable; as clear and acrid as the metallic, chemical scent of disinfectant permeating the room.

Something was threatening his boy. He let himself relax a little further, hoping to identify it.

Hunger.

A deep, insatiable hunger; an old hunger.

Something *wanted* his boy. Something that did not operate by the laws and rules of the so-called normal world, the world Larry had lived and moved in exclusively for the past seventeen years.

But not always. Before that—before he and Miri had moved to Tulsa—he'd had no few encounters with another world altogether. And that feather-light brush of cold down his back that had just alerted him had always been the signal that he was about to have another such meeting. The other feeling, the feeling of danger—that wasn't exactly new, either. But he hadn't felt it in years, and it had never been this strong before.

It had never been aimed at anyone but *himself* before.

He stiffened—and the feeling faded, leaving behind it only bone-deep weariness, and the even deeper relief of a parent whose child is safe.

For now, said something, a certainty deeper than thought. *For now.*

"Come on, son," he said, quietly. "Let's go home."

TWO

Ann Greeley surveyed the twenty-four pupils of her Honors English class and grimaced. And not because they were wearing clothing *she* couldn't afford unless she won the Publisher's Clearing House Sweepstakes—which they were. Not because in general they spent more on one haircut than she spent in twelve months; she'd gotten used to that over the past three years. Not because she knew that the "allowance" most of them got from their parents every week equaled or bettered her salary.

It was because she felt as if she was facing a class full of trendoid zombies.

One and all, with very few exceptions, they hung over their reading assignments listlessly. They were not acting as if they were distracted, but as if they were too emotionally burned-out to care about the assignment or comprehend it. And that was *not* the norm for this class, a class that a kid had to *earn* his way into.

The empty desk in the third row was the reason; Jillian McIver's seat. Oh, it didn't have her name on it, but it might as well have. That had been her favorite desk for most of the year—she'd even come to class a minute or so before everyone else just to secure it. Now it shouted her absence, the rest of the kids so studiously averting their eyes from it that they might just as well have stared and gotten it over with.

The funeral had been on Wednesday, but the kids were still in mourning, and Ann was desperate for a way to wake them up. She'd tried anything and everything—she'd taken a risk that the principal might find out and object to her playing anything more controversial than *Bambi*, and brought in her own videotapes, showing them *The Breakfast Club* and asking them for reviews and analysis. She'd tried asking for reports on their favorite Judy Blume novel. She'd had absolutely no results, and no luck. Response was automatic and dead. Jillian's seat was empty, and that emptiness ate at the whole class like a cancer.

It was ironic that Ann hadn't wanted the girl in her class; despite high grades in English (though never anywhere else), to her way of thinking Jill had been just another mindless mall bunny. The principal and Jill's counselor had both prevailed against Ann's better judgment. "She needs to be motivated and challenged," they'd said. "She's not getting any challenge that she recognizes as such anywhere else."

The latest buzzwords, had been Ann's disgusted thought. *The latest excuse for why a spoiled kid doesn't give squat about school, when her parents don't care what happens so long as she graduates* or *gets married, whichever comes first.*

But for once her superiors had been right. Much as Ann hated to admit it. She was of the cynical, if unvoiced, opinion that guidance counselors were failed teachers who were too inflexible to find a job outside the school system. And that principals were inept teachers who'd been bumped upstairs to keep them from ruining any more kids.

The fall term traditionally began with drama, working in no particular order, anything from modern to classic to Greek. Ann confidently expected Jill to wither under the onslaught of *The Lady's Not for Burning*, and capitulate with *The Seagull*. But that scenario never developed.

Jillian McIver encountered classic literature and freedom of thought, and blossomed. Much to Ann's astonishment (since she hadn't expected that the girl would even be able to read without moving her lips) Jill devoured Jonson, raced through Chekhov.

And then she went on to gobble Molière, Ibsen, and Schiller.

Then they'd hit the section on comedy, and Jill had *really* shown what she was made of. She'd done a synopsis of Aristophanes' *The Wasps* in ValSpeak that had even Ann rolling in the aisles. The girl was a natural comedian, which may have accounted for her popularity. Despite a voice like a whining saw, she could convulse either a listener *or* a reader. And Ann had cherished hopes of nurturing that gift. There was no reason why the girl couldn't become a *real* comic, or a comedic writer. She had the wit, and the talent.

But not the drive.

Gradually Ann had become aware of a curious metamorphosis. Inside the class Jill was one of the shining stars, bright, articulate, witty. Outside that classroom door, Jill was the same vapor-brain she'd always appeared to be.

Inside, she held her own with the Brain Trust.

Outside, she trailed around with the Trend Set, and never opened her mouth except to second someone else's ideas.

It had been, all things considered, rather like watching a multiple-personality case switch personas. It had also been maddening to witness, because the girl was only interested in using her comedic sense to amuse her classmates. She had no ambitions otherwise.

It was the waste of intellect that had troubled Ann the most. That, and the switch to airhead she pulled whenever she hit the door on the way out of Ann's classroom.

Dear God, it was like watching Segovia pump out guitar backups for Muzak tapes.

The kids in the class didn't seem to be bothered by the fact that Jill was one person to them and another to the social crowd. In fact, they seemed to have expected it, and there was a kind of unspoken accord among them not to approach Jill in any way outside the class, unless she approached them first. As if they were all obeying some kind of tribal law of conduct Ann hadn't been made aware of.

It had annoyed the hell out of Ann; among other things, Jill *could* have been a bridge between the academic and the social cliques. If she'd chosen to do so . . .

But she wasn't interested in being a bridge to anything. Once that kid passed the threshold, she had no life outside of shopping and parties. As far as Ann could tell, she never even opened a book outside of school.

Ann could not imagine a life without books, especially for someone as bright as Jill proved she could be.

A life without books . . . There was a book locked up in Ann's desk right now that was Jill's—*I, Claudius*. She'd brought it in under her notebooks and asked Ann to keep it for her so she could read it between assignments.

Presumably because if she'd been seen with it, she'd have had the stigma of being a Brain.

Well, it was all an academic question now; the girl was as dead as last year's leaves, and all her ambitions—or rather, lack of them—were dead with her.

And the kids, ranging from freshman to senior, were taking it much harder than she would have dreamed. The life was gone from the class.

She wasn't just the star pupil with a gift for comedy, Ann thought, watching Derek Kestrel turn over the last page of the assignment, then brood out the window. *She was their passport into the In Crowd, if only by proxy. And it isn't just that she's dead, it's the way she died.*

The accident had not only been freakish, but there were some strange rumors circulating about it, rumors that had reached even the teacher's lounge, that things weren't the way the official story had them.

According to the police reports, Jill was the only one of the four kids in the car *not* wearing her seat belt. And that, given that Ann had personally heard Fay Harper boast of having no less than twenty-three warning tickets for *not* wearing her belt ("It scrunches my clothes"), was very odd indeed. So was the way Jill had died. She'd been catapulted over the front seat and partially through the windshield. But not completely through—and it wasn't the impact that had killed her.

She'd bled to death, her throat slashed open to the spine by the broken windshield. When Jill's head went through the windshield, the glass had fragmented into knife-edged shards that had closed around her throat like a collar of razors.

Yet none of the blood had fountained into the interior of the car. Neither Deke nor Fay had so much as a single drop on them.

There were rumors that Fay had been moving in on Jill's steady; that Fay had told Jill not to object *or* tell Deke Kestrel, or Fay would "take care of " her.

Yet Fay wasn't acting like a teenager who'd gotten her way over a rival; and Ann hadn't met a kid yet who could convincingly cloak gloating triumph or fake grief. Fay was acting "normally," just as distraught as anyone would expect. She hadn't been overly hysterical, nor cold and distant. She'd wept *exactly* as much as one would predict for a girl whose best friend had just died.

Even more telling, to Ann's mind, she wasn't zeroing in on Sandy that Ann could see, which would have been the next move for a girl whose rival was out of the way. At least, she wasn't going after the boy publicly, and teenagers, in Ann's experience, were just not good at subtlety or strategy.

There were other contradictions, though. There were rumors and eyewitness accounts that the quartet had been drinking heavily at the concert and afterward.

According to the doctors' reports and a dozen lab tests, there hadn't been a trace of alcohol or drugs in the kids' systems. Even Jill, who'd been the first tested. Of course, it had been pretty easy to get a blood sample from what was left of Jill. . . .

The official story was that Jill had unbuckled her seat belt to talk to Fay, because the music on the car stereo was too loud for her to be heard from the backseat. That would certainly account for *why* the girl went headfirst through the windshield when the others were only cut by flying glass, or bruised. Fay's story was that the steering went out, cause unknown. According to the police, there was no way of telling what had happened, because the undercarriage had been destroyed when the car went off the road. . . .

Enough already, Ann told herself sternly. *You aren't Miss Marple, and there's no way any of this could be anything except a particularly bizarre accident. Life goes on. You have a class to teach, and they've already lost a week to this. You have to get them motivated again. That's your job. Not trying to make an episode of* The Twilight Zone *out of this.*

She watched the kids finishing their assignment, one by one. Finally the last one turned over the final page, and Ann stood up. Twenty-four pairs of eyes turned listlessly toward her.

"You've all finished C. J. Cherryh's essay," she said. "It might interest you to know that Ms. Cherryh is a very prominent science fiction writer and lives here in Oklahoma."

And used to teach in Oklahoma City, poor thing, Ann thought wryly. *No wonder she went into writing. They ought to issue machetes and Uzis, and award combat pay over there.*

Some of the kids *did* look interested, as if they hadn't imagined that a *real writer* could come from anywhere they recognized. Ann smiled in satisfaction.

Now that they've got that idea in their heads, maybe I can install the notion that they could really become writers. Then I get them to deal with what happened to Jill through fiction. If I can get these kids to put their trauma in writing, it'll help them a lot. That's what all the teaching magazines say, anyway.

"I'm telling you this," she continued, "because I want to prove something to you. I want to prove to you that the people who write books are just like you and me. I want to prove to you that any of *you* could be one of those people, with enough work and talent. And believe me, the work is more important than the talent."

She paced back and forth, slowly, in the little Demilitarized Zone between her desk and theirs. She watched their expressions as she spoke, hoping for the spark of interest that would tell her that she was motivating them again.

Because this class was her reason for continuing to teach. Without it, she'd have gone slowly crazy, like so many other teachers she knew. And if she couldn't get this class going again, she'd lose *her* motivation, for this year, and maybe for good.

If that happened, she might as well take that job over at that advertising agency. The pay was *much* better and the grief factor bound to be less.

"So, what you're going to be doing for the rest of this quarter is this: you are going to learn how to write fiction yourselves. First you're going to see *how* to write, which is why I chose 'Arms and the Writer' as your first reading assignment, so you can understand the importance of choosing the right words." She smiled at them, noting that the new girl in the back, the transferee from Colorado, was looking particularly bright and eager.

Ann had high hopes for that one. Normally she didn't warm much to the pretty girls—they tended to be as bad as Jill, if not worse. And this girl was spectacular—creamy-brown, perfect skin, green eyes, bronze hair, and petite face and figure. But she had been genuinely interested *and* talented, and Ann found herself directing at least half her remarks to the newcomer.

Maybe she'll replace Jill. . . . "Mark Twain also said something of the same thing: 'The difference between the right word and the almost-right word is the difference between lightning and a lightning bug.' Here's your homework assignment: I'm going to give you each a different picture. I want you to write one paragraph about it; choose *exactly* the right words to describe it. Make it not just a description of the scene, but try to describe what seems to be happening, as if you were writing a tiny story. You are absolutely forbidden to use the words 'almost' and 'nearly.'"

She began passing out the pictures, culled from a dozen different magazines she'd gotten at the Salvation Army, carefully matched to her students' individual interests. The only things the pictures had in common were that each contained two people, one old man, one young woman—and it appeared that the old man might be teaching her or offering advice.

"While I'm distributing these pictures, I'd like to ask your help."

Derek Kestrel took his picture listlessly. Ann was particularly worried about him. He'd gone as uncommunicative as a mute.

Not that she blamed him. It couldn't be easy to have a friend beheaded, particularly not when it was virtually impossible to have saved her.

"I need to know," she continued, passing the glossy bits of paper down the row of desks, "if any of you or your parents know a real, professional writer who would be willing to come in and help me show you what you need to do to become a writer." She smiled encouragingly. "The only ones that *I* know have full-time jobs too; they can't take several weeks off just to come in and teach a class."

A couple of the kids roused up enough to look surprised. Ann responded to that surprise as the first genuine reaction she'd gotten from them in a week. "That—having to hold down a 'real job,' or as those writers call it, a 'day job'—is part of becoming a professional writer. Some people *never* make it to full-time, self-supporting authordom. I'd like to have someone here who *has*, who can tell you what it takes and give you a taste of what his nuts-and-bolts world is all about."

She looked around the classroom; to her surprise it was Derek who raised his hand.

"My dad knows someone," he offered tentatively. "There's a lady he used to go to college with. She's a full-time writer; she writes romances."

Two of the boys snickered; half a dozen of the girls looked truly interested, though, and the little girl from Colorado positively came alive. Her green eyes glowed and her cheeks flushed with excitement.

"That's *exactly* the kind of thing I was hoping for," Ann said quickly, to counter the snickers. "Romance writers are very business-oriented people, and there are quite a few men writing in that genre under female pseudonyms. I'm not interested in someone who's been spending the last twenty years trying to write the Great American Novel. I want to bring in someone who can tell you and *show* you what it's like to work at the craft."

"Okay," Derek replied, looking a little more in tune with the rest of the universe than he had a few minutes ago. "I'll ask my dad tonight."

Derek slumped over the leather-wrapped steering wheel, with the engine running and KTHK blaring from the radio. There was no use in trying to move until the last of the aspiring Indy drivers had cleared the school parking lot. He wasn't in the mood to fight their flashy muscle cars with a Chevy Citation; it was sort of like taking on a bunch of F-15s with a Piper Cub.

With a lot of imagination, balls, and skill it *could* be done—in fact, he'd bet Jackie Stewart could do it in a Yugo; he'd heard a story about him trashing Porsche drivers in a rented Lincoln—but Deke wasn't feeling that magical. Magic seemed to be in pretty short supply, lately.

Gray clouds bulked lethargically overhead; the air smelled like rain, but so far nothing had fallen.

It would be just my luck to have it start pouring the minute I pull out of the parking lot.

He was beginning to wonder if he'd used up his entire lifetime quota of luck the night of the accident.

Nobody'd been wearing a belt, but only Jill had taken a header. The car hadn't rolled, though by all the laws of nature and physics, it damn well *should* have.

But that had only been the beginning of the weirdness.

Because Fay had *vanished* from the front seat before the steering went crazy. Deke remembered that, with all the clarity of something that had happened a few minutes ago.

It gave him a queasy feeling just to think about it; made him feel a little dizzy. Or maybe that was because of the concussion. *Sometimes I wonder if that hit on the head made me see things. . . .*

But no, he hadn't been concussed then, *or* even all that drunk. He was remembering right. One minute Fay had been cussing Jill out. The next, she'd *disappeared.*

But when the car came to a stop, hitting the abutment of the overpass with enough force to throw Deke against the dashboard and total the front end of the TransAm, she was back. She was cut up a little, bruised a little, and totally hysterical—but back in the front seat.

And she was buckled in.

And so were Deke and Sandy.

He fingered the buckle of his own seat belt now, and eased the shoulder strap away from the side of his throat. *I wasn't belted, I know I wasn't. So how did I get fastened in?*

The cops had appeared out of nowhere—on a road they never patrolled, since there was a dispute on between the County Mounties and the Jenks Police as to who "owned" it. Somewhere in the back of his skull, in a part that wasn't gibbering about Jill's twitching body right in his lap, a little piece of his mind figured that they were doomed. The cops were going to see all the bottles, and they'd end up in the Juvenile Home for the night, then up in front of the court in the morning, and they'd get it in the teeth for drinking underage—even if he and Sandy hadn't been the one in the driver's seat, they'd still be lucky if any of them got their licenses again before they were twenty-one, and Dad—

Dad would hit the roof. Probably send him to military school.

But there wasn't so much as a single beer bottle anywhere in the car. Not even a shard of glass.

The back of his neck crawled. The whole night was right out of *Twilight Zone.*

The cops had *searched*, too, and hadn't found a thing. What was more, when the doctors pulled blood samples at the hospital, there wasn't anything in *them*, either.

That had totally weirded him out. Though at that point he'd felt as sober as a Baptist preacher, Derek couldn't believe what they told him. But they'd run the tests twice, and every single one of the doctors insisted. All four of them, including what was left of Jill, were clean.

So when the cops and the docs tried to ask him what happened,

he stopped himself before he could blurt out the truth. Truth that
the evidence denied. He'd just sat there with his mouth open, unable to think of *any* story at all.

The doctors put down his stunned inability to answer their
questions to shock. Well, that was okay. He figured he'd just let Fay
give her version and keep quiet. And when Sandy woke up, they'd
probably figure he was hallucinating. After all, what good would
telling the truth do now? It wouldn't unmake the accident, or bring
Jill back, or even make Jill's parents feel any better. All it would do
would be to get *him* in trouble, maybe ending up with having to
see a shrink.

But things got even stranger. When Sandy came to, his un-
coached, unprompted version of the night's ride tallied exactly with
Fay's—and ran completely counter to what Deke remembered.

Fay admitted, tearfully, to speeding "just a little. There wasn't
anybody else on the road. I kind of forgot to watch the speedometer. I can't believe the steering and the brakes went out; my God, I
just had my car inspected and worked on!"

Then she coughed up a real fairy tale, the sanitized Walt Disney
version of the night's outing; *sans* booze, racing, and sex.

And there was something else he felt he should have remembered, but couldn't. Something about a drag-race?

If it hadn't been that he *knew* Fay, and *knew* that the innocent,
playful joyride she described was about as typical of her as finding
the president of Exotic Furriers in a Greenpeace meeting, he'd have
figured he was going nuts.

Maybe I am going nuts, anyway, he thought, watching the last of
the losers in the exit race rev their engines to make up for their
poor showing. *I could believe that he was just covering everything up
really well, but Sandy still doesn't remember what actually happened.*

He pondered that a while longer, staring at his hands on the
steering wheel and wondering just what the signs were of someone
going bonkers. Was it really true that if you wondered about your
sanity you were probably still sane?

A spatter of rain hit the windshield; Deke looked up, startled, and realized that the lot was empty. He looked at his watch, swore, and threw the Citation into reverse. He backed out of his slot with a shriek of abused tires, threw her into drive, and burned as much rubber as *any* of the other rocket jockeys getting out of the lot.

Once out on the street, though, he cooled his jets. Be pretty damn stupid to get a ticket after all he'd just been through.

The rain was just drooling down; barely enough to make him put on his wipers. He knew better than to trust these streets, though—some of those muscle-cars leaked oil pretty fierce. Add oil buildup to enough rain to float it above the asphalt, and you had more trouble than he wanted to take at speed. Hydroplaning was no fun, and he didn't need another wreck right now. So he took his time getting home, watching for slick spots.

And remembered, suddenly, about the English class, and what he'd promised Ms. Greeley.

That was something he hadn't much thought about when he'd volunteered—how he was going to approach his dad about this business with that writer friend.

He began to feel a bit more cheerful with the change of mental track. He flicked on the headlights; it was getting pretty gloomy and it didn't look like this storm was going to die out anytime soon.

When Ms. Greeley had made her pitch, he'd just shot his hand up, because he'd been wanting to meet this Diana Tregarde for ages. Mostly because of the funny way his folks acted whenever they talked about her.

First of all, they *didn't* talk about her when they knew Deke was around, and then it was like by accident. He'd gathered that his mom had met her when Mom was going to college in New York, at about the same time that Di Tregarde and Dad were Yale class-mates. Which was odd, because you wouldn't think that somebody would know people at Yale and NYCU, much less get them to-gether. The other hint he'd gotten was that there was something really funny about the way that his parents had met and that the meeting involved Di Tregarde.

But they wouldn't *talk* about it. Or not much.

"Di introduced us," Dad had said once, with a funny, sly sort of grin at Mom. "I thought I was seeing things—"

"No doubt," she'd retorted—then they'd both broken up, for no reason that *Deke* could see.

Granted, they were probably all hippies together back in the sixties; he'd seen a couple of pictures of them and their friends. They'd looked like the cast of *Hair*; beads, headbands, Indian-print shirts and granny dresses, wire-rimmed glasses. He'd hardly recognized his mom; she'd had crinkly Art Nouveau hair down to her waist, a flower behind one ear, and was wearing a miniskirt so short he wondered how she ever sat down. Hell, her *hair* was longer than her dress!

He grinned, thinking about it. *Mom didn't look bad in that mini, either. Don't blame the old man for jumping her.*

His mom had taken one look at the photo, blushed beet red, and asked him if he didn't have better things to do than look at a bunch of old pictures of people he didn't even know.

That's when he'd *tried* to get them to talk about when they were his age. And they avoided his questions as neatly as a diplomat. Now that was crazy; when his friends asked *their* folks to talk, you couldn't get them to shut up, especially about when they were in college.

But Dad wouldn't talk about college, and neither would Mom. It was like there was this four-year gap in their lives that they didn't want anyone to know about. A gap that was somehow tied in with this Diana Tregarde.

Probably it was something along the lines of the wild stuff Alan said *his* parents used to do—psychedelics, Mazola-oil parties, that kind of thing. And they didn't want him to know the kind of trouble they used to get into.

Deke had always been pretty good at deciphering Parental Codes. Spelling hadn't held him for long, pig Latin baffled him for less than four months, and when they used French it only forced him to become bilingual at ten. But the cryptic references the folks used when they *did* talk about Diana completely threw him. And the way they acted about her—like they didn't want him to talk about her to anyone—you'd have thought she was a CIA agent, or a rock star incognito, or something.

He was thinking so hard that he was startled to notice that he was on his own street, and practically in his own driveway. He thumbed the garage door opener hastily, and pulled the Citation into his side of the garage, just clearing the slowly rising door.

He checked the answering machine for messages, but the only ones on it were the disconnects of "robot calls" and one intrepid siding salesman.

He hunted through the refrigerator for something to eat, but nothing looked good, so he settled for some microwave popcorn to tide him over until his dad got back from the downtown office.

When the corn was popped, though, he suddenly didn't want it. The first bite was fine, but after that it was dry and tasteless.

Because he kept seeing Jill—

Deke dumped his snack down the garbage disposal and plodded up the stairs to his bedroom, where he threw himself down on his bed and beat his pillow into submission with angry fists.

"I'm *not* going crazy," he said aloud, fighting back fear and tears. "I'm *not*. Somebody's lying, and it isn't me!"

Finally he rolled over on his back and stared at the ceiling, at the little constellations of glow-in-the-dark stars his folks had put up there when he was eight.

He wanted, with a desperation he couldn't admit aloud, for his mom to come back from Japan. Things never seemed right when she was gone, this time especially.

But—well, when she was gone, Dad was a bit more talkative. *And* he'd been moping around a lot himself. Maybe if this old college buddy came out, it'd pick Dad up.

And I can see if I can't figure out what the big deal is about her, Deke promised himself. *That'll give me something to think about besides seeing Jill lying across the dash—*

He shuddered, and turned over on his side, burying his face in his pillow.

Dinner was Kentucky Fried—Mom would have had a cat. No veggies, no salad, just chicken and double potatoes and biscuits. Deke and his dad grinned at each other in delicious guilt over the bones. It seemed an auspicious moment to broach the Question.

"Dad—" Deke said as they cleaned up after themselves and disposed of the evidence, lest Mom find it. "You know that writer you used to hang out with? The romance lady?"

Larry Kestrel stopped shoving bones down the garbage disposal and looked at his son with a very strange expression. "Di Tregarde? Funny, I was just thinking—why? What about her?"

Deke plunged straight in. "Ms. Greeley wants us to try writing and she wanted one of us to find a real writer to come in and help for a couple of weeks and I said you knew a writer and she said to ask you if you could get her."

It all came out in one sentence, without a pause for breath. Larry pondered him with a puzzled frown for a moment; then his face cleared. "Is *that* all?" He was so relieved that Deke wondered what on earth he *had* been thinking. "Well, I can't promise anything, but . . . come on back with me to the office; I'll make a few phone calls and we'll see what happens."

Deke followed his father into the inner sanctum—the "den of iniquity" was what his dad called it. Actually it was just a home office where Dad worked on his private projects. It held nothing more sinister than the usual office furnishings and a drafting table and a microcomputer, and the all-important speakerphone. Larry picked up the handset, though, flipped through the Rolodex, and lifted an eyebrow at his son, who was hovering at the threshold.

"Let me talk to your teacher a minute, kiddo."

There was a low-voiced exchange on the telephone, while Deke stood uncertainly beside the door. Finally Larry hung up and nodded to his son, who edged over into the pool of light around the desk.

"Ann seems to like the idea—now I'll see if Di is free. Have a seat; this is going to take some time."

Deke picked a comfortable-looking chair, then sat on the edge of it while his father thumbed the Rolodex again, and punched buttons. A long distance call from the sound of it.

"Mark?" Dad said, the sound of his voice very loud in the quiet of the office. Deke jumped in startlement. The phone on the other end couldn't have rung more than twice. "It's Larry Kestrel." He listened, then chuckled. "Yeah, I know, long time, no hear. How's the job treating you? Oh, really? Sonuva—"

He flushed, and glanced belatedly at Deke. "—ah—gun," he finished, ears flushing. "Listen, I've got a favor to ask. I've got DT's address, but not her phone, and I know she keeps her number unlisted. Could you—?"

He grabbed a pen and scribbled something down on the blotter of the desk set. "Great, old buddy! Thanks! I owe you one—" He listened for a moment more, then laughed out loud. "Okay, so we're even, have it your way. I gotta go, they're an hour ahead of us on the Coast."

He hung up and dialed again. This time when the phone was answered, he frowned for a moment. "Excuse me, but I was trying to reach a Miss Diana Tregarde—is this the right number?"

Deke ran his thumbnail nervously along the seam of his jeans, while his father listened cautiously to the reply.

"Well, I'm an old friend of Diana's, from college. Larry Kestrel." Larry's face brightened then. "So *you're* André. Great, Mark Valdez told me a little about you. I don't suppose the Lady ever told you about the Squad, did she?"

The Squad? What the hell is that? Dad wasn't in ROTC; he'd rather have died! If there's anything more frustrating than listening to one side of a phone conversation, Deke thought, squirming in the chair, trying to find a comfortable position, *I can't think of it.*

His father seemed to be taking an awfully long time, just listening. But finally his face lightened. "Terrific—I'm really glad to hear *that.* Carte blanche, huh? Well, I'd say we all earned it at one time or another."

He listened again for a minute, and laughed. "No, no, I promise,

this is mundane. My kid's English class is looking for a writer to
come talk to them and I wondered if there was anyway I could lure
her out. . . ."

While Deke watched, an expression of incredulous joy flickered
briefly over his father's face; then, after his eyes met Deke's, the expression vanished, replaced by casual cheerfulness so quickly that
Deke figured he must have misread it.

"Kansas?" Larry said, and chuckled. "No, really? I'll be darned.
That's practically next door! Listen, let me ask you something, has
she got anything urgent she needs to take care of back there? Do
you suppose she'd be willing to take a detour and a little vacation?"

Suddenly Deke's father lost all the cheer he'd been projecting; he
looked as if what he was hearing was entirely unexpected.

"Oh," he said faintly. "Oh, God. God, I am really sorry to hear
about that, I really am. I never met Lenny, but she used to write
about him so much it feels like I know him. He sure was a good
friend to her when she first moved to New York, I remember that.
The last time she wrote, she said he was sick, but I had no idea—"

Deke bit his lip to keep from interrupting.

"—yeah, it might be a real good thing for her to have a break, I
agree. And I'll do my best to keep her distracted. Listen, I can pull
some strings, I know a few people; I could get him into one of
those experimental programs, the ones that *aren't* giving out a
placebo run. . . . Oh. He is. No improvement. Shit."

Larry's expression was angry and frustrated, and the tone of his
voice was bitter. It wasn't the first time Deke had ever heard his father swear—but it was the first time he'd ever heard him put quite
so much feeling into it. He wondered what it was that was making
him feel so strongly.

"Yeah, give me the number, please."

Larry reached for one of his drafting pens, and jotted down a
number in careful, neat little numerals.

He repeated it back to the other person, and nodded. "Thanks,
André. Yeah, you too. Do you want me to say anything about—
okay, I won't mention him unless she does. And if there's anything

I can do, you let me know. And I mean *right away*. I'm not just making noises, I'll help if I can. You know our crowd—we tend to make some oddball contacts—I could even get him some of that Mexican stuff if he really wants to try it. I don't advise it, but I'm not in his shoes. Thanks again. I'm only sorry I'll be stealing her away from you for a month." He listened again, and smiled at the reply. "Yeah, I suppose so. You take care."

Deke slouched back in the chair as his father dialed this new number; he couldn't help wondering if this was *ever* going to get anywhere.

His father's face lit up again. "Di? Larry Kestrel. Yeah, the real thing! Same to you, Spooky—"

There was something really odd about the way his dad looked as he listened to his old friend on the other end of the line—something that made Deke feel strange and uneasy. He wasn't sure he understood the sparkle his dad's eyes were taking on, or the way he seemed to be getting younger with every minute.

"Whoa there, milady," he interrupted at last, laughing. "Let me put you on speakerphone. I've been on the horn half the night trying to track you down, and my ear's getting tired. Besides, I want my son to hear this; he's the one that got me to track you down in the first place."

He laughed again at something she said, and thumbed the speaker switch.

"—and your yuppie techie toys!" said a young-sounding female voice. "Honest to gods, Larry, I swear you've been hanging around in bad company! Weren't you the one who refused to own more than two pairs of jeans, because anything more was conspicuous consumption?"

"I got corrupted by easy living." Larry chuckled, looking far more amused than the comment warranted, or so Deke thought. "Besides, the more I buy, the more jobs I create. So what in hell are you doing in Kansas?"

"Oh ye suffering *gods*," she groaned feelingly. "Signings. That's 'autograph parties' to you. Bee-lyuns and bee-lyuns of them, or it sure seems that way. If I never see a mall again, it'll be too soon."

"In Kansas?" Larry said incredulously.

"In Kansas," she replied. "Believe it or not, they can *read* in Kansas. My publisher found out that I was going back to Dallas to pick up a car Mark Valdez found for me, and he decided that since I was going to be driving it back to New Haven, I might just as well stop at every godforsaken shopping mall between Dallas and Kansas City and sign a few thousand books. After all, I don't have anything better to do, right?"

"Do what Nancy Reagan says. Just say no," Larry replied, his mouth twitching as he tried to keep from laughing. Deke was grinning himself.

"He *bribed* me, the skunk," Diana protested. "He bribed me with something I could never afford on my own—a state-of-the-art laptop. With more software than *anyone* has a right to own. And a built-in modem. So I didn't even have the excuse that I couldn't work on the road. How could anyone say no to that?"

"Jeez, Spook, you have no room to twit me about *my* techie toys!"

If he grins any harder, Deke thought, *he's going to split his head in half.*

"So why did you have to go halfway across the country just to get a car? And why from Mark? Don't they have cars in New England?"

"Not ex-highway-patrol interceptors, they don't," she replied, her tone no longer light. "Not with less than ten thousand miles on the engine and tranny; not with both the engine and the tranny rebuilt and retuned until they sing the 'Halleluia Chorus.' And not with most of the goodies still *on* it—and you did *not* hear that from me, laddy-buck."

"I hear you," Larry replied.

"Good. Mark pulled some real strings to get it for me, KK. I've needed something like this a long time, and the offer was too good to pass up. You know why—"

"Yeah," Larry interrupted her. "Yeah, I know—listen, like I said, my kid's here, and we've got a big favor to ask you. Can I talk you into backtracking a little? If you'd be willing to come on back down here, I'll treat you to a month's vacation as my houseguest. I just talked to André, and he thinks you need the break. Granted, Tulsa isn't exactly the pleasure capital of the universe, but as I re-call, you were into culture, right? We've got a couple of decent mu-seums, and a pretty good opera and ballet company—"

"I know about the ballet company," she interrupted. "I saw them do that Ballanchine revival in New York. You're damning them with faint praise if you think they're only 'pretty good.' I'd do a lot to get a chance to see them again—" she continued, sounding wist-ful. "And not just because they're good; they're also darned scenic. It's too bad Jasinsky Junior's married, he's *really* slurpy. But I don't know, Kosmic. It's going to take a lot of convincing to get me to drive back down through Kansas again. What's this got to do with your kid?"

Deke was back on the edge of his chair and bouncing. For some reason—for some reason he couldn't even define—getting this lady to come visit was *important*. He didn't know why; he just knew that it was.

His dad seemed to feel exactly the same way; he was talking to Diana as if he'd forgotten Deke was still in the room. It felt like eavesdropping—and Deke *wanted* to eavesdrop. He tried very hard to think like a leather armchair.

"Ann Greeley—that's Deke's teacher—is doing a section with her Honors English classes on creative writing, and she wants a real full-time author to come in and show them the ropes. Not just cri-tique, but the day-to-day stuff. Watching the markets, revisions, tailoring to suit a particular editor, that kind of thing. Thing is, there's more to it than that. It's not just that she wants the kids to get an idea of what it's like to write for a living, she wants 'em—I don't know—distracted, I guess. Deke and three of his buddies were in an accident this weekend, and one of them—well, she didn't make it."

"Ah. So the kids are taking it pretty hard?"

"Yeah," Larry replied. "She was pretty popular, with this class in particular. Ann's hoping bringing you in will be enough of a novelty to get them all going again. Right now they're all pretty much in shock."

That was news to Deke, who tried not to move, for fear his dad would remember he was there.

"Yeah, I can see that. You say Deke was one of the kids in the accident? Am I thinking what you're thinking?"

"Probably," Larry replied cryptically. "So what's it going to take to lure you down to glorious Oklahoma?"

"Just that you need me—and clean air. Right now—definitely clean air," she moaned. "You don't have any stockyards down there, do you? I think they park a stockyard next to every damn motel in Kansas. I am *never* going to get the smell out of the back of my throat!"

"No stockyards," Larry promised. "You—you don't want to arrange any more of those signing things down here, do you?"

"No!" she exclaimed. "Great Jesus Cluny Frog! These women are *crazy*! They think I'm like one of my damned heroines—they think I write this stuff from experience!"

Larry bent over in a spluttering, choking, laughing fit. The laughter was infectious—and besides, Deke didn't think he'd get to overhear any more stuff about what Ms. Greeley had told his dad. So Deke joined in.

"Oh, right, Kosmic Kid. Go ahead and laugh! *You* aren't the one they're descending on, with their books clutched to their all-too-ample bosoms. *You* aren't the one they're asking for advice on their love lives. *You* aren't the one with the groupies—"

"Groupies?" Larry chortled. "You have *groupies?*"

"Every romance writer has groupies, laddy-buck. Most of 'em thirty-nine going on thirteen. And they want *me* to solve all their personality problems with a wave of my magic wand. Kee-rist. If I could do *that*, I wouldn't be hacking out bodice rippers, I'd be making a fortune as a Hollywood shrink."

"I'll buy that. Okay, no signings, and to sweeten the pot, we just put in a six-man Jacuzzi."

"Uncle!" she cried. "For a Jacuzzi, I'd emeritus a class full of go-rillas! And since I just did my last spot in the barrel, I'll be there by late afternoon tomorrow."

Deke and his dad exchanged triumphant grins. "Okay, sport," Larry said. "Looks like this is a done deal. I'll call your teacher as soon as I get off the phone with Di. How about if you go take care of that homework, hmm?"

Obviously he was *not* going to be allowed to eavesdrop any-more. He capitulated. "Okay. I guess I'd better."

He slid out of the chair, while his dad switched back to the handset and began talking too quietly for Deke to make out what he was saying without making it plain he was trying to listen.

Very obviously he wasn't going to be allowed to eavesdrop.

But he couldn't help wonder, as he headed back up to his room and a dismayingly long history assignment, what it was that a ro-mance writer did that would call for owning a former police car. . . .

THREE

Deke pretended to read his history text, and peered through the half-closed door of his room at his father. Larry Kestrel was pacing again, and Deke was beginning to wonder if this business of having Diana Tregarde come out here was such a good idea after all.

Ever since she'd agreed, his dad had been acting like—like Deke, with a hot date coming up. Diana had told them that she expected to be there "late afternoon," which Deke interpreted as between four and seven tonight. Larry had hardly eaten his supper; he'd parked himself in the family room, and when he wasn't pacing, he was pretending to read a book. This after rushing Deke through his own meal and up to his room "to work on homework." But Deke could see him easily enough from his desk—and he didn't like what he saw.

Larry flung himself back down in the corner of the beige velvet pit-group, and reached for the book again. Deke wasn't fooled. For one thing, Deke could tell his dad was only pretending to read. He hadn't turned a page in the last ten minutes.

Besides, somehow I don't think Dad's the Danielle Steel type. . . .

And he spent more time pacing than staring at the book, anyway. Miss Tregarde was due any minute now, and Larry was getting increasingly fretful.

So was Deke.

I don't know, he thought worriedly, drawing aimless little scribbles on the blotter. *Maybe I made a big mistake. I mean, there's all kinds of "old friends." Maybe this lady used to be a real hot item with Dad, and Mom didn't know. And Mom's clear the hell over in Japan. And it's not like Dad's taken a vow of celibacy or anything. As far as I know, he's still got all his hormones and everything. . . .*

Deke chewed on the end of his pencil and wished he'd thought about this a little more before he'd gone and opened his big mouth.

But maybe I'm getting all worked up over nothing. Yeah, I probably am. Miss Tregarde's a year older than Mom, at least that's what Dad said; there's got to be a good reason why she hasn't gotten married. Besides, all she does is write—I bet she never goes anywhere. Probably she's still stuck in the sixties, no makeup, straight hair, granny glasses, patched-up bell-bottoms, and Earth Shoes. Either that or she's about twenty pounds overweight, maybe getting a little gray in the hair. Sort of like Ms. Greeley. Even if Dad is kind of expecting something to happen, I bet he's thinking she looks the way she did in college. I mean, he told me himself he hasn't seen her since he and Mom got married.

Deke chewed his lip a little, feeling a bit better when he pictured this Tregarde lady as looking a lot like his English teacher—a little matronly, certainly nobody's idea of a sex fantasy.

Just as he reached this conclusion, he heard the sound of a car pulling into the driveway—a car with a big, powerful engine. Of course it *could* be someone using the drive to turn around—

But the engine stopped, and Deke saw his dad leap up from his seat on the couch and head for the door.

Deke abandoned his own pretense at study and bounded out of his room, taking the stairs two at a time and winding up right at his father's heels.

Larry Kestrel pulled open the front door of the house before the driver of the car now taking up a good portion of the driveway in front of their garage could even make a move to get out.

The vehicle had had its driver's and passengers' doors primed, but it was going to be hard for even the gaudiest Earl Scheib paint job to hide the fact that this used to be a cop car. Brake-vented hubcaps, extra heavy sway bars, and most especially the skid plates underneath gave its history away to anyone as car-crazy as Deke. You just didn't see Crown Vics out on the street with mods like those. Like all cop cars, the beast was a four-door, and Deke had the shrewd suspicion that there was a roll bar still in the door pillar.

Sunset painted the sky behind the car in exotic shades of purple and gold, and the interior of the vehicle was so shrouded in shadows that Deke couldn't make out what the occupant looked like. For a moment, while the driver was still involved in getting extricated from the seat harness, Deke's attention was on the car. He itched for a chance to get under that hood and poke around. He had no doubt, given the way the engine had sounded, that this thing was exactly what Diana had claimed—a police interceptor, capable of catching just about any commercial vehicle on the road.

And even more than getting under the hood, he wanted a chance to *drive* it.

But then Diana Tregarde opened the car door and slid out into the last light—and Deke's worst fears were realized.

Jee-zus, he thought in dismay. *She's a babe!*

She was willowy and supple, and looked athletic without looking like an athlete. In fact, Deke had the startling impression that she was in better physical shape than Fay. About five feet tall, she had an overall build like a dancer, and she moved like a dancer, too. Instead of the holdover hippie outfit of peasant skirt and baggy blouse, or patched jeans and ratty T-shirt he'd been picturing her in, she was wearing a leotard that might as well have been a second skin and chic designer jeans nearly as tight as the leotard. She *was* wearing makeup; subtle, just enough to make her look model-like and a touch exotic. Her waist-length chestnut hair was caught in a ponytail, and hadn't even a trace of gray.

She sure doesn't look Dad's age, Deke thought unhappily. *She looks more like a college student.*

She bounded over to his dad (she *ran* like a dancer; she hardly touched the ground) and flung her arms around him, an embrace that Larry reciprocated, much to Deke's discomfort. And the warm and enthusiastic kiss she gave and got didn't make Deke any happier.

She finally let go and backed off a pace, looking Larry up and down with a strange smile. The sunset glow haloed her as if Ridley Scott were directing the entire scene. Deke wanted to be sick; this was a setup, and it was all his fault. The next thing she'd say was "Oh God, Larry, I never realized how much I missed you. . . ." And they'd clinch again, and then they'd hustle him out of the way, and then—

"Why, Kosmic Kid," she said, laughing, "you look positively bourgeois! Where's the wild-eyed revolutionary I used to know and love?"

Well, *that* certainly wasn't in the script! *Kosmic Kid? Wait a minute, she called him that before. What is this, a comic book?*

"Know, I'll admit, Fearless Leader," Dad replied, shoving his hands into his pockets and grinning back. "But love? Hardly. Not from the way you used to abuse me. Oh, I'm doing what you told me I should do, way back when. I got tired of beating my head against monoliths. It's guerrilla warfare now; real subversion. I'm being the thorn in the foot."

"You mean 'pain in the ass,' don't you?" She chuckled, her grin spreading still wider. Deke couldn't help but notice that she stood, not like a dancer, but like a martial artist, balanced and a little wary. And that those designer jeans had the special little inset piece that would let you do a sidekick without tearing the crotch out.

This is a romance writer?

Larry clapped the back of his hand to his forehead theatrically. "Crushed! How *could* you?"

"I couldn't crush you with a bulldozer," she retorted, tossing her tail of hair over her shoulder. "So answer the question already— what's with the yuppie rig, and where'd the rebel go?"

"Undercover." Larry put his arm around her shoulders and pushed her gently back toward the car, leaving Deke to trail along behind them, sneakers stubbing along on the concrete of the drive- way. Next to this "old lady," he felt as awkward and ungainly as a bull calf. Larry continued, oblivious to his son's reactions. "When I'm not separating the wealthy from their ill-gotten gains by trans- lating their vague notions of one-upmanship into their homes and buildings, I'm designing low-income housing, and doing it for a lot less than anyone else will." They exchanged conspiratorial looks. Deke bit his lip. "It drives my accountant crazy."

She raised one eyebrow, like Mr. Spock. Deke wondered how she did it. He'd practiced that for hours in front of the mirror without getting it right.

"I'll bet," she said sardonically.

"I keep *trying* to tell him that money isn't everything, but he keeps tearing his hair out."

"Did it ever occur to you that an accountant is probably *not* the kind of person who is going to believe that little platitude?" They all reached the car, and Diana freed herself from Larry's arm and turned to give Deke a very penetrating once-over, quite unlike the examination she'd given his father. It gave Deke a very funny feel- ing, uncomfortable and a little scary. It felt like he was being tested in some way, but it wasn't any test he recognized.

Finally she held out her hand with a cheerful smile, one that somehow didn't seem superior, the way most adults smiled at kids. "Hi. You're obviously Derek. I'm Diana Tregarde, as you've prob- ably figured out on your own. Di, to you. I can't say I know a lot about you, but what I do know, I like."

Derek shook her hand gingerly, a bit taken aback by her forth- rightness and frankness.

Her smile turned into a grin full of mischief; the corners of her enormous, velvety-brown eyes crinkled up. That was the first sign he'd seen that she was anywhere near Dad's age. Mom took pains to hide *her* crow's-feet and never smiled that broadly as a conse- quence; Diana Tregarde didn't seem to care.

"I should warn you now," she told Derek in a confidential tone. "You're going to have to put up with a lot of nonsense while I'm here. We're likely to start reminiscing about our romantic, wild youth at the drop of a poncho."

"Hey, man," Larry drawled—the accent he was using sounded vaguely Valley, but not *quite*. Derek couldn't place it. "Is that, like, a real poncho, or is that a Sears poncho?"

It sounded as though he was quoting something, but Deke didn't recognize what. Then, as they started to giggle, for Chrissake, he identified it as a quote from one of Dad's Frank Zappa records. "Camarillo Brillo," whatever the hell *that* meant.

Jeez, he thought, half in dismay and half in disgust, as they both looked at his expression and went from giggling into gales of laughter, *am I going to be sitting through reruns of* The Wonder Years *and* Hair *every night?*

They finally calmed down, Di leaning against the fender of her car and wiping her eyes with the back of her hand. "Lord," she said weakly. "I'd honestly forgotten how dumb we all were. At one point that really *meant* something, Deke. If you didn't wear a real, honest-to-gods poncho, handwoven either by some poor Guatemalan peasant or somebody named Moonflower—if you had some kind of polyester fake, you were what we called a 'day-tripper' or a 'plastic hippie.'"

Gods? Plural? This is a romance writer? But she was looking at him expectantly, waiting for a response. He tried to sound intelligent. "Like a poser?" Derek hazarded.

"Yeah." She nodded vigorously. "A real nowhere man, a plastic flower child. Some suit who came out to the campus on the weekends to get high and get his brains balled out by hippie chicks so he could boast about it to his suit buddies during coffee breaks. Or some deb who came looking for Sexual Liberation in easy, one-screw doses."

"Di!" Larry exclaimed, looking shocked.

She gave him a wry *look.* "Come off it, Kosmic. Kids these days have twice the sex education we did by the time they're Deke's age. I'll lay you odds eighty percent of his female friends are on The Pill."

"More like ninety-five," Deke admitted, deciding, however reluctantly, that he was beginning to like Di Tregarde. She didn't talk down to him, and she didn't pretend to be a buddy, either.

"See?" she said. "You can't shelter 'em, KK. Not any more than our parents could shelter us, or Yale could. I've told you before; if they've got brains and a drop of sense, your best bet is to give kids all the facts. Then when they've had a chance to absorb the facts, throw 'em my theory of Teenage Evolution, and ask them the One Big Question."

"What's that?" Deke asked, curious against his will. "The question, I mean."

Di leaned back against the hood of her car, a dark silhouette against the fading sunset. "I know your mom and dad, and they're no hung-up born-agains, so I'm going to assume you *do* know all the facts, including the ones about AIDS—"

"That you only get it with exchange of mucus and semen and blood, and that it isn't just a gay disease," he offered. "That anybody can get it; that the only known protection is a rubber."

She nodded soberly. "Right on; that sums it up." Deke sneaked a look at his dad; he looked like somebody'd hit him in the middle of the forehead with a two-by-four. Stunned. *I can't tell if it's 'cause of what Di's talking about, or because I already know what she's talking about. We had the Big Talk years ago, but we never got around to AIDS.*

"Okay, here's my theory of Teenage Evolution. You know why we—human beings, I mean—start to fall apart when we hit forty?"

He shook his head.

"Because, evolutionarily speaking, we aren't meant to last beyond our reproductive years. I mean, that's what evolution really means—survival of the fittest means *reproductive* survival; the one that spawns the most wins, not the one that lives the longest. Nature favors quantity of life, not quality."

Deke scratched his head. He'd never quite thought of it that way. *I guess that sure explains cockroaches, mosquitoes, and linebackers.*

Di nodded, and smiled a little, as if she had heard his thoughts. "So—given that, the *best* years for the human being to reproduce are its youngest fertile years, so that you've got a chance to raise and teach the young. Basically, in these days of improved nutrition, that's thirteen to twenty-four, or so. Which means, kiddo, that right now your hormones are screaming at you to get out there, establish a territory of your own, grab you some wimmen, and raise you some babies. Like, *now*. *Lots* of wimmen, and lots of babies. Have you figured out what that means to you, personally?"

"Uh—" he replied brightly.

She *didn't* laugh at him, though he'd half expected her to. "Okay. One, establishing your own territory means aggravating the hell out of your old man, so he'll throw you out of the cave and force you to go fend for yourself. Two, grabbing you some wimmen means just that, which is why all the peacock stuff everybody does as soon as they figure out the opposite sex is pretty neat—from fancy cars to fancy clothes. *And* that's the whole rival thing too, so that all you young bucks start locking antlers to figure out who's top dog. I mean, you're supposed to have a harem of about two or three—that means knocking off some of the excess competition. Establishing your territory kind of goes along with that. Three, raising you lots of babies means your hormones are going to have you screwing anything that'll let you. Now the Big Question, Deke."

At some point during this astonishing discussion, Di had scooted up on the hood of the car, where she now perched with her legs neatly crossed. She didn't look like an adult, or even, oddly enough, like a kid. What she *did* look like was ageless, as if she was some kind of modern incarnation of the Delphic oracle, perched on a weird substitute for a tripod.

The Fordic Oracle?

Larry looked more than stunned, he looked paralyzed, with his mouth hanging half open.

This is a romance writer?

"Which is?" Deke managed.

"You aren't a mindless tomcat surrounded by queens in heat, and you aren't a caveman, kiddo." The "kiddo" didn't even come out sounding patronizing, just earnest. "You're a human being, and you have brains as well as glands. So tell me, what are you going to let run your life—your head, or your hormones?"

Now it was Deke's turn to stand there with his mouth hanging open. He'd never heard—things—put quite that way, or that bluntly, before.

"Well," Larry managed to choke out, before the silence drowned them all. "You sure know how to get a kid's attention. I hope you aren't planning on delivering this same lecture to Deke's class."

She grinned, and blinked innocently. "I might. If the situation calls for it."

"In that case, I may have to protect you from a lynch mob." Larry swallowed twice, and managed to get his jaw back in place.

"My brains," Deke said, at the same time.

"Good choice, Deke," Di replied, sliding down off the hood of the car. "Keep that in mind next time your libido goes into over-drive. Your kid is smarter than you were, KK."

"Before or after I met you?" he retorted. "I have the feeling some of those escapades you got us into cost me more than a few brain cells, milady."

She just snorted, but reached for Larry's shoulders and gave him a hug. It looked to Deke like an apology for the teasing. "Listen, I've been thinking about that Jacuzzi you promised me for the last hundred miles. My shoulders are killing me."

"The boiling pot is ready and waiting, Spooky, and if it can't cure your shoulders, nothing will." Larry seemed to have gotten over his previous shock.

"So what are we waiting for?" she asked, skipping around to the rear of the car, popping the trunk just as the automatic floodlights over the driveway came on. "Let's get this junk into the house and get cooking!"

Deke's dad grinned. "Your wish is my command, milady," he said mockingly—but he reached into the trunk and pulled out a trio of purple ripstop nylon bags. Deke grimaced. *Prince had a yard sale?* She looked at him, grinned, and shrugged, as if to say, "It was cheap, what can I say?" Buried in the sea of purple were a black ripstop case and a corner of a briefcase. Di took the former out gently.

"My new toy," she explained to both of them. "Sorry, Deke, no games. The IRS won't let me deduct it if I put games on it."

"The things we do for taxes," Larry sighed, looking just as disappointed as Deke felt.

Deke found himself loaded down with gear, all of it purple nylon. *Now this, I'd expect from a romance writer. This, or rose pink.* His dad got his fair share, though, and to her credit, so did Di, including a beat-up leather briefcase; that case looked heavy. *Very* heavy. Deke had avoided reaching for it on principle; it looked like it held an entire IBM mainframe. Di hefted it easily; another surprise. Larry led the way into the house and up the stairs to the guest room. Di was close behind, leaving Deke to trail forlornly in their wake. His dad and their guest were chattering away at high speed now; their conversation was full of cryptic little references to things he couldn't even guess at.

That was quite enough to make him feel like the one on the outside, but besides that, they kept making sidelong glances at Deke.

I'm not that dense, he thought. *I know when I'm a third wheel.* He dropped the luggage beside the bed and started to leave.

Di touched his arm as he passed her; he stopped, startled.

"Deke," she said quietly, "I had a reason for the lecture. I don't want you to think that *I* think you're some kind of idiot. I—I'm trying to save people. I'm losing somebody I really care about. To AIDS. I don't want to lose anybody else, okay?"

Suddenly that entire conversation Larry had held with the mysterious André made sense.

"Okay," he said weakly, blushing. "Really, it's okay. I understand. And—thanks."

She smiled faintly in reply, and he escaped before he could make a fool out of himself.

But he still wasn't comfortable leaving them—Di and his dad— alone together. He *really* wished his mom was back from Japan.

Diana Tregarde was entirely too attractive to trust with his father. Especially alone.

Di didn't even bother to hide her sigh of relief when the kid finally left. *Nice kid, but—Jesus Cluny Frog!* She just shook her head, strolled over to the bedroom door, shoved it shut with her toe, and gave Larry a look she *knew* he could read.

He grimaced apologetically.

"Ye gods, Kosmic," she groaned, lacing her hands across the top of her head. "How in hell did you and Miri manage to give birth to such a—a—" Words failed her, and she shrugged.

"Square?" Larry suggested, sitting astraddle a chair, after turning it wrong way around. "Three-piecer? Young Republican? Budding IBM rep? Corporate Clone?" He tilted his head sideways and waited for a reply, blinking with mild expectation.

There was a little gray in that lovely, wavy hair, and he was wearing it shorter these days, but otherwise he was about the same as when she last saw him, and definitely in good shape.

Like all the kids in the Squad. Makes me feel like I did something right, anyway—they're fabulous as adults. Mind and body alert and sharp. And damn fine role models.

"Something like 'all of the above,'" she replied. She dropped her hands, headed for the dresser, and began transferring neat stacks of clothing from suitcase to dresser drawers.

The guest room was just as impressive as the rest of the house—which was saying something. If this was an example of Larry's handiwork, he'd fulfilled his promise of talent. If it was an example of his income, it was in the high six figures. This room had a skylight, its own bath, and dry sauna, was paneled in what looked like white birch (and probably was), and was furnished with some truly lovely pieces finished in white lacquer. The gray rug was thick enough to lose change in. But the effect was warm and airy, not sterile; by day it would be like living in the sky. On a practical note, there were *lots* of dresser drawers, and a very generous walk-in closet. Evidently Miri was over the box-and-milk-crate phase.

"Except the Corporate Clone," she amended. "If we can just get your boy's spine a bit stiffer, he *can* think for himself. The hard part is going to be getting him to want to. Which brings me back to the question; how'd a pair of bone-deep rebels like you produce a kid like that?"

Silence. A pregnant silence. She stowed the last of her leotards and turned back to face him, leaning against the edge of the dressing table on one hand.

"I have *no* idea," he said, as she took in his expression of bafflement. "Maybe it's karmic, much as I hate to put any stock in that. It sure would serve me right, given my misspent youth."

"More like it's Jenks," she observed. "Gad. More top-shelf European cars than in Europe. This town looks like Yuppie Central. Capital of expensive bland—no guts, no passion—Jeez, Lar, even the damn *houses* are pastel. And the *people*—cut 'em and they'll bleed tofu."

He shrugged. "The choice was here, or subject him to the Tulsa school system. He'd have come out of there being able to find the nearest muscle car, count to first-and-ten, and figure out exactly how much cash or coke would keep him from getting beaten up *this* time, but that's about it. Di, we average *forty* kids to a classroom over in Union—even if Deke *wasn't* psi, that'd have driven him nuts, and he'd never have gotten the kind of attention a kid with his brains deserves. He does here—they have a special course load for the bright kids, and he's on it. And over in Union, his life expectancy wouldn't be too high in some crowds. The car-crazy kids in Jenks tend to hover over basket cases in the garage. Kids from Union drag-race into the sides of semis."

She paid scant attention to the last sentence. It was the remark about Deke being psychic that caught her attention. "So he *is* psi? I thought so, since you had shields all over him, but that could have just meant Miri's paranoia was acting up. What's his Talent?"

Larry draped his arms over the back of the chair, then rested his chin on them. "No real idea," he admitted. "We bottled him up too fast. We had to shield him back when he was nine—he was picking up everything within a five-foot range. I was kind of hoping he'd grow out of it at puberty, but he didn't."

Di considered that in the light of what she knew about early-developing psychic gifts. "A five-foot range, huh? Not bad," she said thoughtfully. "Not a superkid, but not bad. So why didn't you do more than bottle him up? Or were you trying to keep him out of *your* business—"

"None to keep him out of."

Di looked at him measuringly. "Are you still into hot-and-cold-running esoterica at all?"

Larry shook his head slowly. "No, not since we moved here. Tulsa is about the most psychically null spot you'd ever want to see. Didn't see any reason to keep up the old skills; there was no use for them. Besides"—he nodded in the general direction of Di's shoulder—"this is the home of Oral Roberts University; the Prare Tar is right behind you."

"The *what?*"

"The Prare Tar. That's 'Prayer Tower' to you non-Okies."

"I saw the supposed-to-be-hospital, I didn't see that."

"You have to be on the campus to see it; it only looms subjectively. Anyway, Miri and I figured we'd be better off keeping our heads down and our profiles low."

Di licked her lips, stowing that data away for further examination. "Good move," she said finally. "Probably what I'd do in the same situation. Dear gods, I wish I didn't have to cart all these signing clothes. . . ." She shoved away from the dressing table, and stood hipshot halfway between the bed and Larry's chair. Watching him, his face in particular. She was, after all, still an empath—and she hadn't lost her knack of reading him.

There's more here that he's not telling me. It's got to do with the kid.

She hooked her thumbs through her belt loops and rested her knuckles on her hips. "So," she said, after waiting fruitlessly for *him* to broach the subject. "Talk. You really didn't bring me out here just to lecture for a month to a bunch of rich-brat pseudointellectuals. Or to reminisce about old times and keep you company while Miri's gone. You know better than to detour me for no better reason than that."

"You needed a vacation," he ventured. "That's what André said, anyway."

"Uh-huh." She continued to stare him down, and eventually he capitulated.

"I've—got a bad feeling. Just a kind of hunch." He looked sheepish.

She gave him the patented look of Exasperation. "Kosmic, back in the Squad days your hunches were better than most people's certainties. So what's this so-called bad feeling centered around? Deke?"

"Yeah." She waited. "This could just be normal parent stuff. Parents are supposed to worry about their kids; it's part of the job description."

"Uh-huh. And I'm the Pope. Cough it up, Kosmic."

Problem is, his precognition was always vague, she thought, waiting for him to find the right words. *And he used to be pretty sensitive about that. As if it was* his *fault that he couldn't pin things down.* After watching him grope around for what he wanted to say, she decided to prompt him a little.

"So how long has this feeling of yours been going on?" she asked. "Days? Weeks?"

"Really strong—about a week. Before that, vague, a couple of months. Before that, everything was fine."

He chewed on his lower lip and looked up at her, his expression worried and absurdly young-looking.

"Could all this be normal paranoia?" she asked, knowing that it *wasn't* but wanting to get him to admit the fact. "Or could it be because of that accident you told me about on the phone? If you were picking *that* up, but not that Deke would come through it all right, you'd have been itchy."

"No . . ." he replied, slowly but firmly. "No, it was going on before that, and it's worse since. If what I had been picking up was a premonition of the accident, I wouldn't be feeling anything anymore. And—"

"And?" she prompted. *Now we're getting somewhere.*

"It's not a mundane threat," he said firmly. "I realized that right after the accident, when I got him at the emergency room. I don't know why I didn't figure it out before, but now that you're here, I'm sure of it. But that's as specific as I can get. And *damn* if I can figure out what it is, or even where it's coming from."

She shifted her weight from her left to her right foot, but otherwise didn't move.

"It's like—" he began, then stopped.

"Go on."

He grimaced. "It's not like anything we ran into as the Squad, okay? So I'm just getting little hints around the edges."

Di kept her mouth shut this time; she could sense desperation and fear.

"Di," he said in a near-whisper, "Di, it's like there's something really hungry out there, and it wants my boy. And Miri isn't here to help me protect him."

He never was any good at combative magics, she recalled. *That was Miri's specialty. I remember he had precog, but Larry's biggie was the Sight and clairvoyance. Hell, that's why we named him Kosmic Kid— he was always Seeing things. Things I had to strain to even get a hint of.*

"Do you suppose that's a coincidence?" she asked.

He shook his head. "No, I'm beginning to think it wasn't. Whatever this thing is, it seems like it was waiting for Miri to leave for Japan before it went after Deke. I don't dare contact her; this is very hush-hush negotiations with the Japanese, they're paranoid as hell, and she isn't allowed to talk to *anybody* in the States except superiors in the company. They're so paranoid she told me before she left that the only way I could get to her would be a *real* emergency, because the Japanese would be checking, and she could lose her job. There's no doubt in my mind why it waited for this trip— she's secluded, and half a day away at the very best, and twenty-four hours is more like it."

Di nodded. This was beginning to make very nasty sense. "In our line of work, twelve hours can be all it takes. . . ."

"Exactly." He sighed, and massaged his temples. "You know the other factor here—Deke's age. He's never going to be stronger than right now, when he's got youth *and* energy *and* a fluid mind *and* all that burgeoning sexuality just looking for a place to go."

Di nodded, her lips compressed. "And I'll wager that it wasn't too long ago that he lost the protection of innocence, too. He's got that look—like he's started *knowingly* violating laws and rules, and doing it in a way he knows is going to hurt people if they find out."

Larry nodded *his* head unhappily. "Yeah. And that makes him a legal target, doesn't it?"

"It does. We'll just have to hope he hasn't hurt anybody badly by what he's done—and we'll have to hope he's feeling appropriately guilty about it," Di sighed. "If he's getting his kicks—"

"Not Deke," Larry told her. "I'd stake my life that he's not happy about breaking the rules. He knows we don't lay down the law arbitrarily. And I'm equally sure that he wouldn't hurt anyone on purpose, much less enjoy doing it."

She sagged down onto the edge of the bed. "I hope you're right, Lar. I just hope you're right . . . because you know as well as I do what could happen if you're wrong."

For unmentioned, but not unremembered, was the reason she had answered his call so promptly. The reason she *owed* him, beyond friendship and the help any teacher owed a student.

Melinda Dayton. Unchildlike child, who'd done more than break the rules—

Di did not even need to close her eyes to see Melinda; the one and only time they'd come face-to-face was all too vivid in memory.

Melinda, cowering against the wall of the kitchen of the abandoned shack. Not pretty; Di would have suspected a child that was too pretty, too clean, in that situation. Melinda was plain, a tattered little brown sparrow, with big frightened eyes. Vulnerable, and helpless.

She'd put on a very convincing little act.

Melinda Dayton, who looked so pathetic, had been dismembering kittens at seven, torturing and intimidating her playmates at eight, and at nine had learned how to bring in outside allies to help her do the same to adults.

She'd very nearly gotten Di.

Melinda Dayton, demon-child, who even before puberty had learned the pleasures of cruelty and pain.

Willingly, with full knowledge of what she was doing. Enjoying it. Granny had claimed that there were kids like that, born absolutely evil, wrong, twisted. Who knew the dark and chose it. Di had been skeptical. After Melinda, she believed.

If it hadn't been for Larry, who'd seen past the little-girl-lost eyes to the alien mind behind the eyes—who had spotted the things Melinda had brought in through the gate she'd constructed into the world of nightmares—

I might not have been toast, but I sure would have been hurting.

Some of the traditions she had worked in claimed that once there was a life between two people, they were karmically linked for all time.

Maybe that's true, she thought soberly. *Maybe it isn't. But Melinda or no Melinda, Lar was one of mine, and I take care of my own.*

He was watching her closely, as if trying to follow her thoughts. He looked worried to Di; well, that wasn't too surprising. He tended to think in terms of debts and balances—and maybe she owed him one by those terms. But he'd owed her just as big a debt; maybe bigger, in his eyes.

She'd kept him from killing himself.

That memory was nowhere near as immediate—she remembered more of what she'd picked up from him, and what she'd done; she really couldn't remember exactly what she'd said to him that dark, windy night. Not the way she recalled every second of that nightmare encounter with Melinda.

Not that it really mattered.

The bleak, hopeless despair, that's what had caught her attention; the kind of despair that saw no way out. The kind of hopelessness that drove home to her why the Catholic Church considered despair to be a mortal sin. Emotional trauma that profound could not be ignored—especially not when it carried the overtones of someone with a strong psi-talent.

She'd looked wildly around, using all her senses. The roof of the math building—

She remembered dropping her Coke and sprinting for the door, thanking all the gods that the math building wasn't one of the ones kept locked at night.

She'd caught him ready to throw himself off the top of the building, convinced that he was going crazy because he was "seeing things."

Except that *she* could See what he'd been Seeing.

Poor, pathetic thing, it had been trying to hold him off the edge with hands that could no longer grasp anything material. It was a ghost, of course, the ghost of a classmate who had managed to get some bad acid and take a header out the window the week before. The poor guy didn't even know he was dead.

All he knew was that no one seemed to be able to see him except Larry. He didn't understand what was going on; his mental processes were still scrambled from the bad trip. All he understood was that Larry represented his only hold on the reality that he'd known, and he wasn't about to let him get away.

The revenant had been haunting Larry for two days, turning up anytime, whether he was alone or not. Larry had thought his mind had finally snapped, that the pressures of school and political activism had gotten to him. After all, he was a rational, modern guy, who didn't believe in spirits.

Which meant that he had to be going crazy.

The thing hadn't let him sleep, hadn't left him in peace for most of those two days—and an hour before he'd run up the stairs of the math building, his roomie had quietly dialed the medical center to get them to come haul him away. Larry'd overheard that, and was at the end of his rope. He'd often said he'd rather die than go nuts—just the idea of being locked up in a little white room was enough to make him shake.

Di kept her smile strictly mental. Poor Lar had his share of quirky phobias back then—well, they all did; phobias kind of came with the territory of being psychic.

So when Di had pounded up those stairs, Larry was seconds away from proving he'd meant that statement.

Except that she didn't let him. And before the night was over, she'd put both spirits to rest.

"Well," she said finally, "I'm here now. Anything that wants Deke is going to have to go through me to get him."

Larry grinned with real relief. "God, Di, I was hoping you'd say that. I didn't want to ask—"

She crossed her arms over her chest. "No kidding. You never did. If you had a failing by the time I got through with you, it was that."

"—but I was hoping. So I'm not overreacting?"

She put out mental feelers. *All quiet on the Western Front, but that doesn't mean a damn thing.*

"The truth is, I don't pick up anything now, but that doesn't prove a thing. You know that as well as I do. No, I don't think you're overreacting. I think there's something going on. And one more thing—I think your kid is overdue for an evaluation and maybe some lessons in psi, before *he* winds up doing a soft-shoe on a ledge."

Larry grimaced, but nodded. "I was hoping he'd never have to deal with it."

She snorted. "Fat effin' chance, as you well know. If you don't deal with power, it deals with you. Now about that Jacuzzi you promised me . . ."

"With or without bathing suits?" he asked puckishly. "It doesn't look to me like you've got anything to be afraid to show, even at our age."

Di chuckled. "Lecher. Wouldn't you just like to know—and what would Miri say?"

"She'd say, 'I've always wanted to reenact the murder of Agamemnon.'"

Di laughed. "She probably would. Well, much as I hate wet spandex, in the interests of saving your life, and to avoid traumatizing your child, I guess we'd better use suits. I wouldn't want to shock poor Deke."

"I hate to say this, love," Larry said mockingly, "but I'm afraid you already have."

FOUR

The kitchen was hot, and smelled like fresh garlic. "Keep grating that cheese," Rhonda Carlin told her daughter. "Your hands and mouth can work at the same time."

Monica made a little wiggle of impatience, but picked the grater and ball of mozzarella back up, and resumed her assigned task. It was better than setting the table, anyway; she *hated* setting the table—she couldn't talk to her mom while she was setting the table.

Let *Dan* set the table.

"*So*, anyway, I saw Deke out in the court and he was sort of sitting kind of slumped over, so I went over to him and asked, like, what was wrong." She grated away vigorously so that Rhonda wouldn't interrupt her again, and picked a curl of the cheese out of the bowl to nibble on.

"And? What was wrong?" Rhonda frowned at the lasagne noodles, and Monica immediately felt guilty about asking her mother to make dinner tonight. After all, Rhonda was putting in a lot of overtime at her new computer programming job, and it wasn't really fair to ask her to do something that required more effort than setting the microwave.

"It was, you know, the accident." Monica felt a little chill go up her back when she mentioned it. Everybody at the school seemed to be affected that way—like if they talked about it, they might be next. "He's really down about it."

Rhonda nodded, her black hair curling in the steam from the noodles. "I'm not surprised. So, he was down. And?"

"Well, I said I didn't think he ought to be alone if he was that unhappy, because all he'd do would be to keep thinking about it and getting unhappier." The cheese was done, and Monica handed the white glass bowl to her mother. "And then I said, why didn't he talk about it, because that might help him feel better, and he said with who? And I said, with me. So he did. Or he started to, anyway." She giggled, and her mother raised a sardonic eyebrow at her as she drained the noodles.

"And then what happened?" Rhonda asked, deftly putting the lasagne together, layer by layer. Her sable-brown hands moved like a dancer's, graceful even in performing such a simple household task.

"Well, he started asking me questions, like about Colorado, and what did I like to do, and what did I think of Tulsa." Monica giggled again; she couldn't help it, it just bubbled up out of her. "I told him some stuff, and then I told him I thought the guys in Tulsa were pretty lame, 'cause I've been here a month and nobody's asked me out *yet*."

Rhonda laughed. "Why didn't you just hit him with a brick with your phone number on it?"

"*Mom,*" Monica protested indignantly. "Anyway, he had to go to class, but he said the guys in Tulsa are just slow, and that maybe somebody'll get the idea. And he said I was the sweetest girl he'd ever met, and he kissed my cheek."

"But did he ask for your phone number?" Rhonda asked shrewdly, putting the pan of lasagne carefully into the oven.

"Well," Monica admitted with reluctance, "no."

Rhonda shook her head. "Lame. Just like the others. And what about Alan? Yesterday you were all excited because he'd asked you if you had a boyfriend yet!"

"He's still okay," Monica replied coyly, following her mother into the living room. "He wrote me a note in class today. He's a hunk, too. They're *both* hunks. Besides, Deke knows all about that writer lady that's going to teach us on Monday. She's a friend of his dad's, and she's staying at his house." *That* was almost as exciting as having Deke notice her. "He says she's real nice."

"Did he say anything about whether he thinks she'd be willing to help you?" Rhonda asked, as Monica flung herself down on the couch, upside down, her legs draped over the back, her head dangling down the front.

"He says she might," Monica said happily, examining her nails. "He says I should ask her after class."

Not even her father knew how much Monica wanted to be a writer—not, she reckoned cynically, that he'd care. He was too busy with his new girlfriend to worry about his ex-wife and the two kids he'd gladly shed. Rhonda was the only person who knew; who knew about the boxes full of stories she'd written and never shown to anyone else. Not even her teachers knew.

But she had no idea how you became a real writer; did you just send things to magazines and book companies and see what happened? The writers' magazines, with their articles on marketing and agents and equally bewildering topics, only confused her.

And anyway, she had no idea if she was any good. Certainly Rhonda seemed to think she was, but that was her mother—the same person who'd framed her crayon drawings and hung them on the wall. She'd long ago decided that what she needed was the opinion of a real writer, a stranger, someone with no prejudices on her behalf.

And now it seemed that she was going to be able to get just that. And maybe, if this lady said she *was* any good . . .

I'll worry about that when—if—she does, Monica told herself, then chuckled. *Besides, wanting to know about her makes a good excuse to talk to Deke some more.*

"So what are you going to do this weekend?" Rhonda asked, breaking into her thoughts.

"I don't know," she admitted. "Rent a movie, I guess. And I've got a lot of homework."

Her mother shook her head, but didn't say anything. Monica knew she worried about her kids—she'd been pretty reluctant to transfer to Tulsa in the first place; she hadn't been too thrilled about being a divorced black woman *anywhere* in the South, and she was even more uneasy for the sake of Monica and Dan. "Being black in a mostly lily-white profession can cause enough problems just for me," Rhonda had confided to her daughter. "But you kids—going to a place like Jenks, and not only being black but having a dad who's white—I don't know."

Still, there hadn't been any problems so far, except the ones Monica usually had—jealousy from the other girls because she was pretty. The same thing had happened in Colorado. Monica couldn't help her looks, and she didn't intend to act like a nun or a Brain just because other people felt threatened. The only difference between Colorado and here, so far, was that the guys just couldn't seem to get their acts together. That, and Tulsa was pretty boring most of the time.

Privately, Monica thought her mother worried too much.

"I wish you'd get some friends, honey," Rhonda said, in that *concerned* tone of voice Monica was hearing a lot lately.

"It's okay, Mom," she said quickly. "It's just, you know, coming in like in the middle of the semester. Everybody's got their friends and it takes a while. But Harper was even nice to me today; she told me I ought to try out for pom-poms in the fall. If Harper's nice to me, everybody else will start being nice."

Rhonda's eyebrows climbed halfway up her forehead. "What brought *that* on?" she asked. "I thought she was trying to freeze you out."

"So did I. I don't know; all I know is she's not anymore." Monica went back to checking her nail polish for chips, examining it minutely. "Maybe she changed her mind. Maybe she's figured, you know, people are going to think she's racist if she keeps getting on my case. Maybe now that I've been here for a month she figures I'm not a threat."

"How could you be a threat?" Rhonda asked sardonically. "The guys around here are too *lame* to bother with!"

Monica snorted her agreement delicately. "Anyway, she's going to be graduating in a couple of months; maybe she figures that she doesn't have to worry about competition at this point. She should, though." She grinned at her mother. "It isn't prom time *yet*. I could still end up going with Deke. Or anybody else, if I decided to work at it."

Her mother laughed at her. "Girl, you are so *vain!*"

Monica made a face at her. Rhonda *still* got plenty of looks from guys; more than enough to make her daughter a little jealous. And maybe Dad was a jerk, but he was also a studly hunk. Monica had a mirror; as far as she could see, she'd gotten the best of both sets of genes. Daddy's hair and eyes, Mom's face and build, a blend of both for complexion. *I don't even need to work at a tan,* she thought smugly. *I've got one built in.*

And she didn't see where there was anything wrong with being aware of the fact that she was hot.

"Deke was being *real* nice to me," she told Rhonda, playing with the fringe on one of the sofa pillows. "When he figured out I wanted to know, he told me *lots* about that writer. And he didn't have to, either. He could have gone off with some of his buddies, but he stayed to talk to me. I think he just *wanted* to talk to me, that's what I think. And I think he likes me, so Harper better watch out, or she *will* have to get somebody else to take her to the prom."

The oven timer chimed, and Rhonda pulled herself up out of her chair to go take care of the lasagne. Dan appeared out of nowhere, sort of materializing in his chair.

He's as bad as Garfield, Monica thought in disgust. *All he does is eat. And he* never *gains any weight. It's just not fair!*

She followed her mother into the kitchen, and Rhonda glanced at her with a funny expression as she got the big bowl of salad to carry out to the table.

"You know, *you'd* better watch out," Rhonda warned her. "Harper could be a lot bigger threat than you think she is. She's got money, she's the most popular kid in the school, she's a pretty big frog in that pond."

Monica shrugged. "What could she do to me, really? She can't get me in trouble, and she can't put me on the outs with people who don't even know me."

Rhonda lifted the lasagne pan out of the oven and shook her head. "Sometimes it isn't a matter of what somebody can do on her own, and more a matter of what and who you know. It sounds to me like this Harper chick has more than her fair share of both."

It's show time—

Ann Greeley finished her introduction, making Di sound like the next Pulitzer Prize winner. Di had been waiting inconspicuously at the rear of the class, using just a touch of magic to make sure no one noticed her lurking back there. Now she chuckled to herself, and while Ann took her place at the rear of the class, Di strolled to the front of the uncrowded classroom to face the first of the two Honors English classes she would be teaching. She'd gone over her pitch very carefully with Ann first. She was wearing her usual working togs: blue jeans, boots, and leotard, with her long hair knotted into a bun at the nape of her neck.

She very nearly laughed at the surprised expressions most of the kids wore.

"Hi," she said, half sitting on the edge of the teacher's desk, leaning back a little on her hands. "I'm Diana Tregarde, and I write romances for a living." She smiled, surveying the young, astonished faces around her. "It's a tough job, but somebody has to do it."

The eighteen assorted pairs of eyes stared at her, and she stared back. They looked absolutely incredulous, and Di knew why. She waited, and finally one of the girls, a trendy little redhead, blurted out, "But—you don't *look* like a romance writer!"

Di did laugh this time. "What did you expect?" she asked them all, spreading her hands as she met each set of eyes in turn. "Lace and ribbons? Silk negligee? Torn bodice, with handsome hunk clinging to my ankle?"

She turned back to the redhead. The girl shook her head wordlessly.

"These," Di told them, taking in the ensemble with a gesture, "are my working clothes, mostly because they're comfortable. When I have meetings with my agent or publishers, I do the 'dress for success' thing, gray suit and all, but when I'm working I need to wear something that won't distract me—because I may be sitting at my desk and pounding away at the keyboard for eight to twelve hours at a stretch. Sometimes more. It's never, ever less than eight."

One of the boys raised his hand. "Why never less than eight?" he asked. "I thought writers could do whatever they wanted to."

She leaned forward a little to emphasize her earnestness. "Because this is a job, and I treat it as such. My office may be another room of my apartment, but I go there to work, and I give that work the attention it deserves, just as if I were working for a bank, an oil company, or anywhere else."

Now was the time to be a little more casual. She scooted up on the desk, and crossed her legs. "So, let me tell you what it's really like to be a writer—the way I live my life. It starts out around nine in the morning, because I'm a late sleeper. . . ."

She had them now, and she gave them a précis of what her working day was like.

They seemed fascinated, not the least because her life was so *ordinary*.

Once she started in on this part of the lecture, she had more than enough attention to spare for other things. And now that she had Deke out from under the shields Larry and Miri had put on their house, she could see if there was anything targeting him.

There wasn't, no matter how carefully she looked. Not that the absence of anything malevolent meant that he was safe—in fact, quite the opposite. If there was something after Deke, but it was willing to take its time and use a long-term plan, the smartest move would be to leave no telltales behind. After all, the kid was hardly invisible; he had a set schedule to keep whether he liked it or not. And he was quite visible from a psychic point of view; the shields on him were anything but subtle.

So the absence of telltales only meant that anything after Deke was smart.

She did notice one other thing out of the ordinary about the class, though. There was one other kid with psi, one of the girls in the back row. Unshielded, she glowed with it, though not nearly as brightly as Deke did through the shields. So it wouldn't be enough to give her any trouble, unless there was something out hunting kids with psi-potential, or unless there was a lot of activity in the area.

Now that's worth checking out—Di made a quick scan of the immediate vicinity. And came up with nothing. Absolutely nothing; like dead air. Exactly as Larry had told her, the immediate area was psychically null.

And that *was* strange.

But she really didn't have time to explore that at the moment; she was getting into the part of her lecture where she might start getting some questions.

She turned all of her attention back to the kids, and pointed out that she spent more actual time working than most of their parents, because there was never a break in her work, and in a "regular job" there would be times when there was nothing to do. At that point Deke asked, "What do you do when you've got writer's block? Sit there and stare out the window?"

She laced her hands around her knee and leaned back a little. "This is probably going to sound like heresy—but I don't believe in writer's block. And neither does any other genre writer I know. And you know why?"

Deke shook his head.

"Because we can't *afford* to be blocked. We have bills to pay, and deadlines to meet. We can't afford to be prima donnas, we can't take the time to nurse neuroses. I do one of several things if I'm having trouble with a book. I can go work on another project, because I generally have one book in outline, one being written, and one being revised at any one time. Or I can talk the problem over with one or two friends—and usually, just the act of discussing the problem gives me the solution for it. Or I can go back to the outline, see where I started having trouble, and see if there's an alternate way the plot could go. All sounds terribly businesslike, doesn't it!"

Heads nodded all over the classroom. This was not the way any of them had pictured the craft of writing—and having taught this kind of class before, Di was quite well aware of that. They'd all pictured the inspiration, then the jump to finished product, without a single thought for all the work in between.

She was slowly destroying that illusion.

"That's because it *is*," she said. "This is a business. I have a product—stories. And like any other product, what goes into it is far more work than creativity. That's why I laugh when people come up to me and say, 'I've got this great idea for a book—all you have to do is write it and we'll split it fifty-fifty.' I mean, just think about it. Think about the simple act of typing one hundred thousand words—that's about 400 pages. Not composing them, not revising them—just typing them. It takes me five minutes to get an idea, about a month to outline the book, and then another three *just to write it*. And some fool wants me to do all that work and split fifty-fifty with him? Five minutes against four months? Give me a break!"

The kids chuckled; some of them looked sheepish.

And there go about half a dozen more offers for so-called collaborations, no doubt.

"I'll tell you what I really think writer's block is—it's reluctance to sit down and do the damn work. When you tell people, 'I'm not writing right now because I don't feel like it,' you're not going to get any sympathy. But tell them you've got writer's block—you get plied with wine and cheese and all the 'poor babies' you can handle. Okay, since Deke started it, anybody have any more questions?"

"Yeah," one of the kids in the back said. "If ideas are so easy to get, where do *you* find them?"

She was tired of sitting, so she shoved herself off the desk and moved into the space between her desk and theirs, a kind of no-man's-land. "If I were being really snide, I'd tell you that I belong to the Idea of the Month Club; it's run out of Poughkeepsie, New

York, and you get the regular idea, the alternate idea, and a selection of six featured ideas—"

The kids were all smart enough to see through that, and laughed.

"The truest answer would be that it's easier to tell you where I don't get ideas from. Life is full of them, especially for a romance writer. I can go downtown and people-watch, and see a dozen possible stories go by me. All you have to do is start noticing things around you, and then ask the really important questions—'what if,' followed by 'what then.' What if that model that passed you was in love with some photographer but thought he was gay? What if that worried-looking businessman thinks his wife is cheating on him—and why would she be, if she was? The ideas are there; you just have to open yourself to them."

"Do you ever try and write something the way you think an editor will like it?"

That was the young girl in the back of the room, and Di blinked in surprise. That was one question she hadn't expected.

"Of course I do," she replied. "And I'm sorry if that disappoints you, but it's true. I'd be a fool not to. They're expecting a certain kind of product from me, and I've signed a contract promising to deliver it. Once again, a genre writer can't afford to have feelings of sensitivity about his deathless prose. It's *not* deathless. It may— hell, probably will—be changed before it hits the bookshelves. So when you're a genre writer, you develop a very thick skin, and you learn to be flexible. Not that my editors haven't, on occasion, driven me up the wall with stupid revisions"—she grinned wryly at all of them—"because they have. But that's life. They pay me for the things, and besides, I usually manage to give them what they asked for, but the way *I* want it done."

"So why do you do this?" another girl wanted to know. "I mean, if it's like that much work, and people drive you nuts with what they want, why don't you go do something else for a living?"

"Mostly because I love writing," she answered. "Truthfully. I like telling stories, I like doing it well. In any other job you get people who drive you nuts, too—just ask your parents, or Ann Greeley, here. And I'll tell you something else—most people find themselves in the position of working at a job they're good at, but that they don't enjoy. It isn't too often that a person gets to work at something they really love. And I promise you all, from my own personal experience, if you *ever* find a job that you love to do, go do it, and damn the consequences. You'll live longer—but more than that, you'll be happy. And what you don't spend on ulcer medication and psychiatrists will more than make up for a pay difference."

She could see by the expressions on the faces in front of her that she'd gotten about half the kids in the class to think with that last statement. *Good. In five or six years they're going to be out there making a living—and the more people in the world there are that like what they're doing, the better off the world is going to be.*

She checked her watch; she had just enough time left to give them their first assignment.

"All right, now let's get down to business." She hooked her thumbs into her belt loops and moved over so that she stood directly behind the desk. "The reason I'm here is to give you all a start on learning to write. I say 'a start' because if you're any good, you never stop learning. Some of you will decide that you don't like it; some won't be much good at it. That doesn't matter, and what's more, you won't be graded down for it. As long as you *try*, that's all I care about. But believe me, I *will* be able to tell whether or not you're trying. So. Right now, everyone starts out with a B and you won't go any lower."

There were stifled gasps all over the class. She'd just violated every precedent for classwork they'd ever heard of, and most of them weren't sure how to handle it.

"What does matter in this course," she said, following up on her advantage, "is that you'll have gotten a chance to try your hand at this stuff. And you'll know whether or not you've got the particular combination of skill and persistence this takes. You'll never have to say 'if I'd only' . . . because you *will* have tried. And that is the single most important thing I'll be able to give you."

While they were still in shock, she gave them their assignment. "Now, I want one page of dialogue and description from you tomorrow. A simple scene; a girl and a boy having a fight. *You* choose what it's about. Don't allow them to make up at the end of the page. That's basically it. We'll read them all aloud and see how they work tomorrow."

The bell rang less than ten seconds after she finished speaking, and she congratulated herself not only for completing the lecture on time, but for keeping them so engrossed that none of them had been watching the clock just over her shoulder.

The kids filed out slowly, in clumps of two and three, all of them talking animatedly.

And that's one more gold star in my bunny book. I've got 'em going again.

The bell that had just rung was the one for lunch, so Di was a bit surprised when one of the girls lingered behind the others, hovering right near the door. She'd thought the lot of them would vanish.

It was the girl that had asked several of the better questions, a pretty, delicate child with a café-au-lait complexion and blond hair. Obviously a mixed-race girl, and Di envied anyone who'd been handed such a perfect combination of genes. *Model material if ever I saw it . . . especially in Europe.*

"Miss Tregarde?" the girl said shyly. "I wonder if I could bother you for a minute?"

"Sure," Di replied automatically, "though it isn't a bother. What can I do for you?"

Ann had moved unobtrusively to the front of the classroom. "This is Monica," she offered quietly. "She just transferred in from Colorado."

"I wondered if you'd look at some things I wrote, and tell me if they're any good or not." The girl wouldn't look at her; kept her head down and her eyes on the floor between them.

Now Di understood the intensity, and the look on the girl's face. This was one who wanted, badly, to be a writer.

The question was, did this girl have it in her to *do* what she had to, or was she just a "wannabe"?

"Sure," she replied. "I'll take a look, provided you're ready to handle criticism."

"I—" the girl began.

Di interrupted her. "The fact is—Monica?—the fact is that I can be kind, or I can be honest. I can't be both." That usually deterred the wannabes. "I'm not going to be nice, because an editor wouldn't be nice. It's an editor's job to pick the good stuff out of the crud, and to do that she—or he, my editor's male, though a lot of them aren't—can't afford to waste his time being nice to every poor soul that sends in an unsolicited manuscript. And I'll do one thing that she won't; I'll tell you what's wrong and why. She'll just send you the standard 'This does not suit our purposes at this time' rejection notice."

"That's great, Miss Tregarde," the girl replied earnestly. "It really is. I *want* you to tell me if it isn't any good, really I do. I—I just finished reading *Heart of the Wolf* last night, and I thought it was really terrific. I think I could learn an awful lot from you."

Di gave her two mental points. *Bright girl; read up on me to know who she was going to be dealing with. Okay, she says she's tough. Now we'll just have to see if she really is.* "Fine, if you're really sure. Would you like to take care of this tonight? I don't have anything I need to do."

"If you could—I mean, you know, it would be really great!" The girl looked about ready to kiss her feet.

Di thought quickly. *I'd better pick a public spot to meet her, public enough that if it turns out she can't take criticism, it'll be too embarrassing for her to make a scene. The last thing I need is a hysterical teenager—*

She did a quick take, and recognized the girl from her scan of the class earlier, looking for clues to Deke's hunter.

—make that hysterical, psychic *teenager having an emotional tantrum at me.*

"I could meet you at the library," she suggested. "The one next to

Woodland Hills mall. That could be at about seven if you're up to it."

"I've got a lot of things all ready—I really do. That would be fine—that would be great!" the girl exclaimed breathlessly. She didn't even wait for Di's reply; she just clutched her books to her chest and ran for the door.

Di chuckled and shook her head, looking at Ann with a raised eyebrow. Ann shrugged, and smiled, and began pulling out the next class's assignment from her desk. "Kids," Di said to no one in particular, and followed the girl out.

She couldn't help but notice that Monica seemed to have picked up an escort once she hit the hall. And there was no mistaking who it was, either.

Well. Well, well. Dear me, Mr. Kestrel, I do seem to remember your father saying that you had a steady—and I also recall that it wasn't Monica.

Still, it might just be that Deke was discussing the assignment with the girl. Or that she was asking *him* about Di. It might be innocent.

Then again—they weren't holding hands, or even touching, but there was no mistaking the way they were leaning toward each other, oblivious to everything else.

Partially that's psi-attraction. And partially hormones. Derek, you're flirting with trouble if your steady finds out. . . . Di stayed behind them all the way to the outside door, trying not to grin at the romantic glow Deke was emitting. Once outside the door, they headed for one of the concrete benches surrounding the front entrance, presumably to share confidences and lunch.

Di, on the other hand, was not a student—so she wasn't stuck on school property. She also wasn't a teacher, so she wasn't limited to a half-hour lunch. With Lunch Monitor duty. That was the benefit of doing this without pay. Ann simply arranged for her to be a "guest speaker," and since she wasn't contracted to anything, she wasn't obliged to follow rules. The principal and school board had been so flabbergasted at having her run her "seminar" for nothing that they hadn't balked at any of her conditions.

She could go have a leisurely lunch in a restaurant, far away from babbling kids.

She took a quick look back at Deke and Monica, who were being very attentive to each other, and chuckled again. "Young love," she said aloud, "or is it young lust? What the hell, at that age they can't tell the difference!"

As she turned back toward the parking lot, though, she caught sight of someone else, someone in a fancy red sports car, pulled up at the foot of the sidewalk, very obviously staring in her direction.

At her?

No—behind her. And the only people directly behind her were Deke and Monica—

At that point, whoever was driving the car pulled out in a splatter of gravel and a shriek of tires; the car had been too far away from Di for her to even see what sex the driver was.

Peculiar, she thought, making a mental note to find out who drove a car like that. *Very peculiar.*

Barbecue—pronounced, or so Larry had told her, "bobby-cue"— seemed a good option. It was one of Tulsa's three specialties, the other two being chili and "deep-fried everything."

Since the latter choice sounded pretty vile, she opted for "bobby-cue."

Tulsans, it seemed, barbecued everything, too. She blinked in amazement at the barbecued baloney, and wondered what her old friend Paul Lazinski would say about the unholy concept of barbecued kielbasa.

He'd probably call the Pope and get them excommunicated, she decided, and opted for something a bit less—exotic.

And just a touch of caloric sin. "And cold potato salad," she told the waiter.

"Y'all want that Easterner potato salad?" he asked, making it sound as if it were toxic waste. "Or good Oklahomey potato salad?"

"What's the difference?" she asked, just a little apprehensively.

"That Easterner potato salad, they put in the mayo, an' the mustard, an' the relish," he told her, "but them potatoes, they's cut up in chunks."

"Okay," she responded. "So?"

"In good Oklahomey potato salad, they's *mashed!*"

He grinned as if he had just revealed that their cook was a Cordon Bleu chef in disguise.

Di swallowed. "I'll settle for french fries," she told him faintly.

She took the moment of peace before her "feast" arrived to arrange her facts in order.

One, Larry thinks his son is being stalked. Nothing to support that at the moment, but nothing to contradict it, either.

She played with the edge of her napkin. *Assume he's right; whatever is after him is leaving no fingerprints. Okay, that's not a problem, particularly if it's noticed he's shielded and has decided to move in on him slowly. What that means is that he, she, or it is probably more than just adult age—probably fifty at least. It takes age and experience to be that subtle.*

Which left out any of Deke's classmates playing at magick. Unless one of them happened to be an apprentice to somebody older and wiser. Even then, it was a virtual certainty that an apprentice would have blundered somewhere along the way. And that would leave traces.

One way to be sure; call Fred and ask him if there's anybody that he knows of operating in Tulsa. Anyone working darkside that has taken apprentices usually devours or ruins them, and that would show up in Guardian telltales.

She stared at the water beading up on the side of her glass. *Two, Tulsa is absolutely psychically null. Frankly, I wouldn't want to operate here. I'm going to have to figure out the boundaries, and figure out why. And how long it's been this way. It may or may not have any bearing on this case.*

Rolls arrived; warm, but obviously mass-produced. She ignored them. *Three, Deke is a legal target. He's obviously flirting with that*

*little black girl, and that means he's knowingly violating the implicit
promise made to the chick he's going steady with. That makes him an
oathbreaker, and puts him on the negative side of the karmic ledger,
which in turn makes him open to subversion, or even attack. Even if
he'd been protected up until now, he isn't anymore. Which leads me
to number four—he's hiding something. It's something he's afraid to
tell anyone else. And I don't know him well enough to judge whether
it's mundane or psi-related. It might even be both.* She bit her lip.
With teenagers, nothing's ever simple.

Her order arrived, and she ate it quickly, without tasting it. As
soon as she was finished, she headed for the bank of pay phones near
the rest rooms, and dialed a Kansas City number from memory.

"Guardian Plumbing and Heating," said a tinny voice, faint
Eastern Seaboard accent tingeing the words. "Fred Hunter here."

"Fred, it's Di," she said, laughing in spite of herself. "You know,
one of these days that name is going to get you in trouble!"

"What, 'Fred'? How could that get me in trouble? When are you
going to let me fix that furnace of yours?"

"Fred, you moved to Kansas six months ago. Is business so bad
that you're willing to make house calls to Connecticut? Besides,
there are perfectly good heating contractors in New Haven—"

"The boys in New Haven are a bunch of crooks," Fred interrupted, as she bit her lip to keep from laughing anymore. "They
wouldn't tell you if you had a transdimensional portal to hell in
your humidifier."

"Why would I want a transdimensional portal to hell in my humidifier?" she asked. "It's easier to take the Greyhound down to
Newark. Listen, I've got a serious question. I'm on a personal case.
Is there anybody operating in the Tulsa area that I should know
about?"

"There's nobody operating in the Tulsa area at all worth talking
about," Fred replied. "At least, not according to my sources. Never
has been, likely never will be. Even the Indians won't work there.
Can't tell you why, it's out of my territory. Let sleeping dogs lie, I
always say. No news is good news. Curiosity killed the cat—"

"Okay, okay, I get the idea," she said hastily. "But I'm the one that's down here. I could sure use some local information."

"Sorry," Fred said, sounding sincere. "Wish I had some. But you know how thin we're spread. Hell, we didn't have *anybody* down in these parts till I moved here after that Dallas mess you got yourself into. Good thing you were able to handle it alone. Now about that furnace of yours—"

If I'd had anybody available, I wouldn't have tried. "Fred, you're incorrigible. But thanks."

"No problem," he said. "Call me if you need a hand."

"I'll try to stick to smaller guns," she told him. "I don't intend to pull you out of your territory unless it's a screaming emergency."

"I don't know what you'd call a screaming emergency, Di, but I do gotta admit I got a tricky little problem of my own up here. I'd kind of prefer taking things in order, if you know what I mean."

"Is this the disappearing kids?" she asked. "That sounded pretty mundane in the papers."

"Yeah. I think it was supposed to. Not sure I'd have picked up on it if I hadn't been doing a furnace installation in the neighborhood. Bad feel, Di. Bad feel. Think I got a handle on it, though. Just gonna take a little more time."

Just what I need. Working two juggling acts a state apart. Still— "Are *you* going to need *me*?"

"No; just think it's a job for a professional. I can handle it."

She closed her eyes and tried to invoke her own limited precog. The little she got said he'd be all right.

And after all, he was, indeed, a professional. "All right, Fred. Good luck. Thanks again."

"Same to you, Di." She started to hang up, and thought she heard him say something else. But by the time she'd gotten the receiver back to her ear, he was already gone, and all she got was a dial tone.

Had she heard him say, "You'll need it"?

FIVE

Fay Harper clutched the steering wheel of her brand-new Dodge Shelby and lifted her lip in a delicate snarl. Even as she did so, Deke leaned across the concrete bench and oh-so-casually brushed the black girl's cheek with his hand.

If she'd had the energy to spare, Fay would have called down a lightning bolt to fry them both then and there.

And it would *take* a purely physical attack to get through those damned shields Deke had on him—at least given the energy level Fay was at right now.

Miserable bitch! Double-timing twit!

In complete disregard of school rules that stated no student was to leave the school grounds until classes were over, Fay pulled her car out of the parking lot in a gravel-scattering, tire-smoking show of anger.

How could she have so misjudged that new girl? After the little bitch had failed to get a single date in the first month since she'd moved from Colorado, it seemed as if, despite the undoubted fact that she was disgustingly cute, she wasn't going to be any kind of threat. Fay's ascendancy at Jenks High was going to remain unchallenged.

So Fay had turned her attention elsewhere, to taking care of other competition, to beginning the tiniest moves toward ensnaring

Sandy and parting him from Jill—and as soon as she turned her back, disaster had struck.

A stray dog started across the street in front of her, and Fay hit the accelerator, hoping to ease some of her anger by killing something. Unfortunately, the cur saw her coming, and managed to dive out of the way before she could run him down. It hid between two parked vans, completely protected.

This was *not* her day.

And it was all Derek Raymond Kestrel's fault.

He was letting that sugar-sweet little bit of fluff haul him in like a hooked fish; he was falling for her just as quickly as he'd fallen under Fay's carefully controlled fascination.

It just wasn't *fair*.

She pulled the Shelby into one of the local Sonic drive-ins; this one was franchised and run by a bunch of born-again bigots, and it always gave her a little thrill to eat there. After all, here she was, the Scarlet Woman, the Enemy, smiling and feeding her face right under their noses. They took her money, and never guessed what she was. And she would use the money to carry misfortune to them, making certain that something went wrong after she was ready to leave.

It was too pathetically easy, really, but it was such fun—they were opening themselves to her so thoroughly that she *always* had an opportunity to make them miserable. Their karmic balance sheets would be constantly in the red if only for the way they treated their employees. That they cheated on their taxes and quietly hated their fellow man (in the form of anyone who didn't belong to *their* little fundamentalist sect), all the while professing to love their neighbors—that only made it easier. Hypocritical liars that they were, they were ripe for her tampering. And then there was *his* mistress, and *her* secret alcohol binges—

Lovely. They played right into their hands.

She ordered from a harried-looking middle-aged woman whose red-rimmed eyes testified that Mrs. Bigot had been brow-beating the staff again and threatening cuts in hours.

That was wonderful; that alone would justify something satisfyingly expensive. Perhaps an invasion of cockroaches and a surprise inspection from the Health Department?

It had occurred to her, as she'd watched and ground her teeth in frustration, that Deke was playing into her hands exactly the same way, by taking up with little Rosey Tush. Unfortunately, it wasn't something she could take advantage of; that kind of leverage didn't fit in with the plans she had for him.

Her plans were more complicated than that, because the little twit was exactly what she'd been looking for over the last two years. Perfect, in fact; callow as hell, easily manipulated, good-looking, amusing in bed, and a walking power plant of magickal potential.

And she did *not* intend to turn him loose,

"I have thee, Derek Kestrel," she muttered, "and yet I cannot take thee."

"Pardon?" said the startled carhop, tray in hand.

"Nothing," Fay said, smiling sweetly. "That was how much? And take the tray, dear. I won't need it."

She paid the woman, including a big tip half of which Mrs. Bigot would confiscate, thus increasing the feelings of rancor the staff had for her.

The woman retreated; Fay contemplated her problems with Derek. There didn't seem to be any simple solution, and she bit savagely into her hamburger. There was no hope for it; she couldn't counter his shields and haul him back to the fold. She just didn't have the time or the resources to deal with Deke and his little Juliet right now. Not with the current project she had going.

In a few more days the rivalry between Sandy and Bob would be finally out in the open; ripe and ready to harvest. She'd been playing one against the other for some time now, working them both into a fine froth of jealousy over school status. Now it was time to add sex to the picture. It wouldn't be too long until the lust-spells she'd cast on both of them had them literally at each other's throats. She'd have added Deke to that emotional stew, except that his parents had shielded him too well, and too long ago, to make the shields easy to subvert.

Ah, well. She licked ketchup off her fingers daintily. Red, and thick, it could have been blood. A hundred years ago, it likely *would* have been blood. The rivalry between the two football heroes would have been resolved at gunpoint, in a duel of some kind, or in an ambush. A case of winner-takes-all, where Fay was the only true winner.

She'd instigated more than a few duels in her time. Death and spilled blood were such *fine* sources of power.

Fine, and satisfying. She finished her fries and sighed with nostalgic resignation; it was too bad, but she'd just have to make do with the power surge she'd accumulate when Sandy and Bob finally confronted each other, fought—and hopefully beat the pulp out of each other.

Time to go. And time to visit retribution upon the Sonic drive-in. She considered and discarded several minor disasters, and finally settled on an irreparable leak in the hot water heater, and several more in the plumbing in the Bigots' house. She set the spells on the money Mrs. Bigot had taken from the carhop; they would activate as soon as the old bat touched the handle of a faucet.

That accomplished, she started the car and threw it into reverse, not being too careful about whether there was anyone in the way. There *were* compensations for living in this age. This vehicle was certainly one of them. She'd considered replacing the TransAm with a Firebird, but the salesman had put her off; he'd acted as if he was immune to her looks, and he himself had been far too ordinary to bother with. In contrast, there had been the young man who'd sold her this T-top Dodge Shelby—*he'd* been more to her taste . . . and a tasty little morsel indeed, once she got him home.

Vehicles like this one meant no more dealing with horses, stupid, smelly beasts that they were. She never could abide animals, and the feeling was mutual.

She pulled out into traffic, cutting off a senile old lady who nearly had a heart attack on the spot. The old biddy slammed on

her brakes, and was rear-ended by some nerd in a metallic gold
VW Beetle. Fay smiled and continued smoothly on her way, casting a glamour on her own license plate so that, should anyone
think to note the number, it would in no way match the one registered to her.

As she passed Sooner Federal, she noted that the bank sign said
1:47. She was already late for class—but the sun was shining and it
was much too nice a day to spend further indoors. And besides,
that last little pair of indulgences had cost her; she felt a little weak,
and was starting a moderate headache. Suddenly she had no wish
to return to school; basking on the sun deck, with a strawberry
daiquiri in hand, was much more attractive.

This business of "school" was such a bother, anyway. Not like in
the old days. . . .

As Fay roared into her immaculate driveway, the garage door
opened silently without her having to raise a finger. This was, of
course, as it should be; it meant her Servant was properly anticipating her needs. As usual, she parked across two spaces; she hated
having her car too close to another to get the door open completely, and hence having to squirm to extricate herself from her
vehicle. It was undignified; it rumpled her clothing and her temper. Besides, there was plenty of room; this was a four-car garage
and there were only two cars in it, hers and the Mercedes.

The Merc reminded her, as always, of Wes. Wes, who'd chosen
the stodgy little Merc over the Ferrari he could easily have af-
forded. Who had never understood why *she* drove the Porsche.
Dear, stupid Wes, no taste, no zest for living, who had asked her
plaintively *why* she needed a garage big enough for four cars when
they only had two.

"But what about Fay, dear?" she'd said sweetly. "She'll be old
enough to drive soon, and she'll surely want her own car."

She certainly did, Wesley. She certainly did.

She waxed nostalgic over the Porsche for a moment. It *had* been a lovely car until she'd wrapped it around a tree. And, matters being what they were, she'd had to walk back home and have Aunt Emily report it as stolen. Too bad; no car since had possessed quite the élan of the Porsche.

The garage door closed. The Servant was waiting silently for her, holding open the door to the house, as always. As it *should* be. Fay had returned to her kingdom, where she alone ruled.

As she passed the Servant, Fay took a moment to give it a minute inspection, and was satisfied that it was holding up. If anyone had bothered to examine it closely—which nobody ever did—they'd have been struck by how closely it resembled her.

Well, it was supposed to be her aunt, after all, and so close a resemblance wasn't unusual in near relations. And there was no reason for anyone to take that second look and see that "Aunt Emily" was Fay's double—if you aged Fay fifty years or so.

Not that anyone would *ever* see her aged sixty-eight.

"The doctor called," the Servant said, when Fay had finished her examination of it. "He wants to know when you plan on visiting your mother. He'd like you to come by as soon as you can."

Fay laughed, throwing her head back and baring her teeth in a feral smile. "Why? The last time I showed up, she had to be tranked afterward. He surely doesn't want that to happen again. It looks bad on his record."

The Servant bared its teeth in an identical smile; it tended to mimic her expressions when she was around, since it was an extension of herself. Of minimal intelligence, of course; enough to answer questions and direct the other, flesh-and-blood servants. Building it had taken all the power Fay had left after the transfer. But she'd discovered some time ago that having a Servant during her minority was well worth the cost, especially these days. Modern laws did not permit thirteen-year-old children to govern themselves and a sizable fortune; did not even permit them to live without adult supervision.

"The doctor said that your mother is asking to see you," the Servant replied. "He believes his new therapy is working, and he wishes to put it to the test. He feels that if your mother remains calm when confronting you, it will be a sign that her recovery is near."

"He's an old fool," Fay said scornfully, starting up the rust-colored, wool-carpeted, oaken staircase to her room.

"You pay him very well to be a fool," the Servant replied from the base of the stairs behind her.

That was so unexpected and so intelligent a response that Fay stopped, and turned to look at her simulacrum thoughtfully.

It occurred to her that the thing had been saying some clever things lately. Perhaps . . . too clever. And it had been acting as if it disapproved of some of her recreations, especially the pharmaceutical ones. The problem with a Servant was that if you left it alone too much, forcing it into a position of making too many decisions, it *could* develop an independent intelligence. And when that happened, you could lose control over it.

That would be a disaster, for other than life, Fay had no hold over the thing. It was oblivious to the pain of psi- or levin-bolts, and she dared not injure it in a way that would show. And, like Fay, because it was a part of Fay, it was convinced of its own immortality.

Fay tightened her lips; another annoyance in a day of annoyances. If that was what was happening, she'd have to destroy this Servant and make another. She could reuse the raw materials, of course, which would make the energy expense minimal, but it would still *take* energy, and time—and she could ill afford either at the moment.

"I'll go in the morning," she told the Servant. "Call and make the appointment, then call the school and tell them that I'm going out there. And while you're at it, tell them I went home with a migraine at noon."

The Servant bowed slightly, and moved on silent feet to Wes's den and the nearest phone. Fay continued up the staircase to the master bedroom.

Something was going to have to be done about Monica Carlin. Something to keep that obnoxious little creature occupied with something other than hauling in Deke.

She stopped again on the top step, and smiled as a thought occurred to her. By *knowingly* encouraging Deke, who was going steady with Fay, Monica had opened *herself* to retribution.

She was poaching, in short. And poachers deserved punishment. After all, as far as that little tart Monica knew, Fay was truly in love with the twit. If this were an ordinary affair, Fay would be devastated by his loss.

Now what would throw her off balance—yet be so bizarre that she would be unwilling to tell anyone about it?

Fay bit her lip, and continued on her way to her room. This was going to call for some careful planning. The poolside and that daiquiri were definitely in order.

Deke wasn't paying much attention to his homework; not with Alan on the phone, with one of the best pieces of news he'd heard in a month.

"—so Coach gets the guy in his office, and before he even gets a chance to start name-dropping, the guy tells him he's the DA, and the old crow Bobby-Boy rear-ended is his grandmother!" Alan gloated.

Deke cradled the handset between his chin and shoulder, and typed a few more words on his micro. "Jesus, I bet *that* took him down!"

"The best is yet to come, my man," Alan chortled. "Seems like she had two of the professors from ORU with her. Bobby-Boy didn't see 'em, I guess, or else he didn't think they were important."

Deke stared at the screen, but wasn't really paying any attention to the words on it. "Or else he was too drunk to care," Deke put in.

"Could be. Basically, she had two witnesses to the way he cussed her out, and then cut and ran. One of 'em was taking down the license; that's how they caught him."

Deke chuckled heartlessly, and took a pull off his can of Coke. "Kind of makes you believe in God, doesn't it?"

Alan laughed. "Amen, brethren and sistern. Dork should never have taken off like that; they're gonna have his license for sure. Of course, if he hadn't cut and run, he'd have had a DWI underage."

"Probably," Deke agreed. "I've never heard of Bobby out dragging when he wasn't stoned. So then what happened?"

"I don't know. About then Coach saw that the door was open and closed it. I cut out before anybody could see me lingering and tell Coach I was dropping eaves. God, I'd love to know what's going to happen to Bobby-Boy, though."

That hint's about as subtle as a lead brick, Deke thought. *He knows damn well that Fay's gonna find out, and she'll tell me when she calls tonight.*

"I'll probably be able to tell you tomorrow," he began, when the "call waiting" signal beeped at him.

"I heard that," Alan told him. "I'll catch you later."

"Okay." He let the incoming call through as Alan hung up from his end.

"Deke?" The coyly seductive voice turned his knees to jelly.

"Uh, hi, Fay." He gulped. "Whatcha doing?"

Boy, is that ever a dumb question. She's calling me, of course. Wake up, Kestrel, and start sounding like you know what day it is.

"Did you hear about Bobby yet?"

"No," he lied. "What's up?"

She was only too happy to tell him. Funny, though, although she *sounded* upset about it, there was a faint undertone of something else in her voice. Like she was kind of gloating about it.

"He and Sandy were like, you know, racing a little. And this senile old lady pulled right out in front of him. He kind of tapped the back end of her car. I guess he yelled at her for being such an asshole, and then he pulled around her. But I guess she's the DA's mother or something, and besides, she had two of the religion professors from ORU with her—anyway, he's in a hell of a lot of trouble."

He scribbled a couple of notes while she talked. Alan was going to want to know about this—and how Fay's story differed from the one he'd overheard. "Like how much?"

"Reckless driving, leaving the scene of an accident; the insurance company is gonna nail his ass to the wall, I guess, and the DA came up with some law about cussing out old ladies, because they got him with that, too."

Deke managed to keep from laughing. "Gee, that's too bad. What's Coach doing?"

"It's pretty awful. They already took Bob's license; Coach took the car away from him, and he's grounded for a month."

We'll see how long that lasts, Deke thought cynically, saving down his homework. *Bet he's out partying Saturday.*

"Is this gonna make any difference to those recruiters?" He already *knew* the answer to that one. They weren't calling the UO athletic dorm the "Knife and Gun Club" for nothing.

"I don't think so. Bob says not."

Which meant she'd been getting her information straight from Bobby-Boy. If *that* didn't figure . . .

He flopped down on his bed and stared up at the ceiling. "Well, he's pretty lucky, I guess. What about Sandy?"

"I guess nobody saw him, so Bob didn't squeal on him."

Besides, it wouldn't have made any difference. What could Coach do, drop him from the team? The season's over, and he's graduating. Deke bit his cheek to keep from chuckling. *Bet that really scralled Bobby's nurd!*

"What were *you* doing?" she asked.

"Homework. And thinking about you." *Good touch, Deke.* "I'm *always* thinking about you." *Even better.*

"You're so *sweet.*" How come she made that sound like something she'd have said about a cocker spaniel? "You *know* how much I love you."

"Me too," he said awkwardly, feeling his mind start to go to jelly along with his knees. How did she *do* that to him, anyway?

"Why don't you come on over here, hm? You could do your homework over here."

"I can't," he said hastily. "I've got this assignment for English and I can't get a handle on it. It's a creative writing thing, and . . .

I just can't work on it and be around you, you know? You're too *distracting*, lover. And it's due tomorrow."

And we go through this every night, a small part of his mind that hadn't gone to guacamole thought. *Every night you want me to come over there.* What was she trying to do, get him to flunk out?

"You're no fun." Again, it was like he was hearing two conflicting things in her voice. On top—that she was pouting. But underneath was something else. And he just couldn't make up his mind what it was, or even if he'd heard it at all.

"I can't help it, you know what my dad'll do if I mess up my homework and he finds out about it. And I can't get away with saying I forgot; it's for that writer that's staying here."

"Well, okay. This time. Better not make a habit of it, though. I *might* get tired of you." Definitely a hint of threat there.

"I won't," he replied hastily. And spent the next five minutes placating her, without really understanding *why* he suddenly felt like he was in the wrong.

Monica flipped on the headlights and pulled carefully out of the parking space; her mother waved good-bye from the door of the apartment, then turned and went back inside, closing the door behind her. There was at least one thing Monica liked about living in Tulsa—the apartment complex they'd moved into. The complex itself had anything you could want; *two* swimming pools, a sauna, an enormous Jacuzzi, an exercise room, a clubroom. The apartment was bigger than the house they'd rented in Denver, and it was cheaper—

Rhonda said that was because the Tulsa economy was depressed and rental places were cheap. Monica had no idea; she was perfectly willing to believe whatever her mother said.

She waved at the guard at the gate and pulled out onto the main street. They'd never lived in a place that had a guarded entrance before. It was pretty intimidating at first. In fact, once she'd *seen* the situation and had figured out the kind of lifestyle they'd be having, Monica had been all for the move. Between the lower cost of living out here and the substantial raise Rhonda had gotten to come here, the family was living higher on the hog than Monica had ever dreamed they would—

—until she'd seen her fellow classmates.

And at that point, she realized that these luxury apartments were Jenks's version of low-income housing, and far from being the envy of her classmates, she was going to be considered strictly middle-class.

These were kids who routinely got foreign sports cars for their sixteenth birthdays. Kids who thought nothing of dropping five or six hundred dollars on a date. Who spent more on clothing in a weekend than she did all year. Who flew down to Dallas for a day the way she used to drive over to Colorado Springs—and who flew out to New York, or London, or San Francisco to do their Christmas shopping.

It was not at all what she'd expected.

She headed the car in the direction of Memorial and Woodland Hills Mall. Kind of funny name; no hills, and no woods—but then again, right down the street was "Shadow Mountain," all one hundred feet of it. There were rocks in Colorado taller than that.

It was all pretty much in keeping with the way people thought of themselves around here; like the whole world was centered in Tulsa. Or at least, that was the impression Monica had gotten.

That alone was a good enough reason to want to show the rest of the kids up, at least a little. *If Miss Tregarde says I'm good enough— they can't look down their noses at me anymore. And it won't matter how much money they've got. Money won't buy talent. Money won't make* them *writers. I'll have something they can never have.*

Rhonda understood; when Monica told her the root of her problems and why school was making her kind of unhappy, she'd been both concerned and relieved. Concerned because she didn't want her kids unhappy—but relieved because the problems *could* have had other causes.

"We could move," she'd suggested that very night. "I'd rather not; Jenks is so much better than the Tulsa school system it's pathetic, but we could move—"

Monica was not inclined to take her up on that offer. "I'm not going to let them beat me, Mom," she'd said stubbornly. "I'm not. I'm going to have something that's going to make them want to be my friends."

In the back of her mind she had no doubt what would happen if she actually got published. She'd be a celebrity, like the prom queen, only better. The kids would be impressed because the money she got for a book would be *hers*, and they'd all want to be in her next book. . . .

And, practically speaking—it sure would help pay for college.

Rhonda was the one who'd mentioned that, when Monica had come bursting in with the news that Miss Tregarde was willing to look at her work. And it had been Rhonda's idea that the girl should take the car herself over to the library. They'd have two hours before the library closed at nine. That ought to be enough time for Miss Tregarde to get a good look at her work and critique it, too.

Monica squinted a little; the headlights of the cars in the opposite lane were bothering her, and she was cold. She'd just gotten her license a month ago, and she hadn't driven much at night. And her mom's old 280-Z might not be a Porsche, but it was a bit more to handle than the Pontiac Bonnevilles the driver's-ed class used.

So she was nervous; nervous enough that when she turned off onto a side street rather than fight the mall traffic anymore, she was going about five miles *under* the speed limit. Since most of the other cars on the road were trying to do ten miles over the limit, she'd been getting a lot of tailgaters and horn-blowers. It was a real relief to get away from them.

"Jerks," she muttered, as she took the right-hand turn too slowly to please the last of them, and he roared past her, nearly taking her tail off in the process. "Jenks jerks." She turned the car heater on and rolled her window up, wishing she'd brought a jacket.

The street she chose wound through a half-built subdivision, with empty fields stretching for several hundred yards on both sides of the asphalted road. There was no traffic at all here, which was fine, but there weren't any streetlights, either. After the dazzle of the sodium-vapor lights and the car headlights out on the main drag, Monica felt like she was half blind. The nearest sources of illumination were the lights of the houses hundreds of yards away. She slowed still further, fumbling for the high beams.

She couldn't find them. Wherever they were, they weren't in the same place as on the Pontiacs. She looked down for a moment at the steering column.

That was when the *thing* hit the windshield.

It was only there for a moment, but that was more than long enough.

She got a fleeting glimpse of something horrible, twisted, wrong—

The eyes were what she saw first—evil, yellow eyes, eyes that *glowed*. Then, under the eyes, a round mouth full of sharply pointed teeth.

She tried to scream, but the sound was stuck somewhere in her throat.

The awful thing flattened itself against the windshield. She could see long spindly arms and legs now; the thing seemed to be all head with the arms and legs just attached wherever there was room. It slavered, pressed its face into the glass, and the talons at the ends of those skinny arms clawed and clutched hungrily at her.

She *did* scream then, and jerked the steering wheel sideways, trying to shake it off. It grinned at her and mockingly ran a tongue that was at least two feet long all around its fur-covered face. It clawed once more at the glass.

Then it was gone, leaping off the hood of the car, into the darkness. At that moment the car ran off the road.

She shrieked again, this time in surprise, when the car jolted over the concrete curb. It wound up with its nose buried in the weeds. If she'd been going any faster, she *could* have had a serious accident.

She took her foot off the clutch, the car jumped, and the engine coughed and stalled.

There was dead silence except for the ticking of cooling metal under the hood. After a while, Monica could hear the sounds of traffic off in the distance, even though the windows were closed, but other than that she couldn't hear anything. Certainly nothing—strange. In the glare of the headlights she could see the bank of weeds immediately in front of her; when she looked away and gave her eyes time to adjust to the dark, she could also see that there was nothing in those fields except more dead, weather-flattened weeds.

There was no sign, *absolutely* no sign, that what she thought she had seen had ever existed—outside of her own mind.

She put the gear in neutral and tried to start the car, her hands shaking so hard she had trouble turning the key—and her knees were so weak she had trouble keeping the clutch down. Once the engine caught, she found she couldn't move; she just huddled in the front seat, trembling all over.

It took a while before she was able to think. When thought came, it was a denial of what she thought she'd seen. *I didn't see that. It wasn't real. It was never there. It can't have been there. Things like that don't exist.*

But if it didn't exist, what made her think she saw it?

I'm going nuts. I'm going nuts, just like Gramma. I'm seeing things just like she did before she died.

That was a thought almost as horrible as the notion that she *had* seen something.

The wind blew a piece of newspaper into and out of the cone of light from her headlights. She jumped and screamed—and then laughed, when she realized what it was. And that gave her a rational answer.

It was just an old movie poster or something. Yeah, that's what it was; somebody's poster, the wind blew it into the windshield.

She kept telling herself that, over and over, until she stopped shaking. Until she began to laugh at herself.

Stupid! she told herself. *Getting all shook up over a dumb piece of paper.* She was sure now that she hadn't seen the thing move or make faces at her, that it had all just been her overactive imagination.

I'm not going crazy like Gramma; Mom told me that was senile dementia, and you can't catch it, and you can't get it unless you're real old, like forty at least.

She even managed to get up enough courage to get out of the car and check it over for damage. There wasn't any, to her immense relief.

Like, what would I tell Mom? Gee, I'm sorry, I wrecked the car 'cause I thought I saw the bogeyman?

She climbed back into the driver's seat and carefully backed the car up; she would have preferred to pull forward and around, but she was afraid of something more normal than the bogeyman— what might be hidden under those flattened weeds. Gaping holes that could break an axle, concrete blocks to take out the undercarriage, or sharp pieces of metal that would slash up the tires.

Mom would really kill me if I messed up the car just being stupid. She could forgive an accident, but stupidity would get me grounded for the rest of my life.

The car lurched sideways as first one rear tire, then the other, went over the concrete curbing and hit the asphalt. She held her breath and inched it the rest of the way out, hoping that ridge of cement wasn't high enough to scrape the bottom of the car.

It wasn't, and she let out the breath she'd been holding as the front tires met the curb, and she had to gun the engine a little to get them over it.

She sat there for a minute, with the car heater drying the sweat on her face and scalp. Then, trying not to feel nervous, she took a deep breath, put the car in first, and took her foot slowly off the clutch.

At *exactly* that moment, the thing came back.

This time it landed with a *splat* on the driver's side door, and Monica screamed at the top of her lungs.

There was a second *splat*, and another of the things landed on the hood. It sat there for a fraction of a second, then leapt at her and was stopped only by the windshield.

She and the things stared at each other for a paralyzed eternity. Then *they* moved.

She screamed again, as the things rocked the car, gnashed their teeth at her through the fragile protection of the windows, and tried to claw their way through the glass to get at the front seat and her.

The car hit the curb again, but this time only lurched halfway over it before the engine died. She kept shrieking and waved her hands uselessly at the things, and they grinned and slavered at her. They seemed to be enjoying her fright.

She was still screaming a moment later, when they vanished as abruptly as they'd appeared. She couldn't *stop* screaming, not until her voice was gone.

Then she started crying.

She curled up in a tight little ball on the front seat; unable to move, unable to do *anything*, except to cry, and to think the same thought, over and over.

I'm going crazy. Oh, God, I'm going insane. . . .

SIX

There's something about a library. . . .
  Hey, that's a good line.
  Di paged back in the scene to the point where Claire first entered Lord Burton's library, and inserted the new text. *"There's something about a library, the masculine scent of leather bindings. . . ."* She grinned. *Oooo, I just looove leather. Don't look now, Claire, but Lord Burton's about to insert something other than text. How did I ever manage before I got a computer?* She paged back to the end of the chapter. *Never mind, I know the answer to that. I did a helluva lot of retyping.*

  She contemplated the screen, and decided that this was a good place to close the chapter down. Claire was just about to be ravished. *Little does Lord Burton know what he's in for. Heh, heh. Very good place to stop. Make the reader anticipate what's next.*

  I wonder if I should get a little kinky in the next chapter? Yeah, I think Claire ought to get out the honey and brandy. . . . Surprise, Burty-baby. You—ahem—bit off more than you could chew. I'm going to have a hard—you should excuse the expression—time convincing people you're up to Claire. So much for macho bullshit.

  She chuckled. *My mind's right in the gutter tonight. Not even the gutter, the sewer. Less than a week of vacation, and already I'm feeling better. And feistier. More feisty? Whatever. Boy, is André going to be in trouble when I get back home.*

Still, there is *something about a library.*

Di saved down the chapter, and stretched, easing that ache just under the shoulder blades that every writer she'd ever met complained about.

I must have spent half my life in libraries. Granny's library in the old place, the reading library and the stacks in college—those wonderful libraries in New York— She stretched again and settled back in her chair. *This is an unusually good branch library, though. Tulsa County must have a pretty decent library system. Glad I picked this one, and not the one in Jenks proper.*

She'd found a quiet corner where the steady clicking of keys wouldn't bother anyone, but close enough to the door that she'd be able to see Monica as soon as she arrived. There weren't too many people here to bother, which was a plus. One woman and a set of three kids, all of them loading up and probably about to reach the max limit on their cards, if not their arms—*that* was an immensely cheering sight. There was one old man over in the corner; he looked like part of the furniture. And there were four teenagers scattered at tables, stacks of reference books beside them, three with notebooks, one with a laptop identical to Di's. From the hot outfit and hair that cried out "mousse abuse," Di figured him for a denizen of Jenks, out slumming.

Well, maybe not. There were a couple of very pricey sections in Tulsa proper; the Shadow Mountain condos weren't that far from here. Within—perish the thought!—walking distance, in fact.

The kid looked up, saw her, and smiled before turning back to his book. *I'm being snide,* she thought, a little ashamed of herself. *There are an awful lot of really nice people in this town. Like that cop outside.*

When she'd turned off into the library parking lot, she noticed that there was a car following her. When she got out of the car, it pulled up beside her—

An unmarked fuzzmobile, with a uniformed cop at the wheel. *Oh shit,* she'd thought, *what'd I do?*

"Hi," she'd said, trying not to sound resigned. "What can I do for you?"

" 'Scuse me, ma'am." The cop opened *his* door, and rose—
—and rose.

"My God," she'd said involuntarily, stepping back a pace. "There certainly is a *lot* of you!"

"Yes ma'am," the cop had answered. "I've been told that before. Ma'am, I'd like to ask you—that an interceptor?"

"Well, it *was*," she'd replied, very glad that it was too dark for him to see some of the things that were still installed in the dash. "I got it from a friend on the Dallas PD. I have to drive in New York City a lot, and he thought I needed something with more acceleration and protection that the Hyundai I was going to buy. So Mark got this for me from the Texas Highway Patrol when they surplused her."

The cop's long face lit up. "Gee, ma'am—that's kinda what I thought. Can I—look under the hood?"

"Sure," she'd told him. "There's *something* under there. I'm not sure what, but Mark Valdez said it was legal. Barely, but legal. Big, mean, and nasty, and it makes a lot of noise. Mark called it a 'rat.' With a temper, he said."

Evidently that meant something profound to him. "If you don't mind, ma'am, I know a tad bit about engines. Dad useta run Pontiacs at Kaney Valley Speedway. I could kinda make sure you're street-legal. And if you aren't, well, I don't see how just givin' you a verbal warning would hurt. Not like a lady like you is gonna go out drag-racin.'"

He was dying to get under that hood; it didn't take an empath to figure that out. "Be my guest," she'd said.

She'd moved the car under the light, so he could see better; he wasted no time in popping the hood and diving in.

From time to time appreciative noises echoed out of there. *She* was baffled; while she was a damn fine driver (even Mark said so), the innards of cars were a mystery deeper than the Quabala to her. Only one recognizable comment emerged: "Ma'am," the fellow had said in tones she normally associated only with worship, "I cannot believe they surplused this baby."

"Mark said he had someone work on it for me," she'd said diplomatically.

Afterward, he'd been kind enough not only to tell her that the car was, indeed, street-legal—"barely," he'd grinned—but to give her a rundown on *good* restaurants within fifteen minutes of Jenks—and his dad's garage.

Praise be, there was even an Uno's Pizzeria and a sushi place.

"Yes ma'am," he'd teased. "They got your barbecue sushi, your deep-fried sushi, your okra sushi—you know what most people call sushi 'round these parts?"

"Besides 'ick'?"

"Bait." And they'd both laughed.

I don't think I could stand to live here, but Tulsa has its moments.

She glanced down at her watch; it was past seven. Funny, as eager as Monica had seemed at school, Di would have expected to see her coming through that door by seven at the very latest.

What on earth could be keeping the child?

Di was a Guardian; she had resources most occultists couldn't imagine. Her alarms were sensitive to the brush of power passing by, even if she wasn't the target.

The alarms went off.

What the hell?

There were certain habits she did not break, no matter how safe she thought she was; full shields and alarms went up and stayed up at all times unless she was deliberately taking them down.

In the time it took to frame that startled thought, she had already determined that she wasn't the target, and was tracing the passing surge of power back to its source.

Whoa! She juggled shields, cataloged the overtones, and searched for telltales, all at the same time. She felt like an F-15 pilot with a hundred things to do and a MIG on his tail. *I thought Larry said this whole area was psychically null—hell, I didn't find anything either!*

She wasn't fast enough.

Like the opening and closing of a portal, an arcane "door" in the void that was the Tulsa area; one moment the sullen scarlet beam of magic was there, the next, gone.

It couldn't have been more than a couple of minutes at most. Just not long enough to do anything, especially not when taken so completely by surprise. She blinked and stared at the bookcase on the opposite wall, not really seeing it. *Damn. I wonder what that was all about.*

It hadn't felt good, whatever it was. It *had* been familiar, though; old-fashioned, Western-style sorcery. As opposed to witchcraft, of course. A witch worked with natural balances, rather like a t'ai chi master in that way. If you attacked a witch, if the odds, power levels, and skills were equal, chances were you'd find your own attack turned back against you.

Maybe it's too bad it wasn't *me that it was after. Like* sensei *keeps telling me, there are times when the first to attack has already lost the battle. And I've assisted a few people into a wall in my time.*

A sorcerer ignored those balances. A sorcerer worked with or against the grain; it didn't much matter. Partially that was because an awful lot of the kind of people who became sorcerers were pretty weak in the psionics department. They couldn't sense the natural flows in the first place.

And the kind of person who became a sorcerer also tended to be a manipulator. That wasn't in and of itself a bad thing, provided your motives were reasonably unselfish. Sorcery was a matter of dominances; your will over the material world, your mind over the wills of others, and ultimately, if the sorcerer was skilled enough, the dominance of the master over slaves created or invoked. Again, that wasn't of itself a bad thing; some magickal critters were only under control when they *were* enslaved, and the sorcerer in question did not need to be the one who had invoked them to be the one who controlled them.

You could—as Di *had*—control them right back to where they came from.

Di, as a Guardian, was both a witch and a sorcerer; although by preference, she tended to favor the former. But she *knew* sorcery in all its various forms and flavors; knew it well enough to recognize even when she only "saw" it for a fleeting instant.

She stared hard at the blank screen of her laptop, using it as a focal point of concentration. *Works as well as a crystal ball . . . huh. That's a hoot. A techie witch. Cyberwitch? I'll have to pass that one on.* Since she couldn't trace the power back to its source, she began delicately questing for the signs that would lead her to the target.

She wasn't expecting the second power surge, any more than she had been expecting the first.

She managed to stay with it long enough this time to get the "signature," the characteristic shape and flavoring of the power that was individual to every mage. It *wasn't* anyone she'd every encountered before; that much she knew before she was cut off again.

It *was* stolen power; there was no mistaking that. Though incorporated into a skilled and controlled whole, the individual threads of the work could be identified, and they were all from sources other than the signature. Each had the faint traces of the personality that it had been reft from, and the strong coloring of the emotions that had invoked the energy in the first place.

Nasty emotions, for the most part; fear, pain, loveless lust, anger, hate, envy, and jealousy. Which told Di quite a bit about the sorcerer.

Okay, you, she told the unknown. *Third time's the charm. Poke your nose out again, and I'll have you.*

She waited, ready to pounce the moment that portal opened and the sorcerer used his power—

Nothing.

Until the library door swung open and shut again, letting in a blast of cold air that scattered the papers of the students behind her. And the echoes, the traces, of that same power Di had been waiting for (faint, but near at hand) made her look up sharply.

Monica.

Shaking, green, with all the signs that *she* had been the sorcerer's target.

What in—Monica? She's just a kid! Why would . . . There is something very weird going on around here. . . .

Di shut the laptop down and shoved her chair away from the table. Monica jumped at the sound of the chair bumping across the carpet, and turned white-rimmed, fear-glazed eyes in her direction.

The girl blinked several times, and finally seemed to see her. "M-m-miss Tregarde?" she quavered.

A few feet to Monica's right, the librarian looked up sharply at the sound of her voice and evidently recognized the same symptoms of fear and shock that Di had. She emerged from behind her microfiche reader and the massive desk, and headed straight for the girl.

Shit, I hope she isn't going to cause me a problem. Di took her attention off Monica for a fleeting instant, just enough time to "read" what the librarian was projecting. And felt with relief a solid grounding of worry, with overtones of protectiveness and desire to help. *No wonder there's all these kids studying in here. She must be mother-confessor and trusted adviser to half the neighborhood. Bet she bakes a mean chocolate-chip cookie, too.*

Di and the librarian converged on Monica wearing nearly identical looks of unprofessional concern. The girl reached involuntarily toward Di as the other woman said, in unmistakably maternal tones, "Honey, it isn't any of my business, but y'all look like you're gonna pass out. Looks to me like something just shook you up pretty bad. Why don't you come back to my office and sit yourself down."

The woman gave Di a sidelong glance of inquiry. "I'm one of Monica's teachers; I was waiting for her," Di explained. "Let me get my things, and I'll be right with you."

This is weirder than snake shoes. Why would anyone target a kid like this for a sorcerous attack? Jesus Cluny Frog, she's not even high-psi!

Di gathered up her laptop and her notes, stowed them all in her briefcase with practiced efficiency, and followed in the wake of the librarian and her temporary charge.

The librarian was just as efficient as Di; within two minutes she had Monica ensconced in a comfortable chair, her feet up and half a glass of cold water and two aspirin inside her. At that point, she gracefully bowed out of the picture, telling Di that if they needed anything, she would be at the front desk.

"What happened?" Di asked quietly.

"I—I almost wrecked the car," Monica stammered, twisting the paper cup nervously in her hands.

"How?"

Monica just stared at her, her lower lip quivering, the tears in her eyes starting to spill over.

Di took a firmer tone of voice. "Monica, there's something wrong—and you 'almost wrecking the car' is just the smallest part of it. Tell me. People don't look the way you did when you walked in the door unless something really horrible has happened to them."

The paper cup was a shapeless wad, and two tears were tracking down Monica's cheeks.

Di sighed, and patted her clenched hands. "Monica, when I said 'really horrible,' I meant it. From the way you're acting, you'd rather die than go back outside right now—and I somehow don't have the feeling that you'd react that way to a simple accident, much less a near-accident."

She leaned forward, projecting sympathy as subtly as she could. She had to be careful around this one; as wired as Monica was, even though she wasn't a psychic powerhouse like Deke, she'd be much more sensitive than she usually was. If she picked up on what Di was doing, after being attacked once tonight by magic, she might assume the worst, and panic.

"You—" the girl began, then shook her head and scrubbed the back of her hand across her cheek.

"You can tell me, Monica. I've seen some pretty bizarre and nasty things in my time."

"You—no, you won't believe me!" Monica cried—then burst into hysterical tears.

Di thought about hugging the kid for a split second, and then rejected the notion. She was pretty much a stranger to this girl. She could try to convince Monica to trust her, but this was not the time to use physical contact.

"How do you know I won't believe you?" she asked. "All you know about me is that I'm a writer. But writers see and hear more strange stories than you'd ever imagine. I'm always getting people telling me their life history in the grocery store. If there's one thing I've learned over the years, it's that the strange and *true* stuff is a lot odder than what's in the supermarket tabloids, but it never shows up there; mostly because it *is* true and the people it happened to are like you—they figure that either other folks will think they're crazy, or that they *are* crazy."

There was a tremor of stronger emotion from the girl when she said that. Di followed up on her advantage.

"This may sound like I'm spitting platitudes at you, but it's been my experience that the old saying is true; people who think they're nuts usually aren't. It's the ones who are convinced that they're sane and the rest of the world *isn't* that you have to watch out for."

Monica buried her face in her hands. "What about people who think they've—seen something?" she replied, her words interrupted by strangled sobs.

"Well, if you think you've seen something, there's usually a cause. Like drugs. Some folks are allergic to drugs in odd ways; some prescription drugs have side effects doctors don't always know about. I have a friend who hallucinates on penicillin, and another who talks to God whenever she's given something with caffeine in it."

Monica peeked out from behind her hand. "You aren't BSing me?"

Di shook her head. "Straight up. I could even give you their numbers and you could talk to them if you wanted. Have you been taking *anything* you don't normally?"

Monica shook her head woefully. "N-no," she stammered. "Not even an aspirin until just now."

"Okay, that shoots that one. I have more. There's the weather angle; under the right conditions you can get reflections of things that may be hundreds of feet or even miles away, often very distorted."

She pretended to think for a moment, waiting for the girl to say something.

Monica shook her head. "It wasn't anything like that. It wasn't a reflection."

She nodded. "It's just as well. I didn't think that would fly; you have to get a combination of fog and hot and cold spots and pressure changes to get really convincing fata morgana in the middle of a city, and it's chilly and damp, but not foggy, tonight. So, there's always the idea that you were set up. Have you got any enemies at school, or friends that like to play nasty jokes?" She smiled grimly. "I had *that* one played on me. I made the mistake of letting it be known I believed in ghosts. Some kids in my high school thought they'd haunt my house for me. Trouble is, even then I knew more angles on faking those things than a stage magician, and I caught them at it. Then *I* scared *them*—and afterward, I made sure everybody else at school knew I'd made fools of them by turning the tables on them."

Amazing what anger will do for your ability to project. I wonder if they ever figured out why they ran out of my place screaming at the tops of their lungs?

Monica gave that one careful consideration. Finally she answered slowly. "I—don't think so. It would take a real techie to— do what I saw. The Brains aren't like that at Jenks. I mean, they wouldn't go after anybody who hadn't gone after them first. I like all the techie kids, and I think they like me."

Di leaned back in her chair. Making her *think* had forced the kid to calm down. Good. Now for the move. "All right, then. That just leaves one other possibility. You *did* see what you thought you saw."

Monica's lower lip started to quiver, and her eyes brightened with tears about to spill. Di pointed a warning finger at her. "Hey—that's enough. You were doing fine a minute ago. I told you, I've seen a lot of bizarre things in my time. Remember what Sherlock Holmes told Watson: if we've eliminated everything else and all we've got left is the impossible, then the impossible is the only answer."

"But—"

Di interrupted her ruthlessly. "All that the word 'impossible' means is that nobody's been able to prove something yet. Hell, Monica, there are people in this town convinced that men never walked on the moon, that it was all faked in a movie studio!"

"But—"

"So why don't you tell me what happened? Maybe I can help."

"But—"

"I sure know I want to try." Di let her expression harden a little. "If there's one thing I can't stand, it's somebody that gets his kicks by scaring the shit out of people."

Come on, kiddo. I'm not allowed to stick my nose into your problems unless you ask me to. And I can't help but wonder if this has something to do with what Larry thinks is after Deke.

Di held her breath as the girl visibly wavered between mistrust and a desperate need to confide in *someone.*

Desperation, and the aura of sympathy and trustworthiness Di was projecting, won out.

"I—saw—these *things,*" Monica began, and then the words spilled from her the way her hysterical tears had a few moments before. There were a few more of those tears, too, before she was finished.

Di kept a tight hold on her anger, aided in part by bewilderment. Whoever that sorcerer was, he'd played one of the nastiest little mind games Di had ever seen pulled on a kid. For an imaginative kid like Monica, one who *knew* she had an active imagination, this must have been a nightmarish experience.

And why Monica? That was the part that made no sense at all. There was no sign that she understood or recognized any of what had happened to her. She wasn't even marginally involved in the occult.

Who it was had to be inextricably tied in with that question of "why."

But "what"? That was no problem.

"Wait here a minute," she said, as Monica sniffled into a fist-sized wad of Kleenex from the box on the librarian's desk. The girl started to say something, but Di was already out the door.

There was something to be said for a lifetime spent in libraries. Di knew the Dewey decimal system the way most people knew the streets of their own neighborhoods. Of course, there were some categories that held special interest for her. . . .

She came back in that promised minute with a history book, a colonial history of New England, lavishly illustrated. She was flipping through the section on witch-hunts as she came through the office door and shut it behind her, looking for a particular woodcut. Most histories that covered witch-hunts and trials other than the ones in Salem used that particular picture.

Sure enough, there it was; good old sanctimonious "Barryman Deaton, Witchfinder." Crude though the picture was, Di always thought she could tell a lot about the man from it—the self-satisfied, smug set of his mouth, the cruel enjoyment in his eyes, the stiff spine showing certain knowledge of the righteousness of his cause.

Of course, she could just be reading into the picture what she knew already about the man from family tradition.

Idiot never actually caught a single real witch, she thought cynically. *Only poor fools with bad taste in neighbors. Harmony Tregarde even managed to get the midwives and herb doctors out of Newton before he could accuse them.*

The thing about this picture was that in this one case (as she also knew from family tradition), for the *only* time in his career as a witchfinder, Deaton had caught someone who'd deserved to be caught.

Not a "witch," though, or at least not when Hardesty was caught; Dimwit had caught a magician of another ilk altogether. The Pennsylvania Dutch would have called Hardesty a *Hexenmeister*; the not-altogether-Episcopalian Tregardes of the time had called him a warlock. That did *not* mean "male witch," the way current popular literature had it, but "oathbreaker." Hardesty had been both a sorcerer and the Green Man for another coven, but he had broken the Prime Law of the Wiccans. *Harm none.* His first victims (before he moved to Newton) had been his old associates. . . .

None of that concerned Di at the moment; she was more interested in the creatures surrounding old "Dimwit Deaton" and his
victim. "Familiars," the caption called them. Each of them had a
little scroll apparently coming out of an ear or a mouth, each scroll
ornately lettered with some bizarre name or other: "Thrudsnifter,"
"Lemdoodle," "Fryestappen."

*I suppose Dimwit made those names up himself; they sound about
like his speed.*

She flopped the book down on the desk in front of Monica, and
pointed to the critter crouched down in the far left-hand corner of
the illustration. *The only supernatural manifestation Dimwit ever
saw in his life. What a jerk. And he had no idea what it was he had
seen.*

"Does that look like something you've seen before?" she asked
Monica.

The kid's eyes were like saucers. Di wasn't much surprised. The
depiction was incredibly accurate. Dimwit had gotten an eyeful
when he'd come to take Black Hardesty, and he'd made sure to relate the tale in grand and glorious detail to anyone who'd listen.
He'd been more than happy to spend several days with the author
of this particular treatise on "The Foule and Unnattural Practices
of Witches," telling the story several times, with special emphasis
on his own bravery in "facing the demon and conquering it."

*And a five-year-old with a stick in his hand and courage in his
heart could face an imp down. They live on fear, but any show of guts
sends 'em screaming back to Mommy.*

*It scared the bejesus out of Dimwit, though, and sent him back to
Mommy; it took sixty-two-year-old Glory Fenwick to "disperse the
demon and subdue the heretic." Poor old Glory-Be-To-God; at least
he was sincere. Good thing Harmony managed to get a psi-bolt
through Hardesty's shield and knock him out before poor old Glory
came storming in there with nothing but a Bible for protection.*

*Well, nobody ever knew about Deaton chickening out but the Tre-
gardes and Dimwit, and Glory. Glory was too modest, Harmony
wasn't about to blow his cover, and Dimwit sure wasn't telling. Gods.*

What a jerk; what an appropriate way for him to go, too; getting *drunk two days after he talked to the chronicler, falling down the* *stairs of the local alehouse, and breaking his stupid neck.*

"Come on," she said finally, "let's get out of here. I'd like a burger, and we need to talk."

She picked up her briefcase, and reached across the desk to close the book. Monica stared at the cover, then looked back up at her.

"That—" she said faintly, "that's what I saw."

"I know," Di replied. "I'm *hungry*. Let's get going."

She took Monica's wrist and tugged her to her feet. The girl followed her obediently out to the car—

—which, not so incidentally, was *very* heavily shielded. Not a bad notion at the moment.

There was a burger joint less than a block away; while the kid sat in stunned silence on the passenger's side Di ordered food for both of them from the drive-through window and drove them back to the library parking lot.

"French fries and chocolate," she told Monica, who was still staring at nothing. "I don't have a lot of vices anymore, but I'm keeping those two. I *love* french fries. Combine them with a chocolate shake, and I'm a contented woman." She handed Monica the paper bag full of burger, fries, and Coke.

"That thing in the picture—" Monica stammered, staring at the bag in her hands as if she'd never seen anything like it before. "That thing—that was what I saw. Exactly what I saw."

"Well, that's not *too* surprising, all things considered," Di replied, examining the burger to make sure nobody'd put any mayo on it. Tulsans seemed to put mayo on *everything*, the way midwesterners put ketchup on everything. "If you've done something to piss a sorcerer off, he's going to use the smallest guns he has on you, and those little guys are barely popguns. They make a really good burger here in Tulsa, have you noticed that?"

She was keeping her tone deliberately light. After just proving to the kid that she'd been attacked by a supernatural agency, it would be a good idea to remind her that the mundane world of hamburger joints was still the greater part of her life. There was absolutely no use in letting the girl know how worried Di really was. It wouldn't do Monica any good.

"How can you sit there and eat a hamburger and talk about—*things* like that monster?" Monica cried, clenching her hands on the paper sack.

"Really easy," Di replied matter-of-factly. "First, I'm hungry. Second, I've seen those things before, and they're small potatoes. Thirdly, I'm not just a romance writer, I'm also a practicing witch."

Monica's eyes got big again, and she started to wriggle away; she was stopped by the car door. The locks were all controlled from Di's side. That was one of the police modifications that Mark had left on; pretty useful at a time like this.

Di put her hamburger down and sighed dramatically. "Jesus Cluny Frog, Monica, do I look like one of the bad guys to you? I thought you had a little more sense than these Oklahoma hicks. 'Witch' is just a religion, okay? No baby-sacrificing, no Black Masses, no sending imps out to scare the dog-snot out of kids, trying to make them think they're crazy. We don't *do* things like that. Our number-one law is 'Have fun in this lifetime, but don't hurt anybody.'"

Nice little paraphrase of "An it harm none, do as ye will," if I do say so myself.

She deliberately picked up her burger and took another bite. Monica stopped trying to find the door lock.

"But if you didn't—"

"Who did?" She stirred the shake on the dashboard with her straw. "I don't know. I'm psychic—you don't have to be, to be a witch, but a lot of us are. I picked up on the fact that something was going on just before you came in, but I couldn't tell who or what, and I didn't know you were the target until you came in." She met Monica's eyes; they weren't quite so big anymore. "I'm pretty good, kiddo, but I'm not as good as I'd like. You feeling better?"

Monica licked her lips nervously. "I don't know," she admitted. "I don't understand what's happening. . . ."

"Neither do I," Di said bluntly. "I came here to teach creative writing and I find myself in the middle of a magickal attack. I promise you, you aren't crazy, what you saw was real. Those critters really couldn't have hurt you, no matter how impressive they looked; they're all bluff. The worst they could have done was give you a few bruises. If you'd yelled at them, they'd have split. Remember that if they show up again. What worries me is that this means that *somebody* in this town is practicing traditional sorcery, and that person wants you to be upset. I don't know why. You're not involved in the occult; I could tell if you were. So this is a very bizarre situation. I *would* like to help you, if you'll let me."

The kid straightened up. "How do I know I can trust you?" she asked.

Good girl. Keep that skepticism; that's sound sense if there's somebody with a grudge on gunning for you. "You don't," she replied. "You don't know me—hell, you never even had any hint of trouble before I showed up in town. All you can go by—*if* you decide to trust me—is who my friends are."

She fished in her purse and hauled out her wallet. "Look here," she said, flipping it open and holding it under the light from the parking-lot lamp. In the first pocket was the photo-ID that the New Haven police had given her, with "SPECIAL INVESTIGATOR" printed in red beside the picture.

"This *could* be a fake," Di said. "It isn't, but I'll be happy to drive over to the nearest cop shop and prove it. I've worked for the New Haven cops a bunch of times—here's my permit to carry a concealed weapon in Connecticut. Here's another one for Texas, last year I did some work down in Dallas. This car is something I was able to get because of some friends down there. It used to be a high-speed police car—"

She flipped the switch Mark had hidden under the dash, and the police scanner came on with a squawk and a crackle of static. "If you know anything about police scanners, you'll know it's not legal to have them in your car. Mark's making sure I get the right permissions to keep this one." She turned it off again.

Monica bit her lip; she still didn't look quite convinced, although she did look as though she *wanted* to be convinced.

"You need something closer to home? Deke's dad and I have been real good friends since we were in college together, and his mom and I go back almost that far. They *both* know what I am—in fact, they used to help me a little. So, I've got friends in two different police departments, and some solid citizens right here in Tulsa. Can you trust somebody with friends like that?"

Monica nodded, slowly but not reluctantly.

"Great. You want me to help you?"

"Yes," Monica said. "Please. With the writing too—"

Di laughed. "Right on! Okay, kiddo, start in on that hamburger, and while you're eating, take it from the top. You were over on that side street, and it was dark. Tell me everything that you can remember, and I mean *everything*—"

Deke finished reading Alan's assigned story fragment, and put the last page down on the desk. He restacked the papers neatly, then swiveled his desk chair around to face his friend, handing them back to him.

"So," Alan said, fidgeting a little in Deke's armchair. "What do you think?"

"I think," Deke replied, shaking his head sadly, "that you'd better stick with what you know, like computers. It's pretty lame, Al. Pretty lame."

Alan sighed. "That's what I was afraid of."

Ms. Greeley had two sessions of the Honors class this year, one in the morning, one in the afternoon. Alan was in the afternoon session; they'd tried to get in the same class, but it hadn't worked out. Although Alan was primarily a techie whiz—he'd told Deke that he identified strongly with the Val Kilmer part in *Real Genius*—he generally breezed through all his classes. And Deke knew he'd figured on doing the same with this one.

He'd done just fine as long as they were analyzing someone else's work—but he'd lost it as soon as they started this creative stuff.

The one-page argument scene had been bad enough, but now Ms. Tregarde had upped the ante.

Deke had been expecting a totally new assignment. He'd been a little surprised by what Di had told the class.

"Okay," she'd said, after all the pages were read aloud and picked over. "Now we're going to do what a professional writer would do with that scene. We're going to pretend that this is the climax of a story or even a book. That means that you're going to revise and expand on what you wrote."

She'd turned to the blackboard and begun making a list. "I want a lead-in to the argument; how the fight starts in the first place, maybe even how the two protagonists meet before the fight. If you haven't got a root cause of the fight, I want that in there, too. Lastly, I want a conclusion to the fight."

"How long?" Jennifer wanted to know.

"Minimum of three pages, maximum of ten. Oh, and some of you were swapping viewpoint even in the one pager; that means you kept getting inside both protagonists' heads so that the reader could see what *both* of them were thinking at all times. Don't do that; there's a way to handle it, but you're not ready for that yet. Pick your viewpoint character and stay with him—the boy or the girl, I don't care which. Remember you can only *show* what's in that character's head; your reader will have to guess what's going on in the other character's head from the way you describe his or her expressions. Got that?"

Well, Deke had gotten that all right, but it sure didn't look like Alan had. His two characters just walked up to each other and started fighting for no apparent reason, then shook hands and walked off, also for no apparent reason. And the fight, predictably enough, was about the girl claiming the boy had stood her up.

"It's a yawner, Al," Deke said honestly. "Like, they're bored actors in a bad existential play; they're just walking on, reciting lines they don't understand and don't care about, and walking off. It was bad before, but it's worse now."

Alan sprawled across the arms of the overstuffed beige chair, and picked at his thumbnail glumly. "Yeah. Man, I don't know what I'm gonna do about this quarter, this 'creative' shit." He leaned back and stared at the ceiling. "I'm acing everything else. I *gotta* ace this; I gotta get into MIT or Cal Tech or Rose Poly—I can't do that unless I ace everything. What am I gonna do?"

"Hey," Deke objected, "I don't know what you're so worried about. It's not like you're going to flunk out. Di gave us a B to start with, and she said she wasn't going to grade anybody down unless they didn't try—"

"But a B just isn't good enough," Alan insisted stubbornly. "And I don't want her giving me an A just 'cause she feels sorry for the poor computer nerd."

Deke threw his hands up, conceding defeat. "Okay, okay, have it your way."

"So what am I gonna do? You gotta help me, man. You're doing okay at this stuff—what am I doing wrong?"

Deke thought about the problem for a minute. "Look, let's take this thing from the top. Remember what Di said? About how if something doesn't work, she goes back and changes things until it does?"

"Yeah," Alan replied. "So?"

"So this isn't working for you. Try something else, from scratch. Write what you know. Like when Tracy came after you in the hall and just about took your ass off for what you did to her computer in lab? Di said an argument—she didn't say about *what*. You're just assuming that since she's a romance writer, it has to be like what she does."

"Isn't that, like, cheating?" Alan said doubtfully. "I mean, that stuff with Tracy really happened."

Deke shrugged. "I don't see how it could be cheating. I dunno about *your* class, but most of the guys in *mine* pretty much rewrote the last breakup fight they had."

"Good point." Alan mulled it over for a while. "Real good point. Okay, I'll do it. Can I leave out the part where Tracy dumped her Coke down my pants?"

"Hey, it's creative, right?" Deke grinned. "Make it come out any damn way you want to. Make the Tracy character come out looking like a fool. Make her start the fight 'cause she really wants to screw your brains out and can't think of any other way to get at you. Whatever."

Alan's answering grin was bright enough to light up the whole room. "Yeah," he said, in a contented sigh. "Yeah. Hey, can I see yours?"

"Sure, I printed it before you came over." Deke took the little stack of paper off the printer. "Haven't even had a chance to strip it."

"That's okay." Alan left the papers in their virgin, fanfold state, and began flipping through them. Deke was rather pleased with his version of the assignment. It started out calmly enough, with his two characters meeting in the hall between classes—but then the girl started cross-examining the guy, and making like the Spanish Inquisition when he didn't give her immediate answers. Before long the guy had taken about all he was willing to, and the last two pages was him getting pretty hot about how possessive his girl had been getting. It ended with him telling her he'd had just about enough, and leaving her open-mouthed and shocked speechless in the middle of the hallway when the bell rang.

"A little more of Art replicates Life, huh?" Alan said archly, as he turned over the last page.

"Say what?" Deke said, startled by his response.

"Well, this shit about Danny here being Marcia's boy-toy—strikes me like that's awful close to the way Fay treats you, ol' buddy."

"What would *you* know about it?" Deke retorted; stung, but determined not to let Alan know.

"I've got eyes, Deke. I've got ears. She does some pretty cold things to you, and you just sit there like a dog and take it." Alan put the stack of paper down on the coffee table, and swung his legs back down to the floor. "I'll tell you, man, you could do a lot worse than what old Dan here did. Tell the bitch off. Give her a little hell right back the next time she gives it to you."

Deke found himself in the uncomfortable position of having nothing he could say. If he said Alan was right, he'd look like a wimp. If he said Alan was full of shit, he'd be lying through his teeth. If he told Alan it wasn't any of his business and to butt out, he might lose the last of his old friends.

Maybe if I just tell him I'm in love with Fay . . .

"I suppose," Alan said sarcastically at that very moment, "that you're going to try and tell me that it doesn't matter because you're in love."

What actually jumped into his head at the moment Alan said that wasn't Fay, but Monica. How sweet she was, how gutsy, standing right up and not letting any of the moneyed kids shove her around.

It's too bad I didn't meet her before I started going with Fay. I'd probably be going with her instead. . . .

But he couldn't let Alan sit there and get away with that last remark.

"A lot *you* know," he retorted, throttling down his feelings of guilt. "Half the time, I don't think you even know women exist! If they had hard drives or monitors, maybe. As it is, there's no way you could relate to a guy with normal hassles—"

Alan arched an eyebrow. "Yeah, well, maybe you haven't been paying too much attention to what I've been up to lately. It doesn't take an engineer to figure out female couplers. And *I* never forget I'm the one with the hard drive."

Oh, you poser—"Oh, yeah, right," Deke retorted. "Sure. And when have *you* ever been with a girl? Have you *ever* been with a girl? Third base? Home plate? All the way?"

"Maybe," Alan replied, looking unreasonably smug. "At least I've got a girl that thinks with something besides her—"

"Hey—" Deke said warningly.

Alan shrugged. "Have it your way. But *I've* got a chick with more than two brain cells."

"Oh yeah?" Deke replied, suspicion heavy in his voice. "So who is it?"

"Nobody you know. Now that you're flying with Fay's crowd, you don't notice lesser mortals much." Then Alan grinned, and laced his hands behind his head, leaning back in the armchair. "Your loss, old buddy. She's a hot little number."

"So who is she?" Deke persisted.

"She's in my math class," Alan taunted, "which should tell you something about her brains."

"So who *is* she?"

Alan wouldn't say, which just left him frustrated and annoyed when his old friend left to rewrite his homework.

And it didn't help matters when he called Fay, and she proceeded to get on his case for doing homework with Alan instead of coming over to her place.

Shit, he thought in disgust—at himself, at Fay, at Alan, at the whole damn world. He held the receiver a couple of inches away from his ear and let her rant on until she wound down.

Finally she seemed to sense he was on the verge of finding an excuse to hang up, and her voice softened. She even apologized.

"I'm sorry, lover, I know how your dad is. I guess I'm just jealous of everything that takes you away from me," she cooed, the honeyed words pouring over his bruised ego and taking the sting out of Alan's taunts. "And it's *really* nice of you to help Alan out. You know, I think it's real nice of you to keep him around. *Somebody* ought to find him a social life, or he's going to wind up chained in some cubicle someplace, drooling over computer parts."

Yeah, he thought, basking in the warm glow she was casting over him. *Yeah, what does Alan know, anyway? He probably wrote this chick up on his micro.*

But . . . I wish we didn't have to go through this every time I call. If I'd been calling Monica, she wouldn't have started out by ragging on me. . . .

SEVEN

Diana closed her eyes for a moment, and sent a tentative probe around the house. Not a full probe; she wasn't going to expose herself like that, not even in friendly territory. Nor did she take her shields down. Not after last night.

She touched three presences in the building besides herself. Immediately below her, which meant in his office, was Larry, easily identified by virtue of long familiarity. Two more together, one heavily shielded—Deke—one very bright, simple, and young. A stranger, about Deke's age.

Deke must have a friend over again. Probably Alan; the poor boy is having some real problems with phase three of the argument assignment. Good. That'll keep him occupied. I need to talk to Larry, and I don't want to be interrupted.

She slipped out of her room, moving like an assassin; closed the door of the guest room behind her without a sound. Every time she'd tried to closet herself with Larry, the kid had found some reason to be there or to interrupt. Not this time; it was mildly funny before, but not now, not when she figured she needed to have a serious talk with his dad.

I'm not sure yet what he thinks we're up to, but I may be able to take a good guess. . . .

Thank the gods for thick, expensive carpeting; that made it a lot easier to move quietly.

The bitch is that the kid's room is right at the head of the stairs. If he comes out at the wrong moment, I've got no reason for being out in the hall. If I say something like that I'm hungry, he'll go all helpful and follow me.

She froze for a moment, right outside Deke's door. She could hear Deke's voice, and that of his friend, fairly clearly. They were talking about their homework assignment. Her own name had just come up in the conversation. They were talking about how different her style was from Ann's. It seemed to surprise them that Ann was backing her—giving advice, but not direct help, nor offering any sympathy for the perplexed who couldn't figure out what combination of gimmicks would glean them an A. Alan in particular was looking for gimmicks—well, it worked in other classes. . . .

Lord and Lady—they're not going to come pounding on my door looking for help with their work, are they? I don't even have the excuse of looking for the bathroom, not with the Tulsa Water Festival attached to my room.

But Deke was well trained; the idea evidently didn't even occur to him. Di was a guest, and besides, she was (supposedly) working. You didn't disturb guests in the Kestrel household; you especially didn't disturb *working* guests.

She slipped down the staircase as quickly as she could, and headed down the back hallway to Larry's office.

She found the door closed; evidently *he* didn't want to be disturbed, either. Too bad. She placed her palm lightly against the door and sent out the probe again, just to be sure.

Nobody home but Larry. Good.

She opened the door silently, slipped inside, and closed it behind her just as silently. She waited for a moment with her back against the wood of the door, letting her eyes adjust to the darkened room.

The track lighting was dimmed way down. The only bright illumination was from the light-table; Larry was bent over it with his back to her, hard at work, the warm orange of his aura showing her that he was concentrating.

In that case, better not startle him. I'd hate to ruin several hours' worth of work by making him jump. She reached out with a mental "hand" and gently stroked the edge of his shields.

Funny; he still has the habits I drove into him, even though Tulsa is apparently a null zone, and he's inside his own house shields. She examined the edges of his shielding critically; he might *need* those habits, now. The edges were a little ragged, a bit uneven; heavier around the head, hands, and heart, weak in the back and around the feet. *A little sloppy, but no holes. Good.*

When his aura began to lighten to yellow, indicating that he'd noticed her subconsciously, she tapped lightly on the doorframe.

He looked up, squinting, waiting for his eyes to adjust to the difference between the brightness of the light-table and the dimmer light of the rest of the room. In a few moments, his expression changed from minor irritation at being interrupted to surprise and concern.

Evidently I look like a bearer of bad tidings.

He reached for the left-hand side of the light-table and snapped the switch off. Di blinked; the loss of light was as startling to her eyes as the sudden flood of it would have been if he'd snapped a bright light on.

With a second smooth motion, he reached for a remote control on the table, and dialed the rest of the lights back up to a comfortable level. Not bright, but bright enough to see everything without straining.

"What's up?" he asked quietly.

She made certain that the door was closed. "I've been trying to get you alone ever since last night," she told him, "and your offspring hasn't been cooperating."

He grinned. "Why, Di, I'm a married man—" Then, when her expression didn't lighten, he sobered again quickly. "Not funny?"

"Not relevant." She crossed to his corner of the office and helped herself to a chair. "Got a surprise for you. Tulsa may be a null zone, but it *isn't* empty. I got brushed by some high-level activity last night. Maybe related to Deke, maybe not; definitely from someone experienced. I wanted to tell you last night, but you were working late."

"What?" he asked quickly

"Sorcery. Good old-fashioned High Magick." If the situation had been a bit less serious, she'd have laughed at his expression of flat-footed surprise. "Somebody tried to throw a good scare into one of the kids from the school—the one I was meeting at the library. Sent a couple of imps to shake her up, make her think she was hallucinating or something."

She leaned back into the embrace of the chair, and found herself surrounded by the aroma of old leather. Larry, bless him, didn't waste any time trying to contradict her; if she said the girl had been attacked by imps, so be it, he accepted it.

He chewed on his bottom lip, his eyes shadowed with thought. *Now I know where Deke gets that habit. Or maybe it's the other way around; Larry didn't used to do that.*

"Based on the experiences I had when I was working with you," he said finally, "if the scare tactics don't work, the sorcerer usually ups the ante."

She "fired" her finger at him. "Bull's-eye. Give that man a prize."

He snorted. "Sorcerers and high-powered executives have a lot in common. Arrogance, belief in their own infallibility, and a tendency to run right over anything and anyone in their way."

She stretched, and shifted sideways a little. "I've got a load of questions that we need to find answers to."

Larry, efficient as always, grabbed a legal pad and pencil. "Fire away," he said.

She'd already organized her thoughts; she knew how he worked. He'd always wanted things in order, organized and succinct. The trait had made him an asset both to the peace movement and the Spook Squad, both of which seemed to operate on the Heisenberg Uncertainty Principle. "One, who is the sorcerer? Two, why stay silent so long as to make everyone think there's nobody operating here? Three, why break silence now? Four, why target *this* kid? What's so special about her? *I* sure didn't pick up anything remarkable about her. Deke's high-psi; she's only moderately psychic."

"Good points, all of them," Larry agreed, printing the questions neatly. "By all rights there's no way a teenybopper could have done something to collect an enemy like that. The ability to conjure imps, target them, and control them at a distance suggests a lot of other abilities I'd rather not think about. My only suggestion is that the kid's in the way of something. Money makes a pretty good motive, and there's a lot of money in this area. Any chance she's an heiress?"

He looked up, pencil poised.

She shook her head, little wisps of hair coming loose from the knot at the nape of her neck. "No. Not poor, by any means, but not anywhere near the league of most of the kids in Jenks."

Larry sighed regretfully. "So much for that theory. Okay, I'll add my questions to the ones you came up with. This sorcerer seems to be targeting one kid—any chance the same guy is after *my* kid? What do the two kids have in common that could make them both targets?"

"Not much," she said. "I've been thinking about that myself. High-psi, both very bright, they both go to Jenks, they're both in the same English class. Ann Greeley's, the Honors class I'm teaching. That's it, so far as I can tell."

He pondered that a moment, then shook his head. "The first probable that occurs to me is their English teacher, and I don't think it'll wash. I can't picture Ann Greeley as a sorcerer. Not ruthless enough."

"Unless she's putting on a good act and she's skilled enough to hide what she is from me—no, I agree." It was Di's turn to sigh. "I'm in the same room with her for two hours every day, and *she* doesn't know what *I* am. If she was ever going to work on the kids, it would be right then, when they're concentrating on something else and under her thumb. Pity, that would have wrapped things up very neatly. But even if it *was* Ann, what would her motive be?"

"Search me." He shrugged. "The only motive I can think of would be that the kids are driving her loony, and if that were the case I think both of us would have picked it up. What about it being one of the other kids?"

Di shook her head emphatically. "Not bloody likely; it takes power *and* experience to control an imp. No kid could do it, however precocious. My best guess would be that the motive ties in with the targets being high-psi kids. Not a lot of them in Jenks so far as I can tell. Last question: Why are we in a null zone? Is that tied in? My sources couldn't tell me."

Larry wrote that down. "The more I see, the older I get, the more I'm convinced that there are no coincidences," he stated flatly.

She nodded, the loose ends of hair tickling her temples. "Not when magic and those who use it are involved."

"Right." He shoved the pad away and leaned back into his chair. "I may have an answer to your next-to-last question, if my hearsay has any grain of truth in it. According to at least a dozen people I've talked to over the years, Indian legend, most notably Cherokee, says that there's a goddess buried under what they call 'old Tulsa'; that's the city limits as of about the nineteen-twenties or so. They say that's why that area of Tulsa never gets hit by tornadoes."

Jesus Cluny Frog. Not another demideity ... I had more than enough of that in Texas. "Good or bad goddess?" she asked resignedly.

Somewhat to her surprise, Larry didn't have an answer. "I don't know," he said, shrugging. "I haven't been able to get anyone to tell me. Could be it depends on which tribe you belong to."

"Yeah, I've run across that before. Like if you're an Aztec, Quetzalcoatl isn't the good guy he is if you're pre-Aztec." She tucked her hair back behind her ears absently. "Okay, I'll buy that, just for the sake of the hypothesis. Is she dead, or asleep?"

"Again, no consensus," he replied. "I've got a logical guess, though."

She yawned, though hardly from boredom; it had been a long two days. "Say on."

"Since the legends say that the reason tornadoes don't hit the ground around here is that even the sky gods don't want to wake

her up, I'd say that the logical deduction is that she's sleeping." He
grinned. "She sounds just like somebody I know, a real bitch before
she gets her first cup of coffee."

She made a face at him. "Thanks a bunch."

He contrived to look innocent. "Did I name names? If the foo
shits . . . Anyway, the legends say that nobody, nohow, wants to
wake her up, so they all cooperate to very carefully steer storms
around her. Interesting 'coincidence,' if you like though. The null
area quits at just about the same place as the tornado-free zone.
The 'old Tulsa' border."

She frowned. "So this goddess—or whatever—has a high probability of being the cause of both the null area and the no-tornado
area."

"Looks that way. I can tell you something else," Larry continued.
"I checked, and there's never been a tornado touchdown within
those bounds in all the time that there's been record-keeping in the
area. I'm talking about going all the way back in the newspaper and
military records as well."

"Interesting . . ." She played with a strand of hair, twisting it
around her finger while she thought. "I think I'm going to have to
stick my neck out. I think I'm going to have to check as deep as I
can in this area—find out if I can see below the null and figure out
if there's anything more involved than just a psychic anomaly, or a
critical mass of Fundamentalists. Now, the big question, Kosmic.
Mind if I do that here?"

Larry shook his head after a moment of thought. "No reason
why you shouldn't, so far as I know. You know what you're doing,
you won't breach the house shields, and I trust you. I'll ask you a
big question: What's the odds of this null stuff being tied in with
the attack on the girl and the thing after Deke?"

Too many red herrings. "I don't even want to hazard a guess," she
said truthfully. "There's no way of telling. What I tracked was a real
sorcerer. You don't know what's after Deke. The Indians as a whole
weren't much into sorcery, but there were individual exceptions to
that. Besides that, a lot of colonial sorcerers picked up on their

lore, so the American version of sorcery has a lot of commonalities with Amerind magic."

"You're so helpful."

She made a face. "I'm truthful. And this is not to say that it couldn't be something else entirely. A lot of even the ultra-Christian Spiritualists picked up on Indian medicine, or at least the *appearance* of having something to do with Indian medicine. Ever go back in the old records? An amazing number of the 'spirit guides' the old crowd used to call on were supposedly Amerind. All chiefs, too, or shamans. It runs to about eighty percent."

"What about the rest?"

"Divided about equally between Wise Buddhist philosophers— which gives you an idea of how much most of them knew about Buddhism—and Druids."

"Which gives me an idea of how much any of them knew about Druidic stuff." He half smiled. "Okay, what about this goddess, whatever she is, being the thing that's tapped onto D—"

The door opened, without anyone knocking on it first. Both of them jumped and turned toward the door.

Deke blinked at them suspiciously.

Speak of the devil. If I look as guilty as he does, Deke is going to be damn sure that we're up to something.

"Alan's going home now," Deke said, eyeing both of them dubiously. "Do you mind if I follow him and hang out at his place for a while?"

Di had no problem picking up what was bothering him. If it hadn't been for his shields, the kid would have been projecting so hard Fred in Kansas City would have "heard" him. *He figures Larry and I are either in the midst of an affair or about to start one. With Miri gone he's got me pegged for the Old Flame Returns. And the boy is* not *happy about this. I can't say as I blame him. I'll bet the divorce stats for this area are phenomenal. I'll bet the stats on philandering are even more impressive.*

"That's fine, Deke," Larry replied. Di could tell he was trying to hide his irritation. To her eyes, at least, he was unsuccessful.

He hasn't figured out what his kid is thinking, she suddenly real-ized. *He's so used to thinking of us as working partners—and me as essentially neuter, despite the teasing—that he can't imagine anyone else thinking otherwise.*

"Well, I guess—I guess I'd better get going." Deke shuffled back and forth a little; not wanting to leave them alone behind a closed door, but unable to think of a reason that would allow him to remain.

"Fine," Larry sighed. "That's fine. And Deke—knock next time, okay? You have better manners than that."

"Okay," the kid said unhappily.

He closed the door slowly. Di waited until she could "feel" his presence moving down the hall before continuing.

Larry and me. No thanks. Not my type, Deke, trust me. If I didn't have André—Mark Valdez, maybe, but not anyone else who was ever on the Squad. It's not a good idea to mix business and pleasure, especially this kind of business.

"Whatever is on to Deke," she said, continuing the conversation as if Deke hadn't interrupted it, "is not leaving psychic finger-prints. That means it hasn't done more than try to act *around* him; it hasn't actually touched *him* yet. It could be the sorcerer, it could be this power native to Tulsa, whatever it is. It could be a third en-tity, something entirely different. It is just barely possible that we have three different things acting here—one after Deke, one after Monica Carlin, and the power that's been here all along. I'm not counting that out."

"It could also be that all three, or any two of the three, are acting together," Larry reminded her. "I wouldn't count that out, either."

"I'm not." She wedged her elbow against the back of her chair and leaned her head against her hand. "Basically, I decided to tell you what I'd gotten so far, and warn you that I need to do some se-rious probing of the area. New territory, love. I need some maps. I *also* need to put a telltale on both kids, so that if anything comes after them, I'll have a chance to protect them. I've already got Monica's permission. I'd rather not ask Deke since you don't want him involved, but since he's a minor, your permission will do."

"All right." Larry grimaced. "If that's what you have to do, then that's what you have to do. Are you going to need *my* help on any of this?"

"Eventually."

I wonder if I should tell him just what it is that his only-begotten thinks that Daddy and the Dragon Lady are up to. The kid could make things awfully difficult for Di, especially if she, or she and Larry, had to do anything of a serious magical nature. This attempt at chaperoning them for instance—

No, she decided reluctantly. *No, I don't think it will help. If Larry comes down on Deke like a load of rocks, it'll make him go uncommunicative. If he tries to give him the "there there, baby, everything's okay" routine without being specific, Deke will resent it, and figure we have to be up to something. On top of that, Larry won't be able to tell the kid how he figured out what Deke's thinking. It's pretty obvious that Larry doesn't want to tell Deke the truth about me or what we're really up to, and anything less than the truth will be an evasion Deke will recognize as such. And if anything is going to be the wrong move with Deke, it would be evasion or outright lying.*

In spite of everything, she had to grin at the sour expression Larry was wearing. He had *never* much liked having a psychic gift; he'd only used it because people needed it. She figured he'd been rather pleased to discover how null the Tulsa area was.

"I think you ought to seriously consider giving Deke lessons," she said slowly. "The shields you have on him are all right—but what if something busts through them? You can't be there all the time. And eventually he's going to leave the nest, KK. He's got the Gift—"

"But he's not comfortable with it," Larry replied quickly. "I know, I know—in theory I agree with you. But not now. Not while he still has unbalanced hormones and he might be tempted to *use* what he's got. And not while Miri's half the world away."

She shook her head, but only replied, "He's your kid. I think you're making a mistake, but he is your kid, not mine. Now about what I plan to do—"

"Ritual, or what?" he said finally.

Her grin widened a little. Besides being reluctant to use his powers, the Larry she knew had been very uncomfortable with ritual of all kinds, from Catholic mass to her own. In fact, her Wiccan magics were among the few rituals he found barely tolerable, and that, she suspected, was because they were considerably cut down from the originals that Granny had taught her. She preferred to travel light, arcanely as well as otherwise.

"Or what," she replied. "Pretty basic stuff. It's just that I'm going to have to go real deep, and real far, and that makes it a bit more dangerous. How's your Earth magic these days? If there's such a thing as 'easy' in this business, it'll be tracing the sorcery. Assuming there's traces to read—if the sorcerer has cleaned up after himself, I'll be on a cold trail. The tricky part is going to be reading this goddess. I don't know what it is, and I'm going to be *very* careful. If the business about not wanting her awakened is true, there's probably a damned good reason, and I don't want to be the one to find it out."

Larry growled a little. "Caught me, didn't you?"

"Huh?" she replied, startled.

"I *am* still doing a little magic now and then, and it's all Earth magic. That's why I'm such a good architect, and why I've got the rep I do. My buildings all fit their surroundings, and I make sure nobody pulls a fast one while they're going up. I've caught more than a few subcontractors trying to skimp on me, and weakening the building in the process."

"Oh really?" She gave him a wide-eyed look of respect. "That's one application I never thought of. Good thinking, Kosmic."

He shrugged uncomfortably.

"So—since you're still sharp in that department, let's figure out when it's going to be safest to do this—"

Sometime when Deke is off with his friends again. Safe from interference from outside—and from your nervous and ever-vigilant kid, old friend.

———

Fay stretched luxuriously, smoothed down her silk negligee, and sipped at her fresh-brewed gourmet coffee. She had decided on a leisurely breakfast in bed this morning, since she wouldn't be going in to school. Across the room from her, the Servant was on the telephone to the principal, making excuses.

"—well, Dr. Powell told us last night that her mother started asking for her. He thinks that she really should come out to Vinita now, before Rowena moves out of this phase or slides back to the old one." Aunt Emily's face was an absolute blank; unnerving when you heard the whining anxiety in her voice.

Fay nibbled a croissant, hot and dripping with butter.

"Yes, sir, he thinks it should be today." The Servant sounded completely sincere and entirely human. The performance was truly a marvel.

If I do say so myself.

"Yes, sir, she's getting ready to go right now, but I can put her on. She's very anxious to see her poor mother."

Fay finished the last bite of croissant, and licked the butter from her fingers. Then she put her coffee cup down on the breakfast tray with a sigh of regret, and picked up the radio extension.

Now, let's make this convincing. "Mr. Daniels?" she said, pitching her voice a little higher, so that it sounded strained and anxious. "I'm really awfully sorry about missing a day of class like this, but Dr. Powell was, like, really *insistent*. He said if I came out right away, it might make Momma a lot better—and if I didn't it might"—she broke her voice a little, in a convincing imitation of a suppressed sob—"it might make her a lot worse."

She heard Roger Daniels, the principal of Jenks High, clear his throat awkwardly. She'd just put him on the spot, in an indefensible position. The best he could manage now would be some appropriate posturing. "I realize this is very important, Fay, but you've been missing a lot of classes this year."

And last year, and the year before that, you old fool. "I know, Mr. Daniels," she replied, pitching her voice a tiny bit higher and adding a breathy quality to it. "I really do know. But I've been sick an awful lot. Every time Momma gets worse, I get these, like, mi-graines. It gets so bad sometimes I, like, throw up."

And I've been very careful that nobody credible ever caught me at playing hooky, Roger. I've been careful that no one has caught me at anything the teachers or you would really disapprove of. And I've been oh-so-repentant whenever someone tagged me with so much as a minor slip, like not doing homework or skipping a test.

"I know that, Fay. For the most part you're a model student, a credit to Jenks. But all these absences aren't doing much for your grades." She could hear him leafing through papers; probably checking her records.

If one quarter of what I've done the last three years showed up in those records, she thought with a little smile and a repressed giggle, *I'd have been turned over to the juvenile courts by now.*

"Frankly, Fay," he continued, "I'm rather amazed that UO accepted you. They don't usually accept anyone with grades this low."

You'd be amazed what a quarter-mil grant would make them swallow. They'd have taken me with an IQ of sixty.

"I know, sir," she said, speaking so low that she was a short step away from whispering. "Believe me, I really appreciate it. They talked to Dr. Powell, and he explained everything, and I'm really not going into a terribly hard course, anyway."

Crocheting and Creative Swimming. Which is exactly what you, you old fool, think that all girls should do. You really never have approved of higher education for women. You think we should all become wifies and mommies right out of high school. You aren't fooled, are you? You know this is just a smoke screen so I can catch a husband, about like half the other little tarts in my class.

"I can understand that," he said paternally. "And I'm sure they do, too. And I'm sure that once the excitement of senior year is behind you, you'll settle down."

"And once Momma is well—" she prompted, to keep him reminded of why she needed this excused absence.

"I hope she'll be recovering very soon," he said, sounding sincere. "Well, I'll write this in as an excused absence, Fay. But please, do try and keep these to a minimum for the rest of the year, will you? There isn't that much of it left."

"Oh *thank* you, sir," she bubbled, trying *not* to laugh at the transparent old goat. "Thank you *so* much! I really can't tell you how grateful I am—"

"That's quite all right, Fay," he said hastily. "Now if you're going to reach Vinita before noon, I expect you'd better get on your way. Don't forget to bring me a note from Dr. Powell."

"Yes, sir, I will," she said. "I won't forget. Thank you, sir. Good-bye, sir."

She hung up. "And fuck you very much, sir," she said mockingly to the handset as she put it down on the tray.

The coffee was cold, though, and so were the croissants. She surveyed the remains of her breakfast with disapproval. "Idiot kept me talking longer than I intended," she said, half to the Servant, half to herself. She looked up; the Servant was still where it was supposed to be, perched on the edge of the couch across from her bed.

"Take this away, and bring me a fresh cup of coffee," she ordered. "I suppose I'd better get ready. When is the appointment?"

"One o'clock," the Servant replied, picking up the tray so that Fay could slide out of the king-sized bed. "You have plenty of time."

"Good." Fay pulled the straps of her negligee off her shoulders and let the garment fall to the carpet. She strolled nude into the bathroom, thinking about a nice hot shower with sensual anticipation.

And the only flaw of this entire day is that I couldn't convince Deke to come over last night. The little ninny really is taking his training well. He's becoming quite a skilled lover. Much better than Wes was. But then, I did get Wes rather late in life. Thank God I didn't have to put up with him for more than four years. Thank God the gardener was adequate, even if Wes wasn't. I'd have lost my mind within the year.

The shower was preset; she turned it on with little more effort than a flick of the finger, and stood under the pounding of the massage setting.

This business of school is such a damned nuisance. Such a boring waste of time. I can certainly think of better ways to spend my after-noons and evenings. . . .

The Servant was waiting with a towel when she emerged, and handed her a hot, fresh cup of coffee to drink while the Servant styled her hair and applied her makeup for her.

The outfit awaiting her approval was a disgustingly demure and girlish knitted sweater and skirt. Fay frowned at it, but waved to the Servant to assist her in putting it on. Awful as it was, the cloth-ing *was* the appropriate sort of dress for a seventeen-year-old visit-ing her mother in the hospital.

Even if the seventeen-year-old was the one really in control of the situation. And even if the hospital was Vinita, institution for the criminally insane.

And the mother had tried to kill her own, dear daughter.

A couple of years ago, Fay would have had to stop just outside Vinita to switch places with her bogus Aunt. The law did not per-mit fifteen-year-old drivers to handle sports cars, particularly without a license. Now she no longer had to engage in that little touch of farce; she was able to pull her Shelby-Z right into the parking lot without anyone thinking twice.

If they thought twice about why a woman with as much wealth as Fay's mother was in the state loony bin rather than an expensive, discreet, private hospital, they never voiced the question.

Fay swung her long legs out of the car and emerged to the ap-preciative glances of several of the guards and attendants. One or two even dared to whistle, and her mood was good enough that she flirted her hips at them and gave one a come-hither wink.

The fact was, she reflected, as she led the way up the cracked ce-ment walkway, that this situation was as nearly perfect for *her* as was possible in this day and age.

It's too bad they don't lock loonies up to rot like they used to, she thought wistfully, waiting as one of the guards scurried to hold the glass door open for her. *That would have been perfect. And it's too bad this isn't back in the fifties, when they used to use the criminally insane as experimental subjects. I could have gotten a lot of mileage out of shock treatments, if I could have convinced the doctor to try them on Rowena with me there.* She sighed. *Oh, well. This will certainly do.*

The staff at Vinita, as at any state-run facility, was overworked and underpaid. Most patients never saw a therapist more often than once a week unless they had families that could pay extra for it. And therapy was a joke even for those who could pay. The doctors, besides being years behind the times, were working from inaccurate information, and treatments were based on speculation at best.

The staff, including the doctors, tended to be shell-shocked and incurious; aides and nurses were frequently the dregs of their professions.

For those under state-paid care, there was only one question—if they hadn't committed an act of physical violence, could they be bullied into a simulacrum of health so that they could feed, clean, and clothe themselves? Because as soon as they could, they went out the door, to be "mainstreamed," or "normalized into society," as Dr. Powell liked to put it. If they *had* committed a crime of violence, the question was, could they be coached or bullied into a state in which they could convince a probations board that they were recovered and wouldn't do it again? In that case, it was out the door as soon as the ink was dry on their release papers. Only a few, notorious criminals were the exceptions.

And for those whose care was being paid for privately—

"You get what you pay for," Fay murmured to herself, smiling, as she chose the least damaged of the plastic chairs in the institutional-green waiting room. "Exactly what you pay for."

Dr. Powell emerged from the door at the end of the dingy room after she and Aunt Emily had been waiting for about five minutes.

Looks like he's halfway together this time, Fay observed, noting the key to Rowena's room in his hand. *It's just as well. I don't feel like sitting around for an hour while he tries to remember where he left the damn thing.*

She noted with amusement that his hands were shaking.

Silly man, can't you even get your own scheduling right? Must be time for your snootful, or you wouldn't be so wired. You should have snorted up in your office and made us wait a little longer. If I didn't want you incapacitated, I'd be very suspicious of you right now.

She made a mental note to check with Powell's pusher. If he was getting too heavily into coke, it might be time to think about replacing him.

If he gets caught, it'll be an inconvenience at best, because I'll have to find another incompetent in a hurry. At worst—all his patients and treatments are going to come under examination, and someone may put Rowena in the hands of a real doctor for a while. What a pain that would be. . . .

"She's a lot more lucid," Powell said, blinking his bloodshot eyes rapidly. "I think we're on the right track with the lithium therapy."

Fay hid a smile, and contrived to look awed and overwhelmed.

What an idiot! Even I know that lithium is for manic-depressives, and does nothing for anyone else. Whatever they're calling Rowena now, it's not manic-depressive!

"Oh, Dr. Powell," Fay breathed, looking up at him with sweet, round eyes. "That's *wonderful!* How much longer do you think it will take? I'd *so* love to have Momma back with me!"

She could see the calculations going on behind Powell's eyes; cocaine was an expensive habit to maintain, and Fay's trust fund was paying him very, very well. If he lost Rowena Harper as a patient, his income would drop by a fourth. She was the only private client he had.

"Now, Miss Harper," he said soothingly. "Your mother's problem isn't like pneumonia, where we can tell exactly when she'll get better. The treatment of mental illness is a science, but it isn't an exact one, yet."

Here comes the platitude.

"She has to understand that she's sick, and truly want to get better." He turned to Aunt Emily; telegraphing desperation, if he only knew it. *She* was the other—supposed—beneficiary of the Harper largess. If Rowena Harper was "cured," theoretically Aunt Emily would be out the door, too. "You understand, don't you, Miss Baker?"

"Of course, Doctor," the Servant replied, showing all the submission any doctor could ask of a lay person. "Fay, dear, you mustn't get your hopes up. The doctor isn't going to be able to make your mother better in a single afternoon, not when she's been ill for five years."

Fay allowed her face to fall. *Same song, new verse,* she thought smugly. *Same game we play every time I visit. I really did pick you well, didn't I, Dr. Powell?*

"But that doesn't mean that your being here isn't important," he added hastily. "She really has made some significant progress, and if we can just cement that progress today, it will make an enormous difference in her prognosis."

Buzz, buzz, buzz. "Sound and fury, signifying nothing." All empty prattle and platitudes. You're a marvel, Dr. Powell.

"As I told you on the phone, she has been asking about you for the past few weeks now. It was my judgment that this would be a good time to bring you in. I'm hoping it will give her the boost of reality she needs."

Time for inflating his ego. Fay gave him the same look of submissive adoration that Aunt Emily was wearing. "Anything you say, Doctor," she cooed. "Aunt Emily and I have faith in you."

And if by some chance the authorities ever turned her loose, I'd probably take her over to the faith healers at ORU. She'd have as much chance of "getting well" as she does with you. The only reason I haven't suggested that is because they might believe her. I can't risk that.

Dr. Powell stood a tiny bit straighter and preened under that look. Fay had it down to an art; it was, after all, the same look that had ensnared Wes Harper—and others before and since him.

He led the way past an attendant who did not even bother putting his girlie magazine away or taking his feet off the desk, down the institutional-beige corridor lined with closed and locked doors, all solid, with little viewing hatches at eye level. Fay knew that the attendants were supposed to check on the occupants of these little cells about once an hour. She wondered if they ever got around to it more often than once a day.

Dr. Powell stopped at one of those doors, one Fay knew by heart by now. He opened the viewing hatch, and took a quick look.

"She's fine," he said with satisfaction. "I'll let you in now. This time I'll stay outside. Don't forget, though, I'll be right here the whole time. If you need me, I can have that door open in a minute."

"Thank you, Dr. Powell," Fay replied, managing a credible imitation of someone subdued and a little frightened. "I—I hope you won't need to."

"So do I, Miss Harper," he replied, and unlocked and opened the door.

Rowena Harper sat on her iron-framed cot, staring out the mesh-covered window. Unlike a good many of the inmates here—and unlike the first two years of her tenancy of this cell—she was neat, clean, well groomed; her hair trimmed tidily, her hospital-issue dress clean and unwrinkled. She ignored the opening and closing of the door, continuing to stare out at the clouds.

Fay frowned. This was a new development, one she wasn't sure she liked.

"Mother?" she said tentatively.

Rowena ignored her.

"Mother," she repeated, sharply now. No reaction. "Rowena, Dr. Powell said you've been asking for me."

Rowena turned slowly. Her face was fairly expressionless, but her eyes showed her hostility. She still did not speak.

"Rowena, I had to take time off from school for this. You might at least tell me why you wanted me to come."

The eyes blazed and the hands crooked involuntarily into claws.

"Why do I *always* ask you to come?" she hissed. "I won't give up, Mother. Damn you, *I want my body back!*"

EIGHT

O h, *Mother*," Fay cried in mock dismay, clenching her hands
at chest level to add verity to the performance. "Dr. Powell
said you were so much better—"

She bit her lip as Rowena's face spasmed; Rowena could guess
what she was thinking; probably fairly accurately at the moment.
*But can you realize how relieved I am to discover you haven't gotten
any wiser since last time I was here?*

"*Better?*" Rowena exclaimed, laughing bitterly, holding tightly
to the edge of her thin institutional mattress. "He's giving me
lithium. I can read, I see TV programs—even *I* know how stupid
that is! I wouldn't send my dog to a quack like him!"

"Mother, that's *not* nice," Fay replied, pursing her lips in disapproval and keeping clear of the door so that the doctor could open
it if Rowena rushed for her. The woman seemed to have learned
that much since last time, though; she stayed where she was, seated
on the edge of the bed. Fay smiled tremulously for the benefit of
the camera in the corner. "Dr. Powell has been doing what's best
for you; I'm sure you realize that. And he said you'd been doing so
well—"

"I don't fight him anymore. That way he can't have me tranked,"
Rowena retorted. "God damn you, I want my own body back!"

Fay shrank in on herself, and clasped her arms across her chest.
You can't have it, dear. I'm enjoying it very much, thank you.

"Mother, this is stupid. You know what Dr. Powell says," she replied for the sake of the doctor and any other listening ears—and recording tapes. "He says that's just a fantasy. He says you couldn't face getting older, so you made up this story about my stealing your body."

She smoothed her skirt over her hips, in what could be taken for an ordinary gesture of adolescent nervousness—unless you knew what Fay and Rowena knew. "It's all in your mind. And you're going to have to face facts, Mother. You're in that body, and I'm in this one, and nothing is going to change that."

Rowena's eyes narrowed, and her fingers bit into the mattress. "You bitch," she whispered.

Fay pouted a little, and tossed her head. "And it isn't very nice to call your daughter a bitch."

"You—aren't—my—daughter." Rowena ground the words out from between her clenched teeth.

"There you go again," Fay sighed dramatically, and sniffed. "Mother, I don't understand you! Don't you realize that if you'd just face the facts you could be out of here anytime you wanted to leave?"

Rowena loosened her grip of the mattress and clasped her hands on her lap. "And what?" She turned away again to look out the window. "Go home so you could find some way to kill me?"

For a moment Fay was taken aback. *So she's figured that out, has she? I'm impressed. I hadn't expected her to be thinking that clearly yet.* "Mother," she whispered, pretending shock. "How could you say such a thing?"

"Very easily," Rowena said, turning back and lifting her chin in defiance. "I've had a lot of time to think since that phony started me on lithium. I'm talking to the woman who murdered my father. Why should you worry about getting rid of me?"

"Grandfather Harper died in a factory accident," Fay said with the patience one displays with a retarded child. "And Grandfather Baker died in Korea. When you were two."

It wasn't too hard to engineer the accident, Fay chuckled to herself, *given the miserable conditions at all of Harper's plants. Maybe if he'd paid a little closer attention to the rate at which his workers were getting hurt and a little less to the bottom line, he might have survived a little longer. It was a tad harder to arrange Gary's death; but I'd gotten back up to full ability by then. It's amazing what can be hidden in a combat zone.*

"You know who I mean," Rowena growled. "Your husband. Wesley Harper. Remember him?"

"Daddy—" Fay quivered her lower lip, just a little. It wouldn't do to overact on this one. Fay had only been three when she'd gotten rid of Wesley. "Daddy was killed when he ran off the road. You *know* that, Mother."

That was even easier to set up. When you're driving a dark country highway, late at night, and a thing out of your worst nightmares pops up in the seat next to you, it's somewhat difficult to keep your mind on the road. Another benefit cars have over horses. Horses have a habit of trying to save themselves and their driver—but a car is mindless, and a collision with a tree at seventy miles per hour never leaves a survivor.

"You killed him, Mother," Rowena replied stubbornly. "I don't know how you did it, but you killed him. I bet you killed Granny Baker, too."

She freaked when she found herself in Maria's body. It was so convenient that we happened to be on the yacht at the time. "Granny Baker drowned when you were thirteen, Mother. You know that, too—you were there." Fay was increasingly pleased with the way this interview was working; Rowena was beginning to look like a classic case of paranoid delusion.

"Did you do to her what you did to me?" Rowena cried, pounding on the bed with both fists. "Is thirteen the magic age? Can't you steal their bodies until then? Did you think I'd kill myself the way she did?"

It's partially because sexual maturity makes you corruptible, dear. I have had to wait as long as sixteen years. "Mother, please—" Fay held out her hands coaxingly. "Please, stop saying that. It's only going to make Dr. Powell want to keep you here longer."

She was thinking over the ramifications of this interview even as she spoke. *I'd just as soon she stayed here for another three years. And if I can get her as hysterical as she was when she woke up in that old hulk, Powell will probably go for that. In three years I'll be legally adult; plus by then I should have all my power back. At that point I can arrange for her to drop dead some night when the attendant is drunk or stoned.*

But Rowena didn't look as if she was going to oblige Fay this time. She sagged back, slumped over her knees, hair hanging down limply over her face. "There's no point in even trying to fight you," she said. "I can't win." She sobbed hopelessly. "Why do you do this? How long has this been going on, Mother? How long have you been stealing other people's bodies?"

Longer than you imagine, child. "Mother, I don't know what you're talking about."

"It's got to be great," Rowena said dully, ignoring her protest. "I've been thinking about it a lot, at night. I mean, you party down for a while, till you're maybe thirty and you're wearing the old bod out—then you go find some poor little girl, and get her stoned, and you're all set to party down for another twenty years." She looked up, her eyes glaring at Fay through the curtain of hair and angry tears. "Does it have to be your daughter, Mom? Or can it be anybody?"

"Mother," Fay replied, putting just a little scorn behind her words, "you sound like a bad horror movie."

It has to be my blood-daughter; I've tried others, and all I did was kill them. But you can't know that, can you?

God. It's still so clear; most of the others have blurred in my memories, but not the first.

The first transfer—it had been totally by accident.

She'd settled in Virginia only the year before, she and her very nubile, attractive—and quite corrupt—daughter. There had been one too many close encounters with church officials in London, officials who had been suspicious of her simply on the grounds that she was a wealthy widow with no interest in remarrying. They'd suspected her of immoral behavior, no doubt; they had no idea *how* immoral. The colonies had seemed like an attractive venue— she could buy herself a remote homestead, staff it with slaves, and practice the Arte free from interference. Purity had been equally eager for the move, sensing, doubtless, that she would be trading the jaded and soft deminobles for virile and eminently seduceable men of the frontier. Unpolished perhaps, but also unspoiled. . . .

All started well. She found exactly the kind of place she had been looking for, and at an attractive price. The owner had been eager to sell and return to England. Too eager. She'd assumed he was one of those gentleman-adventurers, more fop than man, who had thought to find gold in the colonies, and discovered that the only fortunes to be made required distasteful hard work.

But it hadn't been hard work that had frightened the man off. It had been the Indians. They survived one attack, but at the cost of half the slaves. Fay (she'd been "Cordelia" then) had been determined she would not be driven off.

Up until that moment, Purity had no notion of what it was her mother did, not really. Cordelia had carefully kept that part of her life from her daughter; there was always the chance that she would need a bargaining chip, and if Purity had known just how choice a counter she was . . .

My dear, debauched daughter. It was so easy. All I needed to do was wait until you were finished with that young farmer, and sleeping the sleep of the sodden. Your cooperation was not essential to my plans. Your body was.

She'd tried a most ambitious sorcery, the invocation of one of the Greater Abyssals, using her unconscious daughter as the proffered sacrifice.

Then a mouse ran across one of the lines of protection surrounding her and erased a fraction of an inch of it.

The Prince of Darkness being notoriously ill-tempered about being summoned and coerced, the creature had gone for *her*—

She could still feel the fear of that moment, as she scrambled backwards and flung all the power she'd gathered over the years in

a single frantic attempt—not at defense, for she had sensed somehow that defense would be futile—but escape.

There had been a moment of pain and disorientation.

*When I could see again, I watched the Prince devouring myself—
and I was my daughter.* She shook her head; she hadn't thought of
that in years . . . decades.

Rowena was watching her with her eyes narrowed, as if she
could see something of Fay's thoughts. "How long?" she insisted.
"How long have you been doing this?"

"Mother, don't be a drag." *Three hundred years and more, child.
If you knew that, you'd know you have no hope at all, and only such
life as I feel like granting you.*

Rowena must have seen something in Fay's expression that
frightened her. She scooted back to the center of the bed, tucked up
her knees, and hugged them to her chest like a small child. "You
know," she said, her voice quavering, "I've been wondering, ever
since Powell stopped tranking me. Like, if you have to do this to a
daughter—that's pretty cold, Mother. That's, like, pretty heartless.
I mean, you get yourself married, and then you have a kid, and
then you do *this* to her. That's, like, worse than a Nazi."

"Mother," Fay said, carefully aghast, "that's—that's sick!"

*Actually, you haven't even guessed most of it. I choose my hus-
bands very carefully; rich and handsome—and not overly bright. Not
necessarily young, either—just so they were handsome in their youth
and are fertile now. It's easier if they* aren't *young; that way I don't
have to go to the trouble of getting rid of bothersome parents. And occasionally I've been able to drive one to death without resorting to arcane aid.*

"You probably *built* Aunt Emily in the cellar or something,"
Rowena continued, a little sob catching in her throat. "That's why I
never heard of her until she showed up with you."

"Mother . . ." Fay shook her head with sorrowful disbelief. "I
just don't know what to say to you. I can't believe you're making
these things up! Are you"—she let her own voice quaver a little—
"are you *trying* to hurt me? Why do you hate me so much?"

You're a lot smarter than I imagined, child. I'd like to know how much else you've figured out. Did you guess that the transfer and the creation of a Servant takes all the power I have? Do you know how weak I am now?

"Trying to hurt *you*?" Rowena laughed wildly, tossing her head back and leaning it against the wall behind her. "Christ, Mother, you're a hoot! Me, hurt *you*? You haven't got a heart; you've got nothing inside you but stone!"

So you don't know. Time to end the farce. "Mother—" She backed into the wall and hid her face in her hands. "Mother, I can't believe you're saying things like this. Nobody's going to believe you, nobody will *ever* believe you! You're never going to get out of here, never! I'm going to spend the rest of my life knowing my own mother is locked up in a loony bin! You're going to *rot* in here—"

Rowena snarled, going into a crouch, hands and lips twitching—

Because when Fay parted her hands, very carefully, Rowena could see what the camera and the doctor couldn't.

That Fay wasn't sobbing, she was laughing.

"You're never, ever going to get out of here, Mother! They're going to keep you so tranked you won't even know what day it is! And there's nothing you can do about it—"

That last was too much for Rowena—she screamed and lunged at Fay—

But Fay and Dr. Powell were ready; the door snapped open, admitting two burly attendants who, if they'd been less Neanderthal-like, could have taken top prizes in body-building contests. The two of them pushed Rowena back down onto the bed, ignoring her screams and her attempts to wrestle free of them. Dr. Powell entered a few moments later; he was sniffing a little, and his hands were no longer shaking.

Finally got your toot while you were waiting out in the hall, hm, Doctor? I wondered why you hadn't interfered by now. It's because you didn't know; you were off snorting your nose candy.

He was carrying a syringe; Gorilla Number One held Rowena's arm still long enough for him to give her the injection. Within a few moments she was so sedated she couldn't even mumble a protest when they put her to bed.

"I'm very sorry about that, Fay," the doctor said insincerely. "I really thought she was making progress. But it's partially your fault. I wish you hadn't said those things to her. You practically drove her into relapsing. I'm going to have to keep her sedated for the next three months at the absolute minimum."

He glared at her as if he suspected her of engineering the "relapse."

He probably did, Fay reflected. Coke tended to make people paranoid.

She decided she'd had enough for one day, and burst into a flood of orchestrated tears.

"My God," Fay said, stretching to relieve the kinks in her shoulders. "What a farce. It seems now like such a waste of time." She'd turned the wheel over to the Servant; for once she felt like being the passenger.

"Hardly a waste," the Servant replied from the driver's side, parroting what Fay had already said half an hour ago. "There's no chance she'll convince anyone that she's cured if she keeps *that* up."

There were times when talking to the Servant felt like talking to a mirror. Or a tape recorder. "But I can think of a lot better ways to spend my afternoons than on a fiasco like that one," Fay said petulantly, watching the eternally boring landscape of Oklahoma rolling by. "In fact, I can think of any number of ways I'd rather be spending my time than wasting it the way I am now. School, for instance. Bloody nuisance, that's what it is. Having to dance around the asinine laws they have hedging in so-called minors— like compulsory schooling. And if that wasn't bad enough, having to waste *more* time in college just to find a suitable man if Deke doesn't work out—" She gritted her teeth. "Up until *this* transfer I could get away with having my own governess to teach me. I didn't have to cool my heels in a classroom. I *could* be spending the time getting my power back. I *could* be spending the time enjoying myself. Instead I spend most of my time being utterly bored, and the rest trying to get around that old fart of a trustee *just* so I can get some use out of *my* money! I don't dare use magick on half the people I need to—if they act out of character, other people will notice."

"You should be thinking about your demons," the Servant reminded her. "They need feeding."

"I know, I know," she snarled, having forgotten. "You don't have to keep telling me!"

"As you wish," it replied passively. Fay looked at its bland face and wondered what, if anything, was going on in its mind. Was she imagining things, or had it really seemed earlier as if it was beginning to act on its own?

She turned away and stared moodily out the side window of the Shelby. Finding inconspicuous victims had been getting harder lately. She'd already taken as many of the kids from Jenks as she'd dared. The ones she'd fed to her allies had been punks or druggies, mostly. Kids nobody would miss—

And nobody was surprised when they turned up dead. But it's starting to get noticed. I heard that a couple of people are saying that there are more problems than usual this year at Jenks.

So that left the kids out. Which meant that she was going to have to go hunting.

"Downtown?" she said aloud.

The Servant shook its head. "You hunted downtown three months ago. You told me to remind you that you might be recognized if you went there again."

She tried to think of other well-stocked hunting grounds. "How about the Fifteenth Street Bridge?"

"The police cleared it out last week." One of the Servant's jobs was to keep up with the news, which was why it spent so much time watching TV.

"Shit," she said in disgust. "The campground?"

The Servant shook its head. "The rangers aren't letting anyone camp there for more than a week anymore; too many vagrants were living there. And the abandoned house at the airport burned down a month ago."

"What does that leave me?" she asked it.

The Servant was silent as it checked its memory for her. "Across the river, or out near Sand Springs," it offered. "One of the other high schools. Or serendipity."

She didn't like any of the choices. All offered hazards she didn't want to deal with, not as low on energy as she was. "Next time you see a place to eat, pull in," she ordered. "I want to think about this a while."

She hadn't had time to blink before the Servant was slowing the car and pulling into the parking lot of a Ken's Pizza right on the edge of the Tulsa city limits.

There was actually a city limits sign right on the weed-covered verge. The pizza parlor was so close to the edge, Fay realized, that while the restaurant itself was within the city boundaries, the line stopped at the edge of the parking lot.

The Servant parked the car smoothly, and as Fay emerged from the air-conditioned interior, she could hear voices, angry voices, from the trash area behind the building.

Her interest piqued, she turned and shaded her eyes against the last rays of the sunset.

Two uniformed Tulsa police, both female, were giving a young teenager on motorbike an unnecessarily hard time. One was examining his license so carefully Fay wondered if she was checking it for wear or flyspecks; the other was reading him a lecture on traffic safety at the top of her lungs, to the vast amusement of a group of his peers in the next block.

Both of them looked distastefully butch, so far as Fay was concerned. She might have passed them by altogether, except for the look of sly self-satisfaction on the face of the one delivering the lecture.

Fay prided herself on being unusually deft at reading people. As she followed the Servant into the restaurant, the reason for that self-satisfaction dawned on her.

They're bullies, both of them, she decided with a surge of delight. *Bullies who put on badges just because it gives them an excuse to push people around. Which means they're not likely to do things by the book. Which also means that they're very likely to actually break the law they're supposed to be enforcing just for the sake of their own ego-tripping.*

Which makes them fair prey.

How marvelous! I begin to believe that my Servant is prescient!

While they ordered, Fay was watching to see if the pair entered the restaurant. They did. A few moments later, the manager came over and spoke with them in a low, urgent voice. The second of the two, the one with dark, curly hair, responded in tones that could be heard all over the dining room.

"Look, I don't give a fart if my jurisdiction ends at the edge of the lot. If I want to bust somebody's ass, I'll bust his ass, and they can argue about it in court."

Good, Fay thought with satisfaction. *So they know. That will make it all the easier.*

The manager left, his ears and neck flushed, and glanced at her out of the corner of his eye as he passed.

Probably hoping we didn't notice, she thought, and yawned, pretending that she hadn't overheard the woman.

When their meal arrived, Fay ate quickly, which forced the Servant to do the same. By the time she was finished, the policewomen were just being served.

Good. Being interrupted at dinner will make them irritated. They'll want someone to pay for their irritation.

"I'm going to the rest room," she said quietly to the Servant as she toyed with the remains of her meal. "When I'm inside, go without paying for our dinner. Take the car, drive about two blocks back the way we came, and wait for me. Keep the engine and the lights off."

The Servant's eyes flickered to the police and back, and it nodded.

Fay got up and flounced off to the women's room, swaying her hips aggressively. She wanted the women to get a good look at her, and to get the impression that she was a spoiled, rich-kid punk. She gave the Servant just long enough to move the car, then emerged, going straight out the door without stopping to pay for the meal either, making sure to choose a moment when the manager's back was turned so that he wouldn't stop her before she left.

Darkness had already descended. She walked quickly in order to be beyond the edge of the lot by the time the two police came out of the restaurant. She noted as she watched for them out of the corner of her eye that the area was half developed at best. That was in her favor. In fact, at the moment everything seemed to be in her favor.

Once she was one step beyond the city line, she slowed, sauntering along, waiting.

She heard them coming; they walked so noisily she could have heard them half a mile away.

"Excuse me, miss." There was a heavy emphasis on the word "miss" that made a mockery of the apparent politeness.

Fay smiled slyly as she turned. *Right on time. And we're all standing on county property.* "Yes?" she replied snidely. "Just what's *your* problem?"

"Did you just leave without paying?" the blond woman said.

"I don't think so," Fay said, in tones that implied she knew very well that she had. She started to turn away, and the first one reached out and grabbed her arm.

"Where do you think you're going?" the woman snapped.

Fay looked at the hand on her arm with a lifted eyebrow. "To my car, of course. Would you mind removing that? You're getting grease on my sweater."

Oh, you fools. You played right into my hands. If you'd just stopped the minute I crossed the line, you'd have been safe. Now, by knowingly violating the law, you've given me carte blanche to do anything I want with you.

"I think you're going to hustle your expensive little rear end back into that restaurant and take care of your bill," the dark-haired woman said nastily.

"I doubt it," Fay answered, with a sneer that was more than a match for hers. "I'll take care of it after I get to my car. I'm in a hurry. Of course, I don't imagine anyone like *you* would understand that, would you? After all, the only thing you types do is sit around in pizza joints and hassle kids."

They weren't expecting a show of defiance from anyone as young as she was. The woman's grasp loosened for a moment, and Fay pulled her arm away and started walking toward the car. She allowed them to catch up with her just beyond a stand of overgrown bushes and young trees, growth that would effectively conceal what was about to occur—

The dark-haired one caught up first and grabbed her arm again, yanking her around with completely unnecessary violence. "All right, you little tart," the woman snarled, "that's about enough crap out of you! Let's see how you like your ass being thrown in jail!"

Come to me, my friends, my companions. . . . She twitched the magick in her mind, the spell that called her allies in to feed. *Here is proper meat for you.*

Fay smiled as the Abyssal Creatures rose up behind each of the officers. They materialized silently, giving no hint of their presence. *I do so enjoy a good farce.*

"I really don't think you're going to have time for that," she said gently. At about that moment, the blond evidently noticed that Fay's eyes were going to something considerably *above* her head, and turned.

The Creature smiled as she started to scream.

I do so *enjoy a good farce.*

Fay leaned back against the trunk of a tree, folded her arms, and prepared to enjoy the show.

They took an artistically long time about things.

Fay could not "feel" the power flow, but she knew from experience that it was there in abundance. She cast the small magick that enabled her to gather it in, and waited, watching her allies at their task with detached curiosity.

This is going to be quite profitable, she thought, moving a little deeper into the gloom beside the trees. *These two were better than I thought. They truly enjoyed exercising their petty authority on the least provocation; it was probably their only pleasure. That kind of petty tyrant always produces a gratifying amount of energy when trapped and helpless. There's going to be enough for my allies and plenty left over for me. Delightful.*

The demonics had the women reduced to quivering rags just as her feet began to hurt a little. *Stupid shoes,* she thought in irritation. *This was getting rather entertaining. I suppose I'd better get them to finish up. A pity. I love watching someone that enjoys his work.*

"I think that's enough, children," she interrupted them gently. "It's time to put your toys away."

The larger of the two looked over at her with sulfurously glowing eyes, and grunted.

"And don't forget to clean up after yourselves," she reminded them as she walked back toward the restaurant.

The spring breeze was comfortably cool, and touched her cheeks like a caress. She savored the sensation, and the faint hint of peony scent carried with it. She noticed with a feeling of gratification that the squad car was still where she'd last seen it, parked unobtrusively behind the restaurant, where no one would notice it for an hour or two at least.

Lovely; no one will wonder where they went until after I'm long gone. And by the time my friends finish, there won't be a single trace that they ever existed. It's quite likely they won't even be missed until shift change. The department may well spend weeks looking for them. I wonder what they'll finally decide?

Her grin widened as a thought occurred to her. *I could see that someone gives the authorities a story about seeing them in that little porn store on Eleventh, buying little toys together. And then see that someone else reports seeing them abandoning the squad, getting into a car and driving off west. What fun! Especially if I see that the press gets the same stories. . . .*

The Tulsa Police Department won't be in quite such a hurry to find out what happened to them, once those *rumors start flying. They'll be very happy to let the mystery fade into obscurity.*

But it wouldn't do at all for the people at the restaurant to remember the unpaid dinner, or the fact that they'd sent the police off after her.

Or, really, for them to remember the police at all.

Always tidy your loose ends, she reminded herself. *That's why you're the success you are today.*

She arranged her expression in a carefully calculated mix of chagrin and distress, and entered the restaurant, rushing up to the fake-wood counter and the girl behind the cash register.

"Oh gosh, I'm so sorry," she gushed to the startled cashier. "I had to visit the—you know—and I thought my aunt had taken care of dinner, and she left, thinking *I* was going to take care of it— I'm *really* sorry. We were halfway home when we both realized—"

She extracted a pair of twenties from her wallet, babbling the entire time and carefully weaving a spell of forgetfulness as she did so.

All she needed was the key phrase to get into their minds. . . .

The manager obligingly gave it. "Didn't you see the cops?" he said.

There was the briefest moment of hesitation; an instant in which everyone who was involved froze while the magick flashed into their minds and worked Fay's will.

"Cops?" she said innocently. "What cops? Oh no, heavens, keep the change, I owe you that much, at least."

The manager blinked uncertainly. "I could have sworn—"

He glanced over at the table where the policewomen had been sitting, but there was nothing there to show who or what the customers had been; just the clutter of half-eaten pizza and used utensils.

"Never mind," he said, shaking his head. "I don't know what I was thinking about. Thank you, miss, it's a pleasure to run across somebody as honest as you."

"Oh, I have my moments," she replied, laughing, and exited the door he held open for her.

The Servant was waiting just as she'd told it to, in the dark and silent Shelby. In the passenger's side, which pleased Fay. Now she was in the mood to drive again.

"You did well?" the Servant asked.

"Very well," she replied, gunning the motor and pulling away with a satisfying screech of tires.

Very well indeed. Now I have a bit of power to spare. Enough to throw a better fright into that Carlin bitch.

NINE

Monica took her time stowing her books away in her locker, eavesdropping shamelessly on the conversation a few feet down the hallway.

"So anyway, from what I heard from Janet, Harper's mom said she was like, a witch, and had put some kind of curse on her. In front of the shrink and everything."

A bitch is more like it, Monica thought acidly.

"God, I'd *die*. So then what?" the walking Bloomingdale's advertisement standing next to the speaker asked.

"Well, *then* Mrs. Harper, like, jumped her. Janet says it took three guys to get her off." The speaker, a tribute to tanning machines, shuddered dramatically. "I mean, can you *imagine* it? Your own mom going after you like that?"

"She's a nut-case," the Bloomie's display said laconically. "You never know what a nut-case is going to do."

"Well, yeah, but still . . . You'd think she'd be embarrassed or something, you know? I mean, even a nut-case ought to have some *pride*. And I'm surprised Harper told Janet."

That's Jenks, Monica thought. *Never mind your poor mother is so crazy she attacks you. Imagine what people will* say.

"She didn't. Jan was on the switchboard when Harper's aunt called her in sick. *Any*way, Fay's got a migraine from it. So no practice tonight."

"Not much point to it right now; what are we doing cheers for? The wrestling team? Tennis? Golf?" The third member of the little group, a chick Monica suspected of wearing glasses only because they made her look like Molly Ringwald, emitted a high-pitched cackle that made Monica's teeth ache. "Shit, give me a break!"

"Oh, right," the bronzed one laughed. "I can just, like, hear the golf cheers. They'd probably make us do 'em in mime!"

That set the Ringwald clone off on a series of gestures that started like boy-scout flag signals and ended obscene. The other two went into gales of laughter and all three migrated in the direction of their next class.

So that's why Harper wasn't here today or yesterday, Monica thought smugly. *Her loss. She's not gonna keep Deke much longer at this rate.*

She grabbed her notebook for the English class and started down the hall herself, feeling very much in tune with the universe. Because in the inside pocket of her purse were three notes from Alan and *five* from Deke.

Just ahead of her she caught sight of Joy Harris, one of the Brains, a skinny, long-legged kid who devoured science and science fiction with equal enthusiasm and wore glasses because she *needed* them. "Hey, Harris!" she called. "Wait up!"

Joy looked back over her bony shoulder, spotted her waving from behind a bulwark of freshmen just getting out of French 2, and grinned, showing braces like a Chrysler grille. She stopped and got over to the side to let the crowd move around her, and ignored the push and shove until Monica reached her.

"Hey, I'm glad you caught me before I forgot," Joy said without preamble. "Carri said to tell you that if you're really interested she'll sell you the Cabri for four. She wants that Firebird real bad, and they'll only give her three on the Cabri."

"*Okay,*" Monica said happily. "I'll tell Mom, and she'll tell Dad that she thinks it's a bad idea, and that'll make *him* cough up some cash just to make her look like a jerk. So what's the verdict on contacts?" she finished.

Joy sighed. "No way. My eyes are changing too fast. The op-tometrist says to wait another year. And besides, I wanted extended-wears and he won't give them to kids. He says we don't follow instructions."

Monica made a face. "He ought to talk to your chemistry teacher. Like, Alan says you're the only one in the class that *always* gets the results like in the book."

"Yeah, I know, but he's an old fart. Mom got a little disgusted with him this time, though—he wanted to know why she wanted a pair in every color, and what did she think she was, a movie star? I might be able to get her talked into going to the guy at the mall—you know, the one you went to—just taking the 'scrip from our regular guy but getting 'em made up over there. If she does that I bet I can get her talked into 'em for me." Joy gave Monica a wistful sideways glance. "I'd really *die* to have green eyes. Although why I bother, with all this barbed wire in my mouth—"

"I think you'd look cute with green eyes," Monica reassured her, "and the braces aren't as bad as you think. Lots of the kids have 'em."

"Yeah, but not with enough metal to make a DC-10 on their fangs." Joy fished a mirror out of her purse, grimaced at herself, put it back, and kept walking. Monica ignored the gesture; Joy com-plained about her braces at least twenty times a day.

"So what's this about Harper's mom?" Monica brought up her *real* reason for catching up with Joy. "I heard some kid talking about her. I didn't know she was, like, locked up." Joy Harris was the unofficial school historian. Not a gossip; she didn't indulge in speculation or rumors—but if it had happened in Jenks in the last ten years, Joy knew about it, every last detail.

"What, the nut-case? Oh, right, I keep forgetting you don't know." Joy shifted her books over—a huge volume on the Etruscans (who-ever they were), topped by three fantasy books with dragons on the covers, and her English Lit stuff. "Harper's mom's in Vinita."

"Isn't that the nuthouse for murderers and stuff?" Monica said doubtfully.

"Yeah, except that it used to be, like, just the state loony bin, and that's what it was when the shit happened and they put Harper's mom in there. When the Bitch-Queen turned thirteen something really weird happened over at this cottage where they kept Harper's horse." Joy's notebook slithered off the top of the pile, and she caught it just before it hit the floor.

"Like what?" Monica asked, taking the notebook away from her.

"Thanks. Like her mom went—*blam!*—off the deep end. Real sudden, for no reason. It was a good thing this aunt of Harper's had shown up for a visit, or God only knows what would have happened." She paused dramatically. "It was bad *enough,* you know? She, like, passed out or something, and when she came to, she ran all the way down to 169 and tried to flag cars down, yelling about how Fay was a witch and had stolen her body."

"Oh, *God.*" Monica managed to feel a flicker of sympathy for the bitch. "I bet she wanted to *die.*"

"Well, that's not the worst, either—right after that, when they were making Vinita into the max-security loony bin, and they had to move all the regular patients out, they were, like, making all the relatives show up to take 'em away. Well, Fay and her aunt showed up, okay, with her mom's shrink? And her mom started in again, about how Fay was a witch, only this time she'd gotten hold of a knife and she went after Fay with it and cut her up. So they left her there, 'cause she'd just proved she was violent, you know?"

"Wow." Monica was awed. "That's pretty gross. I mean, there's that, and there's the way Jill croaked—like Harper sort of attracts disaster, doesn't she?"

"Makes you kind of feel sorry for her. She's almost got a reason to be such a pain. It's like *she's* the one with the curse on her. Even if she *wasn't* the Bitch-Queen, *I* wouldn't want to be her friend," Joy said emphatically as they reached the door of the English class. "Around Harper, seems like if you don't go crazy, you get hit by lightning or something."

"Or else Harper gets tired of you," Monica whispered nastily. "And then you wish you *were* dead or crazy."

They both took their seats, choking on giggles.

Deke passed her another note halfway through the class. She smiled sweetly at him, but Diana was watching, and while Monica didn't think Ms. Tregarde would be mean enough to make her read it out loud, she didn't want to make any trouble, either. So she tucked it inside her notebook for later.

Alan had already given her a note earlier, so that made two to-day, and it wasn't even noon yet. *This is getting kind of fun,* Monica thought, enjoying just a little snicker at their expense. *Deke doesn't have any classes with me* and *Alan and I bet they don't know I've got classes with both of* them. *I bet neither of them knows that the other one's been coming on to me.* The idea was rather exciting, really; her own little secret.

I think maybe I'll just keep it that way as long as I can. I don't think they know that I know that they're best friends. So when they find out, I can just act surprised that they know each other. It's a whole lot more fun this way.

She tried to pay attention to Bart Young reading his assignment aloud, but his scene wasn't very good. The original argument itself was pretty stupid, with one character saying nothing but "Oh yeah? Prove it!" And poor Bart, a gawky guy who looked like a hockey stick with hair, hadn't improved it any since the last time.

Her attention wandered. *I can think of one good reason not to tell them about each other—they'd be ready to kill each other, the way Bob and Sandy are. I wonder if that's over football, or over Harper? Probably Harper, from what Joy says. Bob's been playing footsie with her forever, and I know I saw her making kissy-face with Sandy in the hall after school a couple of days ago. God, Deke must be the only person in the whole school who doesn't know about the way she sleeps around on him. He still thinks Harper's playing by the rules.*

She wondered if she should tell him. Or did he really know, and was just pretending not to?

It occurred to her for a brief, guilty moment that *she* wasn't ex-actly playing by the rules either, but she shrugged it off. *I'll tell Alan and Deke as soon as one of them makes up his mind. I can't tell Deke about Fay—he'd think I was just being bitchy.* It was too bad he didn't spend more time with his friends—the ones Alan hung out with. Instead, from what he'd told her, he spent most of his time either hanging out with Fay's crowd, or at home. Alan was about the only one he saw anymore.

And I bet Fay has a lot to do with that, too.

Her writing assignment was the confrontation she'd imagined between Deke and Harper if he ever *did* find out that Harper was fooling around.

But when she'd read it aloud, he didn't seem to make the connection—although a couple of gasps and snickers told her that everyone else in class had. And maybe it was a good thing Jill wasn't around anymore; she'd have gone straight to Harper with the dirt.

He just didn't see what I was trying to say. Unless he was pretending not to. I mean, it's gotta look pretty lame, her running around on him all over town. Maybe he figures it doesn't look so bad if he doesn't act like he knows. Boy, that's dumb. Everybody has him figured for a real dope this way. But maybe he'd rather look like a dope than a wimp.

But he had to know *something* was wrong; she'd recognized the subjects of *his* assignment right away, and from the way everybody else looked, the rest of the class did, too.

Him and Harper having it out, except that he wins and walks out on her, which he never does in real life. Come on, Deke you only wish!

Yeah, and I wish he would, too.

Bart finished droning, and she woke up to the fact that he was the last one to read his piece as Diana nodded and hitched herself up onto the top of the desk. She seemed to like to sit up there.

Maybe it's because she used to be a hippie.

The writer scooted herself back and folded her legs up, lotus-style. "Okay, remember I said I wasn't going to grade anybody down as long as it was clear that you were trying. You all have been, and if there's any reason why some of you guys that aren't comfortable with this need something higher than a B come talk to me and

I'll see what we can arrange, okay? Because by now it's pretty obvious that some of you were better than others, am I right?"

Monica could see a couple of the other kids, Bart among them, nodding vigorously.

Diana grinned. "It's also pretty obvious that the two best were Monica and Deke. Now what stands out in your minds about those two scenes that make them good?"

Diana led them all in a spirited discussion of what made the scenes work, and what was lacking in the ones the rest of them had done. "And just to keep you two from getting swelled heads," she finished, just before the bell rang, "Monica, you repeated yourself too much and I got the feeling you were padding the thing out to make it ten pages—and you had some *really* choppy sentences. A sentence needs to be more than three words long, folks; if you have a lot of three-word sentences, it's more than time to think about combining them. Deke, your protagonist was pretty unrealistic. There's no indication to *me* of why he ever started dating this chick in the first place. There's no *way* you'd catch *me* going with a bitch like her if I was a guy."

Monica saw him flush beet red out of the corner of her eye, but Diana had turned back to the blackboard and missed it.

"Okay, gang, here's the next phase. It's time to put in some action and a third character." She was writing all this down in a series of two- and three-word notes. Monica thought her eccentric style of printing was kind of neat, like calligraphy. "Follow your viewpoint character right after the fight; bring in that third character and make him or her an ally. After all, some of you just trashed your v.p. character; now it's time to give him somebody sympathetic. But not *too* sympathetic; this is an ally, not a yes-man. And for those of you whose viewpoint character won—what if he's really in the wrong? He needs to get taken down a peg. Even if he's right, there's two sides to every argument, and somebody should point out the other side. For the sake of making things interesting, let's *not* make it the v.p. character's best friend, okay? Somebody who's maybe a friend, maybe a teacher, but somebody who can give him a little grief along with the sympathy."

Diana turned away from the blackboard, and by then Deke had gotten his blushing under control. "Have fun with this, gang. That's what we're all about in this business."

At that moment the lunch bell rang. "See you tomorrow, kids. Monica, can I talk to you a minute? I got a chance to read your stuff last night."

"Sure." Monica gathered up her things; her stomach felt fluttery and uncertain. She was no longer quite so certain about the quality of her work. Sure it was all right for class, but—Diana was a real writer, and she'd asked for a real writer's kind of critique.

"Monica," Di said, pulling a manila envelope out of her briefcase and handing it to her, "I'm pleased and surprised, on the whole. I won't kid you. You've got real, honest-to-God potential. You have a genuine flair for characterization and a solid grasp of the way conversation works. But—"

All through this Monica's heart had been lifting—now it plummeted into her shoes. "But?" she replied doubtfully. "You might as well tell me the worst."

"Your plots are weak," Diana said, with a touch of reluctance. "You make things entirely too easy for your characters. Think about it; a story where everything goes right and your character is perfect from the beginning is boring! Even in fairy tales things start out rotten for the heroine, get worse, and only at the very end does she 'live happily ever after.' You've got to make your character *work* for her happy ending. And making her wonderful, sweet, understanding, no faults at all—what is she, Mother Teresa? If she's that fabulous, she should be a saint. You've got to make her interesting; give her warts, make her human."

"Like how?" Monica asked weakly. "I mean, what should I do?"

"Give her faults; make her impulsive, oversensitive, something. Give her PMS, for heaven's sake. And every time your heroine thinks she's got a clear path, throw something in her way and make her trip over it." Diana shook her head, and lifted one eyebrow at her. "You're taking this very well, Monica. I've got to say I'm relieved—and that I'll be happy to work with you."

"You will?" Visions of book covers with her name on them danced before Monica's eyes. "You really will?"

"Now don't get too excited," Diana cautioned her, a trace of a smile lurking at the corners of her mouth. "You may decide this is a hell of a lot more work than you want to get into. You also have some viewpoint problems, and you have nowhere near enough description, but I'd like to handle all that in the next draft—*after* you straighten out your plot problems."

"The next draft?" Monica couldn't hide the tremor in her voice. "That—sounds like a lot of work."

"It is," Diana replied soberly. "My guess is that once you get a good plot going, you'll have another five or six drafts after that before it's submittable. We're talking a year or more of work here. Just be glad you're writing on a computer; *my* first books were all done on a typewriter, and each draft had to be retyped from the beginning."

"Oh," Monica said faintly.

"I didn't promise you it would be easy," Di reminded her. "But I did say that I would tell you if I didn't think you had it in you to be a writer. And I think you can do it, if you're willing to put the work in." She sighed, and looked a little sad. "So far I *have* had to give bad news to six of your schoolmates—each of whom came to me clasping what they obviously thought was the best story of the year to their hope-filled bosoms."

She heaved a larger, more melodramatic sigh, and clutched a notebook to her chest with one hand while sending the other hand fluttering to her forehead.

Monica giggled. The fact that Diana had turned the others away—but had just said she'd help *her*—cheered Monica up immensely.

Diana grinned back, but sobered again in the next instant. "Now, about your other problem—have you told anyone else what happened. Even your mother?"

Monica shook her head. She'd *wanted* to tell her mom, and she somehow knew that Rhonda would believe her—but she also knew what Rhonda would say about Diana. The family had some cousins in Jamaica—and Rhonda had come a bit too close to some of the nastier aspects of voundoun to ever trust anyone who *admitted* she was a witch.

And no matter what her mother would think, Monica was certain she could trust Diana Tregarde.

"Nothing else has happened to me," she told Diana. "Nothing at all. Maybe it was all a mistake or something."

To Monica's dismay, Diana shook her head. "Not a chance, kiddo," she said regretfully. "I wish there was, but magic has to be targeted very specifically to get *that* kind of result. Nope, somebody out there wanted to send you screaming into next week. Have you come up with *any* idea who that somebody might be? It's *got* to be someone you know, or who at least knows you."

Monica shook her head. "Everybody I know is pretty normal," she said slowly. "There's supposed to be some heavy-metal dudes that are into Satanism in my class and in the senior class, but I've never met any of them and I wouldn't know who they were unless somebody pointed them out to me. Most of the kids that like metal look pretty much alike, you know? There's even a Christian heavy-metal band."

"Heavy-metal Satanists?" Diana said incredulously, and snorted. "Posers. Bush league. The Dan Quayles of High Magick. Not even close to whoever was after you. The kind of knowledge and practice it takes just to call one of those imps is a hell of a lot more than any kid is going to have. And the kind of *control* it takes is something most of them would never even dream of. It takes the same kind of discipline and patience it's going to take *you* to get that book into publishable form, if that's making any sense to you."

Oddly enough—or perhaps not so oddly—it was. "You're right," she agreed. "From what I've heard they aren't into anything more complicated than lighting candles, getting stoned, and running around naked while they play Judas Priest on the CD."

"Pretty much what I figured." Diana nodded. "It looks to me like whoever sent those critters after you is an adult. Call me a kind of magic-tracker; I can read the footprints that power leaves behind, and everything I saw suggested a mature mind. Can you think of *any* adult you've pissed off lately?"

The last time somebody yelled at me, it was for passing a note to Alan—and before that, it was Ms. Greeley giving me a hard time for daydreaming.

"I—no," she said. "Not anybody, not an adult, anyway."

Diana gave her a long, hard look, then nodded reluctantly. "I think you'd tell me if you could. I think you've got the good sense not to go playing games with me. All right, then, we're stymied for the moment. And *maybe* nothing more will happen to you."

Monica noticed that she was clutching that manila envelope so hard her fingers were starting to ache. "Do you really think so?" she asked hopefully.

"No," Diana replied. "No, I certainly don't. I think whoever it is will keep coming at you until you do whatever it is he wants you to. And I'd feel a hell of a lot better if you'd let me put a stronger kind of protection on you. I know you said I could help you, but every time I do something else, ethically, I have to ask first. Think of what I gave you the first time as burglar alarms—well, this is an electric fence."

The deserted classroom suddenly seemed very quiet—and a world away from the student-filled corridor outside.

"Would it—would it hurt?" Monica asked in a whisper.

Diana shook her head and reached out to pat her clenched hand. "No chance. I doubt you'll even notice it's there. But anything that comes after you *will* know it's there, big-time. They'll see it, and that should be enough to make them go away. If not— anything that touches it is going to get its little paw fried."

"And nobody else is going to notice it?" Monica persisted. "I mean, I don't want anybody to think I'm looking weird or something."

"Not unless they're *very* psychic—in which case whoever notices is going to be used to seeing odd things and keeping his or her mouth shut about it." Diana's little smile had a bitter cast to it, and barely stretched her lips. "Think about it. What would *you* say if somebody started telling people he saw glowing lights around one of the other kids?"

"Yeah." Monica could see Diana's point. "Okay, then, I guess it wouldn't hurt. . . ."

"Fine. I had it ready, just in case you were willing. Take this a minute—" Diana handed her a piece of rock, not even a crystal, just a polished black pebble. Funny, though, it felt warm—and instead of cooling as she held it gingerly between her thumb and first two fingers, it seemed like it was getting warmer.

"It's all ready," Diana said, her eyes a little unfocused—or maybe focusing on something Monica couldn't see. "Just—call it. With your mind," she added as Monica started to open her mouth. "Think of wanting to be protected from those things. Want it very, very badly."

Monica squeezed her eyes shut, after a hasty look toward the corridor. She started this feeling foolish, but as she remembered those horrible *things* that had come after her, she stopped feeling like an idiot. In fact, she was able to do as Diana had asked without any difficulty whatsoever.

"Very good." Diana's voice broke her concentration, and she opened her eyes, startled.

"I don't *feel* any different—" she started to say.

Then she noticed a faint glow just out of the corner of her eye. She turned her head to look at it directly, but it seemed to keep moving, staying just within the barest limits of her vision.

"There's—something there," she said, waving her hand vaguely. "But it's only sort of there."

"That's because you're not really looking at it with your physical eyes, you're looking at it with your mind," Diana replied, nodding in a satisfied way. "You're a bit more sensitive than I gave you credit for. When all this is over, if you want some training in how to use it, let me know. I think you should get some kind of instruction, okay? If not from me, there are a couple of books that should suit you fine."

"What is this thing, anyway?" Monica peered at it sideways, but the more she concentrated, the more ephemeral it seemed. But there *was* something there; she was certain of it.

It was scary. Because this meant there was something to all this magic stuff. Monica would have been perfectly happy if Diana had only been cultivating a very peculiar delusion.

Or would I? she wondered suddenly. *Because those things— they're real. And even if Diana claims they can be scared away, I don't want to have to try it.*

"It's like a 'Star Trek' force field," Diana told her. "It'll keep most nasties off your back, and protect you long enough for me to get there if what hits you is more than the shield can handle. Listen, it's gone really gloomy out there, and you don't live that far from Deke. Do you want to meet me after classes this afternoon? I could drive you home."

Monica was tempted, but then she remembered that Alan had asked her what route she usually took to get home. If she walked, she just might "run into" him.

"No, thanks," she said. "Mom doesn't like me to get rides from people she doesn't know—and I'm not sure I want you two to meet. If she figures out what you are, she might freak."

Diana raised an eyebrow, and gathered up her purse and brief-case. "I take it Mom is where you get your psychic abilities."

Monica shrugged, and flushed. "I don't know. Just we've got some relatives in Jamaica that do some pretty gross things, and Mom doesn't want to even talk about it."

"If your relatives are doing what I think they're doing, I don't blame her." Diana held the door open for Monica, and the two of them stepped out into the deserted hallway as the door shut and locked behind them. "Okay, kiddo; how about working on the very first story in the bunch you gave me—turn your heroine into a human being, screw up her life, and put some of the guts into it that you put in that fight scene. When you've got about thirty pages, come show it to me, okay?"

"Okay," Monica said, already thinking ahead to this afternoon, and trying to remember if the Computer Club met after school today, or tomorrow.

It was today. In a way that was good, because it meant she had a better chance of intercepting him alone.

Maybe. If the club members all got started on something and stayed more than the hour the meeting was supposed to take, she'd have to start for home on foot and hope he'd drive her route.

She loitered for a while in the empty hall outside the computer lab, but it didn't sound like anybody was ready to go home in there. It was kind of funny how those Brains were; real quiet even in class, although they could pull some real rude tricks if they were pushed to it. But get a bunch of them together, and it was worse than a pajama party.

She paced up and down the hallway; the janitor came by, pushing the big stainless-steel floor waxer toward the cafeteria. He looked at her curiously, but didn't say anything or even stop; he just kept right on going, leaving the heavy scent of floor cleaner in his wake. Once he was gone, she heard her own footsteps echoing up and down the corridor every time she moved, and the faint murmur of voices and occasional laughter from behind the heavy computer-lab door.

It was getting dark, darker than she expected. The corridor had windows high up, right near the ceiling, and when she looked up she saw heavy, charcoal-gray clouds bulging overhead. There weren't any storms predicted when she'd gone to school this morning, so she hadn't brought a raincoat. If it started to rain, as evil as those clouds looked, she'd be drenched before she got a block.

She eyed the clouds dubiously, then went over to listen at the lab door. This time she could hear one of the machines beeping, and the muffled exclamations of the kids when it made that *blat* sound that meant something had gone wrong.

They're running something, she decided finally. *They could be in there until their sponsor kicks them out. I'd better head home now. Maybe Alan will catch up with me.*

Once outside, the gloom seemed even thicker, even though it didn't *smell* like rain. March had been gorgeous, with balmy temperatures in the seventies and even eighties during the day, and no storms at all. April was turning into a stone drag. Monica shivered inside her windbreaker. The air felt thick and heavy, and even though there wasn't a bit of wind, she was cold. It might not smell like rain, but it felt like it; damp and oppressive.

It could be worse, she told herself. *In Colorado there's still snow on the ground.*

But snow, even the dirty, gritty snow of April, seemed preferable to this.

Alan was *not* worth loitering around for.

I wish I'd called Mom at work and had her pick me up, she thought wistfully, as the damp penetrated her light jacket and chilled her right down to her bones. *It would have given her an excuse to get out of some of that overtime and she wouldn't have minded. I don't think.*

The street she usually took home wasn't much like Colorado. There weren't any sidewalks, for one thing. Joy had explained cynically that this was because Tulsa was an oil town; people were expected to drive half a block to get a carton of milk. Houses sat in the middle of absolutely huge lawns, acres of lawn. Monica supposed they'd be pretty once things started growing, but right now they were a sort of dirty brown-green. Except for the people who had a lawn service come out. You could always tell those; the lawn was a bright emerald.

When Joy told me how they dye their lawns for the winter, I about fell out, she thought, giggling at the very idea. *And how they have contests for "Lawn of the Week." Not garden, lawn—God, these people are crazy out here. Maybe it's the Prayer Tower. Maybe it attracts cosmic rays or something.*

She walked another block, the clouds getting thicker and darker overhead, everything getting dimmer and gloomier.

They may be crazy, she thought forlornly, *but I wish I had some company out here. God, it's dark. I don't blame everybody for being inside, but I wish it didn't feel so deserted around here.*

For the past month whenever she'd walked home those huge lawns had been full of people: yard crews or dads taking care of their own gardening work, little kids playing, guys from school running or having a game of frisbee, girls working on their tans. Now, tonight, she could have been the only person left alive in the universe.

Like that old movie Joy rented, about how everybody dies while this scientist is down in a cave, and when he comes up he's all alone.

Even the lights on in the windows of the houses seemed cold and distant, like there really hadn't been anybody in there to turn them on, just a bunch of timers in empty dwellings, faking the signs of life.

And it's so dark it might just as well be dusk. God. This is creepy. She glanced back over her shoulder, but there wasn't anything, not even a stray cat.

So why does it feel like somebody's watching me?

It materialized, just as she turned back.

This time she saw it arrive—or rather, she *didn't* see it; there was nothing but empty street one minute, and the next minute it was *there*, all teeth and claws and sulfur-yellow eyeballs. There wasn't even a special-effects-type shimmer, like in a movie—just nothing, then the thing was *there*.

She jumped back a foot, and tried to scream, but all that came out was a squeak. The thing growled and drooled at her; she remembered Diana telling her that these monsters were cowards and easy to scare off—

No. *Oh* no. This thing didn't look like it was going to scare too easily. And *she* didn't want to try. Those teeth were each as long as her little finger, and the talons were even longer. And this time there wasn't the dubious safety of the windshield between her and it.

She backed up another step. Another.

And the thing *giggled*, a high-pitched titter, like a dumb blond on a sitcom. Then, before she had time to react, it jumped for her.

She squeaked again, a panicked-mouse sound; it leapt high into the air, twice its own height, and it was coming straight at her—

But before she could move, before she could even do more than raise her hands in a pathetic attempt to fend the thing off, it hit something about a foot from her body. It landed, spread-eagled, in midair, and hung there for a moment, like a bug squashed against a windshield.

She felt her heart stop, and had just enough time to register that the thing looked very, very surprised.

Then there was a sizzling sound, the same sound a bug-zapper made when it caught something big, like a moth or a horsefly. The thing's eyes bugged out, and it looked like *it* wanted to scream, but when it opened its mouth, nothing happened.

Then it was gone, exactly the same way it had come. One minute, defying gravity. The next, gone without a trace. Not even drool marks on the sidewalk.

Monica dropped her books because her hands were so paralyzed and shaking they could no longer hold them. She stared at the spot where the thing had been, and whimpered in the back of her throat.

Then she turned and ran blindly into the middle of the street. She didn't know where she was going, and she didn't much care. There was only one thought in her mind at the moment, and that was to get *out* of there.

She sensed, rather than saw, the approaching vehicle. Sensed it far too late to evade it. There was a shriek of brakes practically on top of her; and *now* she screamed.

The car swerved wildly around her, somehow, and came to a sliding, sideways halt fifteen feet away. At just that moment her knees gave and she dropped to the pavement, crying hysterically, her face buried in her hands.

"Fuckin' Jesus Christ, Monica! I almost killed you! What in hell were you doing, running out into the street in front of me like that?"

The voice was familiar. After a moment her numb, fright-dazed mind put a name to the voice, just as his hands pulled hers away from her face.

Alan.

"Hey, hey, it's okay. I didn't hit you, did I?" He stroked her hair tentatively. "Are you hurt? Are you all right? Talk to me, Monica. Say something!"

Alan. Familiar. Normal.

She flung her arms around his neck and hung on to him, afraid that he, too, would disappear.

He hauled her clumsily to her feet, and coaxed her into the front seat of his car, where she sat shivering from head to foot, hugging her arms to her chest. After a moment, she noticed that *he* wasn't there, and panicked, only to have her heart slow again when he returned carrying her books and notebooks.

"Hang on," he said. "Let me get this parked somewhere, and we can talk."

"O-okay," she stammered, the first coherent word she'd been able to speak.

To her immense relief, he pulled immediately into the parking lot of a nearby church.

Oh, God, thank you. Thank you. Those things can't come near a church. At least I don't think they can come near a church. . . . They can't in movies.

But this isn't a movie.

Well, the movie people had to get their stuff from somewhere. So they probably can't come near a church.

But what if it has to be a special kind of church? She tried to remember every horror movie she'd ever watched. *It's always priests and things in the movies,* she realized. *Maybe it has to be a Catholic church. . . .*

She craned her neck around to see the lawn sign. *I don't know. Does Methodist count?*

Either it did or the frying the thing had gotten had made it change its mind about coming back. Although she waited for what seemed like forever, with Alan way over on his side of the car, staring at her, nothing else happened.

"Monica?" he said tentatively. "Monica, you still haven't said anything. Are you okay?"

"Oh, *God*," she wailed, finally feeling safe, safe enough to let everything go. "Oh *God*, Alan—"

And that was about all she managed to get out before she started crying and babbling hysterically.

Alan reached awkwardly for her over the gear shift, and held her against his shoulder. Before she had a chance to stop herself, she'd spilled the entire story to him.

Then she started crying harder. "You're going to think I'm crazy," she wailed. "You are, I know you are, but it's true, I swear it, there are these *things* after me and Miss Tregarde believes me, and she put, like, this force field on me and—"

"Whoa, Monica, hey, it's okay." He held her a little more tightly and patted her hair. She closed her eyes and started shivering again. "It's okay. *I* believe you, too."

She gulped, and began to throttle down the flood of tears. "You—you do?" she said, doubtfully. "You really do?"

She felt him nod. "I really do. I mean, shit, people don't go running out in front of moving cars just for fun! And I don't know what the hell you'd have to gain from lying, either, or making all this up. You tell the wrong person, and they just might get you locked up, you know? Now why'd you tell Miss Tregarde, anyway?"

"Because she was there, I mean, I was going to meet her at the library the first time this happened. . . ." She told him the entire story, feeling a heavy weight fall away just because she could finally tell *somebody* about it. "So today just before lunch Diana asked me if I could think of anybody who'd want to do this to me, and I said no. And then she asked me if I'd let her put this thing on me to keep them away, and I said yes. So she did." The image of the thing, spread-eagled in midair just at her eye level, seemed burned into her brain. "Alan, the thing tried to *get* me! I don't know what would have happened if Miss Tregarde hadn't—"

"Did it ever cross your mind that *she* could be the one who's doing this?" Alan interrupted. "I mean, none of this started happening until *after* she got here. None of it started happening to *you* until after you met her. And both times these things have come after you when you'd either just met with her, or were going to."

She pulled away from him, and stared at him in shock. "I can't believe you're saying that! Diana's been really, really nice to me! She's helping me with my writing and everything."

"And if she wanted something out of you, that's *exactly* what she'd do," Alan retorted. "What if she needs a virgin sacrifice or something?"

"Then she isn't going to look for one in Jenks," Monica snapped angrily, flushing. "And if this is a sneaky way to find out if I'm— well—I don't think it's very funny, Alan!"

Alan blushed, starting with the tips of his ears and working down past his collar. "Monica, I didn't—I mean—hell, I'm just trying to think about you. I think you're putting too much trust in somebody you don't know anything about!"

"I know enough." She set her chin stubbornly. "She's got a special investigator's card from the Hartford police; she showed it to me. And she—"

She had *started* to say "she's known Deke's dad for ages," but she stopped herself just in time. "—she's staying with somebody in my class," she said instead. *Better not let Alan know I know who Deke is. At least not yet.* "So she isn't exactly some kind of mass murderer."

"Yeah, well, I know the guy she's staying with," Alan replied with a sulky frown. "*He* thinks Miss Tregarde and his dad are having an affair."

Monica burst into peals of laughter, which obviously discomfited Alan. "So because she's hopping into bed with this guy's dad, she's got to be Charles Manson? Come *on*, Alan, that's dumb!"

He glowered.

"And I don't care what you say," she continued, just as stubborn as he was. "I trust her. And I'm going to keep on trusting her."

"Then I guess I'd better get you home," he replied, starting the car and refusing to look at her.

Two can play that game. She turned away from him and stared out the passenger's-side window.

"Yeah," she replied tightly. "I guess you'd better."

TEN

A sharp pain caught Di right between the eyes. The screen of the laptop blurred and vanished as her eyes unfocused; then her vision blanked.

*Jesus Cluny Frog—what—*She grabbed the edge of the desk to steady herself and give her a reminder of where "reality" was. She exerted control; the smoothness of the cool, lacquered wood beneath her palms gave her something to concentrate on. Her vision came back, but she ignored the now-blank screen in favor of vision of another sort.

A fraction of a second later, she knew *what* had happened, and to *whom*, as well. *Monica. Power pulse right in her lap. Hot damn— first shunt some of that off into* my *shields—*

The pain vanished as she took the overflow of energy and gave it somewhere to go.

Now, let's see what's going on out there.

She closed her eyes and focused, following the tie from herself back to Monica. *Something just bamphed in on top of her. That's what caused the pulse. Now what is it, anyway?* She "read" the energy signature just as eddies in the power flows told her that the creature was bracing itself to attack the girl. *You little—no you don't, you twisted bastard!*

She shunted all the energy she'd drained off and plenty of her own besides into the shield around the girl, just at the moment it

impacted against the barrier. She felt it "scream" in her mind. Then
she felt it "die."

*Good riddance to bad rubbish. Ye gods, I hate those things. Bloody
little sadists. Now, let's just follow the shock wave back to your
daddy, and find out what kind of magician it was that gave an imp
that much power to play with. Normally the little creep would never
have dared take on a shield, no matter how weak it looked.*

She stretched her probe out, very carefully, very cautiously. The
very last thing she wanted to do was alert this magician to her
presence. Better to take things slowly; undoubtedly she'd miss out
on some information, but it wasn't worth the risk of having this
guy decide to rush the job on Monica. *There's time. I can afford to
stick around until I've got this guy taken care of. Nothing worse has
happened than Monica getting scared out of her shorts. But if I rush
him, he may up the ante before I'm ready, and I can't be everywhere.
And if the Guardian stuff decides not to kick in, all I've got to depend
on is little old me, and maybe Larry.* Her probe met resistance; a
shield. A shield with the boundaries roughened with pain. *Aha.
The plot sickens. So you felt that, did you? Good. About time the
threefold retribution clause kicked in.*

An *old* shield; layered and reinforced with decades of spell casting. It had the slightly "artificial" feel that she had come to associate with High Magick. It also had the "constructed," crystalline
matrix that told her that the sorcerer had no sensitivity to energy
flows at all.

Her shields, her magic, were a lot more organic. Like her psi-
senses, they were a part of her, and carefully shaped themselves to
her environment without Di's needing to think about it. That harmony with surroundings tended to be a hallmark of neopagans in
general and Wiccans in particular. Although a lot of the New Age
types were building constructs that integrated the crystalline properties of High Magick with some of the organic properties of Wiccan traditions.

Di tended to baffle folks of all traditions; her "base" was organic,
but she built some pretty impressive High Magick constructs when

she needed to—and then there was the Guardian touch. The impression that there was enormous power around her, but not necessarily available to her.

Which is pretty much the case, actually, she thought ruefully. *And not something anybody but another Guardian even recognizes. Not even the folks on the Squad ever knew. André's the only non-Guardian that ever ID'd me . . . but then André's different.*

But although this shield was strong, it had the brittle taste of something put together by rote.

Exactly what I was thinking. Uh-huh. And there's no hint, nothing at all, that it's ever been in contact with worship-centered magic or group magic. Which means that whoever this is has either never been exposed to Wicca or any of the other neopagan movements, or simply decided never to have anything to do with them. V-e-r-y interesting. A pure sorcerer. I didn't think there were any around.

The edges of the shield prickled a little, like the hair rising on the back of an animal's neck, telling her that her probe had been detected. She withdrew quickly.

If I'm lucky, he'll think it was just some random brush-by; maybe even an echo of what Monica did to his imp. I hope he figures Monica did this on her own. The potential is there, if she was scared enough to focus it. It would have been crude—but the way I fried the imp would look the same as if it had been blasted, which is something Monica could do. This could be a lot worse. I'm dealing with somebody who's essentially tone-deaf and color-blind. And if I can't use that to my advantage, I'm going to turn in my union card.

But one thing was absolutely clear now; this was no youngster playing at sorcery. Not with a shield like that. This was someone Di's age, or older. Most likely the latter.

And I would dearly love to know where he—or she, actually, there's no way I can tell through that protection, and High Magick tends not to have sex signatures—has been learning pure sorcery. I suppose it's possible to get it from books, if you've managed to get hold of someone's private notebooks. You'd almost have to inherit them, though, or you wouldn't have the keys to uncode them.

She opened her eyes slowly; they still weren't focusing quite right, but that wasn't too surprising. Magic was always twice as hard to work when you hadn't prepared yourself for it in advance.

She began taking deep, slow breaths, concentrating on physical sensations—the sweet scent of the bouquet of freesia on the bureau, the cool desk under her hands, the warm current of air across her face as the furnace activated. When her focus suddenly sharpened, and she could see clearly again, she let out the last of those breaths in a long sigh, and stretched.

"Oh, my ears and whiskers," she said to the empty room. "This gets more interesting all the time. I think it's time to ambush Larry again. Between doing that research last night, and this, I've got an earful."

She checked the house for Deke automatically; this was becoming second nature, watching for the kid. No muted glow surmounted by her unobtrusive telltale, though; the kid must be over at a friend's place, or staying late after school for something.

Thank the gods for any favors. She chuckled and popped the door to her suite open with no attempt at silence.

"Hey, Kosmic!" she shouted down the hall. "Are you in the kitchen?"

A muffled "yes" from down the stairs and to the right was all the direction she needed. She took the stairs slowly, still not entirely certain of her equilibrium. That was one of the less pleasant aspects of working magic on a regular basis; you sometimes felt as if your body were an ill-fitting garment.

Once she reached the bottom of the staircase, her nose told her that Larry was in the kitchen, and she followed the marvelous aroma she'd encountered through the formal dining room, into an informal breakfast bar, and from there into the kitchen itself.

"Will you marry me?" she asked Larry, who was watching the progress of a truly impressive pizza through the glass window of an eye-level oven.

"Sorry, already taken," he replied. "Besides, you only love me for my cooking."

"Too true, Kosmic. You certainly haven't lost your delicate touch with spices." She inhaled again, blissfully. "Is this for supper? Do I get to make a pig out of myself?"

"As much as you want, and in about fifteen minutes; I timed this to be ready when Deke gets home—this is club night." He cracked open the oven door about an inch and eyed the pizza with a frown of concentration. "I hope this thing isn't going to scorch around the edges again. . . . What brought you down here?"

"Monica got hit," she said shortly. "Same source as last time. *Definitely* High Magick."

"Does that extra *k* on the end seem as pretentious to you as it does to me?" he asked. "Seems like you ought to enunciate it. *Magic-k.* Sounds like a speech defect."

She chuckled a little. "As a matter of fact, yes, it always has seemed a little pretentious. But then I've always figured that half of what sorcerers did was just for show."

"Really?" Larry dug a couple of Cokes out of the fridge and handed her one. "But you're a sorcerer, aren't you?"

She shook her head. "Only by necessity. I'm more comfortable with Wicca. I'm a kitchen magician, Larry. If I have to do something, my choice of tools is pure psionics first, witchcraft second, and sorcery as a definite third."

"So what happened?" He sat down at the kitchen table, and waited for her to do the same. "I'm going to assume, since you trotted down here looking for dinner and not reinforcements, that whatever it was the girl ran into, it wasn't serious."

"Not very," she replied, staring out the kitchen window at the sunset. There was something odd about it. "Oh, it was probably pretty scary, but at least now she knows it wasn't an accident the first time, or something she only thought she'd seen. She's going to be more likely to trust me now, I hope."

"Or else," Larry pointed out, "she's going to notice that none of this happened to her until you showed up in town."

Di grinned. "Too late; she already gave her permission for the shield and telltales. She won't be rid of me until I'm ready. She can avoid me all she wants; I'll still know where she is and what's happening to her. Thanks for stealing Deke's worry stone for me last night, by the way. *His* shield's nicely in place. Now, let me bring you up to date."

After years of briefing sessions, Larry knew better than to interrupt her at this point. He just leaned his arms on the table and listened until she finished describing everything she'd picked up.

"And I've just noticed something else," she concluded as an afterthought. "Look out there—the weather's cleared up."

She waved her hand at the kitchen window; he looked, and frowned a little. "So?" he replied. "Happens all the time in Tulsa. Oklahoma is the state that Will Rogers made the original joke about—you know, 'If you don't like the weather here, wait an hour.' We're a prairie state; weather systems can sweep in and out in a matter of half a day because there's nothing to stop them."

"That may be true—but remember that this goddess thing is somehow tied in to the weather, and I find it a real odd coincidence that threatening rain cleared up as soon as the attack on Monica broke off." She looked outside again; there wasn't even enough cloud cover now to make a decent sunset. "Now I will admit that there's another possibility; weather-wise, this area may be naturally so unstable that the least little upset in the energy patterns around here changes the weather for good or ill. And the insensitive way that sorcerer was wrenching energy around was making some interesting little eddies and back-flows. But—" She held up her index finger in warning as he started to say something. "But— I don't *know* that the area is that sensitive. Do you?"

He shrugged.

"So, where does that leave us?"

"That we don't know if this is tied in with the goddess, whatever it is, but that the circumstances sure make it look suspicious." One corner of his mouth twitched. "I assume that you're more determined than ever to investigate."

"Believe it," she said firmly.

He sighed.

Larry slipped through the door to the guest suite as quietly as he could. Di looked up as her host closed and locked the door behind him. She hadn't needed to shove the furniture against the wall the way they had back in college; the room was more than big enough for her to cast her circle without moving anything out of place. She was holding a small throwing knife about an inch above the pale-gray carpet. Larry concentrated a moment, letting his Sight kick in, and he Saw the faint line of blue light it left behind.

"I told Deke you were too wrapped up right now to eat," Larry told her. "That you were on a hot love scene, and you didn't want to stop."

"That's as good an excuse as any," she said as she finished inscribing the last of the protective circle with a frown of concentration. "That'll cover why I didn't come down for dinner, and why I'll go down and eat like a spring bear when we're done. But I hope Deke didn't catch you sneaking up here."

"I told him I was going for a walk," Larry replied. Di drew the knife point up to meet the end of the circle she'd inscribed. There was a moment when the thin line brightened; at that point she held out her hands, and then there was a kind of half-dome of fainter light, too faint to make out the color, where the circle had been.

"Do you ever do that?" she asked, sheathing the knife at her side and picking up a candle from the dresser. "Go out for a walk, I mean."

It seemed an odd question. "Sure, sometimes. Why?"

She made a face. "Because, m'love, I think young Master Derek has figured out something is going on, and I don't want him to try and bust in on it."

Larry thought about that for a moment, and nodded reluctantly. "He's been acting kind of funny lately, hasn't he? Shit, he *is* sensitive. I don't suppose even shielded I could reasonably have expected him not to notice the kind of things you've been doing."

Di gave him an ironic look, but went on with her preparations, first driving anything that had been inside that protected area out, then sealing it off, using salt and water, the candle, and incense. Larry tried not to let his uneasiness show, but Di knew him too well. When she finished, she wrinkled her nose at him.

"It's all right, Kosmic; that's as fancy as it gets. The floor show is officially over."

He laughed self-consciously. "That obvious, huh?"

"Yeah." She "cut" a door in the dome for him to enter by, and re-sealed it behind him. "You still remember how to do this? All I need is for you to anchor, nothing fancy. I *don't* intend to kick any confrontations off."

"I think I can handle that." She toed a pillow toward him. He dropped down onto it and took a lotus position with an ease that probably would have surprised the socks off his kid. She took a similar pose—without the pillow—across from him, then picked up the candle she'd used earlier, set it in a plain wooden holder be-tween them, and lit it.

Good, Larry thought. *I need a focus, even if she doesn't. I haven't done anything like this in years. Rusty is not the word.*

He stared at the flame, letting it fill his field of vision, and *letting* himself relax. This wasn't so much a matter of concentrating as it was of changing his focus, ignoring everything except the flame. Shutting the senses out of his conscious awareness, one by one, sight the last of all.

This wasn't precisely a trance, although it was quite close to trance-state. As Di's anchor, he didn't dare be in trance (a state of passivity), or he wouldn't be able to haul her in if she got into trouble. The crude EEGs of the psych lab at the university back in the early seventies had shown his brain-wave activity in this state to be very like the patterns when he was creating something at the drawing table.

Definitely not a trance. Refined and directed concentration, perhaps. Except he wasn't concentrating on anything anyone else could see.

He let his eyelids close slowly. Now that he *knew* how to shut his

Sight off, it mostly stayed off, and he rarely thought about what he could sense when he did use it.

For him it worked a lot like real vision, which was what had confused him so much when it had first decided to manifest itself.

A late bloomer, Di had called him. He remembered her words clearly, coming as they had with relief so profound he'd cried and hadn't been ashamed to. "Gifts usually show up when you hit puberty," she'd told him, keeping it all very light, very offhand, as if it were the most natural thing in the world to see things that "weren't there." "You're a real oddball, waiting this late."

He really had no idea *when* he'd started to See things, because what he Saw had the same solidity and reality as what he only saw with his eyes. He'd had no real way of telling which was which until Di came along.

Like now; with his eyes closed, he could still see—or rather, See—her. She looked just about the same, except that she was very faintly haloed with a spectral iridescence. And there wasn't anything else "visible" except her.

Most people didn't Look like that to him; most were fairly faint ghosts of their outer selves. Only the rest of the gang in the Squad—and a couple of the people they'd made it their business to shut down—had been more substantial than that.

If he really opened up, he'd be able to See that spectral radiance around anything alive. Now, however, was not the time to do *that*.

Di stretched out her "hand"—he took it in both of his. Then she was "gone," leaving him holding the end of a glowing cord. Through that cord he could feel things; not much, but enough. If she was in trouble, he'd know. If she needed to be hauled back, he could do that too. As long as nothing cut the cord.

Let's not think about that, shall we? Besides, she's got defenses against anyone trying.

He settled himself patiently. Waiting. Something he was used to doing, one way or another, all of his life.

Wait for clients to make up their minds, wait for them to decide what changes they want, wait for contractors to put in their bids. . . .

And before that, waiting in ambush, waiting for clues, waiting while Di and Miri went off and did things while I just held the fort.

Waiting for Mom and Dad to get back from their latest emergency call. Waiting for vacations, when we could all be together without phone calls hauling them off somewhere. That's why I decided not to be an engineer. I wonder if they know that? I wonder if they ever knew how terrified I was that they wouldn't come back? All those trips to South America—and when the Texas Towers collapsed, and all I knew was that they happened to be in Texas. . . .

I probably ought to tell them.

This, he realized, was one reason why he hadn't done this in a long time. The state of passive hyperawareness made for a bad case of introspection. Every time he went under, he wound up confronting truths he would rather not have known about.

"He thinks too much; such men are dangerous." Boy, Julius, you sure got that in one.

The "line" he held thinned, and thinned again—Di was going a lot "farther" than she ever had back in the Squad days. It wasn't getting any weaker, though, so he decided it wasn't worth worrying about.

Finally the cord of light stopped growing thinner; it remained as it was for several minutes (insofar as anyone could judge time in a near-trance), then began thickening again. At that point Larry knew she wouldn't need him, and set about waking himself up and shutting that extra "eye" down.

He began paying attention to his other five senses in reverse order: first sight, concentrating on that candle flame, then bringing the rest of the room back into view, then body awareness, then the rest. By the time everything was back to normal and he was ready to stretch the kinks out of his joints, a movement across the circle caught his eye. Di blinked once or twice, took a very deep breath, and let it out slowly, then sagged forward, touching her forehead to her crossed ankles.

"So, what's the scoop?" he asked. "You get anything?"

"I'll tell you in a minute," she replied, her voice muffled. "Let me clean up my toys first."

She straightened slowly, turned that movement into a stretch, then turned the stretch into an extension that gracefully pulled her to her feet.

Larry found himself a little resentful—*his* feet were still tingling because they'd fallen asleep.

"You must be made of rubber," he said disgustedly. She threw him an amused little glance.

"You've said that before," she told him, and held out her hands, pushing with them palm-down against the air, as if she was lowering some invisible barrier.

The half-dome of the protective circle shrank down into a glowing trail above the floor.

She took her knife and "uncast" the circle; Larry shivered, looked down at his feet, and concentrated on getting *himself* all locked down. There was something about the way that the light was pulled back into the blade of the knife that made his head ache and his stomach queasy.

When he looked up again, she had finished, and there was no sign in the room that anything out of the ordinary had gone on.

He rose, and forced his stiffened joints to take him over to the plush, charcoal-gray couch. She flung herself carelessly into an armchair, draping herself across the arms of it in a way that reminded him very much of Deke and his friends. She rested her head against the back of it, but was not looking at him.

"So?" he said, when the silence had stretched on too long.

"So, I found *something*," she replied vaguely, her eyes focusing on some point past his shoulder. "Something quite impressive."

"What is it?" he asked, feeling the first stirrings of unease. This vagueness wasn't like her; she generally didn't have to be prompted for information.

"I'm not certain," she answered. "I'm really not certain. It's very big, very old, and not really aware of much. That's all I can tell you."

Something about the way she said that made him certain she was being evasive. He'd seen her in this mood once or twice before. Like Sherlock Holmes, unwilling to say *anything* until he was certain, she would keep what she knew to herself as much as possible. She probably wouldn't lie if he asked her a direct question, but she'd certainly do her best to distract him, and she probably wouldn't tell all of the truth.

And anyway, he didn't know the right questions to ask in the first place.

"Does this thing have anything to do with Deke?" he prompted.

"No," she answered. Too quickly? "No, nor anything to do with Monica. Though it's been aware of the magic currents and the power flows going on around here lately. Vaguely aware, but it's noticed." She sat in silence for a moment, head tilted back, staring at the moon through the skylight. "This isn't finished yet, Larry. It isn't even close to being finished. I just don't have all the pieces." She pulled her gaze down from the moon to stare at him, and he felt a little chill run up his spine. "Look, you'd better get, before your kid wonders if you fell in a hole or something. Do me a favor and go nuke the leftover pizza. I'll be down in a minute."

He got slowly and reluctantly to his feet. "Are you okay?" he asked. "Are you going to be all right up here?" He didn't like the hint of a green glow in the back of her eyes, he didn't like the way she was evading his questions, and he most especially didn't like the odd, masklike quality of her expression—or lack of one.

"I'll be fine," she said, then suddenly shook her head hard, and gave him a gaminlike grin. "You worry too much, Kosmic. It's okay; I just need to sort some things out."

He left, shutting the door quietly behind him, and slipped down the hall and the stairs past his kid's room as if he were some kind of intruder.

But the more he thought about this, the less he liked it. He reached the kitchen, put the pizza in the microwave, and stared at the food through the glass door, frowning.

If this thing she ran into is all that powerful, he thought, *it could be suckering her. She always told us you couldn't lie mind-to-mind, but that a stronger mind can conceal things from a weaker one. This thing could be hiding almost anything from her.*

He closed his eyes and tried to recall exactly what she'd said. And came up with an even nastier thought.

It could even have sucked her in. Power calls to power. Greater power can dominate lesser. It could have her on a string I can't even detect. I couldn't See anything while she was searching, and I should have been able to. Point of fact, I wasn't even aware that anything was there. So it's strong enough to conceal itself. Which means it's a lot more powerful than anything I've ever dealt with before.

As in, orders of magnitude more powerful.

The more he thought about *that*, the unhappier he became.

Especially since he wasn't sure he could trust Di anymore.

"C'mon, Fay," Bob slurred, leaning drunkenly over the back of the black leather couch. He pawed at her shoulder. "Le's go upstairs."

Fay was beginning to regret she'd invited him over tonight after the fiasco with Monica had put her short of energy again. She was regretting even more that she'd given him free run of the liquor cabinet. Bob had been dry since his father had taken his license away, and that had not set well with him.

He's a borderline alcoholic, Fay thought in disgust, *and if he wasn't so good in bed—and so easy to put in a rage—I would never have bothered with him, captain of the football team or not.*

"Not right now, honey," she told him, pushing his groping hands away. "Why don't you watch that tape for a while? I bought it just for you."

That was a patent lie, but he was too drunk to question her assertion or even care if she told him the truth. He turned his wavering attention back to the screen, where several impossibly blond girls, decked out in spike-heeled, black-vinyl thigh boots and imitation Nazi officer's caps, and not much else, were "interrogating" a "prisoner."

Maybe not so impossibly blond, Fay thought, taking a second look as one of the girls achieved an amazingly athletic pose. *I don't think you can dye that.*

The title of this classic was *Sex Secrets of the SS*. Fay had bought it, not for Bob (although he looked—when he was still capable of focusing—as if he was enjoying it), but for Deke. And not for the mundane sex. There were a couple of remarkably accurate depictions of the rites of Sex Magick in this piece of tripe, and she wanted to see his reaction to them. Would he recognize them for what they were? Would he be revolted, or attracted? A few of her spouses in the past had become willing participants in her rituals; as a reward she had allowed them to live until the time of transfer. On one or two occasions she'd even delayed her daughter's menses until the girl in question was eighteen, in order to enjoy the benefits of having a helper that much longer.

She'd set the tape up in the VCR this morning, anticipating that she would be able to coax Deke over after dinner. But she hadn't reckoned on that little Carlin bitch being able to successfully defend herself.

When the imp's here-and-now body fried, releasing the essence of it back to where it came from and out of her power, the energy she'd given it was also released. Like an elastic band now held only at one end, it had backlashed into her, knocking her to the ground before she managed to absorb it. Then it had drained maddeningly away.

So now she was in dire need of replacement energy—and that meant Sex Magick, and that meant Bob, since she couldn't get Deke drunk enough not to notice what she was doing to him.

Bob had lost interest in the pseudo-Nazis again. He was out of his own shirt, and was working his hands up her legs, trying to come at her from the bottom instead of the top this time. *It isn't worth it,* she thought angrily, pushing his hands away from under her skirt. *I should have called Sandy instead. But it was Bob's turn . . . If I'd called Sandy, he'd have figured I want him more than Bob, and he'd have lost that edge of jealousy. Damn. This is not working out right.*

Bob slouched back on the couch, defeated for the moment. Fay curled her legs up underneath her, out of his reach, and considered the afternoon's events. The imp had impacted on a shield, then been blasted. It *couldn't* have been Monica's doing, could it? Fay nibbled her fingernail, peeling all the nail polish off it in tiny bites. But if it wasn't Monica, *where* was she getting her help? Who could it possibly be?

It had to be Monica.

Bob reached for her again, and nuzzled at her like a toothless vampire. She decided to let him; at least he wasn't trying to undress her at the moment. *I had that kind of power the first time I was her age, in my first body,* Fay thought, while Bob ran a thick tongue over her neck and shoulder. *She doesn't seem to be trained, but she could be faking it. Even if she's not trained, I've seen natural shields that strong, and if she was frightened enough, fear would give her the means to blast something. . . .*

No. No, she has to be trained. The imps didn't shock her at all; she didn't run around school the next day babbling about them or make a run for lights and people at the time. It's too bad. She'd have found herself either in a little padded room or in a drug rehab program. In either case she'd be out of my hair.

Bob's hands were suddenly under her sweater, kneading her breasts like they were pieces of dough. "C'mon, Fay," he said, breathing fumes into her face. "Let's go upstairs."

At that moment certain internal alarms stirred, but did not quite go off. Fay herself couldn't sense the stirring of power, but her allies could, and she'd had them set up protections and detection systems for her over the decades. As a man could not actually *see* radar waves, but could view them and their reflections indirectly, so she could track power.

Damn—I've got a line on something here.

She tried to shrug Bob's hands off, then gave in and let him feel her up. As long as he kept his attention on her breasts, she might be able to ignore him.

The power she was tracking was very subtle, and moving cautiously. The origin was in a Magick Fay wasn't familiar with, so it was pretty surprising she'd detected it at all. Only the fact that it was strong made it possible for her to "see" it; it was *damned* hard to track.

Then she lost the trace entirely as Bob began pulling at her sweater, trying to get it off over her head. He'd been taking steroids lately, really strong ones he'd been getting on the street. Fay hadn't minded at first; they gave him energy and a potency he hadn't had before. But now they were making him aggressive, as well. *Too* aggressive, she realized, trying to fend him off and having no luck. She couldn't handle him anymore. He laughed at the surprise on her face at the moment she came to that conclusion. It was not a pleasant laugh.

"Don't be such a cold bitch, Fay, baby," he growled, snaking one hand under her skirt and groping for her panties. "That's what they call you, did you know that? The Bitch-Queen. The Bitch-Queen of Jenks High."

The way he pronounced it made it sound like "Jinx" High, and it startled her. "What else do they say?" she asked without thinking.

"Plenty. They say you're a teaser—I don't take to bein' teased. I'm ready *now*, girl, and you'd better be, too."

He laughed again, perhaps mistaking the look in her eyes for fear.

Enough is enough, she decided abruptly. *He's not worth the game anymore. I can play Sandy off against Deke; I don't need Bob.*

She wrapped the reins of the spells she had cast on him around her mental hands and pulled hard.

He froze, unable to move unless she willed it, and unaware of the passage of time.

She paused for a moment, just long enough to consider exactly what she was going to do with him.

He was of no further use to her in the context of Sex Magick, but there was another even more potent—the combination of Sex and Blood Magicks.

And it was time for the Servant to eat, too.

She loosed her grip on his mind, just a little. "Wait a minute, honey," she said, disengaging his hands and pulling her sweater

down. "You know I don't like to be rushed. Let me get into something comfortable. Come on up in about five minutes."

She slid off the couch before he could grab her (the slick leather
was good for that), and twitched her hips flirtatiously at him. "You
know it's more fun with the stuff in my room," she said. "And we've
got all night."

He looked as though he might lunge up off that couch in a few
moments if she gave him the chance. She didn't. She laughed
lightly, and ran up the stairs.

And planted a compulsion to stay where he was until she was
ready for him.

She called the Servant the moment she'd crossed the threshold
of her room.

This wasn't the first time the Servant had substituted for her;
nor, probably, would it be the last. The trick was extremely useful
at parties, or on those occasions when she'd forgotten whom she
was supposed to be going out with and accepted two dates. But this
would be the first time she'd fed her Servant this way. If the exper-
iment worked, it might be well worth repeating.

She clothed the "old woman" in one of her sheerest negligees. It
hung ludicrously on the stringy body, making a mockery of the
withered breasts. Fay smiled; no one would ever see *her* that way.

I'll be young forever, she thought, the assertion bringing with it
the taste of triumph. *Whatever else happens, I'll be young and beau-
tiful forever. I'll never have to look in a mirror and see myself like that.*

Then she held her hands pressed to the Servant's face and
breastbone, and began a high, keening chant.

When she did hands-on sorcery like this, she *could* feel the
power; she could feel it flowing from her, taking strength with it, as
if she were bleeding from two huge wounds in the palms of her
hands.

She was weak-kneed and shaky when she took her hands away,
but the effort had been worth the result. There, standing before her
in her own silk negligee was—herself.

With one important detail differing.

She gave the spell-born command of release, heard Bob stumbling up the staircase, and directed the Servant to go meet him at the door. She forced her own knees into a semblance of steadiness and headed for her workroom. When the power began to flow, she would have to be ready. And she needed this power badly.

"Take your time, you have all night," she said over her shoulder, as she opened the door of a small cedar-lined closet in one corner of her bedroom and tripped the switch that released the second door at the back of it. "When you're done with him, put him in his car and crash it."

She pushed the few hanging wool coats and sweaters aside and eased the door at the back of the closet open. *How convenient that he put himself in my hands by defying his parents and driving over here anyway, without his license, breaking his curfew.*

"Where?" the Servant asked. "It should be far enough away that you are not associated with his death."

She thought about it. "Over in Catoosa, I think. There are a couple of long, deserted roads out there. And a liquor store that isn't too careful about checking IDs. You might as well make a really hideous wreck of it. Oh, and elevate his blood-steroid level, and make sure he has a stash with him. And don't let the car burn. I want his parents to react properly; I should be able to get a line into them to siphon some of that energy off. If all they have is an unrecognizable cinder, they won't give me half the power they will otherwise."

The Servant nodded. Fay slipped past the soft, heather-toned sweaters, through the redolent closet and across the threshold of the workroom door. She closed it behind her just as Bob shoved open the door to the bedroom.

The light came on automatically as soon as the closet door was closed. She surveyed her lesser Place of Power with a satisfied smile on her lips. From black-velvet-covered walls, to black marble floor, to the permanent altar on the north side of the room, it was perfect. Its proportions were exact, the materials the finest, the workmanship exquisite. Nothing but the best for Fay Harper. Of course, she hadn't been Fay Harper then—she'd been Rowena. And this was supposed to have been an extension to the closet. The workmen who'd installed the marble had wondered, until she'd erased their memories. She'd *rather* have fed them to her allies, but they would have been missed, and as Rowena she could afford the energy expense.

Wes had never known it was there.

She crossed quickly to the pentangle she (as Rowena) had inscribed by expensive use of Magick permanently in the black marble floor of the room; it was cut deeply into the stone and filled with white marble. Had anyone with her training in High Magick been with her, the hypothetical observer would have noticed immediately that it was incomplete, lacking one side. She removed her skirt, sweater, and panties quickly and tossed it all into the corner in an untidy heap, then pulled off Deke's class ring and added it to the pile. The Servant would fetch it all later when she was finished. Waiting within the heart of the diagram were her sword and a piece of simple white chalk. She used the latter to close the incomplete side, and waited.

And listened. Bob was wasting no time in preliminaries; she heard him pulling his clothing off so quickly she heard his shirt tear. Then she heard the impact of bodies falling heavily onto the bed. Then silence for a moment.

Then the bedsprings began to creak. At first she could hear only Bob's grunts, then moans, as the Servant brought him with hands and lips to a complete state of readiness.

Then—

Thrashing; another grunt of deep satisfaction, one she knew well.

Then a scream that spiraled up into the soprano range.

She loosed her spell and sank to her knees within the confines of the inscription. Her strength returned, flowing into her as it had flowed out, and she smiled as the screams continued.

What a wonderful idea that was, she mused. *How clever of the*

Vietnamese to have thought of it. Of course, I improved on it. It was so ingenious to put the Servant's real mouth down there. And I do think the three rows of shark teeth were a nice touch.

She raised her head and laughed, as the screaming from the other room devolved into whimpers.

ELEVEN

George Louvis doodled a few notes on the back cover of his chem workbook and tried *not* to listen to the ghouls behind him. Like everyone else today, they were rehashing the accident that had wiped out Bob Williams.

It had been pretty gory; five miles outside of Catoosa on one of the back roads, a dirt road, no less. That Bob had taken his Porsche down it was a pretty good indicator of how blitzed he was just before he crashed. Stupid. It looked like he'd careened off the road at high speed, and bounced nose-first into a ditch. The car stayed where it was; he'd gone through the windshield and bled to death. The wreck hadn't even been found until this morning, by some kids on their way to the bus stop. George wasn't comfortable thinking about the number of times he'd wished Bob into his grave. Not that the bastard hadn't *deserved* wiping out—

Hell, he didn't deserve the Big One, George thought, a little disgusted at himself. *He deserved to get trashed, yeah; he deserved to get what he was used to dishing out, but he didn't deserve what he got.*

Not that he didn't go asking for it often enough. If there was ever anybody out cruising for a headstone . . .

It had taken some work to get blood, but when the coroner did, it turned out that the fool's blood-alcohol level was through the roof. So, rumor had it, was the level of steroids and THC. George shook his head in disgust.

Man, the guy had anything he wanted in the whole damn world, and he blew it; threw it all away on fast living and cheap thrills. What a jerk. Wonder if any of the other rich jocks are thinking twice about their lifestyles today?

Realistically speaking, he wasn't much mourned, not by anybody in George's crowd. He'd had the habit of throwing his weight around a little too much, of bullying people a little too often, for anyone to even *pretend* that they missed him.

And George could think of one little bird over at Union that might well find the news right welcome. She might well decide to go dancing on Bobby-Boy's grave.

And if she did, George would be plenty pleased to play her the tune to dance to. They had a lot of friends in common, Jannette and him. He didn't know *her*, but he knew about the treatment she'd gotten at the hands of Big Bob's lawyer. When they were through with her, she hadn't a shred of rep left that wasn't bad.

His pencil point snapped as he dug it into the cardboard of the notebook without realizing what he was doing. He started, looked at his broken pencil in vague surprise, and traded it off for a sharp one.

No, nobody's mourning Bobby Williams, except his folks and maybe Fay. And if you ask me, I'd say she carried on just so she could get another so-called migraine and split from class. It's not like he was nice to anybody even on his best days. On his worst, I'd say the only reason nobody ever had him up on assault charges was because his dad bought 'em off.

Still, George was getting pretty tired of hearing about the wreck. It made him feel guilty for hating Bobby. You weren't supposed to hate the dead. And that wreck—God, he hated thinking about it. He wouldn't have put Manson through *that*. Didn't those vampires ever get sick of it?

He tried to concentrate on what the chem teacher was saying, but it wasn't easy, with the whispering going on behind him.

"Yeah, well, I still say he got what was coming to him," one of the Brains, a thin, beaky kid, said aggressively. "The time he came after me, the only thing that saved me was that I was faster than he was."

"Yeah," said one of the others, a guy so quiet George didn't even know his name. "And I hear that the only thing that saved Carol the time he caught her alone in the team bus was that she knew karate. She threatened to break his passing hand if he touched her. *I* think he got exactly what he deserved! *I* think he should have had his d—"

"Shhh!" the Brain cautioned. "You're getting loud."

"I think somebody should have cut it off a long time ago," the other kid replied angrily, though in a much softer tone of voice. "Only I think they should have kept him alive afterward."

"But that's a pretty awful way to die," said Alan quietly. "I wouldn't wish that on anybody. Bob wasn't that bad. He was a real jerkoff, but he didn't deserve that."

George had the feeling that Alan's comment had been mostly for *his* benefit. *Yeah,* he thought sourly, *but Bobby-Boy didn't make a habit of going after* you, *old buddy. You didn't spend half your schooltime trying to dodge the bastard. Not like some of the rest of us.*

Shit, I may go dance on the goddamn grave!

"George?"

He jumped, and looked up at the teacher with startled eyes.

The teacher was looking at *him* expectantly.

"Uh, sir, I, uh—I didn't hear the question."

The teacher looked pained and impatient, and George had the sinking feeling that he was going to pay for his uncharitable thoughts four or five times over in the next hour. . . .

The last chord died away, and Alan was staring at George and the rest of the band with a look of such profound disbelief that George felt a grin taking over his face.

The astonishment didn't fade, either. Alan seemed to be frozen in his seat, an old recliner that had been relegated to the Louvis garage.

"So?" George said nonchalantly, taking an arrogant, hipshot

stance, in half-conscious imitation of every rocker he'd ever seen on MTV. "*Now* what do you think?"

Alan's mouth worked for a moment before he got a word out of it. "I—uh—wow!"

George grinned and raised his chin. "That all you can say? You, Mr. Music Critic?"

Alan shook his head. "I don't believe it, man! You guys were okay before, but now you're *great!* What'd you do, find a fairy godmother?"

George snorted. "Fairy godmother my ass. We've been working at this, and it paid off. We just hit, that's all. We just finally started to hit on all eight cylinders, you know? You play together enough, and you either hit or you fall apart, and we hit. It had to be this year or next one, buddy, 'cause if we didn't get good enough to start the circuit before we graduated . . ."

He shrugged. He wasn't about to let on about the feeling of panic he'd had when he realized that a couple months ago. Nor the feelings of despair before the band finally began to sound like something more than another garage band.

It seemed like we had all the time in the world—and then all of a sudden there wasn't any time left. And that was when I knew I didn't ever want to do anything but the band. Not college, not music school—classical guitar was okay, but not for me. But if I couldn't get it together, and do it fast, I'd spend the rest of my life working some dumb job and wondering why I didn't go for it when I had the chance.

George suddenly realized that in a way, he had Bobby-Boy to thank for that. The bully had been at every single one of the guys, for one thing or another; at some point they'd all decided, separately, that each of them was going to *show him*, somehow. And at that point, they'd all started to buckle down at the one thing they were good at—music.

That had helped, that and the lecture he'd given the rest of the band. About how this was it—and if they couldn't make it, with parents willing to back 'em, and parents with the money to get them the kind of equipment other garage bands could only *drool* over, then they were all just a bunch of posers.

Good old Bobby-Boy, he thought. *And good old Dad. The ridiculous and the sublime. Now, let's see if Lady Luck is really jamming with us, or jiving us.*

"So, what about your brother?" he said, not really hoping Alan would have anything but bad news. He hadn't even told the other guys about Alan's plan, because he didn't want them brought down if it didn't happen.

But Alan settled back in the chair and started grinning, and George suddenly found his own hopes soaring.

"It's a go," he said gleefully. "Doug's prof is all for it; he says it's a whole new art form. KOET said it's okay, so long as we pay for the tapes. Doug's got permission to take the really *good* Minicam, the one they used for the land-rush documentary. And the portable recording system that goes with it. He's going to show Steve how to run the boards, but he says it isn't much different from the mixing he's already doing for you, so everything should be fine. Just two rules. Don't tell him what to shoot, and *nobody* touches the Minicam but Doug."

George had a flash of Steve wanting to play techie and messing up several hundred thousand dollars' worth of camcorder and shuddered. "No problem," he said hastily.

Steve hadn't a clue yet as to what was going on, but he raised his white-blond head at the words "Minicam" and "sound system." "But—" Steve said. "I—"

"I *said*," George repeated, fixing Steve with a nasty glare, "no problem."

"Hey, would somebody mind letting us in on the big secret?" Paul Bellman asked plaintively.

George turned back to his band—*his* band!—and let himself gloat for a minute. They might not make it. There was luck involved with making it in rock, as much luck and connections as talent. It might not ever get any better than this moment. But right now, he had the world by the tail and everything was going right.

"Alan's brother works at the PBS station," he said. "He's there on a theater internship. He's specializing in video right now."

"So?" Paul said. "What's that got to do with us?"

"Only that he's got to do a kind of TV term paper. And the station manager likes his prof and his prof likes rock. And the station manager told him he could borrow the best Minicam and recording gear they've got, and shoot his term paper with us."

"Wait a minute—" Steve was the first to put two and two together. "We're gonna make that basement tape we've been talking about?"

George laughed; he couldn't help himself. "Exactly so, my man," he crowed. "Except—*except*—this is going to be a live concert, with a live audience. I haven't seen a single basement tape yet that was done with an audience. I *know* we're good, but we all know you've gotta have a gimmick. Well, maybe having an audience'll be enough of a gimmick that MTV will take a chance. Who knows? Weirder things have happened."

He gave them a moment to let it all sink in—then without warning plunged into the intro to the song they'd planned on opening the open dance part of the gig with. His enthusiasm was infectious, so much so that the rehearsal was the best they'd had, ever, and he called it a session when they ran out of energy, though not out of interest.

"That's a wrap," he said firmly, when Paul protested. "We all have school in the morning; we aren't ZZ Top yet, guys. I dunno about you, but if *I* flunk out 'cause I was rock 'n' rollin' all night, my old man would strangle me with my amp cord."

"Are you still gonna take everything over to Bob Long tomorrow?" Steve asked.

George checked his watch. "Tonight; he's still open for lessons. If we get it all loaded into the car in the next fifteen minutes, I can make it over there before he closes."

"But what am I gonna do without my axe?" Paul complained. "How are we gonna rehearse between now and Friday?"

"You've got your backup, don't you?" George replied, fixing him with a stern eye. "Look, we can't afford any screw-ups. This gig is either gonna make us or break us. The *least* we can do is make sure the instruments are in top shape."

"But I'll sound lousy—"

"Come on, man, chill out," Steve drawled. "Better you sound lousy to us than that you sound lousy up there on stage. Bob Long's an okay guy; he'll do right by us."

"And he promised he'd have everything working so well our stuff 'll practically play itself," George pledged. "Look, I've been going to Guitar House for *years*. They've never done me wrong yet. Bob knows what the stakes are, and if Bob says he'll have our stuff in top shape by Friday, you can believe it." He grinned, thinking about how it had been Bob who'd taken the unpromising, battered Gibson George had found in a pawn shop and turned it into the crown jewel of the band. "I swear, I think that man can work magic, sometimes."

Fay stared at the ceiling of her room, tracing the subtle patterns she'd had the Servant paint above the bed, ivory on cream. Patterns so subtle only *she* knew they were there; patterns meant to collect power.

But not enough, she brooded. *Not even with that fool's blood and death added to the Sex Magick. Not if I have an enemy. I don't even have the resources to discover who that enemy is, much less defeat him—or her. Shit.*

She played with a strand of hair, and attempted to put her thoughts in order. It was more difficult than she'd expected.

I should never have indulged in the hashish, she thought, resisting the urge to simply not worry about the problem. *But I needed it. Between the frustration of not* knowing, *and the cramps . . . There are times I devoutly wish I had been born male.*

At least in these modern times one can make the Curse a bit easier to endure.

The phone rang, and she reached out to the bedside table for the extension.

It was Deke. Dear, faithful, stupid Deke. She listened to him babble with half an ear, thinking that perhaps she should abandon him as a project. . . . Was he really *worth* the effort she'd been putting into him? Would he be worth cracking those obdurate shields to get at?

Surely there would be more promising material in college—and easier to acquire. If she really *wanted* the child, she was going to have to break through his shielding in order to take him over. *Then* she'd have to get rid of his parents, somehow.

The mere thought of the work it was going to take made her head swim.

Deke continued to rattle on about the Louvis boy and his band. Fay smiled; if anyone had any notion of what *she* had planned for the dance, they'd have had a coronary.

And old Oral would have the Prare Tar spinning like a high-speed lathe.

Maybe I'd better give up on Deke. He's so damned dull, he'd make a saint weep with boredom.

". . . like Monica."

The hair went up on the back of her neck, her lip lifted in a silent snarl, and she curled the fingers of her left hand into claws. For a moment, for one critical moment, she had allowed herself to forget about Monica. No, she *didn't* know who her enemy was, but the Carlin brat was on the top of the list of suspects. And that she had almost forgotten that fact was in itself a telling piece of evidence.

That she had been considering abandoning Deke was another.

I wonder—could it possibly be that I am not the only sorceress to have uncovered the secret of eternal youth and life? Could the Carlin girl be another? After all, we have only her word for it that her mother works for a living—that her mother is her mother. Her life-style may simply be a form of camouflage. She certainly is not poor; she simply does not seem to command the wealth that I do.

Does not seem . . . She could be new at this. Or she could be keeping a lower profile than I. If she knew she was entering the territory of another sorceress . . .

She could have been stalking me *all this time, and I dozed on in blissful ignorance!*

Deke was back on the topic of the band again; she made noncommittal sounds to keep him happy, and thought furiously.

I need more power. The dance itself won't give me that. And I need to be rid of the Carlin girl; she may be just what she seems, but I dare not chance the risk that she is not. But how? And where to get the power?

"... so George took everything over to Guitar House last night," Deke said, as she tuned back in on him for a moment.

"Well, I'm really looking forward to hearing the band," she replied, when silence on his part seemed to indicate that he expected a response out of her.

"Even with the old stuff, they sounded great this afternoon," he enthused. "Listen Fay, I really appreciate you putting a word in for them. I can't tell you how much it means right now. I mean, it's all going to come together for the guys, I just feel it."

And maybe you do, she thought suddenly. *Maybe* you're *what brought that little tart here. If she's been able to get past your shields a little further than I have—if she's seen more potential in you than I've already seen—*

No wonder a few imps didn't frighten her off!

Fay's jaw tightened with a surge of rage. *I will be damned if I will let her have a free hand with you!*

"Oh, Deke," she cooed. "It really wasn't any trouble, not when I was already on the dance committee. You *know* I'd do anything for you, lover."

She spent a little of her carefully hoarded energy on strengthening the spells she had on him. Since they were nonthreatening, simple sex spells, the shields couldn't interfere. She could work on his mind and memories later.

She frowned a little, realizing that she would have to go back to school to do that. *What a bore.* But those spells required at least eye contact.

He went into the predictable routine, verbally strutting for her like a bantam rooster for a hen. She played him out for a little while longer, then let him hang up when she'd exercised her hold over him to her own satisfaction.

As she returned the phone to the bedside table, though, she was frowning. She turned over on her stomach and stared at the head-board, hugging her pillow against her chest and thinking furiously.

I have to do something about that tart. And I have to have the power to crack Deke's shields and see if he's worth my while. The dance in and of itself is not going to accomplish what I need.

An old memory surfaced, of the May Day festivals she had sponsored in the early days. How she, the Lady of the estate, had presided over the licentious revels of her indentured servants, revels that would have had the prudish authorities in an uproar, had they but known about them; revelries imported from the English, Irish, and Welsh countryside and homes these displaced peasants no longer had. There was a tacit understanding between her and her peasants; they called her "my lady," and did not ask what went on in the House. She let them serve out their time in relative comfort, and provided the wherewithal for their celebrations four times a year.

That *she* acquired a considerable amount of power from those celebrations of the earth and the flesh probably never occurred to them.

Most especially in those times when smoldering rivalries broke into open flame under the influence of a butt of brandy shared 'round.

The dance, as she had planned it (with Jill's entirely ignorant help), would only be a pale imitation of those long-ago potent festivities.

Unless . . . unless I can do something to stir things up. I can't feed them brandy—but a good half of them will be drinking or stoned by the time they get to the dance. But how to manipulate them? In the old days I'd supply the music by way of one of my allies disguised as a fiddler—

The music. Yes—yes, I think that will do. Not the musicians in my influence—but the instruments.

She rolled over and reached into the drawer of her bedside table—the one *without* the "toy chest" in it—for the phone book. A few moments of leafing through the yellow pages told her exactly what she needed to know, the location of Guitar House.

It was dark enough behind the building that a casual observer shouldn't notice the Shelby nestled in under the shelter of the dumpster.

She hadn't brought the Servant; she was going to have more than enough to keep her occupied without trying to watch *that* creature as well. It was a bit restless since its feeding; better to keep it at home, playing mindless video games to purge it of excess energy. It was unfortunate that this restless energy was not something she could use. The Servant was, sadly, an energy sink. Anything that went in never came out again.

Too bad Bob didn't know that, she thought, smiling.

She looked carefully about for any signs of another soul before slipping out of the car, slinging her heavy bag over her shoulder, and closing and locking the door behind her as quietly as she could. She found herself smiling in spite of tension and threatening cramps; this was rather exciting, recalling her days of riding to the hunt.

And the days of her unchallenged rule on her own lands, when the quarry hadn't always been a fox.

She slipped over to the back door and placed both her hands over the lock and latch mechanism, whispering the words of the Cantrip of Unbinding. She felt the tiny outflowing of power—it wasn't, thank heavens, a very complicated bit of Magick; mere beginner's work. Then there was a *click* that she felt more than heard, what with the traffic noise just on the other side of the building. And when she tugged at the heavy metal door, it swung open. She paused for a moment before stepping inside, and set the second spell in motion, the one to short-circuit any alarm systems the owner had in place.

Then she crossed the threshold, savoring the moment. *Breaking and entering is such a special thrill . . . even though the only danger is from some passerby or too-curious police officer, I suppose I could eliminate that as well, except that it would alert my foe to my abilities. And I can't spare the energy. A nonspecific glamour like that is terribly expensive. . . . Ah, well, what's life without a little uncertainty? There's a certain perverse enjoyment in taking risks.*

She found herself in a narrow back hallway; it was too dark to see, and she felt her way along one wall until she came to a half-open doorway. She inched her way into the room beyond, closed the door behind her, and conjured herself a light.

As she had hoped, it was a practice room.

She shoved all the chairs and music stands over to one side, then opened the shoulder bag she had brought with her. The first item, folded carefully on top, was a heavy square of virgin canvas; underneath it were a bottle of ink made with her own blood and a brush made with the hair from her head. She unfolded the canvas and spread it out to cover the floor. In a few moments it had been inscribed with the duplicate of the pentangle she had carved into the floor of her workroom.

Only this one was meant to contain, rather than protect.

She spared a fleeting regret, as always, for the fact that she would be unable to see, or even *feel*, most of what she was about to do. She had been told by another Magick practitioner, a member of the Hellfire Club, who had the Gifts of Sight and Sensing, that it was rather spectacular. That was the reason so many aspired to sorcery and so few succeeded; without the Gifts there was only the will and infinite patience, the patience of one blind and deaf learning to pick locks, embroider, and dance. It could be done—she was the living proof of it—but it took so long, so much trial and error, even when one had begun at an age when other children were just beginning to walk about and prattle.

And this would be a much more difficult proposition than when she had called the Abyssal Creatures, the vessels used by her allies to feed by proxy. She needed some new servants for this task;

her allies were too powerful to constrain to anything this petty, and besides, she was young in this body and had yet to prove herself worthy of their full aid.

Sometimes she tired of this continual bargaining and rebargaining, lifetime after lifetime—but when she was at her full powers again, it always seemed, in retrospect, that the game was more than worth the candle.

So; the night wasn't getting any younger.

She spread her arms wide, her fingers twisted into the first of the Signs of Power, and began to chant, holding her pitch to a perfect 440-cycle "A." With each new line of the chant, she raised her pitch exactly one half step, until she had covered a full octave. Then she dropped back to the beginning "A" for the second Sign, the second chant.

Three Signs; three incantations.

On the last note of the last chant, she reached for the little bag of prepared powders she had put in the pocket of her robe, and cast it into the center of the pentangle.

There was a flash of sullen green flame; the lights dimmed for a moment.

She was no longer alone in the room.

There was the inevitable struggle of wills as the demon she had called attempted to wrest control from her. *This* was something she could feel, as their eyes locked and she fought the urge to look away from it; first because it tried to make her fear it, then because of an overwhelming sensation of there being something lurking *behind* her.

She did not succumb to either, staring the creature down— literally; it slouched lower and lower as she kept her eyes locked with its, until at last it pulled *its* eyes away and groveled.

"Very good," she said aloud. "You can get up."

It glared at her for a moment, then subsided sullenly.

It really hadn't had a chance. It *was* a demon, but a very minor one. Nothing like the ones she would be calling on later; this one was hardly a challenge.

She smiled at it to remind it of which one was the master, then laid a strip of canvas across one of the lines of the pentangle to release it.

It crossed the line slowly; one of her allies had told her that crossing out of the gateway of the pentangle was painful to creatures of its type. She waited until it had abased itself at her feet, then gave it careful instructions on how to find the three guitars belonging to George's band. "Quickly," she told it. "You need not be overly careful with any of the other instruments, so long as you are quick to find the ones I need. When you have them, bring them here to me."

It rose and bowed to her, snarling silently, and passed through the wall of the room. In a moment or two she could hear it thrashing about, knocking instruments over in its efforts to accomplish the task she had set it.

It was a bit noisier than she had anticipated, but at least she had ordered it to confine its efforts to the back of the store. Between the muffling effect of the cinder blocks and the traffic noise out on Admiral, the commotion should go unnoticed.

She didn't have time to waste worrying about it, anyway.

She shook the cloth out and relaid it, adding the strip of canvas across the line so that the demon would be able to cross back into the center for dismissal. Then she prepared herself.

She emptied the carryall on the floor, picking out her Wand, tipped with obsidian from Mount Vesuvius, then slipped her Robe over her head and tied her Girdle (braided from the hair of as many of her victims as she could manage) around her waist. She picked out another pouch of prepared powder and the brush and a bottle of thinned white glue.

Carefully she went over all the lines of the pentangle with the glue, then the powder. In the old days sorcerers had only used the powder, and no few of them became the prey of the demons they had called because of an errant breeze or a scurrying insect. Fay had discovered that the addition of the glue made no difference in the efficacy of the spell—and all the difference in the world to her personal safety. It made cleanup a little more difficult, but she'd be burning this cloth anyway, and at home there was always the Servant to take care of cleanup problems.

She would leave the line with the canvas strip across it unpainted until after she had dismissed the first demon.

The noise in the farther rooms ceased at that moment; she straightened just as the demon, burdened with three instruments, kicked open the door. It could make itself ethereal, but not the guitars; though not of a class with the next creatures she would summon, it was bright enough to realize that. Brighter than the Abyssal Creatures, which probably would have tried.

She accepted the instruments one at a time; sure enough, each of them bore tags saying "Louvis" and "reconditioned." Two Fender Stratocasters and an old Gibson with a quarter-moon pearl inlay on the head. The Gibson rather surprised her; it was very nearly an antique and hardly the sort of instrument she'd expect a hard-edged group like the Persuaders to use.

Well, it didn't much matter; the instruments themselves were only the vehicles for her power and her plans.

The demon stood beside her, its face expressionless, but she could tell by the sly glances it gave her from time to time that it was considering testing her hold on it again.

"There," she ordered, pointing to the pentangle. It snarled a little, but complied, taking its place in the center. She didn't need to finish that side just yet—and didn't want to take her attention from this obviously restive creature for even the few moments it would take to paint on the glue and sprinkle the powders—

A judgment that was reinforced when she noticed it inching toward the scrap of canvas crossing the line that would otherwise hold it pent inside the diagram.

She pulled the canvas out of the pentangle while the demon hissed with frustration, and stuffed it into the pocket of her Robe.

The ceremony of dismissal was mercifully short; one line of chanting, one Sign of Uncasting. The thing was gone, leaving behind only a faint scent of scorched cloth and a slightly burned patch on the canvas.

She arranged the three guitars carefully in the center of the pentangle; this was a tricky proposition since there wasn't a lot of room to work with, and she did not want to stack them in any way—and most especially she didn't want to have any part of them cross the lines of protection bounding the center.

Finally she had them arranged to her satisfaction, and completed the new pentangle with glue and powder.

Now for the possession.

For the guitars were to become demon-possessed, an idea that had occurred to her after remembering she'd seen a horror movie recently that had featured a demon-invested object. While a possessed lamp was a fairly ludicrous proposition for her purposes, calling in demons to take the guitars was actually an inspired notion. Once possessed, the quality of music they played would be under her control—and loaded with psychic and subsonic influences. Just as her demonic fiddlers had played her peasants into a state of aggression guaranteed to cause trouble among them, so the possessed guitars would do the same.

Who needs Satanic lyrics, or messages you can only hear when you play the tape backward? she thought with a cynical smile. *By the time I'm done with them, the kids at the dance will have adrenaline and sex hormones giving them such a rush that the ones that don't start a riot will probably go out to their cars and screw each other's brains out! And the beauty of it is, the only people who might suspect it was the music that did it will be born-again fanatics that no one sane would believe in the first place!*

In some ways it was much easier to operate as a sorceress in this age; who would believe that there really *was* such a thing, other than a handful of paranoids, assorted religious crazies, and the odd real psychic or magician? And so far, none of those had proved much of a threat. She seemed to recall some vampire movie where the bloodsucker had told his hunter that the strength of the vampire lay in modern man's persistent disbelief that he existed. The same was certainly true in her case; faced with the "impossibility" of seeing her vanish out of the front seat of the TransAm,

Deke had chosen to consider the entire episode a postaccident hallucination. The community in general had chosen to consider the rash of "accidents" that had plagued her to be a series of unfortunate coincidences, and the deaths of students at Jenks to be sheer bad luck (with a liberal helping of too much money and too little supervision). No one had gone looking for an outside cause, much less a supernatural one.

So long as she kept her creatures under control, her profile relatively low, and her involvement with the supernatural a secret, she could operate with impunity.

Keeping her profile relatively low was harder than it could have seemed. She needed to feed her allies; that was part of the bargain. They needed blood and pain and the energy released with violent death, and they needed it at regular intervals. And these days she couldn't just lure an unsuspecting peddler or trapper into the house. For one thing, there *weren't* any such equivalents; for another, these days they'd be missed. An opportunity like the one that had occurred with the two policewomen came along once in a year at best. The street people who lived under bridges and in dumpsters were a danger-free source, but even they became alarmed when too many of their kind started going missing. As Rowena she had been able to select single, uncommitted men and even women at the various pickup bars, take them home, and allow her allies to take them after enjoying them herself. She had learned over the years exactly how to choose the ones with indifferent families, the ones who were living beyond their means, who would be missed only by their creditors when they vanished. But as Fay, that entire segment of society was closed to her. She had learned only too quickly after a couple of really narrow escapes that the kind of person likely to pick up an underage prostitute had, more often than not, a wife and family who would raise the most incredible fuss when he didn't return from his "late night at the office." She had gone out hunting from time to time, looking for would-be molesters and rapists—but that put *her* at physical risk, not something she courted willingly.

Although it was a little ironic . . . the police never *would* find out who had killed and buried all those hitchhiking kids along old Route Sixty-six, nor discover why the "Rainy-day Rapist" just stopped taking victims.

Well, none of that mattered at the moment, except that she was out of options right now for the means of acquiring power, and this was the safest way she could think of to get it.

She completed the diagram, stepped back as far as the wall would permit, and raised her arms over her head. Her sleeves slid silkily down along her arms as she began the first of the chants and Signs.

There were nine of them this time, not three, and all of them increased in complexity from one to the next. Halfway through the diagram began to take on a dim, greenish glow even to *her* eyes. Three quarters through, and the diagram burned with a fierce green flame that consumed nothing and gave off neither heat nor smoke. As she began the last chant, her arms trembled with the effort of holding them above her head with the fingers contorted into the Sign; she was drenched with sweat, and shivering with exhaustion.

And if she stopped there, the backlash of pent-up power would very likely kill her—if her allies didn't find a way to do it first. There was no safe exit from *this* casting; the only safety lay in perfect performance and flawless completion.

As the final word of the chant left her lips, the diagram blazed up, creating a curtain of dark-green light that rippled like the aurora and prevented her from seeing the center of the pentangle. From the center came a sound—an electronic wail, an amplified snarl that sounded as if the three instruments inside were being tortured.

She lowered her arms slowly, and waited. Waited until the light died down, then died out, leaving behind only the diagram, the lines now covered with a kind of phosphorescent slime. And the guitars, strings still quivering slightly.

And no sign of whether or not her Magick had worked.

Fortunately she had another means of finding *that* out.

She pointed at the first of the two Strats, and intoned a harsh series of guttural syllables; the spell dated back to the spell that the ancient priests had used to make the statues of their gods speak.

"Who are you?" she demanded hoarsely, as the strings quivered.

The voice of the guitar sounded like one of those novelty records from the late fifties and early sixties, the so-called Talking Guitar—using an early precursor of the synthesizer to combine a vocalist with a guitar track.

"Sehkandar," it snarled sullenly. "What do you want of me, oh woman?"

Trapped in the guitar as it was, it didn't have any eyes to lock with hers, but she felt its anger and hatred in its words, and she used her voice as she had earlier used her gaze as the vehicle of her will.

Shortly and succinctly she explained what she expected of her prisoner. And, as she had anticipated, when the demon heard her plan, it lost some of its surliness. It, too, would share in the power the violence she planned to release would bring—and the more violent the kids' reactions, the more the power. It had its own interests to consider here.

Finally it said the words that bound it to her will. "I will obey," it grated; she smiled, and repeated the procedure with the second Strat, with equal success.

Then she turned to the Gibson—

But before she could intone the ritual question of "who are you," the spirit in the instrument spoke up for itself.

"Oh, wow," it said, in tones of complaint. "Oh, wow. What a *bummer*, man! You didn't have to go through all that jive—"

She stood speechless for a moment, then snapped angrily, "Who *are* you?"

"Moonbeam's the name, and music's the game, and what's a nice chick like you doin' in a place like this? Like, what's your sign?"

"*I'll* ask the questions here," she snarled, feeling the situation slipping out of her control. "What are you doing in that guitar?"

"Like, I was about to ask you the same question. I don' much like this gig that you've got goin', and I don't much like the one you've got planned. This's the Age of Aquarius, lady. Peace an' harmony, make love, not war, you dig?"

Fay felt her head reeling. *What* had she gotten herself into? Or rather, what had she put into that instrument?

But as she glanced down at her watch she realized it was too late to do anything about it now. In another five minutes the regular police patrol would be by, and they might notice the Shelby. It was time to go.

"I don't care what you like," she spat, breaking the spell that permitted the guitars to speak and reaching across the lines of the pentangle to take the Gibson by the neck. She shook it a little to emphasize her point. "I don't care what you want, or what you think. You'll do what I ordered, or you'll find yourself inside that instrument forever!"

She picked up the other two instruments and removed them from the canvas; now that they'd given her their pledge, she was safe from them. As for this "Moonbeam," she didn't know what it *was*, but it wasn't a demon. It should be no threat to her.

She stuffed the stained cloth back into her carryall, and left the guitars in the middle of the practice room. After the mess that the minor demon had left in the rest of the store, the owner would probably just be pleased to find them there, and wouldn't worry about why they were there.

She slipped out the door, and out into the hall, taking her witchlight with her. She only extinguished it when she reached the back door. She took a quick look around before dashing across to her Shelby, unlocking it, and slipping in behind the steering wheel.

So far, so good.

She pulled off a little down the street, then turned and made three gestures and spoke five words. With that bit of Magick, she not only canceled the spell that was holding the alarm systems inactive, she *activated* them.

It wouldn't do for the owner to wonder why the alarm hadn't gone off in the shop.

But as she pulled off onto Admiral at a sedate thirty-five miles per hour, she wondered, with an increasing sense of frustration, what could *possibly* have gone wrong with that third guitar.

TWELVE

The history teacher droned on about the Korean War, a dreary subject that made little or no sense to most of the class, Monica included. Monica chewed a nail in complete frustration, contemplated the back of Deke's head, and wondered why in hell she was wasting her time on anybody that dense.

He spends half his time with me on the phone, she thought, copying down the history teacher's notes in an absentminded sort of way. *He spends tons of time hanging around me at school. He knows I like him. He still doesn't know Alan's after me. So why doesn't he do something?*

It made her want to scream. She hadn't been at all backward about telling him what she thought he should do, either. She'd told him right out just two days ago that she thought he should break up with Fay. This, of course, right after he'd finished complaining about something or other Fay had done to him. It had made an excellent opening.

But, as always, he'd had some excuse. This time it was that he'd promised to be Fay's escort to the spring dance.

"It means a lot to her," he'd said lamely, a glazed look coming into his eyes as soon as she mentioned Fay's name. "I can't just dump her like that. What would it look like? Besides, I still like her a lot."

It would look like you'd finally caught on to the bitch, she thought angrily at the back of Deke's head. *It would look like you'd finally gotten tired of getting walked on. But no—And God, I even showed you how much I trusted you by telling you what Diana's been saying about you and your dad, so you'd know she probably* wasn't *after your old man. And you still keep acting like all I'm good for is to be your crying towel.*

This whole school was getting to be a royal pain. The kids were mostly pretty stuck on themselves and all their money, and not even Alan had managed to get up enough guts to ask her out. About the only good thing she had going was Diana T's interest in her writing.

And on top of it all, there were those two—attacks. She still hadn't told anyone about them but Alan. *He* believed her; but he was still suspicious of Diana.

The things themselves, thank God, hadn't come back again. Diana had finally told her that she didn't think *they* would, but that it wasn't likely that whoever it was that had gone after her was going to give up. This, of course, had been wonderful news. And Alan had insisted that *this* meant that Diana was planning something awful.

Monica was getting pretty tired of Oklahoma, all things considered.

I miss the mountains, she realized. *I didn't think I would, but I do. And I miss having places to go, things to do. The only things to do around here are—well—go to the mall, go to parties, except I never get invited to them, or go to movies at the mall.*

She sighed and rested her chin on her hand. It was going to be a very long day.

It got longer as soon as the class let out. Harper was waiting for Deke, standing right opposite the door, wearing a *hot* outfit that Monica would have died to have, every hair perfect, with a sickeningly sweet smile on her face.

I think I hate her, Monica thought grimly, watching her greet Deke as enthusiastically as if he had been away from her for a year. And watching Deke return the favor, just as if he hadn't spent the ten minutes before class complaining about her. *Scratch that, I know I hate her.*

Deke strolled off arm-in-arm with the bitch, completely oblivious to Monica's presence. Grimly she reversed her course and took the long way back to her locker—then, because she had lost so much time, she had to run for her next class, sliding into her seat behind Carri Duval just seconds before the bell rang.

It was algebra, which she hated, because she was only getting a B in it, and she must not have been concentrating because half her homework was wrong. Fortunately this wasn't a graded assignment, but it was humiliating all the same. Even George Louvis's grimace of sympathy when she botched her problem on the board didn't help.

The bell rang for class change; next, thank God, was English. Maybe she could get Deke to notice her there.

Then again, maybe not. *Maybe I ought to see if Mom was really serious about moving back to Colorado, like she said over breakfast. I know she's getting tired of all the overtime. And this shit is getting old.*

Then, just when it seemed as if everything was conspiring to go wrong today, things started to go right.

Sandy's locker was right around the corner from hers, and the acoustics in the hall were such that she could usually hear everything he and his buddies said. Nine times out of ten, this was basically pretty boring and not worth straining her ears over, since Sandy never had anything more on his mind than his next beer or his next lay.

This time, however, his "next lay" proved to be pretty interesting.

She almost dropped her books when she heard Fay's voice coming from around the corner.

The girl's voice was pitched too low for her to be able to pick out exactly what she was saying, but Sandy's reply was clear enough. "Shit, babe, I can't, not tonight. My grandma's coming in for Julie's recital, and we've all gotta go pick her up at the airport. You know, the whole 'Brady Bunch' thing. *Then* we all get to go out for ice cream together. Then Grandma is gonna tell us all about her latest operation, or her trip to Las Vegas, I forget which."

"Sounds like a thrill a minute," Fay drawled. "I think you're just trying to avoid seeing me."

"Give me a break, will you? Grandma's the one with the money in the family, and she's a Reagan-mom-and-apple-pie-nuclear-family pusher. She's *still* not sure she approves of Mom. I'm tellin' you, we have to do this perfect-family shit every time she comes, otherwise she'll leave all the cash to the Salvation Army Girls' Home. If I try an' sneak out on any of it, I'll catch hell. They might even ground me."

"Well, I guess it's okay," Fay said sullenly, while Monica tried simultaneously to look busy and *not* to make any noise. "But baby, I *want* you. I want you *now.*"

Sandy snorted. "What about Deke? You're *supposed* to be going with him, aren't you?"

"He's a kid." There was silence for a moment, and Monica's imagination ran riot. "You're a man."

Sandy cleared his throat; it sounded like he was having a hard time doing so. "Listen," he said thickly. "My car's in the shop, and they let me take the van today. You want to, like, meet me in the parking lot at noon?"

"Van?" Fay replied doubtfully. "I don't know. . . ."

"It's an RV. It's Dad's Boomer Sooner wagon; he takes it to all the UO games. It's like a little living room, you know? Stereo, TV, wet bar, carpeting, miniblinds . . . and the couch at the back folds down."

"Oh," Fay breathed. "Does it?"

"Yeah. Think that'll do?" Sandy sounded very cocky; Monica had the feeling that he might have engineered this little coincidence, especially if he knew that he was going to have to do this Grandma gig but didn't want to miss a shot at Fay. It was true that Sandy never thought much beyond his next beer or his next roll in the sack, but from what she'd seen, he could be very persistent in making sure he *got* them.

"Oh yes," Fay replied, her voice so sugary that Monica wanted to throw up. "That will do. See you at noon?"

"At the parking lot door."

Monica closed her locker and hurried off toward her English class. If Fay knew she'd been overheard—it wouldn't be pretty, and Monica would most likely end up getting the short end. Somehow it always seemed that no matter who was in the right, when Fay tangled with anyone, the principal always backed Fay Harper.

Now how am I going to get Deke out there to catch them? She wracked her brains for an answer all the way to class. *I've got no reason to ask him to meet me out there. He's got no reason to be out there.*

She beat the bell by less than a second; fortunately Diana was inclined to be generous about things like that. She scooted into her seat with an awkward little nod; Diana replied to her half-apology with a shrug and a grin. Then she brought the class down to business. And ironically enough, it was Deke himself who gave Monica the answer she needed.

They were into character development; Diana had told them all that there was no point in trying to re-create "reality" for their main characters.

"First of all, writing exactly what you know will be boring for all of you; second, when have any of you *ever* seen a best seller about a kid from Oklahoma who does all his homework, never gets into much trouble, and basically minds his own business?" The class had laughed, and Diana had spread her hands. "See what I mean? So let your imagination go; so what if whatever you produce isn't what I'd call salable? You'll have fun, and maybe, just maybe, with more experience under your belt and a good editor, someday it *might* be salable."

So Deke's viewpoint character was turning into a race car driver; exactly what *kind* of driver, Monica wasn't sure—his prose was full of things like "group B," "cracked transaxles," and "oversteer." In fact, today's pages were so jargon-intensive that it was pretty clear he was writing for himself and no one else.

That didn't matter. What *did* matter was that he knew about cars. And Monica had been talking to Carri about buying *her* old

VW Cabri, but she really wanted somebody who knew about cars to look at it first.

And Carri's car was out in the parking lot just a couple of rows away from Sandy's van. . . .

When discussion time came, they broke up into groups of three and four to dissect each other's pages. Monica waited until the other two kids had given Deke a hard time for sounding like a columnist for *Car and Driver* ("only without the humor," said Mark). Then she put in *her* oar when he turned to her for help.

"Well, it *was* a little too much," she said as gently as she could. "I mean, like, we're not *all* lifetime subscribers to *Auto Week*, you know? Half of what you had in there sounded like rocket-scientist stuff. The other half sounded like Swahili."

His face fell. "I thought I was just making it sound like it was real."

Mark Shepherd snorted. "You know what *I* think race drivers talk about when they sit around? Taxes. And broads. And maybe airline food. Not 'transaxle overcooked megafarts,' or whatever the hell you had in there."

"But I had no idea you knew so much about cars, Deke," Monica said, grabbing her opening with both hands. "Do you suppose you could do me a favor?"

"Yeah, I guess," Deke said, looking a little uneasy. "Depends on what the favor is."

She leaned over her desk so she could look right into his eyes— and tried to look helpless, not sexy. "I need a car. It's a real drag having to ask my mom to drive me all over—and besides, she's putting in a lot of overtime and she can't always. Carri says she'll sell me her Cabri for four grand, and Mom says that sounds okay to her, and Dad says he'll go half if Mom goes half, and they *both* say it sounds like a good birthday present, but I don't know if the car's any good. Could you like, you know, look at it at lunch?"

"How about right after class?" Deke said promptly, perking right up. "I know what the car looks like; I could meet you over there. Do you know where it's parked?"

"Carri said it's about a row down from a big RV at the edge of the lot." Monica smiled sweetly at him, unable to believe how easy this had been. "I can find Carri in the cafeteria and get her to come on out so you can start it and whatever. If that's okay."

"Sure," Deke said cheerfully.

"If you two are *quite* finished—there's a little matter of our assignment," Mark said, giving them both *looks*.

Deke blushed, and Monica gave Mark the evil eye before returning to more mundane matters.

To lend authenticity to her ploy, Monica intercepted Carri in the hall on the way to her locker. Rather than going out, once she heard what Monica wanted, Carri just turned the keys over to her. "Bring 'em back after lunch, and don't take it out of the lot," Carri told her. "Otherwise I could get in trouble, 'cause we're not supposed to leave the campus and it's my car. Okay?"

"No problem," Monica said. "This shouldn't take long."

She *thought* she managed to keep most of the glee out of her voice, but Carri gave her kind of a funny look before she handed her the keys.

Monica waited what she thought might be a reasonable length of time for her to have taken to look for Carri, then waited five minutes longer than that before heading out to the lot.

Her timing was impeccable. The fight was already in full flower when she pushed the door open. As she squinted against the dust, she saw Sandy slam the door of the van and make tracks back toward the building; then she saw Deke's back. He was gesturing wildly. She heard Fay long before she saw her; her shrill voice cut across the rising wind.

That wind made it hard to get the door open; she had to really fight the door, and even then only got it open enough to squeeze through.

Do I go over there? she debated. *Yeah, I said I'd meet Deke; I'm not supposed to know about the thing with Sandy and Fay. But I'd better just look curious.*

"You were *spying* on me, you little geek!" Fay shrieked, as Monica made her way slowly between the rows of parked cars.

After a moment of thought, Monica decided, given the look of rage on Fay's face, that she'd better not head directly for Deke. Instead, she loitered out of Fay's line of sight, pretending great interest in a brand-new Miata.

"I was not!" Deke spat back. "I have more right to be out here than you do! I was coming out here to look at a car, not to climb into a rolling bedroom and screw my brains out with some oversexed jock!"

Monica leaned down and peered into the car's interior.

Fay's expression darkened. "Since when do you tell me what to do, Kestrel?"

"Since we're supposed to be *going* together, Harper! How long have you been doing this, anyway? Ever since I gave you my ring?" Deke sounded sick and disgusted. "Boy, I must look like a real jerk. I'll bet the whole school knows about what's going on. Who *else* have you been messing around with? Bob? Jim Glisson? The entire goddamn athletic department?"

The wind was rising more by the minute; it whipped Monica's hair around and blew dust into her face so hard that it stung. She shielded her eyes with her hand and stayed right where she was. This was too good to miss.

"What's it to you?" Harper sneered. "You don't own me!"

"Well, you've been fuckin' well acting like you own *me*! And I got news for you, babe, I like to know where something's been before I mess with it! Seems to me the only place you *haven't* been is peddling your ass down on Denver!" Monica took a quick glance at Deke. He was white; his eyes were wide and the whites showed all around the irises. His hands were clenched into fists but held rigidly down at his sides, as if he might be afraid that he would hit her if she took one step closer.

Fay spluttered for a moment, unable to get a single coherent word out. Then she ripped Deke's ring off her finger and held it up. "Listen, asshole, I don't have to put up with this! I can give this thing back to you anytime I want—and have somebody else's ring on this finger in thirty seconds flat!"

Deke drew himself up to his full height and looked down his nose at her. The wind was howling now, making it hard to hear what his reply was. Monica moved closer; to hell with the risk if Harper saw her and put two and two together. She didn't want to miss this. As it was, she missed the first couple of words, though the rest was plain enough. "—I'm not sure I want it back—unless you get it disinfected first."

Fay snarled like an enraged beast—and threw the ring in his face. Deke ducked, and simultaneously his right hand shot up.

And somehow he *caught* the thing.

Fay stared at him, then at his hand.

"You're not even a whore, Harper," he said. "You have to give it away, 'cause nobody'd pay for what you spread around. It's too easy to get. It's a damn good thing you're a rich bitch, 'cause you sure couldn't make a living—"

Her hand shot out; there was a *crack* like a rifle shot as her palm connected with his face.

His right hand was already in a fist clenching the ring. He started to draw back to deck her—and then their eyes locked.

Deke froze.

And Monica felt—*something*—poised to strike him. She couldn't see it, she couldn't hear it, but she knew it was there all the same. And she knew that Fay Harper had something to do with it.

"No!" she cried, a tiny sound, lost in the howl of the wind; but she reached out her hand as if to protect Deke, and—

Some force stretched between them; some force reached between her and him, and interposed itself like an invisible barrier between him and Fay Harper. Like the thing poised to strike Deke, she couldn't see it, but she could feel it. And she remembered some of what Diana had told her about how magic worked for the people with the Talent for it if they just believed hard enough. She *believed* with all her strength.

Fay's head snapped around; her angry gaze swept the lot and came to rest on Monica. Monica stepped back an involuntary pace or two before the red, unthinking rage in those eyes. Fay Harper didn't even look human at this moment.

She held up her hand to ward—whatever—off. The menace had transferred itself from Deke to *her*.

Oh, shit. Now *what have I done?*

The wind hit her like a middle-linebacker; she staggered and braced herself against it. There was some force besides the wind trying to get at her, the same one that had been targeted for Deke. She felt that instinctively; the only thing she could think of to do was to stand and refuse to give way to it. . . .

She heard what sounded like a frustrated growl, only it was all inside her head.

Then the wind whirled around her in a vortex, some kind of magnified dust devil, and pulled at the notebook she was clutching at a velocity of about fifty miles per hour. Her fingers slipped and the cover tore; the loose pages of her writing assignment flew out, and the wind grabbed them and sent them halfway to Kansas before she could even blink.

She made an ineffectual grab after them, then turned to face Fay Harper with suppressed fury in her own eyes.

You did that, you bitch! I don't know how, but you did that!

But Fay's own expression was not one of triumph, but of thwarted anger. She stared at Monica for one moment more; then, as the wind shoved at Monica so hard she had to brace herself against the car next to her just to stay on her feet, Fay whirled and flounced off to her Shelby-Z.

She yanked the door open, flung herself inside, and slammed it shut. And in direct defiance of school rules, pulled out of the parking slot and onto the street in a cloud of burning rubber from the front tires. She gunned the engine and tore out of the lot, leaving a long streak of black rubber on the pavement and another at the entrance to the school. In seconds she was out of sight, leaving Monica and Deke staring at each other; Deke accusingly, Monica with a feeling of shock.

Deke was the first to move; he strode up to her and grabbed her by the elbow. "Inside," he shouted above the wind. "I want to talk to you."

As soon as they got inside the foyer door, he wrenched her around to face him. She didn't recognize him. His face was contorted with anger, his eyes glazed. She'd never seen him look like this, not even when Bobby-Boy had been at him. He did not look like the Deke she knew.

"You set this up," he snarled. "You set this whole thing up. You *knew* she was going to be out there with Sandy. You *knew* what was going to happen when I found them. Didn't you?"

Monica looked down at her feet, feeling a combination of guilt and anger. Since she *had* set Deke up, she could hardly deny his accusation with any real feeling. But she *hadn't* tricked Sandy and Fay into sneaking out there!

"You little bitch," Deke spat, the strange light outside making his eyes look as if they were glowing red. "You jealous little bitch! I thought you were my friend! I thought I could talk to you! I thought I could *trust* you!"

"I am!" she cried, stung. "You can! I—"

"I can't believe a single word you say," he interrupted, voice dripping with disgust. "You're just like every other girl; you can't just be a friend, you've got to have everything your way, you've got to have some kind of collar on me, like your little puppy. You've just been making up all these fairy tales about what a good friend you are. Just like you made up all that stupid shit about how you want to be a writer and what Ms. Tregarde's been telling you; you just did it so I'd pay more attention to you, so that I'd think you were better than Fay or something! I *knew* you were just making that shit up, but I thought, okay, she wants to be a writer, she just daydreams a lot. But I guess you wouldn't know the truth if it walked up and hit you one! Probably *everything* you've ever told me is a lie!"

She clutched her hand at her throat; that *hurt*. It had taken a lot of soul-searching and guts to tell him those secrets. The only reason she'd told *him* was because he'd been agonizing over finding out that Diana and his dad had been spending hours together in Diana's room with the door locked. And she just wanted

to give him the real reason for them spending all that time together. Not that they were having an affair—that they were working, helping her. She *couldn't* tell him what they were really
doing, but she did let him think they were critiquing Monica's
own book. . . .

She had been thinking all this time that he believed her. After
all, *Alan* did, even about the magic attacks on *her* and that there
was somebody after her, which was a helluva lot harder to believe!

But Deke didn't. He'd been stringing her along.

She tried to think of something to say, and couldn't. She tried
to think of some scathing put-down and failed. And anger at his
treachery just built up to where she couldn't stand it any longer.

So she pulled back her hand and belted him a good one. No stupid little slap, either; a solid blow to the chin that rocked him back,
forced him to windmill his arms to keep from falling down, and
made his eyes water.

Before he could even *start* to recover, she wrenched the door
open against the wind and stalked back out; back straight, eyes
stinging, throat tight.

If that bitch Harper can leave in the middle of the day, so can I,
dammit!

She didn't hear running footsteps behind her; she just sensed
someone back there, someone too small to be Deke. She kept right
on going, at a fast, stiff-legged walk.

"Monica," Ann Greeley shouted above the wind. "Monica, wait!"

She stopped right at the edge of the parking lot and turned reluctantly.

"What?" she asked, pouting, *knowing* she was pouting, and unable to keep herself from pouting. *I can't talk to anybody right now.*
I just can't.

"Monica, where do you think you're going?" Ann asked reasonably, catching her by the elbow and keeping her from going anywhere, at least temporarily.

She'd had just about enough of being grabbed for one day.
"Home," Monica said tightly. "I'm going home. I don't feel good."

Belatedly she remembered Carri's keys, still in her hand. They'd bruised her palm when she'd hit Deke. . . .

"You can't do that," Ann pointed out; it was hard to sound gentle when you were shouting over a windstorm, but somehow Ann managed. "You can't leave during the day. You have to get a nurse's excuse, and then your mother has to—"

"My mom's working," Monica interrupted. "And I don't feel good. Harper left—"

"She did?" Ann said, wrinkling her brow in puzzlement. "Are you sure?"

That was too much. "You don't believe me!" Monica cried, bursting into hot tears of anger. "*Nobody* in this whole school believes me! You believe *Harper* when she tells you *anything*, but not me! It doesn't matter what I say, I could have the Pope backing me up and you'd all still say I was lying!"

Ann stared at her with the wind blowing her hair into her eyes and practically ripping her clothing right off her body. She let go of Monica's arm and grabbed her skirt in a futile attempt to keep it under control as it blew up toward her waist; Monica didn't even bother.

"Here," Monica wept, grabbing Ann's wrist and shoving the keys into Ann's limp hand. "You probably won't believe *this* either, but Carri Duval loaned me her keys so I could look at her car. Ask her yourself. Of course, you *probably* think I stole them. I don't care *what* you all think anymore, and I don't care what you do to me. You can all go to hell! I feel awful, and I'm going *home!*"

She threw the tattered remains of her notebook at Ann's feet, and turned on her heel, leaving Ann staring after her with her mouth hanging open in dumbfounded amazement at her outburst.

I don't care, she told herself, hugging her arms to her chest to keep the tears inside. It didn't work very well. Angry tears kept escaping anyway, burning their way down her cheeks. *They're all a bunch of phonies and posers. They all hate me, and I don't care what they think.*

She walked fast, as fast as she could, trying to outdistance her troubles.

She kept her head down, as much to keep the dust out of her eyes as to keep anyone that might be passing by from seeing that she was crying. It occurred to her, in some isolated corner of her mind, that she hadn't really believed in those Oklahoma dust-bowl stories before. Now she had to. It was as dark as twilight out here; she had to lean at a forty-five-degree angle to keep the wind from blowing her over, and the sun was little more than a vague disk in the sky, about as bright as the full moon on a cloudless night. The sky itself was a dirty yellow-brown, about the same color as a cardboard box.

I hope I can make it home—

She was getting tired quickly; finally she had to shelter for a moment in the lee of somebody's house. Her anger and her unhappiness were long since put into the back of her mind. As bad as the weather had turned, they'd probably send everybody home right after lunch. So she not only wouldn't be missed, unless Ann snitched on her—which she probably wouldn't—she wouldn't even get into trouble.

Of course, she thought, tightening her lips with anger, that meant that neither would Harper.

Her legs burned with fatigue, and she wasn't at all surprised to see that her clothes were getting to be the same dirty brown color as the sky.

I'm gonna have to wash these about twenty times just to get all the dust out, she thought unhappily. She was afraid she was going to cry some more, so she concentrated on her anger instead. And how everything, *everything,* was Harper's fault. *I'm gonna have to reprint everything in my notebook. I'm gonna have to somehow remember everything everybody said about the story and fix it. Goddammit. It's not fair! Harper's the one that's been cheating on Deke; she's the one that started all this shit in the first place. She drove off and she'll have her aunt phone in some phony excuse for her, she got to drive home and I have to walk through this shitty storm, I'm gonna be filthy, and she probably won't even have dust in her hair.*

She sounded bitchy, even to herself, and she didn't care. After a rest, she steeled herself and walked back out into the wind. If anything, it was worse than ever. She saw cars being rocked by it as she stumbled past them, and massive limbs were creaking and thrashing and snapping off every tree in sight. She finally decided to move into the center of the street; it was safer.

And on top of everything else, she couldn't help but remember, *Harper can basically get anybody she wants as her date for the spring dance tomorrow night. She wasn't lying about that. And I still don't have a date. Alan's too damn lame to ask me, and Deke's a bastard. Damn it, it's not fair!*

Ahead of her, a phone line snapped and went down, lashing the ground like a whip. She sidestepped the whole area gingerly.

I hate this school, I hate this town, I hate this state!

She made a kind of chant out of all the things she hated, using it to give herself the impetus to get through the storm, to cut through the wind.

I hate the kids, I hate this weather. . . .

Three more blocks to go, and another line snapped, practically on top of her. *This* one was a power line, and it came down in a shower of sparks, missing her by a few feet at most.

She screamed and jumped out of the way, her heart pounding with fear.

Then, from somewhere, found the unexpected strength to start running.

She only slowed when the wall around the complex was in sight. When she reached the guard shack at the entrance to the apartment complex, she was halfway afraid the power would be off. It wasn't, but the guard at the gate cautioned her against using anything that might have problems if there was a surge, like a computer or a VCR. "I'd stick to the radio and electric lights, if I was you, miss," the guard said. "And keep some candles and matches handy. Weatherman says this isn't going to let up until about midnight."

"Midnight?" She swallowed. "Does this happen a lot?"

Because if it does, she thought with a kind of forlorn hope, *Mom isn't gonna want to stay in this state much longer. Tornadoes are bad enough; she's gonna have a fit about this.*

"About once every five or six years," the guard replied, squinting against the dust. "One of those oddball things the weather does in the springtime."

Not often enough for Mom to get mad about it. Damn. She nodded, and forced her tired legs to get her as far as her own door and into it before she collapsed on the couch in the living room. Her brother popped out of the kitchen, his mouth (as usual) full.

"We lost power at school, and a buncha windows got broken by stuff, so they sent us home," he informed her. "Mom called and said they're expecting to lose the lines over there any minute, so she might get off early, too. And she said if you wanted something hot for supper, you'd better either cook it now or we're probably gonna have to do hot dogs in the fireplace. Okay?"

"Okay," Monica replied wearily. She tried to think if the hot water heater was gas or electric. The one in Colorado had been electric. . . .

"Is the hot water gas, or what?" she called out.

"Gas," her brother replied promptly.

Good, that means I don't have to hurry up and get a shower.

She let herself sink into the couch cushions; every muscle in her body was twitching with exhaustion, even the little muscles in her hands and feet. Every time she moved, she could feel the gritty dust that had somehow gotten inside her clothes. It was pretty gross. And in about a minute more she'd go get that shower. In a minute. When she wasn't so tired . . .

I wish this was tomorrow. If it was tomorrow, they'd cancel the dance until next week. Then I'd have a whole week to get a date. Even if I had to ask Alan to go myself!

She clenched her jaw angrily. *Dammit, I'll show them all! I'll go without a date! They can all go to hell, I don't need them, I don't need anybody—*

The phone rang. Figuring it was her mother, Monica stretched out a weary hand to the extension on the end table, and caught it before the answering machine got it.

"Carlin residence," she said automatically, continuing with her standard anti-burglar response, "Monica Carlin. Mom's in the shower right now, can I take a message?"

But the voice on the other end was young and male—and familiar. "Monica? Uh—this is Alan."

A quick glance at the clock showed it was only one-thirty. *They did let everybody out,* was her first thought after a moment of blankness. *Alan? What does he want?* was the second.

She sat up and bit back an exclamation of pain as several muscles in her back and neck protested the sudden movement.

"Monica? Are you okay?"

"Yeah. Uh—hi, Alan. Yeah, I'm fine, I just had to walk home. Gee, I was just thinking of you."

"You were?" His voice rose in surprise. "Monica, I know it's kind of late, but—I'd like to ask you something."

"You would?" *If there's a God . . . oh, please.* Please *let him ask about the dance, please, please. . . .*

"Yeah. Uh—do you think—I mean, you don't—uh—could you possibly be free for the dance tomorrow night?"

There is a God. Suddenly the world was a wonderful place.

"Gee, Alan," she said flirtatiously. "I don't know. I'd *love* to go with you, but I don't know what the kids at Jenks wear for these things, and I don't know if I've got anything really hot, you know?" She lowered her voice coyly. "I wouldn't want you to be ashamed to be with me."

As he stammered something about being proud to be with her even if she was wearing a garbage sack, she thought about Deke. And what his face would look like when he saw her there with Alan.

Revenge was sweet. There *was* a God.

"How in hell did I let you rope me into this?" Di muttered at Ann Greeley in the sanctuary of the cramped, two-stall ladies' room in the teachers' lounge. She scowled at her reflection; it scowled back. Her agent Morrie might have recognized her in her current getup from all the writers' teas and publishers' cocktail parties he'd

Mercedes Lackey

dragged her to, but none of her friends would. The normally straight brown mane of her hair had been twisted into a fashionable creation reminiscent of an Art Nouveau print. Her dress continued the theme; flowing cream-colored silk and heavy lace insets at the throat and shoulders, in a Pre-Raphaelite style that made her appear fragile and seductive at the same time.

"I look like one of my damn heroines," she complained to the mirror. "*How* did I let you rope me into this? I hate chaperoning!"

"But the kids think you're fabulous." Ann chuckled. "Did you hear what Alan said to those friends of his?"

"What, the band kids?" Di turned away from the mirror and leaned against the sink. "By the way, they look pretty pro. I was impressed. No, I didn't hear what he told them. What was it?"

"'See, I *told* you she looked just like Stevie Nicks.'"

"Christ on a crutch," Di groaned, covering her eyes with her hand. "Oh, that's *just* what I need, a room full of adolescent males with the hots for me because I look like Stevie Nicks. Terrific. Ann, I am *not* the type to enjoy the role of Mrs. Robinson!"

"Which is why you'll make a good chaperone," Ann had the chutzpah to point out. "You're as hip as any of these kids, but you never forget you're twenty years their senior—"

"Thanks for reminding me," Di muttered. "I really needed that. Should I have brought my knitting?"

"They figure you understand them; they respect you. They'll listen to you."

"You think." Ann started to remonstrate; Di held up her hand. "All right, I'm here, aren't I? Just remember what I told you. I don't break up clinches, I don't arbitrate in lovers' quarrels, and I don't keep kids from smoking in the john. And I don't care whether or not what they're smoking is legal. Unless it's heavier shit than grass. What I *will* do is break up fights, keep kids from *driving* out of here if they're drunk or stoned, try and put the fear of God into anybody doing heavier drugs than grass, and keep anybody from raping or getting raped. And that, my dear, is the extent of my involvement."

"You have a far more realistic view of our student body than most of their parents do," Ann said dryly. "Or the teachers, for that matter."

"I can afford to," Di replied just as dryly. "They aren't my kids. I don't live here. I'm not dependent on their parents' goodwill for my salary and continued employment. I can be just as blunt as I want to, and just as realistic as the situation calls for."

"You also must be a lot tougher than you look, if you're planning on restraining high-flying adolescent males." Ann gave her an interesting look; not at all doubtful, just speculative.

"Karate. Second *dan* black belt," Di said modestly. "I'd be higher, except for two things. I don't compete, and my *sensei* teaches cross-discipline stuff so we'll know how to handle martial artists from other schools. So we don't exactly have what you'd call perfect forms, and you have to have perfect forms to compete."

Ann laughed a little. "You're going to play Bruce Lee in that dress?"

"That's the reason why it's so full. And silk has another advantage; it doesn't tear easily." Di eyeballed the paper towel dispenser, and spun into a *kata*, with the dispenser as a target. Front kick, side kick, back kick, and finishing with a second side kick; hitting the dispenser very lightly, the kind of pulled blows that showed truer skill than full-contact karate. She wasn't even breathing heavily, and she'd only lost one hairpin. "My jeans are all karate cut, with the extra gusset in the inseam. Last but not least, you'll notice I always wear flats." She grinned.

Ann nodded. "You'll do, my dear. You'll do. If you ever want a teaching job—"

"Bite your tongue!" Di laughed. "I'm not that tough. You couldn't pay me enough."

"That's what I say every spring—and every fall I'm right back here." Ann said over her shoulder as they left the teachers' lounge, "You take the punch bowl; see if you can keep the little psychotic darlings from spiking it, will you? I'll take the stage corner and try and keep them out of the curtains."

Di sighed, smiled sweetly at one of her erstwhile pupils who seemed to have been struck dumb by the sight of her in a dress, and tried to keep a weather eye out for Monica. Fortunately the canned music wasn't bad. She hoped the band played half as good as they looked.

But Monica, and the threatening ruin of her reputation among the teachers, was foremost in her mind. *If I can just talk to her alone for a little, maybe I can repair some of the damage she did to herself. She's just damn lucky the principal sent everybody home halfway through lunch period because of the storm, or she'd be in even deeper kimchee than she is now. As it is, nobody knows she left the campus; they're assuming she stayed until everyone was turned loose.*

Teachers are well known to have detection systems that rival Stealth bombers and spy satellites. Within five minutes of the moment Monica had stormed off in her cream-colored huff, half the teachers in Jenks had heard some version of the blowup. By the time school was canceled, it was the talk of the faculty lounge.

The way the current (and most popular) version had it, Monica was a first-class troublemaker. According to *that* version, Fay and Sandy were set up by Monica; Deke caught them together and came to some unwarranted conclusions—thanks to Monica making a lot of little innuendos beforehand.

But Di had heard part of the story from Deke himself—and the version of intercourse Sandy and Fay had been about to engage in when he caught them *wasn't* "talking." Yes, Monica had all but pushed him at the van during the critical time period—but she hadn't set the pair up. They'd arranged their little tête-à-tête all on their own.

And everyone seemed to have forgotten that.

Yeah, well, Fay is teacher's pet for everybody except Ann and me; Ann just basically could care less about the little bitch because she never even tries in class, and I haven't done more then see her at a distance since I got here. Di leaned back against a column, trying to ignore the half-dozen moonstruck adolescent males who were lurking in her vicinity. *Jesus Cluny Frog, guys—where the hell were you back when* I *was in high school? Back when* I needed *you?* Three of the six weren't at all bad looking, if a trifle nerdy.

They were all on edge, though, and it wasn't just because of the dance. But before she could figure it out, she saw someone else standing a little apart from the crowd.

There was a seventh kid who wasn't giving her puppy-dog eyes; he was just watching her. She couldn't help but notice him; he had an aura of vitality that practically glowed in the dark. He was something really special—not classically handsome, not even close, but so cutting-edge he'd stand out in New York, with wicked good humor gleaming out of those big green eyes.

You're going to be a real lady-killer, my lad, she thought with amusement. *And it won't be long, either. These provincial posers don't appreciate you. Just you wait until you get out in the world—*

He lifted an eyebrow at her—then headed straight for her.

Lady Bright. He can't possibly have the audacity—

He did.

"Care to trip the night fantastic, my lady of the camellias?" he asked, offering his arm. "You'd make Alphonse Mucha swoon with rapture."

"I'm a chaperone," she said sharply.

"Does this mean your legs are broken?" he retorted. "Come on, you're dying to dance, I can tell. And it's too early for anybody to get the guts to dump anything in the punch bowl. That won't happen until the lights are down for one of the couples' dances."

She looked at him; at the mostly empty dance floor; at the wistful expression his broad grin wasn't quite hiding.

"Oh, come on," he whispered. "Half the guys here want to dance with you, but they're too chicken to ask. You'll do wonders for my rep."

That did it. *What the hell. There's no law about the chaperone not having a little fun.*

She allowed him to sweep her out into the middle of the floor, where she proceeded to do both her t'ai chi instructor *and* all her professional-dancer friends proud.

And the boy wasn't half bad himself.

They cleared the floor, drawing impromptu applause from the kids that gathered on the edge.

"I feel like I'm in a music video," she laughed, after the third song. "Enough, I'm out of breath, and I've got to get back to my job"—she leaned close so she could whisper—"and I don't think there's too many girls who'd turn you down tonight, not after *this* little exhibition."

The wicked sparkle in his eyes told her that she'd hit the mark, but he escorted her demurely enough back to her station.

The kid—whatever his name was—was the only light spot in the evening, though. Yesterday's windstorm had died down some, but it wasn't over. The sky was the color of a grocery sack all day; Di had decided that it wasn't quite so hard to believe the old dust-bowl stories of the sky being black at high noon. She was just glad that her silk dress was washable, and that she'd changed here instead of back at Larry's.

And that she'd brought a can of antistatic spray. There was an incredible amount of static electricity in the air. She was wearing rubber-soled flats and had liberally sprayed her dress, but nearly everyone else was getting shocks when they accidentally touched something metallic. The kids were nervy and restless; even the adults were on edge. Di had seen just this kind of nervous tension in California once, when she'd been around Orange County while the Santa Ana was blowing. The experts claimed that the hysteria generated by the Santa Ana was caused by the static and the positively charged ions caused by the constant high wind. Whatever the reason, it set everyone jumping like cats in a dog pound.

And there was a sense of something stirring, ever so slightly, elsewhere. *She doesn't like it either,* Di thought suddenly. *She's still sleeping—but this wind is disturbing the surface of Her dreams. Whatever She is. Definitely female, but nothing I've ever crossed before.*

Ever since Di had communed with the edges of the dreams of the One Below, she'd been vaguely aware of what She was sensing.

Di hadn't wanted to get too close; it would be only too easy to get pulled into those dreams, and damn hard to get out again.

She *was* the reason for the psychically null area here. She tended to influence psis; either She made them uncomfortable and they moved as soon as they possibly could—

—or they get sucked in and never come out again. Wonder why nobody's ever noticed that an unusually high number of catatonics come out of the Old Tulsa area?

Di shook her head; she tried *not* to think about the One Below too much. Just thinking about Her brought you in closer contact. The dreams of the One Below were *not* the kind of thing Di preferred to have loose inside her skull.

This storm, though—it had nothing to do with Her. The legends were right; *nobody* wanted Her to wake up. She was dangerous and touchy, and Di hoped profoundly that this anomalous weather didn't disturb Her even a little.

It would take an awfully long time to brew five thousand gallons of coffee. I don't think She'd wait.

At that point there was a *squawk* from one of the stage amps the band was setting up, and Di jumped, then grinned sheepishly at some of the kids nearest her, who'd reacted the same way.

"Static," said one kid. "Gremlins," said another. There was a nervous giggle—

The amp squawked again; one of the mikes was on and did a feedback squeal that set Di's teeth on edge.

"Shit—" said the kid on stage, the one Alan had introduced as the bass player, unaware that the mike was live. There was a nervous laugh at that and the rest of the chaperones glared; the kid blushed the most spectacular shade of firecracker red Di'd ever seen in her life.

"Uh—sorry—" the kid mumbled into the mike; it began to squeal and he turned it off before it could pierce their eardrums.

Some things never change, Di thought, looking around at the decorated auditorium. *The only difference between what we've got here and* my *high school dances is the cost of the trimmings.*

The theme of the dance—there was evidently a law somewhere that high school dances had to have a theme—was "Spring Fling."

I hated themed dances when I was a kid, and that hasn't changed, thank you.

Someone in his or her infinite wisdom had decided that "Spring Fling" meant some sort of bizarre connection to medieval Scottish May Day celebrations. There was an abundance of tartan, all inappropriate and in ghastly colors, and an overabundance of inappropriate paper flowers and garlands. And the Major Decoration *(where is it written that "there shalt be a papier-mâché Monument?")* was a Maypole. Complete with crown and streamers.

Dear gods, does anybody here really know what a Maypole means?

No. Not possible. Unless . . . there's a couple of teachers here that are the right age to have been flower children. Including Miz Greeley over there—

She caught Ann's eye and nodded toward the—ahem—erection. And raised an ironic eyebrow. Ann started to grin and covered the grin quickly with her hand.

But the shaking of her shoulders told Di everything she needed to know. Ann Greeley, at least, knew *exactly* what Maypoles meant, and found it hilariously funny.

I wonder if it could have been her idea in the first place?

But at that moment, Fay Harper, the Spring Queen, made her appearance on stage surrounded by her court.

And suddenly nothing was quite so funny anymore.

THIRTEEN

T here's something very strange going on up there, Di thought, staring at the crowded stage. *Somebody up on that stage is doing a shield that's as good as Deke's. And I can't tell who. Or, most importantly, why.*

And it was impossible to tell *where* that shield originated. The four members of the Persuaders were already up there, plus the assistant principal, the Queen and King, the escorts for the six Princesses, and the Princesses themselves.

Like trying to pick out one goldfish in a tankful.

The stage wasn't exactly crowded, even with twenty people standing on it; as with everything else, Jenks had superior facilities for their would-be thespians. Although no amount of bunting and tissue-flower garlands was going to conceal the fact that this was the cafeteria by day, and Di was just as glad she wasn't on the cleanup committee; this place was going to be hard to get in shape after the dance was over. In Di's time dances were held in the school gym— but apparently the pristine condition of the precious hardwood basketball court took precedence over convenience of cleanup.

According to Ann, that Fay would be Spring Queen was as predictable as the coming of spring itself; there was no surprise there. But standing on the right as her escort—though *not* as the Spring King—was Deke.

Now that *was* a surprise. As late as just before dinner, Deke had

been swearing that Fay was a bitch and he'd rather die than take
her to the dance.

*So something changed his mind in the last two hours. I wonder
what?*

He didn't look too happy up there, though. He was hunched up
a little, face sullen, and he oozed Bad Attitude. The latter was
hardly surprising, since at Fay's other hand was the Spring King,
Sandy, who was doing an Attitude number right back at Deke. On
the other hand, this sulky brat didn't look much like the Deke that
Di knew; *something* had certainly been playing with his mind and
his hormones. Deke could be awfully easy to manipulate.

That something was undoubtedly his date. Di took an instant
dislike to Fay Harper. She was blond and gorgeous, and at the moment looked like the proverbial cat that ate the canary. Exactly the
kind of chick that used to make *Di's* life miserable back when she
was in school. It was pretty obvious to Di what was going on here;
Fay was playing Deke against Sandy, and neither one of the boys
was bright enough to catch on to what she was doing.

There was more to it than that, though. Di had gotten a peculiar
feeling the moment she laid eyes on Fay Harper—a feeling as
though there was something very wrong about her. It was an uneasiness that ran deeper than the animosity Di would have felt
anyway, given that the girl was obviously a manipulative little tart.

Di didn't get much of a chance to analyze her. The vice-
principal took over the mike to announce the crowning of the
Queen, and Fay moved, with false and simpering modesty, behind
him, out of Di's line of sight.

The static discharge from his clothing was playing merry hell
with the sound system. Every time he touched the mike, it
squealed. It didn't help that he was wearing what Di thought of as
the Plastic Teacher Suit (Ann called it the Sears Sucker Suit; "whole
herds of polyesters died to make Sears great.") The static he was
creating could have powered Tulsa for a week.

Finally he gave up, and gestured to one of the band members
to try to make the introductions and announcements. The boy

(Di remembered he'd been introduced to her as George) did his best, but the mike kept interrupting with howls and shrieks so often that the kid just threw up his hands in frustration, took the tinsel crowns from the vice-principal, and did the whole ceremony in mime.

And still that uneasy feeling persisted. *There's something in the air, and it isn't static. Something's going down.*

Sandy marched up to the mike and turned it back on, and Di braced herself for another shriek from the tortured electronics.

He cleared his throat self-consciously, and the mike popped threateningly, but didn't quite act up.

"I guess all of you know that the Spring King was supposed to be Bob Williams." His face looked like a plastic mask in the harsh stage lights, and his words sounded stilted, as if he'd memorized them.

He probably did. I bet I can predict the rest of this little speech. "Bob isn't with us anymore; he's gone to that big football field in the sky."

"Bob isn't with us anymore. I guess somebody up there must have needed a good team captain." The microphone popped again. It sounded, oddly enough, like laughter.

Give me strength. Who wrote this piece of tripe, I wonder? Just about then Sandy hesitated, and Di saw the vice-principal's lips moving in an attempt to prompt him.

Aha, I might have known.

"Bob always gave everything he had for Jenks, one hundred and ten percent. He never missed a game, no matter what. He was the best football player Jenks ever produced." Feedback through the amp made the speakers whine petulantly.

And the less said about his academic achievements, the better.

"We'll all miss Bob. He had a heck of a future ahead of him. It's going to be real tough to fill his cleats."

The vice-principal leaned forward, and Di got a good look at Fay Harper's expression. She wasn't quite sure how she'd been expecting the girl to look—at least a little moved, maybe. But whatever she'd been anticipating, however vaguely, it *wasn't* the deadpan Fay was wearing. Sandy cleared his throat again and prepared to continue with his recitation, but the sound system chose that moment to break into a screech that probably vibrated the fillings out of people's teeth.

Sandy just shrugged (looking relieved) and retired to his spot beside Fay to the equally relieved applause of the audience. Then Fay stepped forward.

It was only at that moment that Di saw how odd her gown was. If it hadn't been that the thing was a very modern shade of baby blue, it *could* have come straight out of a costume exhibition of the Revolutionary War. Beribboned, ruffled, and panniered, with a neckline that was just short of pornographic, all it lacked to make it perfect was a powdered wig. Di wondered what on earth had possessed her to buy it—and where on earth she'd *found* it.

Most girls Fay's age would have looked awkward in a dress like that. Ninety-nine percent wouldn't have known how to handle the wide skirts and panniers.

Fay carried herself as gracefully as if she were Marie Antoinette. Di had to admit to grudging admiration for the girl. It took a certain amount of chutzpah to wear a dress so entirely out of step with the neon lamé and hot-pastel organdy currently in fashion. And it took native grace to be able to *move* in something like that.

Fay's little gratitude speech was as clear as the proverbial bell. The sound system didn't misbehave once during the entire proceedings.

Given Fay's reputation, Di couldn't help thinking, *it's probably afraid to. So, what's next?* She looked around, trying to find a source for her feeling of impending disaster, and couldn't spot a thing. As she scanned the crowd, identifying and dismissing every marginally psychic kid she could spot, the six Princesses and their escorts picked their way gingerly down the slippery wooden stairs to the stage, heading straight for the Maypole.

That was enough to distract Di from her search. *They can't be—* she thought, incredulously. *They* can't *be. Good gods. They are.*

Sure enough, each one of the twelve grabbed a streamer, and began to sort themselves into a ring of facing pairs. Boys facing girls, boys to be circling clockwise, girls widdershins.

Does anybody out here know what that Maypole dance really stands for? Di spotted Ann at the edge of the crowd, trying to bury her giggles behind a cup of punch. The fact that the cup was empty was a dead giveaway.

Yeah, she knows what's going on, all right. Yeah. Let's hear it for Fertility Rites in the Modern High School. Coital Rituals 101, first door on the left. Di bit her lip to keep from giggling herself. *I wonder if Ann even bothered to try to keep them from going through with this when she heard about it?*

From the way Ann's shoulders were quivering, she probably hadn't. And it was an odds-on bet she hadn't even tried to tell *anyone* what she knew.

And the rest of the teachers are all seeing innocent little flowers of romance performing a quaint little Victorian custom. She double-checked the Maypole; straw crown, green ribbons, phallic knob on top . . . completely authentic. *Oh, my ears and whiskers, it's about as Victorian as I am!*

One of the guitarists up on stage fingered an opening passage, and the twelve kids raised their streamers in unison, preparatory to going into their dance.

—and suddenly Di sensed the stirring of power, and the scene didn't seem quite so funny anymore.

The rest of the band joined the first guitar, playing something slow and fairly low-key, while the twelve kids began weaving in and out with their ribbons, moving at a slow walk.

Twelve . . . and the pole makes thirteen. It's the Sex Magick version. Lord and Lady, somebody out there knows what he's doing! Now if the band starts speeding up . . .

The band did.

. . . I've got potential trouble on my hands. Scratch that; I have real trouble on my hands.

Ann Greeley? Despite having dismissed her before, Di was forced to consider her the prime suspect now. She fit all the parameters—adult, in contact with the kids, and demonstrably knowledgeable. She didn't have an apparent motive, but that didn't matter; the motive could be something Di just hadn't spotted yet. She didn't have the "feel" of a magick-worker, but Di suddenly realized that if she wasn't at all psi, Di would never know she was a sorcerer until she actually cast some sort of spell in Di's presence.

Di tore her gaze away from the Maypole dancers, who were skipping around their circuits without a single flaw in the weaving, faces set in the blank masks of entrancement. Even more ominously, the rest of the students had begun to crowd onto the dance floor and by *their* dancing were raising more power to feed into the Maypole ritual.

Di finally saw Ann making a lateral for the punch bowl, and threw a full probe on her, a probe which included Di's own rather limited ability at mind reading.

And got nothing. Ann wasn't interested in power, she didn't even realize there was anything unusual going on; Ann was making sure nobody'd dumped anything into the punch besides sherbet and fruit juice.

But the power was going *somewhere*. And there was a lot of it. Maybe, she realized with a feeling of dread, enough to wake up the One Below. . . .

She was going to have to ground it, and fast. The way the ritual was *meant* to go, with the power going right back into the fertility of the earth.

She couldn't scan for the culprit, make sure the One Below *didn't* wake up, and drain off the power harmlessly at the same time. She hesitated for a moment, then sensed the unknown sorcerer pulling the energy as fast as the dancers could generate it.

Not this time, bozo, she thought grimly. *You just ran up against an expert in Sex Magick. You should have tried something other than a pagan ritual, mister. We're on* my *home turf here.*

She tapped straight into the spell casting, taking the power and grounding it the way her granny had taught her. She could tell that the other was surprised when the energy stopped feeding into him; felt him groping around for some way to stop her. But he didn't have any feeling for the power flows, and he had found a way to use the pagan ceremony either completely by accident or through a lot of study. He couldn't tell where she was tapping in, and he

didn't know how to block her. And he didn't have time to figure
out how to get around what she was doing.

*I just love being made default High Priestess with no advance
warning.*

But despite the fact that she could feel her enemy nearby—was
probably close enough to touch him, in fact—she was just too busy
to try to single out which of the people on or near the stage was the
sorcerer. Sweat trickled down the back of her neck as she struggled
with the reins of power. Like controlling a horse that wanted to
bolt; she dared not take her concentration off her task or it would
escape from her. If she'd had a chance to prepare for this, it would
have been different; she'd have been in a trance of her own, and not
fighting to hold the power, stay conscious, and ward the sleeping
Leviathan. The muscles of her shoulders began to cramp with
strain, and she put her back against a pillar to keep herself upright.

The kids continued to dance, and the band continued to play, all
oblivious to the arcane fencing going on under their noses. All except for the green-eyed kid, who had his back to the wall, his eyes
frantically scanning the crowd, his face set and a little frightened.

*He feels it too—and he doesn't know where it's coming from or go-
ing to, either. Shit, I'm scaring the hell out of a budding psi. Sorry
about this, kid. I've got my hands full at the moment.*

That was when things took a turn for the worse. The music the
band was playing started to change.

Strange undertones crept into the sounds two of the guitars
were putting out. The music made the hair rise on the back of Di's
neck; the only thing she could think to compare it to was the stuff
Dave's band had done—

But this wasn't music meant to generate psychic energy. *This*
music carried undercurrents of hatred and anger. This was music
designed to incite violence. None of the band members appeared
to notice what was going on with their own music—

In fact, they looked oblivious to everything around them, completely caught up in what they were doing, paying no attention
to the audience. Up on stage, only Deke and the vice-principal

were left besides the band; Sandy and Fay were already gone.

Two of the kids to Di's left collided accidentally on the dance floor. Five minutes ago, they'd have ignored the collision, or at worst, grinned and gone on dancing.

Not now.

They rounded on each other, snarling, fists clenched, every muscle tensed to attack.

One just happened to be black; the other, white.

The stage was set for disaster, the curtain was about to ascend, and she had her hands full. Too full to even try to stop it.

Lord and Lady, I've got too many balls in the air, and if I drop any of them—Come on, *I need some help here!*

She felt that little something extra that made her a Guardian finally kick in, giving her the equivalent of one more hand—

—and with it, instructions.

She sent a surge of power at the band without knowing why she was doing so, knowing only that she had to.

The third guitar cut across the music of the first two. *Literally* cut across it; what the third one played canceled the undercurrents of the others completely. Peace and harmony and sheer good fun caroled out, Woodstock and a sixties Beach Boys concert combined.

The expression of pure hatred on the white kid's face faded. Between the music and the crowd noise, Di was too far away to hear what he said, but it was evidently an apology. The black one looked down at his clenched fists as if he was surprised to see them attached to his wrists, and sheepishly nodded and backed off.

I don't know what's going on here, but I sure as hell know which side I'm *picking!* She stopped grounding out the energy she'd been taking from the Maypole spell casting and instead of feeding it back into the earth, sent it straight at that third guitar.

Whoever that other magician was, he figured out what Di was doing immediately. He stopped trying to find a way to pull control away from Di, and began feeding the other two guitars from whatever stores he had already, and whatever he could glean from the other dancing kids.

The two enemy guitars—Di recognized them, absently, as Stratocasters—howled like a pair of demented Sirens, and threw out their song of destruction. And Di's ally, a Gibson probably older than most of the kids here, reacted like a t'ai chi master, taking their music and transmuting it. Picking up their riffs and purifying them; turning their own force against them.

It *was* recognizably music; anything that wasn't might have attracted attention and broken the spell the Strats were trying to weave. Everything depended on their being able to keep the kids in that kind of half-trance the first notes had sent them into—and keep them dancing. The Gibson couldn't break the spell, but it could change it, and that was exactly what the instrument—or whatever was inhabiting the instrument—was doing.

The kids were the rope in a tug-of-war conducted by a trio of latter-day Pied Pipers. All they heard was the music and the beat; they were deaf and blind to the subtle manipulations of their emotions. It wasn't fair, but there wasn't much Di could do about it. All she could do was support the side that intended to set them free when the fight was over.

The Gibson was going strong, but Di wasn't sure how long *she* could keep this up. She wasn't sweating anymore; she was shivering with reaction and weariness. Her knees felt so weak that it was only the pillar at her back that was keeping her on her feet.

I need some way to end this. I need some way to overwhelm them.

Then she saw her opening. And so, she sensed, did the Gibson. It pulled back a little, preparatory to giving its all. Desperate for a way to finish the battle, she dropped everything she was doing and sent her ally one last, frantic burst of concentrated power.

The Strats felt it coming, and tried to rear a wall of sound to deflect it.

But the amps had taken enough for one night.

Between the static charge in the air and the dueling magics, they couldn't take any more.

There was a final note from the Gibson that stopped the kids in their tracks, froze the band cold, and made even the Maypole dancers drop their ribbons and clap their hands over their ears. And at that point, two of the three stage amps died.

But they went out in a blaze of glory; shooting flames and smoke everywhere, in a pyrotechnic display that rivaled anything Di had seen name bands do on purpose.

The Gibson wasn't done yet—it still had a partially live amp, and it was moving in for the kill. Di fed her ally one last burst, and together they blew the circuits on the Strats—

Which was calculated to send whatever was *in* them back to whatever hell they came from.

The Strats wailed as their circuits fried. The two Strat players cursed, yelped, and dropped their instruments, frantically hauling the straps off over their heads. The amps were still burning. For some reason the fire alarm hadn't gone off; Di suspected it had been turned off at the office to prevent kids turning in false alarms during the dance. She also suspected that there would be heads rolling over that in the morning. But for now, it was just as well.

The vice-principal and another teacher jumped up on the stage with a pair of carbon-dioxide fire extinguishers and began spraying everything and everyone indiscriminately.

The first of the two Strats gave a last dying shriek as the thing inhabiting it lost its grip on the guitar. There was a power surge that flickered the lights. Then the *guitar* went up in a shower of sparks, and the resulting short circuit blew every fuse in the building.

There were a few screams as the lights went out but not much more than that. Di dropped her shields enough to ascertain that the kids were all mostly dazed. There would be no lasting harm, but the shock of being put *into* a trance state and then blown out of it again was going to keep most of them a bit confused for the next few minutes.

Most of them, but not all.

"Oh, man," came a mournful voice from the stage. "Oh, *man*. If we're gonna blow amps and guitars every night, we *gotta* get better-paying gigs. . . ."

———

Deke headed straight for the can the minute the lights came back on. He felt like he was going to be sick, even though he hadn't had much to eat and not a thing to drink that wasn't perfectly harmless.

It had been a long day, and it didn't look like it was over yet.

First the vice-principal had called him on the carpet for fighting with Fay in public. Then Fay had been all over him every chance she got, pouting and trying to make up to him. And Monica had *avoided* him all day, even going so far as to sit on the opposite side of the English class from him.

And somehow, some way, Fay had managed to get him talked into first coming over before the dance, then giving her his ring back. He still wasn't sure how she'd done it; the entire afternoon and early evening were lost in a kind of tired haze. When he got to the dance, he wasn't mad at her anymore; he was mad at Sandy for making it look like he and Fay were going to—

Going to—

Now he didn't remember what it was. But it was all Sandy's fault.

Then he'd taken Fay to the dance—in *her* car, not his—and all this weird shit started happening.

First off, there was Sandy, acting like Deke was poaching on *his* turf.

Then there was that stuff with the sound equipment; George *never* had trouble with his equipment before.

That was when he started feeling sick. He had gotten down off the stage without Fay, who managed to vanish at some point during the Maypole dance. He remembered her looking startled, then angry, then completely enraged—then she was gone, about the time the music started to go thermonuclear.

He'd had a pretty good idea where she'd gone, because Sandy disappeared a few moments later. But he was feeling too dizzy and light-headed to care.

Then the band blew up.

When the lights came back on, it turned out that the damage was a lot less than it had looked like. Basically two of the three guitars were totaled, and two of the three amps. The sound system itself was okay, so the vice-principal grabbed George's sound guy to play

DJ and told everyone to take five; they'd start the dance back up once the stage was cleaned off.

Deke had about had it. He'd decided he was going to confront Fay about vanishing on him and head home; *walk* home if he had to. But every time he started to track down Fay and demand an explanation, he felt sicker.

He went to the sinks and started throwing cold water on his face. *God, it's hot in here,* he thought. *When the band was playing it was so hot I thought I was going to smother. Shit. Like I couldn't breathe—no, more like somebody was sucking the breath out of me.*

The door to the johns creaked and Deke glanced up at the mirror reflexively to see who it was. "Hi, Alan," he said wearily.

Alan was looking pretty smug. "Hey, what's wrong?" he asked, giving Deke a look of concern mixed with condescension. "It's pretty early in the evening to tie one on, buddy."

"I didn't 'tie one on,'" Deke replied with as much heat as he could manage to dredge up. "I haven't had a damn thing to drink except a Coke. I think I must be catching something."

"Too bad," Alan replied, messing unnecessarily with his hair. "Don't give it to me, okay? I finally got together with that girl I was telling you about. We just *might* go somewhere private. Depends on if they can really get the sound system working again or not."

Deke's stomach turned over, and he clutched at the sink until his knuckles were white. "Yeah, fine," he mumbled. "Great, nice going. Hope you finally manage to get laid. It'll do you good."

He looked up at Alan's reflection.

Oh shit. Boy, I really put my foot in it this time.

His friend bristled with anger and pulled himself up as tall as he could without standing on his toes. "This is for those who don't deserve the very best," Alan said, holding up his fist with his little finger sticking out of it.

Then he stalked out, leaving behind the scent of bruised dignity.

Now why in hell did I say that? Deke asked himself. *God, what kind of a jerk am I? Alan didn't deserve to be insulted. What in hell is wrong with me?*

He finally went into one of the stalls and sat with his head between his legs until he felt a little steadier. *First I take Fay back, then I dump on Alan. It's like I'm my own evil twin or something. Maybe I am catching something. Maybe that's what the problem is.*

One of the teachers came in, making the rounds, and took pity on him when it was obvious that he wasn't drunk or stoned. The teachers' lounge wasn't far away; it was cool, and dim, and stocked with everything a teacher might need to face a class full of bored adolescents—everything short of Valium, anyway. Two Maalox later, and his stomach settled at last, he felt ready to face the rest of the school, and to deal with Fay. He straightened himself up as best he could, and headed out into the hall.

And ran straight into Monica.

"Monica!" he exclaimed. "Hi! I—uh—"

"Hello, Derek," she said coldly, in a tone so chill he could feel ice forming on his eyebrows.

She turned away from him without another word, and started to walk off down the hall toward the cafeteria. He looked around quickly; there was no one else around. This was a good chance to try and apologize.

"Monica, wait!" he called desperately. "Look, I—uh—about yesterday, I—"

She stopped, and looked back over her shoulder at him. "Yes?" she said, in tones of complete indifference.

"I—uh—I was a little hot." He flushed, and his stomach did another flip-flop. "I lost my temper, you know?"

"Oh, really?" she replied. "Is that what you call it?"

She turned away and started to walk off again, her back stiff and straight. "Monica, wait!" he cried desperately. "Can I talk to you later? Please?"

"No, you can't," she said frostily, without turning around. "I've got plans. For the *whole evening.*"

She stalked off with all the pride of an outraged dowager, trailing disdain behind her like a cloak.

Shit, he thought glumly, staring after her. *Shit, I really screwed*

*that one up, too. Good job, Kestrel. Now you've got Monica and Alan
pissed at you.*

Then, suddenly, he remembered something. When he'd been up
on the stage with Fay, he'd noticed Monica in the crowd below.
And Alan had been next to her. What if that hadn't been coincidence? What if they'd been together?

*But how could she have met him? She—oh shit. That math class.
He's in it, too.*

He started to hurry after her, to find out who she'd come with,
but Fay intercepted him just as he got to the cafeteria door.

"There you are," she said playfully. "Sandy and I were wondering if you'd fallen in."

From just behind her, Sandy glowered at him.

"They've gotten the sound system put back together," she told
him. "They're just waiting for me to get the dance started. Sandy
thought I should do the first dance with him, but *you're* my escort,
and I think I ought to do it with you."

It was all in the open now; she was playing Sandy against him and
vice versa, and loving every minute of it. And he couldn't help himself; he took Fay's arm like some macho cowboy grabbing his dance-
hall girl in an old western. And she was as desirable now as she'd
been distasteful half an hour ago. "Yeah," he said aggressively. "Yeah,
I think so, too. You *did* come with me. And you *are* my steady."

Before Sandy could say anything, he hustled Fay out into the
center of the floor. That seemed to be the signal everyone was waiting for; somebody started a Stevie Nicks tape, and he put his arms
around Fay like he owned her. . . .

But out of the corner of his eye he saw Monica. Dancing with
Alan.

Aw hell—

How dare *she move in on my territory! How* dare *she steal my power!
When I get home, and I'm alone, I'm going to break something.* Fay
relaxed bonelessly—outwardly, at least—into Deke's arms and

turned up the sexual heat. She'd managed to get Deke back under her control; and now he was so worked up tonight that his face was white and his stomach must be churning.

Poor little boy. So easy to manipulate. But I'm still going to kill something before the night's over.

She moved her hips in tight against his, reminding him of everything she'd done to him on all the nights before this; reminding him of all the things he *could* have from her. Promising things with her hands under his jacket. It was hard to maintain this pose of calm, when inwardly she was screaming with rage at the loss of all that power. Only the coke and grass she'd done right after the demons were exorcised enabled her to stay in control.

Body language is so eloquent. And if it could say what I felt, you'd be short a body part or two, Deke dear.

She'd made up her mind last night, after she'd cooled down from the fight. Deke had done the unthinkable; he'd broken free of her control. So there *was* something worth digging for under that shield of his. He was the best prospect she'd seen yet; the signs were all right. If she let him get away, there might never be another target as easy, or as tasty.

So she set herself to winning him back. Because as soon as graduation was over, she intended to move on him. First she'd have to get rid of those inconvenient parents of his; then she could get him to marry her. Deke would have a tidy little fortune by inheritance, especially if she made certain his parents died in some kind of double-indemnity accident. Added to her own wealth, Deke would never actually have to work a day in his life. In his *short* life . . .

But the parents were going to have to go. Absolutely. There was no doubt that his father had brought in that witchy female, that Tregarde woman—and Fay had no doubts whatsoever that it *hadn't* been primarily to give Deke's English class a creative writing teacher.

She was probably the one responsible for the shield over the boy in the first place. If it hadn't been for the lines she had on him before he was shielded, Fay would never have been able to work Deke at all tonight. The hooks were set, though, and with Deke's tacit consent, when he'd given her his ring right after the accident. Not even an Adept could work a passive shield against something like that.

But this writer was a wild card Fay didn't like. A rival, a competitor, on *her* carefully staked-out ground. *She* was certainly the one responsible for foiling the attacks on the Carlin brat. She'd suspected the Kestrels at first, but no more. If Deke's parents had the Gifts or the Power, they would have used it by now for more than simply shielding their son. They hadn't, therefore they didn't have it. But they knew it existed; they may have even guessed the threat Fay was to their child. That was undoubtedly why Larry Kestrel had brought the witch to Tulsa. And once here, the potentials were obvious. . . .

And it's why your life is going to be cut much shorter, old man, she thought maliciously, leaning on the son's shoulder, and swaying in place to the gentle song that was playing. *Then I'll produce the next vehicle, and dear little Derek will have a fatal accident, too.*

She was rather looking forward to that. Derek had cost her dearly in the past month or so. Her nerves were fried; as scorched as the remains of the amps now being carted away by the members of the band.

All that power—right in my hands, and she took it away from me. That bitch. I should have known *what she was when she started draining the Maypole. I planned that ceremony, and the power I was to get from it. I planned everything, right down to the costume, the copy of the one I used to wear, and that was a bitch to have sewn. That power was mine, I earned it, I set it up, and she stole it. And I lost even more fighting her.* Fay's jaw clenched. *Then she nearly gave me a stroke with backlash. If I hadn't had shunts set up into the Servant, I'd be unconscious. I want that power back, and I want it back now! And I want her gone!*

Her hands caressed Deke's back automatically. Her mind seethed with anger. *Sandy. He was useful as a smoke screen during the confrontation, but not as useful as I hoped. Someone just might tell Deke we were off necking, and I don't need that. I hadn't intended to get rid of him quite so soon, but he's a nuisance, and he's been worked up to the proper pitch. And I've got everything I need right here with me.*

Then home, and I drain Deke, then some coke, bennies—that's an-
other thing modern times are good for. Drugs. I'd have had to make do
without the boost. Coke was the only stimulant I could get back then.

Right. A new plan. I should have set one up beforehand. Never mind,
it doesn't matter. This will probably work out better in the long run.

The dance came to an end, and Deke pulled reluctantly away from
her. She smiled up into his glazed eyes. "I've done my little duty," she
whispered. "I'm not in the mood for dancing, or for putting up with
Sandy anymore. He acts like he's high, or something. I think we
should go home." She licked her lips sensuously. "I can think of other
things to do tonight besides dance. You still have the keys, don't you?"

"Right here," he said, blinking owlishly at her.

"Then why don't you go get the car. I'll meet you at the front
entrance."

He blinked again, then turned away from her and wound his
way through the crowd. She'd had him park at the back of the lot,
in a place she knew would be hard to get out of once the lot started
to fill. And *he* knew if he so much as scratched the paint on the
Shelby, he'd never hear the last of it.

So that would keep him occupied for a good fifteen or twenty
minutes. Long enough to deal with Sandy.

The Servant was also here, having driven the Merc over, playing
the doting relative right down to bringing the camera and taking
pictures of her being crowned. She sidled through the crowd until
she came to its side.

"I need the drug," she said softly.

The Servant handed her the packet, but didn't let go of it.

"I believe this is a mistake," the Servant replied, just as quietly. "I
do not think this is a wise decision on your part."

Fay resisted the urge to tear the tiny packet of PCP out of the
Servant's hand. "You aren't *supposed* to think," she told it coldly.
"You're supposed to do as I order you."

"You created me to see to your well-being." The Servant's expression was calm and serene. "I am attempting to perform that
function. You have not been acting in a wise or thoughtful manner

of late. You have been impulsive, irrational; you have been acting, if I may say so, like a child. This unreasoning insistence on ridding your path of that girl-chit, for instance. She is no threat to you, except that you make her one. Perhaps it is because of the stresses on this body you wear, perhaps the transfer was more of a strain than you had guessed, or perhaps you have indulged too much in spirits and drugs—"

"I've lived over three hundred years, and I've made the transfer more times than I remember," Fay whispered angrily. "I know what I'm doing now! And *you* are nothing but a puppet I created to serve me!"

"Very well." The Servant released its hold on the packet. "I exist but to serve you."

"And you would do well to remember that." Fay palmed the packet of PCP and shook her hair back. "Wait until you see Sandy going after that little Carlin bitch, then follow him. I want to make sure nothing goes wrong."

The Servant looked as if it would like to say something, but then shrugged slightly and nodded. Fay bit her lip angrily, and only the sweet taste of blood made her wake up to what she was doing. *I think it's time, and more than time, to be rid of that thing. It's out-lived its usefulness. Damn. It couldn't have picked a worse moment to go independent on me. I'll have to create a new one at a time when my reserves are a lot lower than they should be. Then again . . . I did want to kill something tonight. . . .*

She turned her back on the Servant, letting it see how angry she was with it, and regretfully abandoned the idea of destroying it tonight. *No, I'd better be a little more careful than that. It's possible I'll have to keep the thing around longer than I would like. Unless . . .*

Unless I can persuade Sandy to extreme excess.

She licked her lips thoughtfully, as she spotted Sandy spiking the punch bowl with Everclear.

Perhaps I can, she thought, fingering the little packet in her hand. *Perhaps, with the help of this, I can. And rid myself of Monica as well.*

FOURTEEN

Fay threaded her way through the crowd, smiling and nodding at those who made eye contact with her, but not devoting a great deal of attention to anyone except Sandy. She reached his side just as he poured the last of the bottle into the punch bowl and slipped the bottle up his sleeve.

"Hey, lover," she murmured, slipping up behind him and sliding her arms around him from the back. He turned, a little clumsily; she avoided his elbow and snuggled up against him again before he'd even noticed that she'd pulled away.

"I've got something better than *that* with me," she whispered. He grinned and nuzzled her neck; the booze on his breath was enough to get her high just by contact.

"Well, why don't you just work a little magic and produce it, hm?" he mumbled, working his tongue into her ear.

"Not *here*," she protested, with a little giggle. "I've only got enough for the two of us. Let's go out back, okay?"

She wriggled neatly out of his grasp, and caught up his hand before he could protest. She tugged impatiently when he blinked dully at her, and he finally followed her, like the fool he was, through the crowd, past the double glass exit doors and the Servant, out to the second parking lot behind the cafeteria.

Once there, his instincts took over, and he pulled *her* into the shadows beyond the lighted doorway. She allowed him to back her into a corner, encouraging him with hands and lips and tongue. The stiffened, low-cut bodice of her dress allowed him nearly as much access as if she'd been bare-chested, a fact no few of the ladies of Fay's acquaintance back in her youth were very familiar with.

When she thought he was sufficiently engrossed, she extracted the packet of PCP from the pannier of her dress, palmed it, and placed it against the side of his neck. Once it was in place, she used some of the last of her magic to dissolve the gel of the packet and leach the drug directly into the major vein in his neck.

He started a little when it first began to seep in and pulled away, sensing that something was out of the ordinary, perhaps. He made as though he was about to say something; she drew his head down with her free hand and opened her mouth under his.

He took the hint.

She kept him occupied and under control until the drug had a chance to get into his brain; then, when she could tell by his increasing aggressiveness that it was hitting him, she let loose her second spell.

It was a hypnotic, and one she'd used on him before, though never in tandem with PCP. He stiffened and stood up rigidly straight as the spell took effect.

"Relax," she ordered, and he did so. She pulled his head down against her shoulder and stared off into the bright-and-dark patterns of shadow and parking lot lights as she whispered her orders into his ear. . . .

At length he pulled away from her and went back into the cafeteria. She waited a moment, then strolled casually around the outside of the building until she reached the front portico, where she waited for Deke.

It was pleasant enough out here; a little chilly, but not bad. The wind had died down sometime during the duel she'd had with that witch. There was dust all over everything, but she sat down on one of the concrete benches under the portico anyway. She wouldn't be wearing this dress again, so it didn't much matter if it got soiled. Having it made and wearing it had been a purely symbolic act, to accent her differences from the rest of the world and to evoke the mood of bygone times when it had been her indentured peasants performing the Maypole rite

Well, that gets Sandy and *that little nuisance Monica out of my life,* she thought with angry satisfaction. *Even if the Tregarde woman is protecting her arcanely, she won't be looking for a physical attack. And when Sandy gets done with the little tart, at the very least she'll be ready for a nice, long stay in a hospital. He might even kill her; I'm not sure how far he'd go if she fought back. And even if all he does is damage her, they'll put Sandy away in the juvenile home so fast he won't even know what's happened. Even all his daddy's money and influence won't buy him out from under a charge of rape and assault under the influence of an illegal drug.*

The Servant was presumably following him to make certain nothing interfered until the Carlin bitch had learned her lesson. Fay folded her hands in her lap, and nodded to herself. This was as fool-proof a plan as she'd ever come up with. Even though her primary plan had failed, she was still able to come up with backups on an instant—and the power released by the pain and fear of a budding mage was worth that of all the ordinary children at the dance put to-gether. Now all she needed was a way to negate the Tregarde woman.

Retrench and cool off. Plan ahead. Don't let a little failure throw you into confusion. . . .

Yes—the Tregarde woman could wait. If she'd known what Fay was, she'd have attacked directly, instead of working through the guitar. So she hadn't figured out who her enemy was. She had no notion of Fay's resources, nor would she ever be able to learn where Fay's major Power Place was. She would probably think to-night's failure would set Fay back enough that she wouldn't be able to counterattack for days.

Little do you know. First Monica, then you, witch. I wonder what it is you want? Maybe I ought to let you make your offer before I shut you down. How long were you going to string Monica along before you used her? And I wonder what on earth the Kestrels offered you to protect their brat. . . .

Deke was pulling up next to the portico in her Shelby; the night was young, and she had more plans for insinuating herself even more deeply into his emotions.

She smiled sweetly at him as he leapt out of the car and ran to hold the passenger-side door open for her.

She rose, and he looked at her uncertainly. "Do you—" he said awkwardly, holding out the keys.

"Oh no, not tonight," she murmured, caressing his arm lingeringly as she passed him. "No, tonight *you* drive, lover. I'll just sit here and—relax."

And she snuggled up against his shoulder as he pulled the car out onto the street.

When I get done with you tonight, little boy, you'll never even think about anyone else ever again.

The kids swirled past the eastern corner of the cafeteria, avoiding it, and not at all aware that they were doing so. Di had managed to track down the young psi who'd inadvertently found himself stuck in the cross fire, and she didn't want to be disturbed while she talked to him.

". . . so there was just some real heavy shit going down, and you got caught in the middle," Di told the green-eyed youngster, feeling quite apologetic and a little defensive. "I'm sorry, but sometimes these things just happen."

The boy who was Spring Thing, or King, or whatever, drifted by them. Di didn't much care for his glazed eyes and rigidly set expression, but he wasn't doing anything out of line, so she ignored him for the moment.

"Yeah, I guess." The kid rubbed the back of his neck and looked around uneasily. "Weird things kind of happen around me, always have, but I can't say I like it."

"I can't say I blame you." Di shrugged. "It could be worse, trust me. You could have my job."

"What, writing romances? Ooo, pretty scary." The kid seemed to be recovering his aplomb fairly quickly. "Or did you mean cruising high schools for wicked witches?"

She gave him a raised eyebrow. "I'm the only witch around here that I've been able to spot—" *Wait a minute, did he pick up something I missed? Could the sorcerer be a female? Hell, why not? I'd been thinking "he," but there wasn't a sex signature on the spell casting.* "—and last time I looked I was on the side of the angels," she finished without missing a beat. "Unless you know something I don't."

He spread his hands in a gesture of denial. "Hey, not me, lady! I like to keep my profile low, if you know what I mean." He glanced significantly down past his feet. "I wouldn't want to wake anybody up, you know? I hang around the art classes so I don't stand out . . . much."

"Not much more than an anthurium in a bouquet of daisies," she replied dryly.

"Tasteful comparison." He smiled wickedly.

She was about to make a scathing retort, when every alarm she'd put on Monica went off at once.

Lady Bright! She didn't even stop to excuse herself; she just whirled and set off at a dead run for the opposite entrance to the cafeteria. Somewhere outside that door Monica was in deep, deep trouble, something no shield could handle—and even if Di *hadn't* put those alarms on her, the emotional distress she was giving off would have alerted Di to the emergency. She ignored exclamations and protests as she ducked through the crowd, shoving people out of the way if necessary. She was vaguely aware that the kid was following her; she hoped he had the sense to know when to stay out of the way.

All her training told her that there was some serious mayhem going on outside. And now that she wasn't juggling magic, she could and would do something about it.

She stiff-armed the doors at top speed; they flew open and she dove through them, then stopped dead. She peered through the dust-laden air, trying to spot her quarry in the crowded expanse of the back parking lot. The wind had stopped after her duel with the sorcerer, but the dust that had been kicked up was still sifting down, making a haze that was hard to see through when the lights from the parking lot shone on it.

But then she spotted movement and heard an angry shriek; the combatants reeled into the pool of brightness under one of the parking lot lights. She took off like a sprinter, trying to identify them as she ran. The aggressor was the Spring King, and he was making chutney out of Deke's hacker-buddy.

Gods—what the hell is going on here? Who started what?

She noticed that Monica was not doing the expected—she *wasn't* standing out of the way and screaming like a ninny. She was trying to pull the jock off, dragging at his collar and beating on his head with her shoe.

Good Lord . . .

It wasn't doing a lot of good; he was paying about as much attention to her as he would have to a mosquito.

In fact, in the next second, he shrugged Monica off. She went tumbling across the pavement. The hacker flung himself at the jock, and took one on the chin that sent him down—so for the moment, the fighters were separated by about three feet. That would be enough. Di put on an extra burst of speed and blindsided the jock with her shoulder, knocking him off balance and sending him staggering into a car. She bounced off him in a more controlled manner, and used the momentum of her bounce to position herself between him and the other two kids.

Before he had even begun to recover, she was in a balanced, "ready" stance, and—

—dropped back an involuntary step as he focused on her and the sheer force of his rage carried the blind emotion and some of his thoughts past her shielding.

It felt like a blow to the temple. But more startling were the images she got. The hacker hadn't been his primary target; *Monica* was. The hacker just got in the way when he went after her, and scrambled neurons took over.

Now Di was the one in the way. And the glazed look in his eyes wasn't from spiked punch, either. The yellowish sodium-vapor light glared down on both of them as she tried to figure out what he was on. It was something that was making him oblivious to pain, something kicking his adrenaline into "high" and shutting off his reasoning processes entirely.

He seemed paralyzed for a moment, and she took her opportunity to drop shields and "read" him quickly.

Holy— There were the magical fingerprints she'd been searching for in vain all over his psyche.

"Lady!" She recognized the voice of the green-eyed kid. He was yelling from behind the shelter of a parked car to her left. "Lady, watch it! I think he's dusted!"

Now everything made some sense. *Angel dust, PCP, yeah, that would explain it. But not the tampering with his mind. Somebody was finally a little careless, and as soon as I get a minute, I'm going to find out exactly who . . . if I get that minute.*

So *that* was the picture; the unknown had decided to go after Monica mundanely. Sending someone else to do his dirty work.

"I'm getting the principal!" the kid shouted from the darkness, as she heard him take to his heels. *"Don't let him grab you!"*

Great advice, kid. Now tell me how to keep him from grabbing me!

She concentrated on the jock, and saw the tensing of his muscles that meant he was going to rush her; she stood her ground until the very last minute, then danced out of the way.

And tried to remember what she knew about angel dust. *PCP is going to sharpen his reflexes; he's already a trained athlete and he outweighs me by a bunch, and right now I could break both his arms and he wouldn't even notice.*

He bounced off the car and spun, faster than she would have given him credit for; he spotted her again and lunged for her. She escaped by a hair, and only by kicking the back of his knee and following that with a punch to his kidneys. And although the contact was solid and would probably leave a bruise the size of her head, it just barely staggered him.

She sensed his attention wavering for a moment, as if something was trying to "reset" him. *Oh hell. Monica is over there playing Florence Nightingale to her boyfriend. Great, just great. I'd better make sure I keep myself between him and them, or he may go for them instead of me.*

In fact, at that same moment he spotted them, and his attention was split between Monica and Di for a second.

Then it centered on Monica, and he took one step in the girl's direction.

Oh bloody hell. Better get him back . . .

She pulled a flying side kick just to wake him up a little. She connected better than she'd had any reason to hope; he went reeling into the trunk of a Caddy, and hit it with both forearms, with enough force to dent the trunk lid. She came down much too close to him for her own comfort and skipped out of his reach with adrenaline sending little electric chills down her back.

When he turned around and spotted her again, his attention wasn't divided at all.

His face twisted into a snarl of completely unthinking rage. *Great, Tregarde. Now he wants to kill* you. *Smooth move.* His anger clawed at the outside of her shields and she winced at the impact of it.

Then something occurred to her, and she took a closer "look" as she skipped sideways to avoid his lunges at her.

Wait a minute. He's wide open. If he can affect me, *even though he's a normal, I'll be able to hit* him! *Maybe that's why his buddy used it on him; dust must leave normals open to magic and suggestion.*

"Hey!" she yelled, wanting to make sure he focused on her entirely. She waved her arms at him, as if he was an animal she was trying to herd. "Hey!"

He focused *entirely* on her; his whole world narrowed to just her, and he lunged for her.

She backpedaled, gathered her strength, then let him have it with a full-force psi-bolt; if it worked on him the way it would work on a psychic . . .

It hit him just as he lurched forward.

The result was spectacular; his eyes suddenly rolled up into his head, and he plowed face-first into the asphalt at her feet, like a stunned ox.

She stopped backpedaling, and heaved a sigh of relief. *Well, that was—*

"Look out!" Monica screamed.

She glimpsed movement out of the corner of her eye, and she spun to one side, narrowly avoiding the attack of—something.

It was human-shaped, but its aura said that it wasn't any such thing; it was mage-created. An artificial construct.

Which didn't matter except that it was likely to be faster than she was—and as impervious to pain as the dusted jock.

It had leapt out of the shadows and back into them so quickly she didn't have a chance to see or sense more than that. It snarled, hidden deeply in the shadows between two cars; a hoarse rasp that didn't sound like anything human. Di sensed that it was going to attack again.

All this registered in the time it took her to jump away and orient herself.

If it's made by magic, magic will take it down. And I've been playing High Priestess all night. I may be tired, but I've got a full charge, and I'll bet it doesn't know that.

Before the thing had a chance to move a second time, she got ready to hit it, this time with a levin-bolt, a torpedo of pure magical energy.

She caught it just as it sprang at her and entered the pool of light; it spread-eagled there, caught by the force of the blast, shrieking. It stood there for just a moment, arms thrown wildly over its head, face twisted and contorted. Then it was gone.

Entirely.

But in that moment before it winked out, Di had a chance to scan it briefly, and the unknown's fingerprints were all over it, too.

Gotcha. By the gods. She slumped against the trunk of a car, her knees going weak with reaction. *As soon as I deal with the wounded, friend, I'm going to have you dead to rights.*

She looked down and to her right, at the prone body of the dusted jock. Amazingly enough, the jock was moving, groaning; starting to come to and actually trying to lever himself off the ground.

"Jesus Cluny Frog," Di muttered. "I don't believe this! What's it take to stop this guy, a tank?"

She stalked over to his side, and stared down at him. He was definitely trying to struggle to his feet and to full consciousness.

Hang if I'm going to waste another psi-bolt on him.

She removed one of her flats, weighed it thoughtfully in her hand and gave him a scientifically placed tap on the head with the heel—one well weighted with another psi-bolt. He gave a grunt, and collapsed back onto the pavement.

She slipped her shoe back on, and walked slowly over to the other two just as the vice-principal came puffing up in the wake of the green-eyed kid.

She ignored both of the new arrivals for the moment; she wanted to assess the damage to the two victims.

Though the sodium-vapor lights didn't do much for either kids' looks, the hacker was obviously the most damaged, so Di concentrated on him.

In contrast, Monica looked a little disheveled, and one sleeve of her dress was torn, but she was mostly radiating anger, not shock or pain.

Honey, you were lucky. You don't know how lucky.

Di hunched down next to the two of them; Monica was helping support the boy in a sitting position, and holding a handkerchief to his bleeding nose.

"I don't think anything's broken," the girl said hesitantly, looking up at her. "He can move everything, and he's not dizzy; he said he just hurts a lot."

"I'll bet he does," Di said absently. She tilted the boy's head up so she could see his eyes. Both pupils reacted equally, and though his nose was bleeding, it didn't look too badly damaged. "I don't think you're concussed," she said. "Although I think a real doctor ought to look at you. You're going to have a lot of bruises and a pair of black eyes that are going to make you look like a raccoon in the morning, but other than that, I think you're going to be okay. How are *you* feeling?" she asked, turning to Monica.

The girl scowled. "I'd like to rip Sandy's head off and shove it up his—" She caught herself, and took a deep breath to calm herself. "I'm sorry. I'm mad, that's how I feel."

"Good. You should be." Di stood up slowly.

She had gotten a pretty good chance to assess the vice-principal earlier, and she had a fair idea of what his notion of "handling the situation" would be. Basically, he'd try to cover it up. *CYA, you officious little bastard. Well, not this time.*

She scowled at the vice-principal, putting everything she'd ever learned in dealing with overweening idiots into her glare. "Well," she said. "You certainly have a *fine* school system here."

The vice-principal was taken rather by surprise. He'd obviously been preparing to bluster right over her, intimidate her into keeping her mouth shut, forgetting that she *wasn't* one of his teachers.

"Wh-what?" he stammered.

"Just a *fine* school system," she repeated acidly, "where some lame-brained jock stoned to his eyebrows on PCP can attack two perfectly harmless kids and *then* try to beat up a helpless woman. Wonderful. Just *wonderful.* I really admire the level of control you have over these kids."

"I—uh—"

"You—" she continued, turning to the green-eyed boy, who was obviously enjoying all this to the hilt. "Go call an ambulance. *That* idiot over there should be under restraints when he wakes up. And *this* poor child should see a doctor. A real doctor, in a real emergency room."

"Yes *ma'am,*" the kid said with relish.

"Don't you—uh—think it would be better if we called the students' parents and let them handle it?" the vice-principal said weakly.

She gave him a look that made him shrink at least two inches.

"No," she replied, venom dripping from each word. "I don't." She turned to raise an eyebrow at the young psychic. "What are you waiting for?"

"Not a thing, ma'am," he said quickly, and trotted off toward the school.

Twice more the vice-principal tried to convince Di to let him call the parents and cancel the ambulance. Each time she withered him with a glance. She knew damned well what he was up to; when the hospital got hold of Sandy they'd run a blood test, and there would be no covering up what he was on. And that would make local headlines, for certain.

The kid was quick. The ambulance arrived before Sandy came to again, and before the vice-principal could make up his mind to push any harder.

Di made quite certain that the paramedics knew what she knew. "Listen," she said quietly as the first of them bailed out of the emergency vehicle and grabbed his kit. "The only reason the cops aren't here is because nobody got seriously hurt."

That stopped him in his tracks. He took a good look at the vice-principal hovering in the background, at the hacker, and at the unconscious jock.

"So?" He took his time about setting up. "Why don't you tell me more?"

Di did.

He had a quiet little consultation with his partner when she got finished giving him the facts. She couldn't help but notice that afterward they were very gentle with the young hacker—and *very* careful about securing the jock to the gurney with some heavy restraining belts. . . .

She leaned against one of the cars, feeling every bruise, mental and physical. *Ye gods. This is more than enough for one night. And I still have to use those little traces I picked up to figure out who's behind this.*

She blanked for a minute, lost in weariness. She shook herself awake as the vehicle pulled away, with the jock in the back guarded by one of the paramedics, and the hacker in the front with the other.

Monica refused treatment, and Di wasn't going to force her. The girl stood staring after the flashing lights of the ambulance, dark shadows under her eyes.

"Okay, kiddo," Di said, coming up behind her. "Now what do you want to do? You could go talk to the cops if you want to press charges. *I'm* certainly thinking about it."

Out of the corner of her eye she saw the vice-principal wince and pale.

"I just want to go home," Monica said tiredly. "I just want to forget this ever happened."

"If that's what you want, I'll take you," Di offered, before the vice-principal could say anything. "I've about had enough for one night." She leveled one last icy stare at the man. "Tell Ann Greeley I'm giving up, please. I'm just about chaperoned out."

The green-eyed kid had vanished somewhere after calling the ambulance. *Just as well,* she thought. *I'm not up to much more tonight.* "Come on, Monica, my car's over in the front lot."

"But—" the vice principal protested weakly. They both ignored him, and walked off together into the darkness, shoes clicking in unison on the pavement.

"How awful do I look?" Monica asked mournfully, when they were out of hearing distance.

Di smothered a chuckle. "Not bad, really. I don't think that sleeve's going to be repairable, though. If I were you, I'd just cut the other one off, too. Might make a nice little sleeveless number with some careful tailoring."

"I don't think I ever want to wear it again," the girl said in a subdued voice. "Not ever." She glanced at Di out of the corner of her eye. "Diana—what—really happened back there?"

Di pulled the last of the pins out of her hair and shook it loose. "Whoever was after you went after you again," she replied, checking her dress for damage. There wasn't much that a good dry cleaner couldn't handle—the one advantage of expensive materials and tailoring. "This time he—or she, I'm not sure which—went after you physically, probably thinking I wouldn't be guarding you against that kind of attack. He got that meathead stoned on PCP and sent him out to beat you up. Your boyfriend just got in the way."

"Oh," Monica said, in a small and frightened voice. "I thought it was just—I mean, everybody knows Sandy does drugs, I thought—"

"Trust me. It was deliberate, and aimed at you," Di said firmly. "Monica, you can't keep telling yourself that this is all just something that isn't really happening. It *is* happening, and denying it isn't going to make you any safer. Wasn't it you who warned me about that other thing?"

Monica shuddered, and shrank in on herself. "I thought it was just one of Sandy's buddies."

They had reached the car, and Di unlocked the passenger's door for her. "Did you?" she asked, holding the door open so that Monica could get in.

"No," the girl said unhappily. "I guess I didn't."

"Good," Di said, climbing into the driver's side and sighing as her tired body sank into the upholstery. "Now we're finally getting somewhere. . . ."

Monica's mother—blessings on the fates—had been so worried about Monica that she hadn't asked too many personal questions of Di, and she hadn't wasted any time getting the child into the apartment.

That gets one child safely home. And I don't think I want to be Sandy's parents when Rhonda Carlin gets hold of them. Assuming she doesn't call the cops first. Thank the gods it isn't much farther to my own bed.

Di drove up into Larry's driveway feeling weary to the bone, and all she really wanted to do was go have a hot shower and go to bed.

Fat chance. There was still work to do.

Deke's car wasn't in the garage, which meant he wasn't home yet; well, it wasn't even midnight, so that wasn't too surprising.

If I'm going to try tracking down this bastard—or bitch—I don't want anyone untrained around anyway. Not even one of the targets.

She let herself in with her key. Larry wasn't obviously around, which meant he was either buried in his office or watching a videotape in his bedroom. She doubted he would have Felt the ruckus; that wasn't one of his abilities. Just the Sight, and a little bit of other things. That was just as well; she didn't want to tell him what had happened just yet. Not until she had all the information in her possession.

So, first things first; the hot shower. She emptied her mind and let the needle-spray wash all her weariness down the drain with the dirt and perspiration from the fight. That was a little mental trick that usually worked for her, at least for the short term, and it did this time, too. As she'd thought, her dress, amazingly enough, was in perfect shape, except for a couple of stains that would wash out. Well, perhaps not so amazing; it was heavy silk and cost a small fortune—but was worth it, seeing the amount of abuse it could take and bounce back from.

Think next time I make a ritual robe it'll be silk. It'll probably out last me.

She braided her wet hair and coiled it in a knot at the back of her neck, slipped on a leotard and jeans, and laid out four candles in the middle of the rug. This was the "quickie" version of a protective circle; she lit each of the candles in turn, evoking the powers of the four compass quarters, and then sank to the floor in a cross-legged position and picked up the threads of magic she'd detected on the jock, and on the construct.

She let herself drift into a light trance. *Now to follow the traces back to where and when they were created. That should keep my quarry from sensing what I'm doing; if I invoke retro-cognition he won't send up any alerts in the here and now.*

Unless of course he's laid a trap back there for me. She acknowledged the possibility, then dismissed it. *That's the chance I'll have to take, I guess.*

She allowed all the identifying factors to sink into her mind, the

way a bloodhound would memorize a scent. Then, like the bloodhound, she began "sniffing" for that same scent.

But this time she was sniffing about in the recent past; about two
hours ago, to be precise. Just *after* the duel, when the sorcerer presumably set his compulsion on jock Sandy.

Ha! She found the "scent"; followed it back to the moment when
it was strongest, then invoked that rather wayward Talent of retro-
cognition—the ability to "see" things happening at some time in
the past.

That involved putting herself another layer deeper in trance, then
disconnecting her "self " from the here-and-now; when it worked,
she generally got a little lurch of dislocation and disorientation.

Even though her eyes were closed, she felt that identifying surge
of dizziness—and suddenly she was "there," right outside the cafeteria door, getting a camera's-eye view of the entire scene.

Sure enough, there was good old Sandy, putting the make on the
Spring Queen—

Or was he?

He *wasn't,* she realized. He was just standing there, not moving
at all. And the spell casting that was swirling around like a blood-
colored haze about Sandy and the girl was centered on the girl.

And there were webs of power tying the girl to a woman Ann
had said was her aunt, when the chaperons were introduced to
each other. She was standing just inside the cafeteria door.

Aunt? Well, the woman *looked* just fine, but not to Di's en-
hanced senses. The so-called aunt was the construct who'd attacked Di earlier tonight.

And yes, constructed by that little adolescent brat.

It didn't make any *sense!* No eighteen-year-old girl should have
that kind of power!

Her own surprise was enough to tip the delicate balance of
powers in her own magic, and Di felt her grasp on the scene slipping. She *could* try to get the vision back, but—the Talent was un-
predictable. And it didn't feel as if it was likely to cooperate again
tonight.

She drifted back up out of trance, and finally opened her eyes on her perfectly mundane bedroom, feeling stunned and a little confused.

This is crazy! No kid that age is going to have the kind of acquired skill and patience it takes to work spells like that!

She blinked, and thought about it again. *Okay, I could be wrong. Look at Olympic athletes; at eighteen they've got that kind of skill and patience. It's obviously a fact; I can't change it. Fay Harper is the sorcerer.*

Which explains the attack on Monica; she's a rival. She may even be moving in on Deke for all I know. And it explains the feeling of threat Larry had concerning Deke. That gal is a man-eater if ever I saw one, and if she's a magician, there's more ways than one she can take to use a guy up.

Oh, shit. They arrived together; by now they've probably left together. Deke's with her now!

She didn't need to be in trance to check on him. All she had to do was close her eyes and relax; the shields and alarms she put on top of Larry's protections were easy enough for her to track. Usually.

But when she finally picked them up, they were very faint.

She's got the kid on her territory, she realized. *Under her shields and her protections. Hell. I can't go in after him. I don't even know exactly where her territory is. It might be her house; it might not. And five'll get you ten she got her hooks into him before I even set the shields.*

She opened her eyes again and ground her teeth in frustration. *I've got no choice,* she decided. *It's going to have to wait until after Deke gets home. I don't think she'll try anything tonight. Even if she does, he's got Larry and Miri's stuff on him. She can't kill him; consensual hooks won't allow that. She can't even drain him dry. And I think she's planning on something for him. Hell, she's only seventeen, eighteen—if she was finished with her toy, she wouldn't have taken his escort at the dance.*

I hope I was a good teacher. Larry and Miri's shields have held so far. I hope they still do.

*And he's got my stuff on him. At least I know that line of work bet-
ter than she does. I don't think she can do anything to him I can't
counter. I don't think she can work any permanent damage through
those old hooks.*

I hope it'll be enough.

Scratch that; I just hope she doesn't *try anything. That's my* best
hope at the moment. *I hope she isn't thinking beyond the moment
and the Sex Magick she plans to do to him. I hope destroying her
construct gives her a migraine and she sends him home! I don't think
she could have ID'd me in all that mess, so at least I'm in the clear on
that. That should buy us the time we need.*

She pulled both her knees up to her chest and hugged them,
staring at the northern candle.

*And I'll have to go dig up Larry and tell him the truth. Then we're
going to have to figure out what we're going to do about her. Shut her
down, obviously. If she keeps playing around recklessly with magical
energy the way she has, she'll wake up the One Below.*

Good night, I don't even want to think about that.

*No, this is going to take more than just me, or even just me and
Larry. I need a third set of hands. It can't be Bill, he's busy—*

Mark. Mark Valdez.

She pulled herself up off the floor, blew out the four candles,
uncast the circle, then plodded wearily over to the bed and the
bedside table that held the phone.

Looked like the night had just started.

She dialed Mark's number after consulting her phone list in
her purse. It rang twice, then—thank the Lord and Lady—was
picked up.

"Valdez," said a familiar voice.

"Mark?" she said hesitantly. "I'm not interrupting anything,
am I?"

A quiet chuckle. "Di. No, though if it had been last night you
might have. Sherry's out of town doing a trade show; she won't be
back until Thursday. The grandparents have the munchkin. Aunt
Nita offered to take him, but Sherry wouldn't hear of it."

"Sounds like things are progressing—" She made the statement into a question.

He chuckled again. "With patience. And fortunately, most of the designers she meets seem to be either married or gay. Or both. So, what can I do for you?"

"You working this weekend?"

"No," he replied. "I'm collecting some comp time and catching up on my sleep. Or I *was*. I take it you have other plans?"

She sighed with relief. "I do. How soon this morning can you catch a plane up to Tulsa? I'll make a reservation for you by phone and have the ticket waiting at the airport. . . ."

It was going to be a very long night.

FIFTEEN

I t was three a.m. by Deke's watch when he pulled his car into the garage. It felt later than that; *days* later.

He'd barely managed to get home. He'd been tempted to stay with Fay, and only the nagging of his conscience telling him that his dad would worry if he didn't come home by dawn got him out and moving. He felt as if he were running on fumes, and three quarts low to boot. It had been one strange night.

He managed to get the car in beside his dad's Z without damaging anything, although he did run the tires into one of the concrete parking bumpers Larry had installed. He'd put them in all three slots to keep the family from inadvertently shoving their vehicles into first instead of reverse and totaling both car and insurance rates. Tonight Deke was glad of the things; he might well have put his car's nose right through the garage wall and never have noticed, as tired as he felt.

He was almost tempted just to fall asleep in the front seat.

Then I'll wake up with a stiff neck. Nope. Not worth it. I want my bed.

He dragged himself out of the car, wincing a bit as some of the muscles he'd strained complained at him.

Keep this up, and I'll be a damned sexual athlete too. Or dead of exhaustion. Whichever comes first.

Fay had vanished for a moment, pleading a sudden migraine,

just as they got to her house. He thought she was going to let him cool his heels to humiliate him, but when she'd come back, pale and wan looking, she'd been all over him. Somehow, some way, he'd managed to give her everything she asked for. He still wasn't quite certain how. And he'd come real close to believing in vampires tonight, what with the way she leeched onto him, and because he felt absolutely drained when she finally turned him loose to go home.

He didn't expect the house lights to still be on when he opened the garage door. And he doubly didn't expect his dad's voice to call out to him from the living room.

"Deke— would you please come in here a minute?"

Oh shit. Now what have I done? I don't have a curfew on the weekend, and I didn't drink anything. Thank God. And I didn't do anything out of line at the dance.

"Dad, I'm *really* beat," he called back. "Can't it wait until tomorrow?"

"I'm afraid not." His dad actually sounded apologetic. "Please, we really need to talk to you."

Oh shit. His heart suddenly sank as the fact that his dad had said *"we* need to talk to you" sunk in. There was only one other person in the house this late at night.

Diana Tregarde.

Oh shit. I was right. They've been having an affair. He's going to tell me he wants a divorce from Mom . . . and that he's in love with that Tregarde lady.

Sure enough, when he reached the entrance to the living room, they *both* were there, Diana and his father. It sure looked like a setup for the "D" word.

But they weren't sitting together. In fact, his dad was sprawled out over the couch, while Diana, looking as dragged-out as Deke felt, was curled up in one of the overstuffed chairs.

They weren't dressed up, either, and that was the way his friends at school had said It Was Done.

"They always pick some weird time when you aren't expecting

anything. First one of 'em, your dad or your mom, asks you to come talk about something. When you get there, the Significant Other's sitting real *close, and they're both dressed up, like they want to impress you with how serious they are. Basically they look like they're going to a funeral. Then you get the Big Speech about how people change, and sometimes things don't last. . . .* " That had been part of Jill's sarcastic little stand-up routine on "the 'D' word."

He waited hesitantly in the entrance for a moment, until his father gestured for him to come in.

"Come on and sit down, Deke," he said. "This is going to take a while, and you're going to be wanting to sit down for most of it."

That was one of "the lines" his friends had warned him about. *Oh holy shit. He* is *going to tell me he's getting a divorce.*

"Deke, this has been a very strange evening," his dad began awkwardly.

Deke sat gingerly on the edge of the sofa, positioned exactly between the two adults, thinking, *Yeah. I'll bet it has.*

"I think you know that Di volunteered to chaperone for the dance. . . ."

"Not exactly 'volunteered,' " Di muttered. "It was more like I was drafted."

Deke nodded, puzzled. This wasn't exactly what he'd been expecting.

"And before dinner you were swearing that you weren't going to take Fay—that you'd go alone."

He nodded. *Where the hell is* this *going?*

"Deke," Di said, "I saw you up on the stage as Fay's escort, and you left with her early in the dance. I figure that means you've been with her for most of the evening. So what changed your mind about her?"

Huh? He'd been all set for the big divorce speech; this took him totally off guard. "I—I don't know," he faltered. "I mean, I met Fay by accident at the gas station. I guess it was an accident; she couldn't have known I was going to go there. And we started talking and I just followed her over to her house, and—and I guess she talked me out of breaking up," he finished lamely. "It seemed a pretty cold thing to do to her, break up just before the prom, you know? I figured we could at least, like, keep up appearances until we graduated. And, I don't know, I started to like her all over again. I think she's changing. . . ."

"Judging by the way you look, I'd venture to say that you were keeping up more than 'appearances,'" Larry commented dryly.

Deke felt himself blushing.

"Larry, stop it," Diana said sharply. "Deke, think about it; that's important. When you *weren't* with her, you were thinking for yourself. But once you *were*, you were doing exactly what she wanted. Right?"

"Uh—I guess—" He couldn't think of a better response. "I mean, I sort of wanted it, too—"

"That's not what you said at four o'clock this afternoon," his father reminded him. "Wait a minute, don't say anything yet. Di's got some stuff she wants to tell you that is going to sound right out of Vinita, but I'll back her on it, one hundred percent."

Diana pushed a strand of hair out of her eyes with a tired little sigh. "Okay, here goes. First off, magic is real, and I'm a practicing witch."

Deke started to laugh; he couldn't help himself. "Oh come *on*," he said. "You're trying to weird me out, right? Or else you're saying this shit to see if I'm on something."

Di shook her head. "Larry-love, you pull your shields off him and I'll pull mine. Then we'll give him a demo. Don't worry, I've barricaded the house already; nothing less than a deity is going to break in."

"Christ, *that's* comforting," Larry replied sarcastically. "Considering what *you've* dealt with in the recent past."

"Give me a break," she retorted. "We're just dealing with something human where Deke is concerned. Just *do* it, okay?"

Deke looked from one to the other of them, seriously alarmed. *They've gone off the deep end. Or else she was already there, and she took Dad with her. Jesus Christ—*

But just about then was when he felt something leave him, something he hadn't noticed was there until it was gone, like when his ears cleared after being deadened when he had that case of flu and all of a sudden he could hear right again. He felt oddly naked, like his clothing had been stripped off without him noticing.

And *then,* when he looked up in startlement, he saw Diana—

Well, he saw *someone* in the chair she'd been sitting in.

But that someone looked a lot taller. And she glowed with a bright, hazy purple aura that haloed her entire body. Crackling blue energy crawled over both of her hands and arced across the space between them.

Maybe, if it had been daylight and he'd been rested, he *might* have handled it better. Maybe he'd even have been able to come up with a snappy comeback, like "Ever think about working for Steven Spielberg?" But it was late, and he was exhausted, and he *was not* prepared for any of this. Especially when the vision raised one of its hands and pointed at him.

He yelped, and lurched violently away from the apparition, and found himself tumbling over the back of the couch. He hit his head going over, and saw stars for a second.

When they cleared, his dad and Diana were bending over him, helping him to his feet, and they both looked perfectly normal. And that "clothed" feeling was back. He was *very* glad.

"How in hell did you do that?" he squeaked, his voice breaking like a kid's.

He sat down heavily on the couch as Diana and his father exchanged a look of weary amusement. "Magic," she said, shrugging.

He scowled. "That's not funny."

"No. But it's true." She went back to her chair and flung herself down into it. "Your dad and your mom and I used to work together in college. You know the movie *Ghostbusters*? Something like that, only we mostly used ourselves rather than gadgets. When we had the money for gadgets—which wasn't often, may I add— we used those to catch the phonies and expose them. *We,* with the Talents we were born with, did all the real ghostbusting."

He felt his jaw sagging open and closed it with a snap. "You? *Dad?* Jesus Christ—*Mom?*"

"Deke, do you remember that scrapbook your mother doesn't like to talk about!" his dad said, leaning his head on his hand. "That was us. The 'Spook Squad,' we called ourselves. The reason we haven't wanted to talk about our little adventures back then isn't that your mother and I have bad vibes about those days—we had a blast, actually. It's that—"

"It's that *you're* a psychic, kiddo," Diana interrupted, her head on the arm of the chair, her long hair brushing the floor beside it. "You have psis on both sides of the family, so that's hardly surprising. You showed real early that you have some kind of psychic Talents, and your folks didn't want you to freak when you were little. So they didn't talk about it, and they shielded you, so you wouldn't know. That 'shield' thing is what your dad and I just pulled *off* you, so you can figure the kinds of things you might have seen without it. And later on, well, no kid likes to be different from the other kids; it looked to them like you were no exception. And on top of that, since you didn't seem to want to believe in the stuff, they figured you didn't *need* to know about your abilities, at least until you were older, and maybe better able to handle having them."

"I—I'm a psychic?" he said weakly. "I am?"

"Sure," the writer said matter-of-factly. "Why do you think you saw me the way you did? That's *one* of your Talents. It's called the 'Sight,' or 'Second Sight.' You know, your dad has it, too; you can probably do other things, but we don't know what they are yet."

"I'm a psychic?" He gulped. "Does that mean I'm crazy?"

Diana gave a long-suffering sigh. "Am I crazy?"

"Well . . . let me get back to you on that."

"Thanks, kid." She grimaced, and her mouth tightened. "Now listen up; this is deadly serious, and I mean that quite literally. There's big danger in being psi, and you in particular have a problem right now. That's why your dad asked me to show up here. *He's* been getting the feeling that you were in danger for a couple of months now, but he couldn't tell where it was coming from. Your mom might have been able to, but she was in Japan. He started to really panic when you had that accident, and the feeling only got worse instead of going away. So when you came up with that business with your English class, it seemed to him like the perfect opening to see if I'd come on down and give him a hand in figuring out what the hell was going on. You know the rest."

This was all coming at Deke too fast. "I'm a psychic. And I'm in *danger*? From what?" He looked imploringly at his dad.

"She told you, I couldn't tell." His father shook his head. "That's not my area of expertise. All I knew was there was something out here that wanted *you*, that endangered you."

"Oh." He couldn't think of anything else to say.

"Okay, so I got down here, and from all the info I got, I figured your dad was right. But the first person that *I* saw attacked magically wasn't you. It was Monica Carlin." Diana looked at him expectantly. She probably wasn't disappointed by his reaction.

"Monica?" His voice broke again. "But—Monica?"

"Believe it," Di replied grimly. "And tonight I have the bruises to prove it. Because tonight it happened again, at the dance. And *tonight* I was in place to find out exactly who was after her, and why."

Then she proceeded to tell him a story about Monica and Alan that he *never* would have believed if his dad hadn't been sitting right there, nodding his head in agreement.

"And you can call Monica or Alan in the morning and ask them yourself," she concluded. "They *both* have physical injuries to prove that Sandy went after them, and they *both* saw the thing that attacked me after I put Sandy out. And they saw it vanish after I hit it with magic. But don't try calling Sandy, because you won't be able to reach him."

"Why not?" he asked dazedly.

"Monica's mother called the cops after Di took her home, and pressed charges," his father said, with grim satisfaction. "So did Alan's folks. The cops went over to the hospital, and as soon as the blood test came back positive for PCP, they hauled Sandy over to the juvenile detention wing."

"But—" Deke protested, bewildered. "Sandy wouldn't do dust. He's an athlete, they'd bust him off the team—and you *know* they're going to cancel the scholarship offer they made him for UO after this. He drinks like a fuckin' fish, but he'd never do anything that'd show up on a blood test!"

He was a little too tired to be careful of his language, but his dad didn't seem to notice.

"Exactly," Diana agreed. "That's the point. The person that wanted Monica out of the way *got* him stoned to the gills on PCP, and did it in such a way that he wouldn't know she was slipping it to him. And that very same person is the one who created the creature that attacked me, and is the one that is posing a danger to you. Fay Harper."

"*What?*" he yelped.

"You heard her," his dad replied. "And I'm backing Di on this. It makes everything fall into place."

"She was after Monica because you were attracted to Monica, and she wanted the competition out of the way," Diana continued remorselessly. "She used Sandy probably because she'd used him up and he wasn't useful to her anymore, so she didn't care what happened to him. I went over there to the hospital after I figured out who our enemy was, and checked Sandy out. Honey, even without the dust, there isn't much left of him but some basic reactions and emotions. The boy's a burnout case if ever I saw one."

For the next hour or so, until the sky outside the picture windows began to lighten with the dawn, they alternated lucid, reasoned arguments about Fay. And the worst part of it was, the crazier the arguments were, the more they made sense.

Like the way I feel whenever I'm with her—like I can't think about anything except *her,* he thought, when Diana described how fascination spells ("the *real* meaning of the word 'enchantment'") worked on a guy's brains and hormones. *Like how when I'm with her, and I get bored or sick of the scene, and then she just turns and smiles at me and all of a sudden it's okay.*

And when she described, with the clinical detail of a Dr. Ruth, the way Sex Magick worked—well, that *really* hit him where he lived. Except he didn't want to talk about it. Not with his *dad*, for Chrissake.

And he really didn't want to admit just how deep Fay had gotten her hooks into him. So he just sat there and listened, and felt sicker and sicker. Then they asked him questions about Fay, a lot of which didn't make any sense. Like whether she had a little room with just a table in it, or owned a cabin somewhere. He answered them as best he could, but he realized with every question they asked how little he really knew about Fay. It was as if he never, ever saw anything of her outside of school, parties, and her bedroom.

When they finally finished with him, and he still hadn't said anything, they just sat and stared at him for a while, like they expected him to explode, or turn into a frog, or something.

His head hurt, his stomach hurt; he basically felt like hell. And he didn't even want to *think* about this anymore. Maybe in the morning it would all turn out to be a bad dream. And even if it didn't—

Well, he'd deal with it later.

Right now, *he* felt like a burnout case. And he wanted a chance to talk things over with Alan. And Monica.

And apologize, for real. Maybe they'd accept the excuse that Fay was messing with his head, after tonight.

"This's all too much for *me*," he said, throwing his hands up in the air. "I'm going to bed. And after that—I'm going to stay clear of Fay."

He waited for their reaction, wondering if they were going to jump him and tie him up or something. At the moment, anything seemed possible.

Instead, they just looked at each other, then at their empty coffee cups, then at the brightening sky outside. And shrugged.

"That's probably the smartest thing you've said in a week," Diana opined. "I think it's time we adjourned this little session."

"Sounds good to me," his dad replied, climbing up out of the depths of the couch. "Come on, old buddy." He held out his hand to his son.

Deke took it, and his dad hauled him to his feet while Diana extracted herself from the chair.

"After you, Alphonse," she said, gesturing to the two of them to proceed her up the stairs. They did; Deke's dad first, then Deke, then Di following after she'd turned out all the lights.

Deke pulled open the door to his room and started stripping off his clothes on the way to the bed, just leaving everything where he'd dropped it. He had just enough strength left to pull the covers over his head and turn out the light, but not one ounce more.

And just enough consciousness to think, before sleep descended like a lead curtain, *And to think I was afraid Dad and Diana were having an affair.*

Christ. Now I wish they were.

The alarm went off in Di's ear. She groaned, but hauled herself out of the tangle of blankets she'd created. It was too damn early in the morning, and she'd gotten less than three hours of sleep—

But Mark's plane was due within the next forty-five minutes, and she was going to have to be there to meet it. And she'd gotten by with less sleep before this.

She turned on the light, and headed for the bathroom to put herself into some semblance of order.

There were certain things she could do to kick her metabolism up and stave off weariness; certain disciplines she could invoke that would enable her to replace some lost sleep with food. They were temporary, and she'd pay for them later, but that would be *after* this whole mess was over with.

I need to move on this, and move on it fast, she thought grimly, telling her body what she would be requiring of it while she pulled on her clothing and brushed her teeth and hair. *Before too much longer, Fay is going to know who I am and that I'm the Enemy; she has to. I wasn't making any pretense at hiding, and besides, I'm the only new game in town. She's going to want my innards on a hook for destroying her Servant last night. If I'm lucky, she'll be at low power for the next few days and I can shut her down at a reasonable cost.*

Lady Bright, she's just a kid. . . . She was just using her power like any other kid would if you gave them that kind of—

Hell with that. I'm not a social worker, I'm a Guardian. I don't want to take her out, but if I can't reason with her, I'll have to. She's screwed up at least three kids that I know of, and who the hell knows what else she's been up to? And even if she really didn't think about what she was doing, or hasn't figured how wrong it is, she's putting too much strain on the local environment. Even without the One Below to think of, she's playing merry hell with the weather systems every time she does something major. Lady bless. These spoiled Jenks yuppie brats are all alike; don't think past their own noses and their own wants. Even Monica has a touch of bitch in her, and Deke's been trampling all over his own friends.

I hope this teaches them a lesson. I hope she's not as psychotic as some I've had to take down.

She was dressed, clean, and out the door with her keys in her hands within ten minutes of the alarm clock ringing. *I'm going to have to do this absolutely right, because I may not get a second chance,* she thought, as she pulled her car out of the driveway. *I want this confrontation on my terms, with me on the high ground and with my allies around me, and while I'm at full strength. So I'd better prioritize things before I pick Mark up, so I can give him a decent ops plan.*

There wasn't a great deal of traffic around on Saturday morning at seven a.m. She even accelerated onto the 169 on-ramp without the usual hassles of dealing with the local drivers, who didn't seem to understand the meaning of the word "merge." She cranked down her window to get some fresh, cold air on her face. It was almost as good as a cup of black coffee.

Number one priority has got to be to find the physical spot that this girl is using for her major ceremonies. I've never seen a sorcerer yet who put that where he lived. She might be the exception, but I doubt it.

High Magick was incredibly ritualized; most sorcerers had a small workroom where they could do simple spell casting and summoning, like Sex Magicks and simple Blood Magicks, but for the really major rituals, a huge room and some very specific trappings were required. In the old days of witchfinders, it was simply too dangerous to keep that sort of setup where you lived. And in modern times, it was too damned inconvenient. If you lived in an apartment building, had parents, nosy neighbors, or human servants—well, people tended to get really curious about cries and screams, strange people coming and going at odd hours, really awful stenches and clouds of smoke. . . . And Di didn't even want to think about the havoc that could result if somebody stumbled over even an innocent spell in progress. And with High Magick, that was increasingly likely the more skilled you were at it. The more elaborate rituals of High Magick tended to require a series of spells that would be cast over a period of days, or even weeks.

It was much safer to have a little vacation cabin somewhere, or a second place out in the country, out where there weren't a lot of people. And if you had the kind of money that Fay had, acquiring that sort of property was as simple as calling up a real-estate agent.

So she'll have her secret sanctum, and it will be someplace that she thinks is safe, but will be within about an hour's drive. She won't be willing to be farther away than that. It'll be some place that isn't public, that she can secure from interlopers and snoops.

She passed a slow-moving pickup and told her growling stomach that she'd give it a real good breakfast in about half an hour.

It didn't believe her, having heard this promise before.

I wish I could use Deke, but without training he's probably useless. So that leaves me and Larry to trance out and triangulate, and Mark to bodyguard and drive.

That place—wherever it was—would be the gate to Fay's main reserves of power. When they found it, they could do two things. Di could safely disrupt any major rituals that were in progress— and it was a pretty good bet that there *would* be one, and maybe more—and Mark and Larry could drain the power reserve while

Di went off to confront Fay while she was at her weakest.

But it would all have to be done today. Before *she* realized that Di knew what she was doing. Before she had any idea that Di might go on the offensive.

That was the one advantage in dealing with a bad apple like Fay: she'd probably assume Di was another like her and could be bought off. Once she knew who her "rival" was, she'd be waiting to hear the challenge and the price Di would ask to go away. She'd never figure Di wouldn't stand around to hear the counteroffer.

They never figure someone would have any interest but his own at heart.

The Tulsa airport was gratifyingly easy to get to—and Mark's plane must have been right on time. She pulled up the "arrivals" ramp to see him waiting at curbside for her, waving.

She stopped the car right in front of him and popped the door. He slung an overnight bag into the back and slid into the passenger's side without a single word; she pulled the car out again so quickly that they couldn't have spent more than thirty seconds stopped at curbside.

"Well?" he asked, as she took the on-ramp back onto the highway.

"Mark, m'love," she replied, "there's only one thing that could make me happier than seeing you right now."

"Oh?" he said, raising a thick, raven-wing eyebrow at her.

"And since archangels don't make house calls," she continued, "I don't think you're going to have to worry about competition. Did they feed you on that plane?"

"Feed me? On Cattle-Car Airways? Are you serious?" He laughed. "I was lucky to get a seat that had a working belt!"

"You know," she mused out loud, "I should have suspected something when they told me they'd give me a discount if you could bring a giant rubber band with you. . . ."

"That was for the motor," he told her. "They had holes in the floor for the guys in back of me to stick their feet through. They got their seats at ten percent off for being the landing gear. You know, you should never buy a ticket for a plane that has a smiley-face painted on the nose."

"I'll remember that," she laughed. "And listen, big guy, thanks for coming. Now, how about some breakfast? I'm starved, and you should be."

He gave her a closer look. "You're starved? You look more like you're running on empty. Writing IOUs to your body again, hm? It must be worse then you told me."

"Well, it gets complicated." She pulled off at the Twenty-first Street exit. She'd discovered a great place with a breakfast buffet, and at this time of the morning it wouldn't be crowded. "I hate to tell you this, but there's a maybe-deity involved."

She saw his swarthy complexion go paler out of the corner of her eye. "Tell me I didn't hear you say that."

"So far it's okay," she told him. "The thing's asleep. The kicker is, we *don't* want her to wake up. . . ."

"Okay, so what am I looking for?" Larry asked. This was feeling just like the old days—

Except I'm a little stiffer, a little slower, but a lot smarter. Let's hope if it comes to a showdown, smart turns out to be the most important.

"He wasn't in on the Madam Mysteria thing, Di," Mark reminded her, as he lounged back in one of the living room chairs. "That was about two months before we hooked him in, remember? Mysteria was doing her thing right at the beginning of the fall term, and we got Larry at midterms."

"Thanks, I'd forgotten that," she said with a touch of chagrin. "So who was the other sensitive? Jake?"

"Yeah. Remember, he bailed out of school and went back to Montana. He just couldn't take all the people. Can't blame him. Heard from him a week ago; he's still working that Forest Service fire-watch job, and happy as a clam." Mark didn't look as if he'd aged much more than Di. *Working as a cop must be keeping him in pretty good shape.*

"So what am I looking for?" Larry asked again, before they could get off on a reminiscence kick.

"A negative spot," Di said. "A great big energy sink. Fay's major workplace is going to be shielded against detection, but because it's a place where energy goes in but doesn't come back out again, we're going to have a kind of magical black hole out there. Not a place where there *isn't* anything going on, but a place where every available bit of energy that walks by goes in and stays there. You'll have to be in trance to do that, with your set of Talents. That's what makes these things a little hard to find."

"Great," Larry groaned. "The Zen of Magic; looking for the place that isn't there."

"Exactly." She managed half a grin. "It's kind of too bad you aren't like Jake; all we had to do was move him around until we found a place where he was suddenly comfortable. Now the reason we need two of us is that we're going to act as checks on each other. Partially we'll triangulate, partially we'll just make sure that one or the other of us isn't getting thrown off. It's easier to double-check when there's two of you working." Di was meticulously packing a small bag with all manner of odds and ends that she'd brought down to the living room. Some she'd just swiped from the kitchen, with the wry comment that it was a good thing Miri loved him. . . .

After seeing the bottle of asafetida in with the rest of the herbs, Larry was inclined to agree. And that had been *before* they found the hemlock.

He couldn't help but wonder if Miri'd been keeping her hand in, now and again, all these years. She *was* the one of all of the Squad who had been the most interested in witchcraft, as in the practical, spell-casting side of Wicca.

And when he recalled the way certain chauvinistic, abusive executives Miri had worked under had come to grief—well, it certainly gave him food for thought.

Pleasant thought, actually. It meant that while he'd always known instinctively that he would never have to guard his back or sleep with one metaphysical eye open while Miri was around, he now had evidence to prove his belief wasn't misplaced.

Di packed the last of the little bundles away and zipped the bag shut—then looked up at him as if she had read those last thoughts.

And smiled, a brief flicker across her otherwise solemn face. "I wish she was here, too. The gods know we could use her. But Mark and I managed all by ourselves down in Texas, and this isn't anywhere near as nasty an opponent."

Always provided that "goddess" hasn't suckered you, Larry thought worriedly. *There's always that chance. And there's the chance that Fay Harper could be working for the goddess.*

"Okay, are we ready?" she asked, getting to her feet.

Mark rose unhurriedly, and looked up the stairway. "What about that kid of yours?" he asked.

"Di put even stronger shields on him last night," Larry said. "I renewed mine, and we doubled the house shields. Besides, when I looked in on him he was sleeping like two logs. He won't be going anywhere for a while."

"Good," Mark replied, and ran his hand through his thick, black hair. "Let's lock and load."

Larry's range wasn't anything near Di's, which slowed progress down considerably. They were hampered in the fact that it was Saturday and the county offices were all closed. If they'd been open, a simple check of the property tax rolls would have shown them what property (other than the house and surrounding grounds) Fay and Fay's family owned. That would have narrowed their initial search down by quite a bit.

So it was plain grunt-work; starting at the far south end of town and moving north and east, stopping every four or five blocks to "look" for what was essentially a black hole, something which would be revealed only because of the distortion it left around it.

They stopped for lunch at the sushi bar Di thought so highly of. Both Larry and Mark opted for *cooked* teriyaki and tempura, and watched with awe and a little trepidation as Di devoured a small mountain of raw fish and rice.

She took a great deal of delight in eating her raw octopus and squid with gusto while Mark looked away and Larry winced.

Lunch over, they went back to business. The roads were getting crowded, and the interference from all those living, active bodies cut down on Larry's optimal range. It wasn't until late afternoon that he finally got a "hit," clear over on the north side of town past the airport.

He came up out of his trance to see Mark and Di staring at him from the front seat with expectation.

"Me, too," he said, as soon as he could talk. "I got it. That-a-way." He pointed east and a little north of where they were now.

"Pretty much what I got," Di agreed, pulling open the map of Tulsa they'd brought along. "Look, Mark, let's try this route." She pointed at a little county road that intersected with Mingo, the street they were currently on. "Go about half a mile and stop, and we'll try again."

"Okay." Mark put the car in gear and whipped it around in a tight U-turn, picking up the county road at the intersection a few hundred feet back in the direction they had come. Almost exactly half a mile later, he pulled over onto the verge beside some sorely puzzled cattle, and Di and Larry went back into trance.

And came back up immediately. "That way," they said in chorus, pointing ahead and slightly to the left.

"I don't think it's more than half a mile," Di added. "I've got a feel for distance now, and I don't think it can be more than that."

Mark consulted the map, smoothing it over the steering wheel and squinting at the fine print as Di and Larry looked over his shoulder. "If that's the case, this would be a good candidate," he said, pointing. "It looks like there's a gravel access road that intersects with this one in about another half a mile. There's probably farms all along here, and a farm would be a good place to put something like a sorcerer's work base. You could bring animals out there and nobody would notice, and if it's the first farm after the turnoff, your neighbors wouldn't see cars going by at odd hours."

"Let's try it," Di agreed. "We won't lose anything by going straight there, and let's stop and check out the very first farm along that gravel road. We may end up saving ourselves a lot of time."

It didn't take that long to get there; this was rural farming country, with grazing cattle and freshly plowed fields on either side of the county road, so there wasn't any traffic to contend with. And when they turned off on the gravel road Mark had indicated, they found themselves driving through a tunnel of cottonwood trees.

"This road isn't that bad," Mark shouted over the crunching of gravel under their tires. "What kind of cars did you say this chick drives?"

"Mostly sports cars," Larry offered. "This one's a Shelby, the last one was a TransAm, I think; the one before that was foreign."

Mark drove around a washout, the first bad hole they'd seen in this road. "None of those would have any problem getting in here," he observed. "And if you turned off your lights as soon as you pulled onto the road, the only way anyone would know you were here would be if they heard you. Whoa!"

He slammed on his brakes and they skidded to a halt beside a cattle gate that barred another graveled road, this one a one-lane drive.

"Okay, gang," he said, turning the engine off. "Do your thing."

Larry didn't need to drop all the way into trance; he could feel the place pulling at him the minute he closed his eyes and dropped his shields. "This is it," he said, reshielding immediately and opening both eyes wide. "Jesus. You mean to tell me a kid my son's age is responsible for that?"

Di shook her head. "I know it seems impossible, but there it is. For the record, I agree, we just hit pay dirt. Okay, Magnum, now that we're here, how do we get in?"

"That's the other reason why you asked me to come on up, isn't it?" Mark grinned. "Just leave it to me."

He popped the door and strolled up to the cattle gate, taking something out of the back pocket of his jeans, a small, hard case a little bigger than a wallet.

He reached for the padlock, then interposed his body between it and the road—which also blocked *their* view of what he was doing. He stood there a moment, then pushed the gate open wide, and came back to the car.

"Haven't lost your deft touch, have you?" Di said, as he slid into the driver's seat and backed the car up a little.

"It's a useful skill for somebody in my position," he agreed. "Nothing like being able to go where you need to. Some of the other guys like that high-tech lock-gun, but hey, this little kit doesn't need batteries, you know? Boy, I'll tell you, it's amazing how careless people are, leaving their gates unlocked like that."

"Amazing," she agreed. "Let me get out; I'll get the gate closed behind us."

She hopped out, and Mark pulled the car into the graveled drive, stopping just past the gate. Di swung the gate shut behind them, but did not relock it; she just secured it with a broken branch, then ran back to the car and jumped in.

Mark continued onward, through more huge cottonwoods, this time several deep on either side of the drive. The gravel drive took a dip and a sharp left just past the gate—and abruptly became an expanse of asphalt, as smooth as anything in Tulsa County.

"Even if I hadn't trusted you two, *this* would have told me we hit pay dirt," Mark said after a moment. "Either that or I would have started looking for a big, flat, mowed field, the kind you can land a private plane on."

"As in drug runners?" Di asked.

Mark nodded. "Look at this, it's a perfect setup. The first part of that county road is in great shape, but since it's graveled, you're not going to get too many curiosity-seekers coming down it. Then the drive; also graveled, and looks like it could get bad, until you go around that curve and out of sight of the county road. And *this* won't even be visible from the air because of the trees overhanging it."

"I can't believe this is the work of a kid," Larry said, puzzled. "I'm not sure that I'd be able to think of things like that."

"Let's wait until we see the house," Di cautioned.

And at just that moment they came around another cluster of trees, and saw it.

A falling-down, tilting derelict of a place.

It hadn't been anything spectacular to begin with; a basic two-story farmhouse, tall and narrow, the kind of simple wood-frame dwelling you saw all over rural Oklahoma. But now, it was a total wreck. Every window had been broken out; the doors flapped open in the breeze, and the right-hand porch support pillar had given way, leaving the porch roof drooping without any support on the right-hand side. Any vestige of paint had long since peeled away; the house was the shabby dead-gray color of unpainted, weathered wood.

Larry stared; he couldn't believe it. Nobody had been inside that heap for years; if they *tried* to get inside, the floor would probably collapse on them. How could he have been so wrong?

"Are you seeing what I'm seeing?" Di said quietly from the front seat.

"Uh-huh," Mark replied calmly. "What's a brand-new pole barn doing out here, where the house isn't fit to live in?"

"Yep." Di tilted her head to one side, and Larry finally looked past the wreck of a house to what lay, partially concealed by its bulk, behind it. A relatively new barn of corrugated metal. Freshly painted, too.

"And why are the electric lines running to a barn?" she continued calmly. "Looks like two-twenty service along with the regular line. And unless I miss my guess, a phone line. First time I've ever heard that hay had to make phone calls."

"Good question," Mark replied. "Want to go find out?"

"Yeah," she said. "Larry?"

He was already opening his door. "You couldn't keep me away," he told her, staring at the building. "*I'd* like to know why it needs a chimney. I always was too curious for my own good."

"Sweet Mother of God," Mark muttered for the fourth or fifth time, as they stared at the interior of the pole barn.

The big double doors had never been intended to be opened; they found when they approached the front of the building that the doors had been welded shut, all along the edges as well as in the middle. On the side they found a smaller, padlocked door—and an air-conditioning unit.

Mark had quickly picked the lock on this door, too; and when they opened it, Di had pulled a flashlight out of the bag she'd brought, and found a light switch.

But what they saw when the lights came on was nothing like they'd imagined.

The original metal of the walls and roof was paneled over; the building seemed a little shorter inside than out; probably the small door at the far end led into a partitioned-off utility and storage room. Certainly if the place had an air-conditioning system it also had a furnace, and there was no sign of one in this room.

The air was stuffy, and held a faint, sickly-sweet hint of incense. And the work on the interior must have cost the owner several hundred thousand dollars.

The floor was covered with a mosaic design of geometric figures; one large, central figure, and four others in each of the corners. The central figure was composed of several circles nested within each other. Each circle had inscriptions of some kind around the perimeter. And within the innermost circle was, not a pentagram alone, but a pentagram within a hexagram.

At the heart of the pentagram was a huge slab of stone; probably native limestone. The rough block was topped with black marble, and there were manacles set into each corner of the slab.

Beside the altar was a reading stand, with a huge book still on it. Beside the reading stand was a smaller table with an assortment of objects on it, ranging from a single crystal goblet to a supple, brightly gleaming rapier. In each of the points of the pentagram stood a man-high, wrought-iron candle holder, with a half-burned black candle as thick as Larry's wrist in it.

The walls had been paneled and then finished with black lacquer, and they gleamed wetly in the subdued electric light. Lighting came from three massive chandeliers depending from black wrought-iron chains.

And there was a veritable forest of more candlesticks, ranging from a foot tall to man-high. All the candles were either dead black or blazing scarlet.

"So what's going on in here?" Mark asked, having recovered from his shock while Larry continued to stare. "Anything current?"

Di tilted her head to one side and narrowed her eyes. "Yes," she said finally. "An appeasement ceremony. It's due to complete in about two months. And she wouldn't be able to build another construct here until that's over with."

"Anything you want us to do?" he asked.

"Not at the moment. Just stand there and let me go pull some fuses." She opened her bag and pulled out a jar of water and a blue cardboard cylinder of prosaic Morton salt. "Just call me a one-woman UXB squad."

She pulled the spout loose and made her way carefully around the edge of the largest circle until she came to the side opposite the entrance. Then she stepped over the first of the perimeters, and began walking around it in a clockwise direction, sprinkling salt before her and muttering something under her breath.

When she got to the place where she had entered, she stepped into the second circle and repeated her actions.

When she reached the circle containing the hexagram, pentagram and altar, she replaced the salt in her bag and took out some of the herbs she'd taken from her own supplies and the kitchen. These she crushed in one hand and broadcast over the figures, then opened the jar of water and threw it on the altar.

Both Mark and Larry jumped as something shrieked, and the altar hissed and steamed where the water hit it.

Di didn't even flinch. She took the heavy book, threw it on the steaming altar, and removed a square can from her bag. As she squirted something all over the book, Larry caught the distinct odor of lighter fluid. She emptied the entire can onto the open book, saturating the pages, then tossed the can to one side and pulled out a Bic.

There was a second scream as the book went up in blue and green flames. Di watched it for a moment, then turned and took the nearest of the heavy, four-foot-high wrought-iron candlesticks from the point of the pentacle nearest her. She weighed it experimentally in her hands, then smashed it down onto the mosaic pattern at her feet.

After two or three blows, the tiles powdered.

"Okay, guys, it's safe to come in here," she called softly. "You want to give me a hand? Grab one of these and make sure all the lines of all the figures are broken in some way."

Mark strode over to her and took another of the candlesticks. Larry moved a bit slower; even with his shielding he was seeing things out of the corner of his eye that he didn't much care for.

But he noticed after a few moments that they didn't seem to be able to move; that, in fact, they seemed to be frozen in place.

At that point Di came up beside him, still methodically hacking away at the lines of the diagrams. She noticed him staring at one of the things, a particularly ugly little blob of filth. Or not-staring, since he could only view them by looking at them sideways.

"Don't worry about them," she said reassuringly. "That's what the routine with the salt was all about. They're stuck; I froze them halfway between this world and theirs. They can't get out and they can't get back. This way they can't warn Fay about what I'm doing."

"Oh," he said weakly. *God, it has been a long time. I am really out of practice. . . .*

And out of the habit of taking this sort of thing in stride.

"I'm taking this all very well, aren't I?" he said to Di.

She laughed. "Don't kid yourself; this is *not* the kind of thing I do every day. This gal is using some *powerful* stuff, and there's only one advantage that I have over her—it's all old. Real old, like three hundred years or more. I know some shortcuts she evidently doesn't, and some ways to nullify what she did that she evidently didn't know to guard against. And I will be damned if I can figure out *where* she learned all this."

Just the thing to make me feel at ease. Thanks, Di.

"Are you going to just stand there?" she asked finally. "Or are you going to help us?" Behind her the last flames were dying on the altar. They were still blue and green.

"Oh, shit."

Larry stared out at the setting sun, frozen by the realization of how much time had passed.

"What's the matter?" Di came up beside him, emptying out the last of the stuff in her carryall—more herbs—and strewing handfuls at random.

"We've got a problem," he said grimly. "There's a big birthday party tonight for one of Deke's friends, a kid named Brad Sinor. All of Deke's friends are going to be there—and Deke's probably left for it already. We didn't tell him not to leave the house—we just told him to avoid Fay."

"So what?" Mark asked.

"So Fay *has* to know about it. I don't know if she was invited, but you can bet she'll be there."

"Oh, shit," the other two said in chorus. Di looked from one to the other of them, her face set and blank.

"I deliberately destroyed this stuff in such a way that she *won't* know it's happened until she actually shows up here or tries to call something tied in to what she was doing here," Di said finally. "But there was something else I needed you two to do—drain out her power reserves. You both know how, right?"

Larry nodded reluctantly, as Mark said, "Yeah. Haven't done it for a while, but I think I can handle it."

"Good. Neither one of you is up to handling a sorcerer, even a young one. I think she may try to blow through Deke's shields; I think she's getting desperate enough to try whatever she wanted him for." She took a deep breath. "Larry, this is it. You're going to have to trust me. I need you to do what you can here, and let me handle Fay. Otherwise we're *all* going to lose on this one. Will you do that?"

Larry struggled with his paternal instincts, which were screaming at him to go rush to his son's rescue, and finally won. "Go," he said thickly. "Do it. We'll hold the fort here. Brad's address is in my Rolodex. Brad Sinor."

She didn't wait for another second; she spun around and tore out of the building at a dead run. And in a few seconds more, they heard the car start up and the screeching of tires as she peeled out back down the road.

Larry looked at Mark, who just grimaced. "Okay, old buddy, looks like we're on our own. Let's do it."

They walked to the ruined center of the diagrams, and stood back-to-back, preparing to tap into the stored energy and let it drain harmlessly away.

"Hey," Larry said suddenly, "she took the car!"

"I noticed," Mark replied, "but there's a working phone in that storage area. I know, I checked it. When we're finished here, I vote we call a cab."

Larry sighed. "I'm really taking this all very well, aren't I? So who pays for this cab?"

"Who do you think?" Mark retorted, bracing himself in a wide-legged stance.

Larry found himself grinning weakly in spite of the seriousness of the situation. "She does?"

"Right. So let's get this over and blow this pop stand."

"Right on," Larry replied, and prepared to tap in.

SIXTEEN

H oney," Rhonda Carlin said worriedly from the living room,
for about the fifth time, "are you *sure* you want to go to this
party?"

Monica looked away from the mirror, sighed, and hunched her
shoulders stubbornly. "Yes, Mom, I'm *sure*. I'm okay. There's gonna
be a lot of rumors about what Sandy did to me—"

"He didn't do anything to you," Rhonda interrupted, sounding
even more worried, "did he?" She pushed the door to Monica's
room open slightly, and their eyes met in the mirror.

"No, Mom, he didn't. Honest. But he probably would have if
Alan and Miss Tregarde hadn't been there."

Rhonda still had that somebody's-hurt-my-baby-and-she-won't-
tell-me-about-it look on her face, so Monica figured she'd better
reassure her. Again.

*For about the fifth time. You'd think she was the one Sandy went
after.*

"Alan was right with me; Sandy just sort of came up behind us
and grabbed me, and that's when my dress tore—then Alan jumped
him. He didn't wait around to see what the hell Sandy wanted."
Monica slipped her dress over her head and continued, though her
voice was a little muffled. "Sandy beat up on him a little bit; then
Miss Tregarde came out and saw what was going on, and waded
right in. She's a black belt in karate, did she tell you that?"

She thought it was probably a good idea to leave Rhonda with the impression that Diana had taken Sandy out with martial arts instead of magical. Monica still wasn't quite sure what Diana had used to knock Sandy out—she'd just stood there and pointed at him—but it sure had been effective.

Probably more effective than karate would have been. Monica had heard stories of kids on dust—how they'd broken and dislocated bones and hadn't even noticed until they came down off the high. Sandy hadn't even *noticed* when she'd beaten on his thick head with her shoe.

Too bad it wasn't a spike heel, she thought vindictively.

"Well, all I can say is that it certainly is a good thing Miss Tregarde took an interest in you," Rhonda replied. "And if you think it'll kill some nasty rumors to go to the party, then I guess you should do that."

Monica straightened the seams of her dress, and fussed with her hair a little. "Alan's taking me," she said. "Black eyes and all. So no matter *what* anybody thinks, they're going to *see* both of us, and they can ask us about what happened for themselves if they really want to know."

"All right, honey," Rhonda replied reluctantly. "If that's what you want."

What I want is a chance at whoever put Sandy up to this, Monica thought grimly. *And I can't wait to find out who that is from Diana. And when I do . . . they're gonna find out that Monica Carlin learned a few nasty tricks from her daddy before he decided Mom didn't fit his career image.*

"You *do* look like a raccoon," Monica said to Alan as they strolled up the walk to Brad's house. They'd had to leave the car a block away; Brad's driveway was full, and so were both sides of the street right by the house. "Miss Tregarde said you would, and you do."

"Thanks," he said sourly. "And everybody's gonna know I got bailed out by a lady. Sandy was waxing my ass before she showed up, and everybody in the world is gonna know that."

"I don't see how," she objected. "Sandy can't talk to anybody except his parents, I haven't said anything, and neither has Miss Tregarde. And old Soames didn't get there until after Miss Tregarde put Sandy out."

"What about what's-his-name, the car nut? Tannim?" Alan wanted to know.

"He never talks to anybody," she replied, dismissing him with a toss of her head. "Except about cars. And art. And rock 'n' roll. *He'll* probably talk about the size of the dents Sandy put in that Caddy. Besides, he doesn't hang out with the same people you do."

"I guess," Alan acknowledged grudgingly. "Maybe I won't look like such a wimp."

"Alan, you jumped on *Sandy Foster,*" Monica said in exasperation. "He's a *football player.* And he was *dusted.* And you took him on all by yourself! People aren't going to think you were a wimp, they're going to think you were crazy!"

"Well, I didn't know he was dusted, did I?" Alan replied, beginning to sound a little more pleased with himself. "Yeah, I guess that was kind of crazy, wasn't it?"

"Yeah," she said, grabbing his arm and snuggling up to him. "It was."

At precisely that moment they came into view of the front entry to Brad's house; it was a big, sprawling, Spanish hacienda-type place, and had a front courtyard full of red pottery and plants, enclosed by a wall pierced by a wrought-iron gate. You couldn't see if there was anyone standing around in there until you were practically on top of the gate, but whoever was inside the gate had a terrific view of people coming up the walk.

Monica cursed her wretched timing, because there was Deke, along with half a dozen other kids, watching her snuggle up to Alan.

He had a really pained expression on his face, and he grabbed Monica's arm as soon as they passed the gate. "Listen, Monica, I have to talk to you right now—" he began.

Then Alan pushed him off.

"Just you watch who you're grabbing, *old buddy,*" Alan said angrily.

"Just who do you think you're pushing around?" Deke snarled back. "I know Monica a hell of a lot better than *you* do!"

"Oh yeah?" Alan retorted cleverly. "You want to make a bet on that?"

They stared at each other with the same fixed stare and stiff-legged stance as a pair of rival tomcats. Monica braced herself for the explosion. They kept looking over at her out of the corners of their eyes, and there was suspicion beginning to dawn there, as well as the antagonism.

I think Deke just figured out I've been playing up to Alan, she thought guiltily. *And Alan just figured out I've been playing up to Deke. Oh, God. And here I am in the middle. . . .*

"Hi, everybody!" The brittle, sharp-edged laughter and too-familiar voice made all three of them start.

Fay Harper swept in the gate with a blithe smile for everyone. "Deke, dearest, *there* you are! Let's go find something to drink, I'm *dying* of thirst—"

She touched Deke on the arm as the boy started to recoil, a look of—fear?—on his face.

Monica stared numbly. Because the minute, the very *second* she touched Deke, his expression changed, just went blank, and so did his eyes. Fay laughed at nothing, and whisked Deke off before anyone had a chance to say a word. Monica felt sick to her stomach over how Deke's expression turned puppylike with bemused adoration.

Why did I ever bother *with him*? she thought in disgust—when Fay turned back to the group at the door and finally spotted *her*.

Fay's smile turned icy and poisonous, her eyes narrowed, and she clutched Deke's arm possessively. Monica didn't need to know body language to read the message written for her there.

I'm going to get you, you little bitch. He's mine, you tried to split us up, and I'm going to get you for it if it's the last thing I ever do.

Fay turned away and hustled Deke out of sight inside the house. Monica wanted to scream. *She either figured out or found out I was the one who set Deke up to find her and Sandy out in the van. That must be what Deke wanted to talk to me about. No wonder he was mad. And when he figured out about Alan, he was even madder.*

Her heart was somewhere down in her shoes. *Jesus, I just ruined the rest of the school year. Deke probably hates me, and I know Fay hates me—and if Fay hates me everybody in school except the Brains and the Nerds and the Crazies is going to avoid me just to keep off Fay's shit-list. The only good thing is that there isn't more than a month of school left.*

And at least Alan still wants me.

She let Alan lead the way into the house; let him find a place for them to sit, over in the big rec room by the pool, where everyone was dancing. It was too cold to swim, but the pool cover was off and somebody had thrown dry ice into it so it was bubbling and steaming like something out of a George Lucas movie. It looked kind of neat, and it gave her something to watch while Alan went off after a Coke for her.

But Alan never came back, and after waiting for him for at least ten minutes, Monica swallowed her pride and went looking for him.

She pushed her way through the dancers and checked all the public rooms; the family room where four guys were playing Nintendo and had collected an excited audience, the living room where a bunch of people were watching a bootleg copy of *Rocky Horror Picture Show* on the big-screen TV, the den where the Brains had all gathered around Brad's father's computer—he wasn't even in the dining room where the food was laid out.

But that was where she ran into Laura, the Saks queen; she was talking shopping with Joy, who was going to Dallas next weekend and wanted to know what was hot. Monica signaled Joy frantically, and her friend broke the conversation off to wave her over.

"Hi!" Joy said, her eyes gleaming with excitement behind her glasses. "What's this I hear about Sandy beating up on Alan? I heard they were *fighting* over you!"

"Not exactly," Monica said, her eyes searching the room for Alan's red jersey. "Sandy was dusted, and I guess he was just looking for something to hit. Listen, have you *seen* Alan? He was supposed to get me a Coke, and he just, like, disappeared."

"Gosh, no," Joy said sincerely. "I wish I had. Mark told me he had *two* black eyes—"

"Oh, was that Alan?" Laura said, with an artificial giggle. "No wonder I didn't recognize him! He was here just before Joy got here."

"He was?" Monica turned to see the girl looking at her with a touch of malicious enjoyment. "Did you see where he went?"

"Oh, yeah, I sure did," Laura replied with relish. "He went off to the back of the house with one of Fay's buddies from Union, one of the cheerleaders—you know, that real fox, the one with blond hair down to her ass."

Brad's parents are gone for the weekend—and the back of the house is where the bedrooms are. And if Laura doesn't know that, I'll eat my shoes. She noticed Joy giving her a sympathetic look, and schooled her face into what she hoped was a mask of amused indifference. "Oh, did he finally catch up with her? He said he was supposed to meet her here. Well, good, that means I don't have to keep watching for her."

Laura's face fell, though she covered it up pretty well. *So Fay set me up to get humiliated, did she? Oh, fine. Just fine. Maybe I'll see if Mom can get me transferred over to Union. Shit, I'd better see if Joy can get me home, too—right after I go find someplace to have a good cry.* "I'll see you later, okay, Joy?" She winked, and swallowed down a painful lump in her throat, smiling brightly. "I'll give you the *whole story* about Sandy jumping us last night. Did you know the cops arrested him?"

Both Joy and Laura looked surprised.

"I thought maybe you hadn't heard." Monica smiled again, even though it hurt. *I'll fix him. I'll teach him to go off with some bitch-friend of Fay's and leave me out here alone.* "If it hadn't been for Miss Tregarde, Sandy would have cleaned the parking lot with

Alan's face. Anyway, I'll tell you all about it later. I've got somebody waiting for me."

She swept off before either of the two of them could stop her, and made her way out into the garden. Brad's parents had landscaped the place in a major way, with all kinds of neat little gazebos and benches with trees and things over them; there were even a couple of ponds, one with a fountain, one with a waterfall. Monica had hoped to find someplace out here to have her good cry, but every place she looked there was another couple necking. She finally found a spot by one of the ponds, right near the edge by the blue-lit waterfall; there was only enough room for one person to sit, which was probably why nobody'd taken it over for a petting session.

She stared into the water, keeping her face carefully averted so that no one coming up behind her would be able to see her crying.

But she didn't even get a chance to start before she heard Alan calling her.

He can't possibly have had time to do anything with that bimbo, she thought, frozen with surprise. *It hasn't been that long, not more than fifteen or twenty minutes. So either he struck out—or he likes me better.*

Oh hell, it doesn't matter. I'll get even . . . later.

She heard footsteps behind her and turned, ready to fling herself into his arms, relieved and grateful to the point of being ready to cry again.

Only what stood behind her wasn't Alan.

It was too dark out in the garden to see very much—only that the thing was taller than any basketball player, wider than any weight lifter, and very, very black. There was a little reflected light coming off the waterfall, and what Monica could see of the thing's face in that light made her squeak with terror.

It grabbed hold of both her arms, and not all the squirming in the world would tear her loose. Her knees went numb and gave out; but she didn't fall. The horrible thing held her up with hands like a pair of cold vises, as if she weighed nothing at all.

"Hello, Monica," it said caressingly in Alan's voice. "I'm very pleased to find you. My mistress wants you to come to *her* party now."

She squeaked again; tried to breathe, and found that she couldn't. All she could do was stare into those horrible, sulfur-yellow eyes, too numb to even *think*. Then the thing *smiled at her*.

And she fainted dead away.

Fay Harper wanted some heads. And she wanted them *now*.

That Tregarde woman's by first choice, followed closely by Monica Carlin's and Alan's. Then Sandy's, for screwing up.

Then that goddamn Gibson guitar. I don't even know where it went. The band did a better vanishing act than I could have, and I don't have the resources to track it down.

Her head pounded with the backlash from the destruction of her Servant. She ground her teeth and paced her room, occasionally picking up a small, fragile ornament and hurling it against the wall. It didn't do a great deal of good, actually. What she *wanted* was to hurt something.

But she didn't have any pets, the Servant had been obliterated, and the human servants had all vanished the moment the first signs of temper appeared. And *she* didn't have the authority to fire the bastards. Only "Aunt Emily" could do that; that was the way her trust fund and guardianship were set up. And there wouldn't *be* another Aunt Emily for another few days at the very best.

She didn't even dare call up an imp to abuse. Not with the low state of her resources and the fact that she'd have to tax her powers heavily to create another Servant.

Oh, she wanted to *hurt* something!

It was bad enough that the Tregarde bitch had completely *ru-ined* the Maypole spell. It was evident now that this little piece of sabotage was meant to challenge Fay—the destruction of the Servant had been the assurance of that. That spell would have given her enough power to make up for any losses over the past few months and "pay" for a new Servant—or several Servants. It was worse that the bitch helped whatever was in the Gibson overpower her demons, costing her not only the two allies but the added power that would have enabled her to break through Deke's shielding and eliminate his bothersome parents.

Right at the moment when Fay was about to get to Deke in a major way, the backlash had hit her. She'd drained him the best she could, and reinforced her controls on him, but she'd had to send him home, and everything else she'd planned for that night was a lost cause.

And the bitch had kept Sandy from getting rid of that *damned obnoxious Carlin tart!*

That was insult on top of injury; it was almost worse than the injury itself. The more Fay thought about it, the more enraged she became. She stopped her pacing just long enough to do another line or two of coke, and somehow all her anger at the Tregarde woman transferred to Monica.

It's all her fault, she snarled, hurling a crystal dragon against the wall. *It's all that little whore Monica's fault. If she hadn't gotten in the way, that woman would never have found out about me until it was too late to stop me!*

There were no more breakables in the room; she forced herself to stop pacing and sit, hands clenched in her lap, trying to think of an alternate plan, the coke making her mind come alive. At least there was no Servant here to chide her. . . .

I've made a mistake. The little tart must *be the Tregarde witch's protégée,* she decided. *That must be why she's been so diligent in protecting her. That must be why Monica showed up here* before *the woman did. The Master invests a certain amount of his power in his apprentice—if I destroy the one, I'll cripple the other.*

Her lips curled away from her teeth in a savage smile.

I haven't met anyone in the last three hundred years who could best me in an open fight. I doubt I'm going to now. All right, Tregarde. It's war. And the first act in war is to hit the opposition where it will hurt the most. I'm going to take out your precious little negress, your dear little darkie apprentice.

But first—I need a clearer head.

She rose and went back to the bathroom, to the special little concealed drawer in the vanity. It wouldn't do for the servants to find her personal stash, after all; they'd probably give way to temptation and help themselves.

She cut herself two more lines of coke—*moderation in all things my ass*—and sniffed them delicately. The rush cleared her head and gave her a burst of energy that left her overcharged and buzzing at the same time.

The Servant hadn't approved of the drugs—but then, the Servant hadn't approved of most of what she'd done, not lately.

Why should it matter? she thought dreamily. *I'll be discarding this body in twenty years, at most. The last time I was this young, I was stuck in Traverse City, Michigan—where I didn't dare enjoy myself, or the entire town would know. Which was precisely why I got married as soon as I found someone wealthy and stupid enough. And then I had to play proper society wife until I could get rid of the idiot. And when I finally got loose, what did I discover? That I was living in the backwoods of a hick oil town, and all my contacts to the pleasures of life were up north. So why* shouldn't *I enjoy myself? I've earned it!*

She suddenly remembered just where both of her targets— Monica *and* Deke—would undoubtedly be tonight. Brad Sinor's party. She hadn't been invited—but that hardly mattered; he wouldn't dare throw *her* out.

Ephemeris, ephemeris, where did I put it? She also realized belatedly that tonight was the night of the dark of the moon. And if it was astrologically as good as she *thought* it might be—

She found the ephemeris under a pile of romance novels, and leafed through it. *Well, it's not perfect—but it's not bad. And it's better than it's likely to be for the next couple of weeks. . . .*

Without any conscious decision on her part, she began dressing for the party, choosing an outfit she'd invested with a very powerful enchantment keyed to Deke.

Red for lust. You lucky boy, you. Lust. And blood. But we won't talk about that. It won't be yours, anyway.

She hadn't intended to use this just yet, but it was time to strike, while the Tregarde bitch thought she was off guard.

They'd never know what hit them.

Let's see. I can buy off my allies by giving them Monica to play with. The moon phase is certainly right for that. She giggled, sliding the smooth silk of her blouse over her head. *That should give me all the extra energy I need to deal with the Tregarde woman. But to do that, I'll have to build up enough extra power to pay off a fiend to do the snatch for me. And I'll have to get Alan out of the way. . . .*

She smoothed the blouse over her hips and admired her reflection in the mirror. *Wouldn't dear little Alan love to get a taste of this! I'll bet he's never been laid in his life.*

The perfect solution to her dilemma appeared like a burst of light, and she spun on her toe in front of the mirror, laughing.

Of course! I can call up a succubus with hardly more effort than it takes to snap my fingers! They'll perform just for the sex, which means the energy is all mine. I'll take her with me, and get her to seduce Alan. Then while she's screwing Alan's brains out, I can be concentrating on keeping Deke under my thumb. Then I give Deke to it. That'll keep him busy long enough for me to get away with the tart trussed up in the trunk. And I can call the fiend with the energy the succubus takes from Alan, and pay it with what I have it take from Deke! It's brilliant!

She turned to face the mirror again, as elated now as she had been enraged before. *It's perfect. While she's draining Deke down to nothing, my ally will be locking the little bitch in the back of my car. Talk about poetic justice! It can't miss.*

And they'll never know what hit them.

If it had been anyone but Di at the wheel, the car would have been pulled over half a dozen times. But somehow the cops never seemed to see her roaring past, bending traffic laws to the breaking point.

But there was an even more reckless driver pulling out of Brad's block as Di came screaming in. Someone in a red sports car, driving like they owned the entire universe. Di didn't pay it a great deal of attention; the driver was alone at the wheel, and Di had more urgent matters to attend to.

She pulled the car right up over the curb and parked it on the lawn; bailed out and barged straight into the house and the party without a single "excuse me." In the living room she grabbed the first person she recognized, one of the kids from her class, Terry— literally grabbed him; seized him by the collar and dragged him down to her level. "Urk—" he said, his eyes bulging. "Uh—Miss Tregarde, what are you doing—"

"Alan," she said. "Deke, Monica. Are they here? Have you seen them?"

She inadvertently tightened her grip. He made a choking sound and waved wildly at the room behind her. Since he didn't seem to be signaling for help, she let him go and turned quickly.

Alan was just staggering into the room, disheveled, glaze-eyed, and absolutely drained. And reeking of Sex Magick and the unmistakable overtone of succubus.

There was absolutely no mistaking what *he'd* been up to. And if *he* was off getting his brains turned into mush, that left Monica alone.

She muttered a curse at the general stupidity of teenage boys— and men!—who thought with their gonads, and stalked across the room, giving him the same treatment she'd just given Terry— except that she grabbed his shoulder instead of his throat.

"Come on," she said forcefully, as he goggled at her. "We've got to find Deke and Monica."

"Uh, yeah," he replied, following her because he'd lose his arm if he didn't. "Sure, anything you say, Miss Tregarde."

They hadn't gone much further than a deserted little office before they ran into Deke. Who looked even more drained than Alan.

Jesus Cluny Frog! Isn't there one *kid in this world that thinks above his beltline?*

But if Deke was *here,* that meant he wasn't with Fay. Di sighed with relief—

But Deke stared at both of them, and the first words out of his mouth were a blurted "Where's Monica?"

Oh, shit.

"How should I know?" Alan snapped back. "Janice said she'd gone off with *you!*"

"Janice who?" Deke and Di asked simultaneously.

Alan ignored Di. "Fay's trendoid friend from Union!" he shouted at Deke. "She said Fay was ripped and you left her and took off with Monica!"

Oh, double shit. Di grabbed Alan's shoulders and shook him violently. He stared at her stupidly, evidently not expecting that much strength in someone so tiny. "Who's this Janice?" she growled.

"Fay's buddy. The girl I was—" Alan blushed bright red.

Di shook him even harder. "You little cretin! You left Monica alone on the say-so of something that came with Fay? That *wasn't* a—"

"Hi, guys!" chirped a bright, seductive voice. "Want to party somewhere in private?"

Di whirled and faced the owner of the voice, a blond with long hair down to her tailbone, the face of an angel, and the body of every male fantasy in existence. She ignored Di entirely. Not surprising. Succubi literally didn't see the female of the human species—just like incubi didn't see the male—unless they had been deliberately targeted that way by their summoner. The two boys went slack-jawed and glaze-eyed, and their poor, worn-out little bodies were probably doing their damnedest to produce the appropriate salute.

It was fairly evident that Fay had left this "Janice" to cover her trail and maybe work some delaying tactics with the boys. She couldn't have expected Di to show up, or she wouldn't have left such a minor demon as a smoke screen.

The succubus slinked a little closer, and the boys licked their lips in an absurd echo of each other.

That might have worked if I hadn't shown up. Instead, this is going to work in my favor. I'll bet Deke still doesn't believe in the magic angle to all this, and I think even Alan still has a few doubts. Time to wake them up.

She gathered her power and blasted the shell of illusion surrounding the creature, revealing "Janice" for what she really was.

She was still a knockout—provided you didn't *mind* a lover with three-inch talons in place of fingernails, teeth like a shark, a long, pointed tail, and batlike wings that would have brushed the walls to either side of her if they hadn't been partly furled.

The boys' eyes bugged out, and Alan gripped Di's arm in a sudden spasm of unabashed fear. But before either one of them could do more than gasp, Di dropped *her* outermost shield. The one that hid the kind of power she controlled.

Now the succubus could see her, all right. *She* gasped, folded her wings protectively around her, and vanished in a cloud of what smelled suspiciously like Opium.

No brimstone for succubi, thank you. Lord. Little tarts always were show-offs. It's a damn good thing they're not as interested in combat as they are in sex. . . .

The boys were both standing stunned, their mouths hanging open, their faces dead white. Di could see identical thoughts running through their tiny little brains.

We screwed that?

She grabbed them both and hauled them around to face her.

"That *friend* of Fay's was a demon. Deke, dammit, I *told* you Fay was a—a witch of some kind! How the hell could you go and let her get her claws back into you like that?"

"Uh—" Deke couldn't look her in the eyes.

Alan just stared stupidly at her.

Di wanted to bash their heads together. "And where's *Fay*?"

Deke looked confused. "She just—left. I didn't ask her why. Then that blond came in—"

Di groaned. "Fay has been after Monica's hide ever since she came to Jenks, you idiots! And while you two were screwing your brains out—assuming you *have* any—Fay was probably kidnapping Monica! Now where the hell would she take her? The farm out near Catoosa?"

"But—" Alan began.

Deke was finally getting his act together.

"No, not there," he said, shaking his head. "That Sex Magick stuff—what you told Dad and me—the first time we—" He coughed. "—uh—"

"Spit it *out,* kid!" Di said impatiently.

"I thought she was just kind of kinky, like she just liked doing it outside. You kept asking me about cabins and things, and I guess I kind of forgot about this. She's got this place, this little place; it's a stable at the end of the runway where her dad used to keep horses. She never *lived* there or anything, and it's kind of run-down. I guess I must of figured it didn't count. We'd go there sometimes when we were in Tulsa and she couldn't—you know—wait—"

He gulped, and finished weakly, "She's kind of—enthusiastic. She used to say she liked the place 'cause she could scream all she wanted and nobody would ever hear her over the planes."

Shit, I'm a real idiot myself— Di thought in disgust. *She'd have to have an outside facility for some things, and any experienced sorceress would have a backup Power Point. She has to have figured out that we had her old place staked out when she tried to call her succubus. I would have checked my stronghold before I did a major spell, and I'll bet she did, too.*

Lord and Lady. I can't take the time to go pick up Larry and Mark. I'll have to use what I've got.

Two kids. Gods help me.

They were untrained, unknown quantities. Alan didn't even register much above normal. But they were all she had.

"Stand by for a shocker, kid," she muttered, pulling *all* the shields off Deke. "'Cause I'm going to have to figure out what you're good for."

Deke had been surprised at what Di looked like before—when she was still wearing *her* outermost shield. Now he practically fainted. She didn't blame him; doing a quick scan on him, she'd already figured that he was just as Sensitive as his father ever was; he had some Wild Talent she couldn't figure yet—

And he was a living Power Point. He could quite easily shunt energy to, or drain it from, anything he chose—once he was trained. No wonder he'd survived Fay so long.

And no wonder Fay wanted her claws in him. At least a hint of that must have gotten through the shielding, and it must have driven her crazy, even if she couldn't identify it.

"Come on, you two," she ordered, shoving them in front of her and out the door. "Let's *move!*"

She briefed them on what they might expect when they got there, or tried to. It was a little difficult, since she didn't know what *she* was expecting. She could at least tell Deke what she expected *him* to do. He'd long since passed the stage of suspension of disbelief; he just hung onto the back of the seat and nodded at whatever she said.

She hoped she was getting through to them. She wasn't sure how clear she was being; it had been a long time since she'd had to brief mundanes under combat conditions. And it was a little difficult to talk and drive like a maniac at the same time.

Alan just looked at her forlornly. He wasn't *saying* anything, but she knew he was feeling utterly useless.

"Look," she said, trying to think of *anything* Alan could do. "In the glove compartment. Can you shoot?"

"I'm on the Jenks target team," he said, fumbling it open. "And I was with the Police Explor—Christ!"

"It isn't as big as it looks," she said acidly. "Shit, I can handle it." Alan removed the .45 revolver gingerly and stared at it. "If a little bitty broad like me can shoot it, so can you."

He just gulped and stared at her, and pulled the handful of speed-loaders out as well.

She didn't even have time to sigh with exasperation; at that point,

Deke shouted *"There!"* and she slid a bootlegger turn into a half-hidden gravel drive on the side of the four-lane county road, a little turnoff that was buried in overgrown bushes.

They bounced through a series of washouts and over a one-lane bridge—

And suddenly the headlights spotlighted Fay, her blond hair and red silk harem pants and blouse unmistakable.

And beside her was Monica, held between two of Fay's little pets.

Di slammed the car into park and yelled *"Now!"* as she bailed out of the driver's side of the car, hitting the gravel and rolling into the weeds at the side of the road. Alan went out the other side, just as he'd been told. Deke stayed with the car—as *he'd* been told, since he didn't have any shields of his own anymore, he needed the ones on the car.

Come on *Deke, get your ass in gear!* Di could feel him fumbling around in the energy currents as she picked off Monica's left-side guard with a levin-bolt.

It shrieked and went up in a pillar of flame. She heard the gun go off as Alan shot at the right-side demon. The bullet wasn't more than a distraction, but between it and Di's actions, a distraction was all that was needed. Monica pulled free of the thing and came pelting back toward the car.

There was an inarticulate scream of rage from the sorceress.

And at that point, all hell—literally—broke loose.

Di didn't even have time to think much more than *Holy shit!* before she was running for her life, trying to put as much distance between herself and the kids as she could.

Fay was pulling power from sources even the most reckless of sorcerers would have left untapped—sources that bled into the protections around the One Below, sources that kept Tulsa's weather relatively stable, and sources that would leave her owing her soul a hundred times over to her allies. Levin-bolt after levin-bolt came winging at Di out of the darkness—and other things as well. Di was pretty certain they *weren't* illusions; illusions took a certain amount of mental control, and it was pretty obvious that Fay had lost any semblance of that. Di treated the things as though they were summonings instead of illusions, and they certainly went up with little screams of anguish when she hit them with her own levin-bolts.

She stumbled through the tangled brush and over tree roots, trying to keep her head down, trying to stay *alive*— Deke still hadn't figured out what he was supposed to do, and she wasn't sure he would in time to save her.

If she doesn't kill me, her allies are going to make chili out of her for what she owes them. They may do it anyway. But right now— She made a dive for the cover of some bushes as an ugly little thing with a long poisonous stinger made a dive for *her*. She managed to pick it off as it sheered away, but that gave away her hiding place, and a levin-bolt splashed off her shielding. *—right now I'm a bigger, shinier target than she is. Shit. I got the innocents out of the line of fire; very noble, but I'll bet that means that Guardian Magic isn't going to kick in.*

Wonderful. Just wonderful. Thanks a bunch, fellas.

A rumble of thunder overhead alerted her to yet another danger. Fay's uncontrolled magics were boiling up the atmosphere, and the granddaddy of all thunderstorms was building up at preternatural speed.

There was another storm brewing *beneath* the ground. The protections were thinning. The dreams of the One Below were taking on a disturbed quality.

Mark and Larry— She made a quick check; felt with relief that they were all right; still draining the site, like an attentive swimming-pool crew, oblivious to what was going on in Tulsa because of the shields around the place. *I have the power to take her down. But I* haven't *given her fair warning. And dammit, I can't do it while she's taking potshots at me!*

Within a few moments, the thunder and lightning were so continuous that the entire landscape was strobing around her, and she couldn't even hear the screeching of Fay's creatures.

The One Below was dreaming of storms, too.

She was right at the edge of the area covered by the headlights. *Not* a good place to be. She scrambled up out of her bushes, tried to backpedal, and tripped over something hidden in the darkness. Then a strange and stomach-lurching feeling distracted her for a moment, and, signaled by something deep inside her, she looked up.

Lightning played across the entire sky, illuminating the clouds whirling around a hole in the thunderheads.

A funnel-cloud.

And there was a definite stirring beneath the earth now; something beginning to wake and take an interest in the proceedings. The last of its dreams shredded away—

It wasn't pleased at having its dreams interrupted.

And was going to make every living thing within reach pay for being awakened.

Its reach was very long. . . .

Long enough to call down a hundred tornadoes on Tulsa, and send them ripping through every neighborhood in the city until there was enough peace for the One Below to drift back into dreams again.

Di spent a split second reckoning up the worth of her Oath, and her options.

I haven't got any. I'm going to have to bet it all.

And hope she hasn't learned the "reflect your enemy's power back at him" trick. Everything she's done so far is three hundred years old, and that trick dates from 1854. Please, oh gods—

Or there isn't going to be a Tulsa in the morning.

She made her "mirror"; grounded and centered herself, bracing it as well as she possibly could—

And dashed out into the cone of light from the headlights; then stood up in plain view, as if caught by surprise.

Di could feel the surge of triumph—and saw the blast of power coming straight at her.

The parabolic "mirror" held—and funneled the sorceress's power right back into her teeth.

Di's arcane "eyes" as well as her physical ones were blinded as a half-dozen lightning bolts lashed down, attracted by the pull of the power. Her "ears" were deafened by the scream of rage and pain, even as her physical ears were buffeted by thunder that literally pounded her to her knees.

And overhead, the storm died; while underfoot, the One Below growled in satisfaction and drifted back into sleep. . . .

After a while, sight came back, and hearing, and Di picked herself back up off the ground.

Oh, gods. Everything hurts. Absolutely everything. Maybe I'd have been better off if she'd fried me.

She staggered wearily back to her car; and as she came closer, she heard the sound of voices.

The boys.

Arguing.

Over just whose girl Monica was.

I can't believe this! she thought, gritting her teeth to keep from screaming. *Okay, granted Alan couldn't See anything but those two demons, and Deke probably couldn't See most of what was going on because he was trying to figure out what to do and had his eyes closed—but dammit, I'm out there getting my ass trashed, and— Lady of Light, if I had the strength, I'd strangle him!*

Monica could not believe what she was hearing.

I was kidnapped by a witch, she thought, stunned into silence. *I was going to be given to a couple of demons. I was nearly killed, we were all nearly killed. There was almost a tornado, we all saw it! And all they can think about is whose girl I am?*

The argument had started right after the huge bolt of lightning, when she'd cowered on the ground between them. That was when they both looked up, when *their* hands met, and each discovered a rival on the other side of her. It was probably all due to the fact that they were *all* an inch away from hysteria, but it was about to reach the point of blows, and suddenly she couldn't take it anymore.

"You—*assholes!*" she screamed shrilly, her voice cutting across both of theirs.

They stopped yelling, and stared at her.

"You can go fuck *yourselves!*" she screamed, shaking her clenched fists at both of them. "You're crazy, both of you! I'm going *home!*"

With that, she turned on her heel and flounced up the rutted road, with the lights of the car behind her, heading for the airport. If nothing else, she figured she could get a cab there, and her mother could pay for it when she got home.

They're crazy! They're both insane! If Fay ever shows up again, she can have both *of them!*

The light behind her grew brighter, and she heard the car engine right at her heels. She stumbled off the track into the grass, and the car pulled up beside her.

She peered suspiciously into the car, ready to tell the guys off, as the overhead flickered on. It was Diana; alone.

"I'm with you, kiddo," the witch said tiredly.

"God," Monica said, awed by the gray pallor of the woman's complexion, the sheer exhaustion that made her eyes look sunken clear into her head. "You look awful!"

"I feel awful," Diana replied. "Like death, only worse. How about a ride home?"

There were shouts behind them, as the boys suddenly realized that they were being left in the lurch. Monica looked back and could barely see them, stumbling along and waving frantically. "What about them?" she asked.

"Let 'em walk. It'll cool 'em down. By the time they get home, they'll be buddies again. They just needed something to take their nerves out on."

Monica managed a tremulous grin, then yanked the door open and jumped into the passenger's side. Diana Tregarde gunned the engine just as the two boys reached the side of the car, and pulled away, leaving them in darkness and a cloud of dust.

"Don't you think they could have done something instead of fight?" Monica asked plaintively.

"Yeah. Except that they're male. You know," Diana said as the boys' forlorn cries died behind them, "I'm twice your age, and I *still* don't understand men."

Dr. James Powell rubbed his hands together nervously. He hated to lose this patient—she'd meant a great deal in the way of a steady income to feed his coke habit—

Powell, that was one incentive you didn't need, he scolded himself. *You've been cold turkey for a month now. You can do just fine with the rest of your practice. And you got into this business to cure people, not make them dependent on you! Go back to being a doctor, not a goddamned drug addict!*

"You can let Mrs. Harper in now, Sherri," he told the secretary.

Rowena Harper moved gracefully through the door to his office and took the chair opposite his desk.

"Well, Mrs. Harper," he said quietly. "There's no doubt in anyone's mind. When you passed the certification board, it was only a matter of the paperwork. I want you to know that I was very happy to give you your release papers. And I'm happy to see you leaving us today."

"I never doubted it, Dr. Powell," she said, in a low, throaty voice. "I want *you* to know that I'll always be grateful to you for your help."

"I'm just sorry that it took such a shock—"

She bowed her head. "My poor daughter. What a horrible way to die. Lightning. Who would ever have thought something like *that* would happen to her? I still find it hard to believe she's gone. And yet—it's a paradox; if she hadn't had that terrible accident, might I not still be locked in my little world of delusions, insisting that I was her?"

"It's possible, I suppose," Powell said carefully. "I've learned never to discount anything when it comes to the mind."

She sighed, and twisted her hands in her lap. "I suppose it's just as well that I was so thoroughly drugged when it happened. You were able to break the news to me gently that way. Somehow I think that's why when you lightened the dosage, I was able to come back to my real self."

"That's entirely possible," Powell repeated. "Now, before you go—are you certain you'll be all right? All alone in that big house?"

"I won't be alone," Rowena said, still looking down at her hands. "Will I, Emily?"

Powell jumped; he hadn't noticed Rowena's sister Emily when she'd come in, nor that she had sat down on the couch behind Rowena. She was so quiet and subdued, she might well have been Rowena's shadow, or a piece of the furniture.

"No, Rowena," the woman said, in a soft, mouse-timid voice. "You will not be alone."

Rowena rose, and Powell realized that he could not delay the moment any longer. "All right," he said, rising to his own feet. "You take care of yourself. And stay in touch. You may need some help in adjusting. You might find yourself with too much time on your hands."

"I'm certain I'll be able to keep busy," Rowena replied, looking up at him. For a moment he thought he saw a hard, calculating look in her eyes. "I have a great deal of unfinished business to handle. A great deal," she repeated.

Then the look was gone, replaced by simple, warm gratitude.

It's the nerves, Powell figured, clenching his jaw. *Coke damages the nerves. I'm going to have to stop being so paranoid.*

He opened the door for her, and she and her sister slipped by him, both of them thanking him again, in sincere, effusive tones.

He watched her walk past his receptionist's desk and out into the hall. *God, she moves like that daughter of hers; at least she does now that she's sane again. Sometimes she even looks like her. Maybe that was the root of the delusion. There might be a paper in that. . . .*

Lord, she could be that sexy little thing all over again. Right down to the come-hither walk. . . .